"SUPPLE AND EVOCATIVE . . .

The Hawaiian chapters are a sensory blowout—the scent of ginger, the taste of mango, the sound of frying squid. . . . Pack *Song of the Exile* for your next trip to the tropics. . . . Richer than a box of macadamias."

—*San Diego Union-Tribune*

"With a keen sense of place and history, Davenport's well-researched and exquisitely crafted novel explores the myriad facets of racism worldwide. A historical novel in the most vibrant sense of the term, *Song of the Exile* brings the past alive with grace and subtlety."

—*The Baltimore Sun*

"The strengths of this novel are many. Davenport is a superb storyteller. She always keeps her readers engaged in her novel's story and caring about her characters."

—*The Seattle Times*

"[An] utterly absorbing story . . . *Song of the Exile* is about love and war, hopes and dreams, the individual and history. It's the perfect beach book, an escape to a Hawaii that springs to vivid life beyond the postcard views."

—*New Orleans Times-Picayune*

"Roiling, romantic . . . Rich and textured . . . There's music, passion, refugee camps, cruelty, and all the strange bedfellows bred by destiny."

—*Boston* magazine

"Davenport weaves into her lush narrative indelible portraits of Honolulu's narrow back streets and hot music clubs, Hawaii's complex coming to statehood, and of the pain, disfigurement, and shame that was the legacy of the war's tragic legion of so-called comfort women."

—*Elle*

"Haunting . . . A powerful tale of love and loss."

—*Publishers Weekly*

Selected by The Quality Paperback Book Club®

Song of the Exile

Kiana Davenport

BALLANTINE BOOKS • NEW YORK

A Ballantine Book
Published by The Ballantine Publishing Group

www.randomhouse.com/BB/

Library of Congress Card Number: 00-190616

ISBN 0-345-43494-3

Manufactured in the United States of America

Cover illustration by Honi Werner

First Hardcover Edition: July 1999
First Trade Paperback Edition: July 2000

10 9 8 7 6 5 4

Ha'ina 'Ia Mai Ana Ka Puana . . .
Let the Echo of Our Song Be Heard . . .

—From *The Echo of Our Song: Chants and Poems of the Hawaiians*
Translated by Mary K. Pukui, Alfons L. Korn

Hope cannot be said to exist, nor can it be said not to exist . . . it is just like roads across the earth. For the earth had no roads to begin with, but when many men pass one way, a road is made.

—Lu Hsun, *Call to Arms*

To the memory of those brave women
sacrificed in World War II,
and to "Eva" of Singapore,
"Margaret" of Kowloon,
"Sunny" of Honolulu
. . . who survived

Part I

Hele Malihini

To Go to a Place as a Stranger

RABAUL

NEW BRITAIN, 1942

". . . SOON THE 'IWA BIRD WILL FLY. HUGE MAMMAL WAVES WILL breach and boom. It will be Makahiki time. Autumn in my islands . . ."

She sits up quickly in the dark, taking her body by surprise. Her fingers roam her face, a face once nearly flawless. She drags her knuckles down her cheeks.

Outside, electrified barbed wire hums. She feels such wrenching thirst, she sucks sweat coursing down her arm. Then carefully she rises, gliding like algae through humid air. She listens for the sea. For that is what she longs for—waves cataracting, corroding her to crystals. From somewhere, gurgling latrines. Even their sound is comforting.

A kerosene lamp is steered into the dark. Sunny watches as dreamily it floats, comes down. A soldier's hand, the hand of memory, places it on the floor, revealing a yeasty, torn mosquito net. Inside, a young girl on a narrow bed, so still she could be dead.

In watchtowers surrounding the women's compound—twenty Quonset huts, within each, forty women—guards yawn and stroke their rifles. One of them half dozes, dreamily composing an impeccable letter to his family in Osaka. "Mother, we are winning. . . . The Imperial Japanese Army will prevail!" He is growing thin.

In one hut a young girl, Kim, pulls her net aside. Burning with pain, she crawls into Sunny's narrow bed, into her arms, and sobs.

Sunny calms her, whispering, "Yes, cry a little, it will help you sleep."

"It's hardest when the sky turns light. I think of my family who I will never see again. I want to run outside, throw myself against the fence."

Sunny sighs, breathes in the smell of sewage, failing flesh. "Kim, be strong. Think of music, think of books—normal things we took for granted."

"I don't remember normal things." Kim scratches at her sordid legs, a girl of sixteen. "I don't remember life."

Sunny shakes her gently, feeling mostly bone. "Listen now. When the whistle blows for mustering, we'll stand up straight, eat whatever scraps they throw. No matter how filthy the water, we'll drink. With what is left we'll bathe. We'll do this for our bodies, so our bodies will know we still have hope for a future."

"What future?" Kim whispers. "Two years of this. I only want to die."

"Hush, and listen. Death would be too easy, don't you see?" Sunny sighs, begins to drift. ". . . In Paris now it would be cool. We would stroll the boulevards." Her voice turns dreamy. "We might even take a cab."

Kim looks up, asking softly, "Will the drivers be rude again?"

"Oh, yes. And my French is so bad. Maybe this night we would go to Chez L'Ami Louis."

"Oh! The food is rich, so excellent." Kim momentarily comes alive, for this is her favorite game. Imagining.

"What wine shall we order? The house Fleurie?"

"And paté. And oysters! Will you dip mine in horseradish, Sunny?"

"Of course. And I will scold you when you pocket the matches, such a tourist thing."

Her voice softens. She thinks of Keo, their time in Paris. Rocking in lush geometries of morning light, nothing between them but heartbeats. Then spinning under marble arches, through terraced parks, young and careless and exiled. Not seeing Paris collapsing around them, not seeing their lives were crumbling.

"How happy we were. Grabbing each moment, so alive."

"I have no such memories," Kim weeps. "I never shall."

"Of course you will! One day this will end. You will heal. Life will help you to forget."

". . . Yes. Maybe life is waiting in Paris. Beauty and adventure. And shall we walk this evening down the Champs Elysées? Shop for the softest kid gloves? And cologne? Or maybe take a café and wait for Keo. I'll close my eyes, pretend I'm there, just looking on."

"Shh," Sunny whispers. "Soon it will be daylight. If they find us together, they'll beat us again."

She feels tears come: hunger, torture, incessant pain, the knowledge that she and this girl—all of them—are dying.

"Don't think so much. It will consume you. You will never survive."

"Survive. For what?" Kim's voice grows loud; girls sit up listening behind their nets. "You talk of life. How can we face life after this? How can we face ourselves?"

Sunny's voice turns urgent. "We must live. Or what have we suffered for? Will these years have been for nothing?"

Under her pillow is a makeshift map, drawn so she can remember where they are, where they were shipped to months ago. Here is the town of Rabaul on the island of New Britain, east of Papua New Guinea, just north of Australia. Here is the Pacific Ocean and, far to the northeast, Hawai'i. Honolulu, home. Farther out is the world, the great oceans. Far across the Atlantic, there is Paris. Yesterday. But, always, her mind snaps back to Rabaul.

Exhausted, weak beyond knowing, Kim sinks back on the filthy mattress, stale grains of rice matting her hair. "I want to sleep, I want to dream. Oh, take me back to Paris, shops, cabarets. Tell me again how you and Keo rode in a car with the top down. . . ."

Paris, Sunny thinks. We were so innocent. Not understanding trains were already leaving stations, streets were darkening with blood. She sighs, begins again, dreamily, and as she talks, girls struggle from their beds, move down the aisle, brushing her mosquito net. Some so thin, their movements seem delicate, some so young they are children, ghosts weaving through a scrim. Wanting only to listen and dream, they sit with arms entwined, heads bowed against each other.

". . . I remember, French women were so chic, and arrogant, always rushing off to rendezvous. I tried to imitate them, to be caustic and quick. It was not in my nature. . . ."

"And did you paint your nails each day?"

"And did you drink champagne?"

She smiles wearily. "Oh, yes. Sometimes we danced all night. Then stood on little bridges, waiting for the sun."

Kim curls against her, like a child. "Tell us again about your sweetheart. Was he always kind?"

Sunny weeps a little, and they wait.

"He was an island man, very kind. And shy. A musician, have I mentioned? So gifted, he played in famous cities. New Orleans. Paris. He was known."

Girls shudder and sigh, as if her words are talismans, miracles that will transport them, save their lives.

"Keo was not my first, but he was my only. I thought I chose him, now I see I was the chosen. It's so nice when someone reaches for you. Try to imagine. A young man, not terribly handsome, not very tall. Dark, very dark, and proud. Even at home in Honolulu, he always stood apart. . . ."

KE ALANA

Awakening

HONOLULU, MID-1930S

DAWN COMING PURPLE OVER THE KO'OLAUS, HE STROLLED UP Kalihi Lane, west of downtown Honolulu. A lane so narrow he could reach out his arms, almost touch bushes on either side. A world remote, unspoken for, so modest there was the temptation to hate it. There was the fear this was all he would know.

Wood-frame bungalows going to termites, their porch steps scalloped by generations. Each separated by wire fences snaked with chenille plants, crown flowers, golden trumpet vines. The heavy scent of ginger, plumeria. Each day he left this lane with the breath of an animal running. And each night he returned.

Some nights he felt the lane reach out to him, beautiful in moonlight. In every yard, chicken coops, orchids rioting in lard cans, blue sobs of jacaranda. And mango trees drooping with lianas, shell ginger hanging like pink jewels. Overhead, scraggly palms stretched back and forth across the lane, forming a feathery vaulted ceiling like a long primeval foyer leading him into a forest of shy and friendly tribes.

Sometimes he stood very still and listened. Mr. Kimuro snoring on his left answered the piping snores of Mr. Silva on the right. Mary Chang's phone rang, and across the lane Dodie Manlapit sat up in bed. He heard the sea, he heard its call. He laid his hand against a tree. *I have not lived.* At lane's end, he stepped into a tiny yard, a carless garage, climbed the steps of a bungalow, and quietly removed his shoes.

On a stool in the hallway his mother, Leilani, already astride the day. Husky-armed, mocha skin unwrinkled, face flawless as a child's, she sat gabbing on the phone with Aunty Silky, who worked the six-to-six shift at Palama Women's Prison.

". . . listen, girlie, was scarlet fever, no cholera, dat took her, so much coming at us in dose days. She nevah sat up. Just blink and die. Dat's when some buggah stole her crystal necklace. And whatchoo t'ink? Last year Milky Carmelita show up fo' Pansy's wedding wearing dem same damn crystals! '*Auwē!* I near went die. Wait—here come my son, da midnight owl."

He stood in cool drafts, drinking guava from the bottle, then closed the Frigidaire and kissed his mother's head in passing. Sprawled in his tiny room, younger brother Jonah, his walls a grid of baseball mitts and rowing paddles. Malia, his sister, in her room, snoring in a chair, eerie white face mask, head helmeted with pleated metal meant to train her curly hair.

In their shared room, older brother DeSoto, on leave from his ship in the merchant marine. Keo pulled off his waiter's shirt and trousers, hung them carefully, and crawled into the bottom bunk. Listening to the faltering tenor of his brother's snores, he covered his face with a pillow, steeped in the distillate of envy and frustration.

He's crossed the Pacific seven times. Seen Antarctica. Known women in Java. Manila. I've never been off this rock. Just a guy who carries trays . . .

HE COULD HAVE BEEN BORN BLIND, SIGHT SEEMED SO WASTED on him. As a child, he fingered everything, not trusting what his eyes beheld. Then, for years he walked with his nose up like a dog, relying on smell. When he was ten, his ears became his eyes, his head always turned, an ear thrust forward, sounding out life. Folks thought he was simpleminded.

In 1921, when he was eleven, Kamaka 'Ukulele and Guitar Works opened on South King Street. Keo ran errands after school, fetching tea and Luckies for the workmen. One of them was deaf, a Filipino with his own unique method of determining perfect resonance in constructing an ‘ukulele.

"All in da fingahs," he said, gently tap-tapping, sensing by his nerve ends vibrations of the sound box.

He covered Keo's ears, placed his fingers on the box of a pineapple-shaped ‘ukulele, then strummed. He did the same thing on a standard guitar-shaped ‘ukulele, so Keo could feel the difference: more mellow sounds of the pineapple uke because of the internal volume of the box.

"Human ears not always accurate," he said. "Sometime ears in fingah tips."

When he was twelve, the deaf man gave him his first ‘ukulele, selling it for five dollars. Keo sat in the dark and stroked the thing, listening with his fingers. Sound came to him then, pouring into him like light. Within weeks he could play any song heard once. But when he tried to go beyond himself, attempting wild variations on island songs, "Palolo," "Leilehua," "Hawai‘ian Cowboy," his playing was blundering and crude.

Keo did not know how to be moderate, to gently coax his instrument so it would hum and glow. Instead, he corrupted its sounds into whining exhalations of stunned wood, playing so hard calluses grew on his fingers. There was no one to guide him, to mesh his wild cogs, no one to help him articulate.

At fifteen, finding a worn-out radio, he rewired it and taped the crumbling shell. Each night, staring at distempered walls, listening to truculent snores of his brother, Keo twisted dials until he heard a crackly reception from the mainland. Choral groups. Concertos. Music called "classical." Listening, he felt a keen, prehensile yearning of his heart toward music he couldn't comprehend. Currents passed through him, so strong his body smelled like something scorched.

From ‘ukulele and guitar it seemed a slow-motion glide to piano. Sometimes he slipped into the Y, where bands entertained the armed forces. The crowd was mostly white, a few Negro soldiers on the side. Keo edged his way toward the bandstand, trying to observe musicians, how they held their instruments, how they controlled their breathing. Because he was civilian and local, MPs always shoved him outside.

One night he stepped into a room of punching bags, moldy leather gloves. Rank odor of sweat and sawdust. Something massive in the corner caught his eye. That was how he discovered the Baldwin. He pulled off the filthy canvas, opened the creaking lid, and wiped the keys. After that, several times a week he slipped into that room and sat at the piano.

At first he didn't care how it sounded, only cared how keys resonated to his touch. The thing was out of tune, strings mildewed, felt hammers hung with insects. Still he got so he could play almost recognizable songs, anything heard once. He played dregs of Bach and didn't know it. Rachmaninoff. Ellington and Basie. He played hour after hour, then dragged himself off to wait tables at the Royal Hawai'ian Hotel. On his day off, he played the Baldwin straight through the night and into the next afternoon. He didn't know what he was doing. Such a torrent poured out of him, his nose bled.

Each night after waiting tables he joined the band in the Royal Hawai'ian's Monarch Room, strumming 'ukulele, fox-trotting with rich, lonely tourists. He was striking rather than handsome, but his dark, mahogany skin seemed backlit, his impeccable presence was like something charged, and women were drawn to him.

Keo learned to tell by their perfume which woman would thrust her hips against him, wanting sex. Imperceptibly he would move her across the floor to Tiger Punu, who women couldn't get enough of, or Chick Daniels, matinée-idol handsome, first 'ukulele in the Monarch Room. Or one of the other "golden men" whose names had the ring of rampant health: Surf Hanohano, Turkey Love, Blue Makua, Krash Kapakahi, the Kahanamoku brothers.

Long-limbed, muscled, they strode Waikiki sands like laughing, bronzed gods. Beachboys in the daytime—teaching swimming, surfing, paddling—serenaders at night, the "golden men" had even been immortalized in Hollywood films, so that rich white women came seeking them out. At dawn they left women slumbering in their Royal suites and drove home, exhausted, in rusty pickups. In working-class Kalihi, Palama, and Iwilei, they sat in tiny kitchens, counting their tips.

Keo stood apart from his friends. White women scared him. He imagined beneath that pale sensuality lay ravening appetite. As if they'd come to collect scalps. He had no desire for them. Lately he had no thoughts of women at all. His blood accumulated in the wrong places. All he wanted was the piano, his fingers on the keys.

One day while he sat at the Baldwin, a USO volunteer entered the room. Blond and pale, she stood behind him listening. Next time, she brought a Victrola and records. "Avalon." "When We're Alone." Keo copied each song almost note for note. Sometimes she hummed songs while he followed, stalking melody and tempo. Then he would play each composition start to finish.

One day he found the piano tuned and polished. He sat down, bewildered. While he played, the woman locked the door, spread something on the floor, and asked him to make love to her. She said she had never "done it" with a native. She was thirty and divorced. He was nineteen. She said once, just once, for the experience.

He watched his dark, swollen penis enter her, like entering a pale flute-edged conch, blue veins spidering her thighs. When he came, he thought his brain had burst, his skull detached and sizzling. He would die insane, stuck inside a *haole*.* He screamed, struggled to pull out of her, but she did something with her hand and he was hard again. They were there five hours, moaning and bleating. He didn't even know her name. He never went back. By then it didn't matter; he played soundless chords on any surface, kitchen tables, his busing tray, sideways on his bedroom wall. His fingers drummed incessantly.

MOONLIGHT ON WET FANGS. DOBERMANS FLINGING THEMSELVES against a fence trying to get at him. Keo snarled, sending them into spasms. Inside the fence, dew turned lawns an orient of pearls. A tin heiress's Indo-Persian fortress on the sea past Diamond Head. To build the house more than two hundred men had labored a year laying the foundation, excavating five acres of lava.

It had been like watching the construction of the pyramids—hovering dust clouds, hammering sun, age-old calligraphy of heaving

*Haole—meaning "white, Caucasian"—is pronounced how-lee. A Hawai'ian-English glossary is provided in the back of the book.

dark men. The actual house had taken several years, and during that time the heiress refused to build toilets for local laborers. They were forced to relieve themselves in the wreckage where they worked, wearing urine-soaked kerchiefs on their faces so they wouldn't choke on dust. She named her fortress Wahi Pana, legendary place. Locals called it Wahi Kūkae, place for excreting.

Keo watched limos slide through her gates. Lights igniting the main house, several bands. All he had to do was give the guards his name: she was expecting her "golden men" from the Royal. He looked down at his toe-pinch leather shoes, knife-pleated trousers. He looked across the lawns. He had no business here. What he needed wasn't here. He turned away, remembering his mother, earlier, ironing his pants.

"Why you going dere? Dat rich *wahine* eat you boys alive, toss you out when she get bored."

His sister, Malia, had argued in her studied, drawing-room English. "Mama, that's how it is with *haole*. The trick is, while they're using us, to use *them*."

Malia, becoming so chic she no longer fit. She had begun to sound like someone not local but not quite white. Someone stuck in between.

Their mother, Leilani, stopped ironing and stared at her.

"Girlie, you talk to me like dat again, I put dis iron smack on yo' behind. You coming too *high maka-maka*."

Malia leaned back as if struck. "But you're the one said *pau* Pidgin in this house. No more talking like *kānaka*. You said learn 'proper' English."

Leilani shook her head. "True. But bumbye you coming too good fo' us."

Malia's voice turned soft and weary. She held out scabby arms. "Mama, look at this. Rash from cheap-starch uniforms. Chambermaid all day at the Moana. At night, dancing *hapa-haole* tourist hula for the same folks whose toilets I scrub at noon. Why shouldn't I have airs? I earned them."

Malia, golden-skinned, verging on voluptuous. Polynesian features gathered into something just short of beautiful. Only daughter, born between the first two sons, she was "cursed" with drive and cunning. Her drawers full of French perfumes thieved from hotel guests. Designer labels snipped from hats and dresses, resewn into hers.

She was a fraud, but Keo loved her deeply. Something in his sister calmed him down.

"I'm proud of you," he told her. "You going be somebody."

"You." She pushed him away. "One day you talk Pidgin, next day 'proper' English. Cunfunnit, make up your mind!"

He smiled. In his youth he'd pushed himself, learning "proper" English. Even without university degrees, Leilani vowed, her kids would sound educated, look educated, wear real leather shoes instead of flapping, rubber slippers. Still, Keo always slid back to Pidgin; it kept him in touch with himself.

Now he turned off Kalakaua Avenue, strolling the sands past the Royal. Farther down stood the U.S. Army installation, Fort DeRussy. He moved up near the open dance floor of the officers' club, watching couples move in circles. The Negro military band played moony renditions of "Body and Soul," "You Are Too Beautiful," their eyes tragic with boredom. One of the Negroes suddenly stood and pointed his horn at the ceiling, making it sob. Couples stopped dancing and listened.

The song was still recognizable, but he played it like someone shaking his skin loose, he was so tired of the world. He didn't bob or sway, just stood apart in ancient grooves. Then at some crucial point the horn turned on the player, the song and his wild talent grappled. He blew it slow, then fast, blew it so it screamed, then crooned. It cursed, then turned docile and familiar. He must have felt too naked. The song eventually won out, flowed into easy rhythms so couples moved round the floor again.

Band taking a break, the man strolled out on the sand, sweat pouring down his face.

Keo approached. "Say. You were great."

"Naw. Great don't reach this far. Not on this fuckin' rock." He turned, peered close, saw Keo was local. "Oh, man, I'm sorry. Thought you was one of the boys from the base."

Keo laughed softly. "I don't mind. Is that a clarinet?"

The soldier looked him up and down. "You sure don't know nothing. That's a tenor sax."

He walked back to the bandstand, returning with the horn, the thing shimmering and furtive like a weapon. Keo touched its big primordial mouth.

"That part don't mean much," the Negro said. "Up here"—he danced the valves with his fingers—"is where you make it happen."

He saw the reverence with which Keo stroked the thing, the way he listened. "You like music? You play?"

"Uke, guitar . . . piano."

"What you play on piano?"

"Anything. All I gotta do is hear it once."

"Read music?"

"I don't need to," Keo said.

"Hey! You pretty hip for a cat can't tell clarinet from sax. This I gotta see."

He went back to the bandstand, leaned down to the drummer, and motioned for Keo to wait in the shadows. An hour later they packed up their instruments.

"We're jamming back of Pony's Billiards, off Hotel Street. Just 'dark' boys. Want to sit in?"

Keo stepped back. "I'm not a pro. I've never played with strangers."

They laughed good-naturedly. "Let's see how good you listen. I'm Dew. This here's Handyman."

In that way he became a camp rat, following Dew's band from base to base on weekends—Fort DeRussy, Schofield Barracks, Tripler Air Base—and afterwards, all-night jam sessions in back rooms of billiard parlors and bars. Still, he couldn't screw up the nerve to play with them, awed by their dark, obverse nobility, the ferocious investitures of their sounds.

"So this is jazz."

"Jazz, ragtime—it's all just torching," Dew explained.

He grew to love their slang, their names, even their coloring—a wash of blacks, mahoganies, tans, jaunty yellows, not unlike Hawai'ians. He studied the massed residue of sweat caught in smoky lamplight, washing down dark faces like wet jewels, as one man stood and blew his horn in the softest, most elegant way. Telling of lost dreams, lost realms, misguided innocence and honor. Another took the drums apart, took songs apart with deafening crashes and wallops sliding into tom-tom rhythms, crazy cymbal flourishes, then put them together again with brushes, gentle splishes and splashes.

Keo pounded tables, wanting to scream, wanting to tell them what it meant being there, being with them, forever freed from silence. They teased him, wanting him to play. He wasn't ready, knew he wasn't good enough. Still, his love of rhythm and tempo, and syncopation, his inability to express it, endeared him to them. They adopted him, took him to taxi dance halls where Filipino bands mixed Latin rhythms with big-band sounds. He still couldn't read music, had no way to practise or improvise. He slept with the radio to his ear, absorbing all he could get, even in dreams.

One day six husky Hawai'ians staggered up Kalihi Lane, a lidless upright Steinway missing keys balanced between them. His father, Timoteo, had found it in the dump behind Shirashi Mortuary, where he was head janitor and coffin repairman. That night after work, Keo stood gaping. Warped hammers hung with leis, sprung wires taped haphazardly, its dark, squat front reminiscent of a bulldog with missing teeth.

He bought manuals and tools, repairing it one key, one felt hammer at a time. His hands took on the smell of glue and lacquer. Neighbors heard the nightly whine of planing, wood shavings curling in air like flimsy locks. His mother sat frowning at the black mass uglifying her garage.

"Why you need dis? Why you no just listen radio? Good kine music on 'Hawai'i Calls.' "

He was patient. "Mama. I'm going to be a serious musician. Not some joker playing 'Hukilau' for tourists."

Sawdust settled on her cheeks. "Then why you no play music of *kāhiko*, ancestors? Real Hawai'ian kine, wit' gourds, skin drums."

"I'm going to play jazz."

"What kine music dat?"

He wanted to say it was like confession, and doing penance, a way of playing that exhausted each man's genius and dementia. He wanted to say that after jazz, all other music would be dead.

Some nights, brother Jonah passing him pliers, a wire cutter, he worked on the Steinway till dawn. Then he walked down to the ocean. And he drank the sea he swam in, nourished and submerged. For that quiet time, nothing mattered. He had his dream. He had the sea. Wet peaks that soothed him, time untying him with salty hands.

RABAUL

NEW BRITAIN, 1943

RAIN. INCESSANT RAIN. NETS ROTTING, WALLS BECOMING MOLD. A girl is shot for trying to signal Allied planes. Doors are bolted, windows painted over; there is little oxygen.

Mustering at dawn, lining up for morning "bow" outside each Quonset, only half the girls are strong enough to stand. Hands held at their sides, feet exactly side by side, each girl inclines from the waist, remaining thus to the slow count of five. Others half squat or lean on sticks, fainting while guards yell "BANGO."

They count off in Japanese, "Ichi, nee, san, she, go, roku," *the strongest calling out for their weaker neighbors.*

Caught bangoing *for others, they are whipped, made to kneel on bamboo poles for hours. Nearly eight hundred girls had been shipped to Rabaul—military bastion of more than a hundred thousand men, major supply base for Japan in its drive to take New Zealand and Australia. Now, barely five hundred girls survive.*

Those strong enough spend hours over washboards, scrubbing soldiers' uniforms. Noses run from chloride of lime poured into latrines. Some guards take pity, slipping into laundry rooms with potato tops, carrot skins, a moldy slice of bread. One guard brings butts of cigarettes, forbidden matches.

"We not all mean," they whisper. "We good, and bad, like everywhere."

"Set us free," girls beg. "Help us dig under the fences."

One day, half crazed with hunger, Sunny challenges a guard. "You've made us slaves. You starve us. You will hang."

The man steps closer. "You stupid girl. Soon all peoples everywhere Japanese subjects." He kicks her backside, knocking her down, kicks her stomach and her face until he tires. "You very big mouth! Next time, I cut off your tongue."

Girls kneel and tend her, some so thin rags hang from them as if from nails. Still there is the daily grind: Six o'clock mustering, lining up for "BANGO." *Gray rice morning meal. The emptying of slop buckets, cleaning out of Quonsets. Waiting in long lines for latrines. For those still able, there is "weekly exercise," mindless trudging in circles round the compound, swinging of arms, bending of backs to start up circulation. At dusk, the evening "bow" to guards, to inspecting officers. Then again the shouting out for* "BANGO."

"Ichi, nee, san, she, go, roku . . ."

Up and down the lines, women whisper news. Another Allied bombing of Tokyo, defeat of Japan's navy in the Coral Sea. Defeat at Corregidor, Midway. An Aussie in the men's POW camp keeps a homemade wireless packed in dirt beneath his cot. Once a week men gather, listen to broadcasts from Australia. Weeks, months later, news reaches the girls in the compound half a mile across the base. Now a Chinese girl, three months pregnant, knowing she will soon be shot, whispers news from the men's camp.

"Allies have captured Guadalcanal. . . . Admiral Yamamoto killed at Bougainville! Japs defeated at Lae and Buna . . . Jap soldiers starving, eating their shoes . . . rumors of cannibalism."

Jubilant, girls cover their mouths and laugh. They laugh at the slightest provocation, sometimes exploding with mirth, so guards point bayonets. Words have become too difficult, tears too expected. Laughter is their only outlet. Without it, they might kill themselves or each other. Laughter expresses everything—grief, pain, love, hate. Sunny even laughs when she sees her face reflected in a piece of glass. Then quickly she turns away. It has been a year since she looked into a mirror.

And, because they are humans struggling to survive, even outlive each other, girls study one another—Chinese, Indonesians, Malays,

Koreans, Filipinas, Eurasians, even white women kidnapped from fallen cities—Singapore, Hong Kong. There is enmity, snobbery among them. And in the total lack of privacy—public nudity of the bathhouse, open latrines of planks set over concrete blocks that overflow—there is even hate.

The whites—British, American, Dutch—are thought of as slavers, imperialists, stupid and spoiled. Mix-blood Eurasians are considered lazy whores. Indonesians, Malays, Filipinas are conniving thieves, sometimes spying for guards. Koreans are sneaky, greedy, ruthless. Chinese, on the low rung, are considered squalid. The few Japanese girls, former prostitutes, are the lowest of all.

"I wish them all dead," Kim cries. "Everyone is so selfish. Charo, the Manila girl, hoards potatoes in her mattress. At night I hear her fighting off rats. Su-Su won't share a cigarette, not one puff. Maria stole an egg. She ate it raw, even the shell, while we drooled. An egg! It has been years. . . ."

Sunny holds her like a child. At twenty-four, she understands this is her motherhood. This is all there will be.

"Don't you see," she whispers. "They want us to hate each other, it keeps us weak. Keeps us from being human."

Yet in the crisis of each Quonset, women nurse each other, hold each other. Sunny has, in fact, witnessed acts of such unalloyed tenderness, she had to look away. Sometimes she thinks she has never loved human beings so devotedly as in these years imprisoned in this hut. She tries to memorize every detail, devour unique things about each girl. She gives them what love and humanity she has in thanks for the miracle of their existing here with her, suffering as she does.

"What would it be if I were forced to endure this all alone?"

Tonight, tomorrow, they might die, but today they gaze at each other, promising to always remember. Girls in each Quonset are kept apart, controlled by separate groups of guards. But at morning and evening muster, and at chores throughout the day, they signal with shrugs, they whisper through walls. Some connection, some coincidence: the same country, same city, same name! Even just the same shape eyes. Sometimes a note is passed, a promise scribbled on a rag.

"Endure. Endure. If I escape, I'll find your family, I'll tell them you are brave, and well."

Their voices drone on in the dark. Many are children, girls kidnapped so young—eleven, twelve—they've never menstruated. This is all they know. For others, some nights grief rinses into remembrance. The beauty of mountains overlooking mirror lakes. Beauty of bare feet on warm roads, running through grass with good, rough dogs. Planting in a father's field beside the father. Weeping in haystacks with lovers. The beauty of grace before a meal. The luxury of thought. Symphonies. And reading verse. They talk of dreamed-of clothes, scented hair. Taste of fresh fruit, coffee. They weep for the lost touch of a husband, a betrothed.

Sunny listens, talking less, giving less away as, more and more, she retreats.

". . . Up the road I race on my old Schwinn. Metallic blue and yellow. There on the left, Mr. Tashiro's house, wide front yard, smart new Ford. There on the right, the Nanakoas, handsome, husky folks. The son is tall and flirts, though I am only thirteen. Up and up to purpling heights! Homes hidden by coco palms, ironwoods. The hour stands still. If I hold my breath I hear blooming, fruiting things. And clattering mynahs full of evening, making banyans burst with song . . ."

"Up, up toward Alewa Heights, slower as road steepens, legs aching, blood pumping in my head. Far above, mountains, rain forests, far below, green valleys, and the sea. Dr. Hong checking his porch for termites. He works with Father at the clinic, doesn't invite him home because he's Korean. Never smiles at me. There ahead, Mama! Standing on the lawn. So graceful-Hawai'ian, so beautiful. Sweet-smelling, like pakalana, *Chinese violet. She turns and floats to me. . . ."*

"Now I'm on King Street, friends beside me in a car. Look, there's Casino Ballroom, dancing, jazz. We pull in, rowdy as gangsters. Now I'm swaying on the dance floor. Heat. Rum and Coca-Cola. Someone in that crowd will change me, save me from my narrow life. I wake up to his profile. Keo . . ."

She thrashes, calling out his name.

Nā ʻIke Naʻau

Revelations That Come from the Gut

Honolulu, mid-1930s

Saliva shaken from brass joints, men taking apart their instruments. Even when they finished playing, he sat paralyzed, his body an organ of hearing. He wanted what they had—a future. Jazz. When they talked of mustering out, going home to Memphis, New Orleans, Keo felt sick, something in him physically revolted.

He watched his mother darning women's prison uniforms, his father's face tinted gray from years of breathing formaldehyde. Younger brother Jonah, still in high school, part-time beachboy at the hotel where his sisters and cousins were chambermaids. All stuck in a life of servitude. Jazz seemed his only deliverance.

The night before Handyman, the drummer, transferred back to Chicago, they gathered for an all-night jam, sliding from blues to ballads, from ensemble choruses to solos. Keo tossed down drinks, working up his nerve, finally approached the bandstand. These were pros, they could tell if a man had talent just by the way he cleared his throat. The piano man stood, bowed him to the bench.

Keo sat down. "For Handyman."

The band winked back and forth, then launched into "Stardust," New Orleans style, everyone stomping, roaring in together. They settled into Memphis style, establishing a theme in the first chorus, then each man taking a solo, each executing his own variation. When his turn came, Keo inhaled, starting slow and cautious. Then he went berserk, galloping through "Stardust" like a madman, on into "Black Bottom" and "Sister Kate," thundering blindly into Bach, Stravinsky, Chopin's Études—music he had absorbed from a broken radio every night for months and years. Music he couldn't comprehend, like hot, slippery glass that dripped through the seams of his slumber, marking him forever. The others leaned forward, stunned.

What Keo played was on the verge of being recognizable but was obliterated by left-hand explosions coming out of nowhere. There were nervous seconds of fingers shimmying up and down keys, a dance that congealed into a sleepy pause, a meditation, one finger tapping a key like a clock's second hand. Then he went berserk again, like two men playing different songs but somehow blending them, then staggering off in different directions. This wasn't music, it wasn't jazz. They could not name what it was.

He played on, possessed, pounding out all he knew or felt. Then he invaded compositions from the here and now—dance songs, pop melodies that screamed through his fingers as he slaughtered sound. Miraculously, by way of tortured, twisted paths, he came back to "Stardust," but the chorus shattered, haunted and brand-new. Sweat poured down his face and arms, puddling the keys. His fingers slid off and fell into his lap. He picked them up and played till he was blinded, lungs sobbing, his forehead on the keyboard. He had played nonstop for twenty-seven minutes. They stared at him in silence.

He raised his head, looking round. "The truth. Am I . . . any good?"

Dew cleared his throat, answering softly. "Tell you what you *ain't*, Hula Man. You ain't ordinary."

After that, nothing stopped him. He still couldn't read sheet music, could hardly tell one wind instrument from another, but he was learning. Musicians mustered out of the army, others took their place. Keo waited for them outside Hickam and Schofield, then played with them all night in backs of barrooms.

Some nights he couldn't sit still, felt the need to physically embrace sound. In the midst of a piano solo he'd kick off his shoes, jump up from the bench, and dance. No one knew what he was doing—knee movements to the Hawai'ian War Chant, something from

Kabuki, a matador's ballet. He danced like he played, a thing unleashed, leaping, darting, turning his body into the instrument. Somehow his crazy movements cohered, a necklace strung with wild rhythms firing up the band. They blew until they were all but howling, then Keo flung himself back down on the bench, attacking the keys.

Dew loaned him records, Jelly Roll Morton, Fats Waller. For background, the mythic ragtime sounds of King Oliver. He bought a used Victrola. Neighbors sat out in the lane with folding chairs and fans, watching his head bowed at the piano, trying to follow the music.

"What dis 'ragtime'?" Mary Chang asked.

Ricky Silva frowned. "Must mean time fo' put rag in yo' ear. Strange kine music—sound more like car crash."

Sometimes Keo hung his head for the ferocious miracle of Armstrong, playing his records until they were warped. And this other genius Earl Hines, who played like no one he'd ever heard. Other men, stride pianists mostly, were still locked into ragtime-seesaw rhythms. But Hines did anything he wished with beat, using single-note stabs with his left hand, chords and long single-note lines with his right. What Keo was attempting, Hines had already perfected. A whole new geography.

Keo aped his style. Breaking up passages of songs with double-time or out-of-tempo explosions while still using a sort of metronomic beat. He decorated songs with tinsel sounds, small hesitations, then slaughtered them with sharp attacks, sometimes ending them with what sounded like a vibrato on a vibratoless instrument. He practised until he couldn't tell a Hines recording from his own rendition. But here was the difference, and he knew it: he was copying someone else. It wasn't original, wasn't pure jazz.

He tried carving out his own idiosyncratic sounds, digging for the marrow of a song, the truer truth. After a while something came, something a little of his own. He took a melody like "Sunny Side of the Street" and, wanting to understand the street, the weather, the mood of its folks, he let his mental eye wander until it stuck—a shaft of sunlight, a rover that crossed over, someone's worries left on a doorstep. He froze that detail, dissecting it, fingers sweeping up and down keys, until it became the essence of the street, the landscape, the meaning of the song.

Some nights Malia sat listening. "I thought jazz was original. Seems to me you're copying someone else's style."

He stared at her. "It's *my* interpretation—"

She waved her cigarette. "Brother, you're playing a song someone else composed, you're interpreting it by miming this guy Hines. How original is that?"

He threw his hands up in the air. "You want original?"

He laid into a monster boogie-woogie that slid into a Charleston of the twenties, then a throbbing tango that dragged down to a dirge, the moans of dead things dragged from graves. Then back to the monster boogie-woogie that had folks toe-tapping in the lane.

Malia bent over laughing. "You're a wild one. But you'll outgrow this."

Keo sat up, stunned. "Outgrow jazz?"

"Piano." She dragged on her cigarette, exhaling theatrically. "You can't really scream on piano. And you need to scream."

He ignored her. She loved drama, loved saying things that threw him off. But one night he pounded the keyboard so hard, he broke a finger. He couldn't even wait tables. For days he haunted pawnshops, not sure why until he saw the trumpet. He held it in his hands, smelling it, studying it. In a park, he put his lips to the mouthpiece and blew. It sounded awful, like something being slaughtered. Still, it felt good, felt right, the right size. He lay down, looking at the sky, the horn resting on his chest.

He dozed, hearing songs he and this horn would play, thoughts and feelings he would express, all the facets of his life. The man who waited tables at the Royal. The "golden beachboy" catering to tourists. The jazz-driven camp rat. He would explore all these men with this horn and, in time, he would abandon them. There would be room for nothing but jazz. He would learn to play this horn so well, it would talk back to him, his fingers following its urge before he knew what he was playing. He walked the streets of Honolulu feeling just-born, that he could live forever. He had found a form of expression he could carry with him.

One day his older brother, DeSoto, took him out in his canoe. After hours of drinking beer and gutting *'ahi*, Keo fitted the mouthpiece into place and blew his horn, tongue thrust carefully against his teeth, the force of air expunged from his lungs making his gut tight. His sounds were dwarfed by the sea and—recalling his days at Kamaka ʻUkulele, a deaf man teaching him how fingers could be ears—he concentrated on depressing valves, lowering the pitch, "hearing" through nerve ends in each finger.

DeSoto listened, then finally asked, " 'Ey. Why you stop piano? Was beginning to sound real good."

Keo hesitated. "This trumpet, well . . . it's like it's connected to my brain, my mouth, to what I want to say as soon as I feel it. With piano, you have to wait till the message gets to your fingers." He shook his head. "Maybe I'm a fool."

DeSoto grabbed him by the arm. " 'Ey! No need explain. Practise. Practise. One day you be on fire wit' dat horn. I seen plenny bands in Tokyo, Hong Kong. Big t'ing now, jazz. Folks talking Louis Armstrong, Duke Ellington, dat dead *haole* wit' funny name—Big Spida' Back."

"Bix Beiderbecke." Keo laughed, loving his brother.

"Tell you somet'ing, Keo. Best place fo' practise—best fo' solitude—right here." He pointed to the sea, mantas soaring in the distance. "Give you time build up—whatchoo call it, confidence. You take my boat out anytime, I give it you."

Keo studied his brother. Prototype Hawaiʻian—husky, fearsome—brooding brow, wind-sculpted face of ancient voyagers. A loner, always a little outside of time. Named after a dream car his father would never own because he had had kids instead, DeSoto had left school at ten to help support the younger ones. His only language was Pidgin, yet he had crossed the Pacific seven times, seen Antarctica, Bombay. When he was home, he spent his days fishing.

"Brother," Keo asked. "I always wondered . . . what do you think when you're out here alone?"

He shrugged. "Tides, weathah, what kine fish I going catch. How I going cook it. Steam. Fry. How much gingah, how much soy. How ʻ*ono* it going taste."

Keo tried again. "What do you think of when you *pau* fishing, *pau* eating?"

DeSoto studied him. "Whatchoo looking fo'? Key to existence? Dis da key. Right now. Nobody own tomorrow."

After that, he paddled out alone, far beyond surfers and fishermen. He would pull in his paddles, wipe his mouthpiece, and blast away with his trumpet. Some days he lost sight of land, canoe swirling in waters so deep the ocean turned blue-black. Sometimes a whale followed, oboeing to his bleating horn. Even dolphins leapt, answering him in click-song.

Days he played past exhaustion—spent lips, spent lungs—he would lie back, point the canoe toward shore, and hope the tide would take him in. Some days he knew terrible thirst. After a while he got used to it, confused the thirst with burning drive. Years later he would remember those days—exhausted, empty, half drowned by crashing waves. And he would wonder if, in fact, he had been practising, or finding out how much he could bear.

LEILANI SWAYED REGALLY DOWN THE LANE CARRYING A LARGE empty bowl. She smiled up at the tofu man, breaking his heart a little, his eyes going doggy because she was so lush, real old-kine Hawai'ian beauty. Brown skin burnished with gold where the sun pulled out her cheekbones and fleshy shoulders. Black hair a waterfall. Eyes deep, chocolate as *kukui*, teeth taro-tough and radiant. She leaned against his wagon, brooding. In large Saloon Pilot cracker cans, blocks of tofu floated in fresh water. She dipped a finger midst the swirling creamy squares, and saw her shivering reflection.

The tofu man leaned down. " 'Ey, Leilani. How Keo doing? Still playing strange kine music?"

She flung her head back. "You wait. My boy going come famous. Blowing horn mo' modern dan *manaka 'ukulele*!"

She swayed back up the lane with her bowl of tofu, head high, afraid they were laughing behind her. She had begun to dread the fish man, the *poi* man, neighbors in the lane. Even the sound of squid deep-frying, rice pots chortling on stoves, conjured for her kitchens full of gossipers, folks whispering her son was *pupule*, that he talked to his piano and screamed into a horn.

His finger healed, his lips grew sore, and for a while he went back to piano. Neighbors heard him muttering in the nights, slapping at mosquitoes, pounding faulty keys. But now and then he played something they recognized, played with such longing, such a going-to-pieces, in their beds folks turned and held each other.

Some nights he was aware of Jonah sitting in the dim garage.

As a boy Jonah had felt a rivalry with Keo, motivated not by envy but by self-defense, a need to be recognized as more than "younger brother." Now tall and muscular in his teens, Jonah had become a star athlete, an honor student. Secure in himself, he grew closer to Keo, almost protective.

One night, sensing his presence in the shadows, Keo turned to him. "Jonah. What you doing there?"

"Watching. Listening."

"You understand this jazz?"

"No . . . but I like watch you go fo' broke. Good example fo' me."

His admiration gave Keo strength. Someone was there, urging him on, halving his frustrations and fears by sharing them. Some nights after he played to exhaustion, they walked down to the sea, arms round each other's shoulders.

Dew would soon be mustering out, headed home to New Orleans. Now he coached Keo on horn, helping him read sheet music: how to decipher written notes, fill in gaps with proper chord sequences, take advantage of conventional breaks—basic things that gave him direction.

"I can't teach you to play. But I'll tell you this—before you can be original, you got to know what's traditional, what rules you gonna break."

He took the trumpet and blew notes with such clarity, such seeming ease, Keo almost hit him in the mouth. "I thought you only played *sax*."

Dew laughed. "I'm a musician. You better be one too, and not look down your nose at other instruments. You need them even when you're soloing." He relaxed a little. "What I just blew was nothing. One day you'll dance all over that. You got fire in you, Keo. But don't get vain."

He took him to Filipino dance halls, listening to bands from Manila. Keo found them excessive and flashy, even the crowds were flashy, competing and fighting. During police raids, hundreds of knives would hit the dance floor. But now and then someone caught his eye. A woman turned, hands on hips, willing to bear his weight for an evening.

He was mid-twenties then, with normal drives. Some nights he'd take a woman to a hotel, pay what she asked, make love, laugh, even stay a while. He was always considerate, always detached, caught up with his horn. It was a kind of communion he shared with the thing, a love with no jealousy, no betrayal, a sense that whatever he invested in it, it would give back. Sometimes he pressed his nose against the brass, inhaling, stroking the horn's flowing lines. This was his, his alone; whatever sounds came out of it could not be duplicated by another human.

Some nights he propped up music sheets and played straight through without faltering. Then he laid the horn down, studying little flags and squiggles that made him think of seahorses and bald, drowning men. He started again, slower, with embellishments not in the score—sly skitterings, a swan-dive arpeggio. Sometimes it worked, and sometimes not.

Still, he resented reading music. What he wanted was to blow out all his juices, let it go, never the same a second time. He wanted to paint sounds of violent, dripping colors. Then he wanted his music to gentle down from violent to penitent, from physical to felt, so folks would gasp, *"How on earth? How on earth?"* He wanted to exhaust them, so they would go home and forgive each other.

Maybe Malia is right, he thought. *Maybe I just need to scream.*

With most of his friends mustering out, he went back to taxi dance halls, studying the bands. In the late 1920s Filipinos coming to Hawai'i had brought, with their native music, rich Latin sounds, influence of four centuries as part of the Spanish empire. This natural feeling of rhythms primed them for blues and jazz. They had evolved into Hawai'i's first corps of dance musicians, now playing in ballrooms all over town.

Keo backed away from it. "Their playing is a joke. You were the one who said real jazz is mental. If it's danceable—it isn't jazz."

Dew looked at him with real affection.

"Boy, you keep thinking that way, you'll end up playing all alone. What these guys play isn't 'pure' jazz, but they offer exposure to new sounds. All us military guys so far from home—where you think we get our juice, our inspirations? These Filipinos, and mainland bands. Dammit, Keo, stop picking my brain. Find your own inspiration."

He answered softly, like a child. "But you're the best—"

"You mean 'cause I'm 'colored,' 'cause me and my friends were raised on pig-feet/whorehouse blues?"

Keo shook his head, unfazed. "I've listened to you for two years now. Nobody plays blues or jazz like Negroes. King Oliver. And Armstrong. That clarinetist, Bechet? They're geniuses."

"Which is what you *ain't*. Yet. You just want to grab that horn and use it like a blowtorch. Boy, you got to learn to be a team man, build on what's established, play with who's around. You got to be generous with other guys, harmonize and complement."

He hesitated, as if he were about to explain the afterlife, an incorporeal realm. "Keo, you've never seen the big time—Chicago, Kansas City, New Orleans. Maybe you will, you're good enough. I'll tell you one thing. You don't respect the rules, those boys will wipe you off the bottom of their shoes."

Two weeks after Dew shipped out, Keo started playing part-time at Rizal's Dance Hall, sitting in after midnight when the second trumpet took a break. Filipinos were passionate, fiery; their exuberant sounds introduced him to new points of view, new attitudes. He followed the rules, and began blowing brass duets with the first trumpet, the band playing a jazzy sensual tempo couples danced to. It wasn't the raw, improvisational jazz he loved, but it was a form of blues, with enough surprises to keep him alert. He memorized his sheet music, so he knew each trumpet arrangement by heart.

When the band struck up, he played the score exactly as written. But sometimes in rehearsals he skidded off toward the edges, improvising, knowing he had gone too far when the bandleader narrowed his eyes. Because he couldn't blow wild, he began to concentrate on tone. In time a quality crept into his playing, something came out of his horn he'd never heard. Keo began soloing, with such restraint and intelligent phrasing, bandsmen looked at him with interest.

One night, playing "I Should Care," he blew such sweeping, lilting arpeggios, couples stopped dancing and listened. He played on, pulling truth into focus, the rhythm section sliding in—piano, bass, drums—adapting to his sound. When it was over, the crowd applauded, shouting Keo's name.

Eventually soldiers came to hear him, serious jazzmen. He wrote

Dew, keeping him abreast. Records arrived from New Orleans. Ellington, Basie. More Sidney Bechet. And wah-wah gutbucket sounds Keo hadn't heard before, blues and jazz played on horns muted with plates, cups, hats. He found the sounds ugly, unorthodox. He thought of gutbucket as cheating. But as he listened, Keo began to like how a horn could be controlled.

One night he put a rice bowl over the mouth of his trumpet, palpitating the bowl while he blew, giving the sounds a wavering, watery address. He switched to a derby hat, copying a photo in *Downbeat.* Excited by the new sounds, he wrote Dew long letters—how he was absorbing and learning.

In the lane, Leilani held her head a little higher.

HO'ONALU

To Form Waves, to Meditate

NIGHTS AT CASINO BALLROOM, LISTENING TO BANDS. ONE NIGHT a face stood out from the crowd, pale and arrogant, yet somehow melancholy. She stared at him so long, he felt a slippage in his joints, his membranes burned. He felt if he didn't look away, all the rules would change; more would be required of him than he possessed.

A few nights later, blowing trumpet at Rizal's, he saw her again. Staring as if she were shaking him down. While he stood in the alley having a smoke, she suddenly appeared.

"I wanted to tell you how much I enjoy your playing." Her voice low, almost shy.

"You follow jazz?" he asked.

"Not really. But I know when I hear excellence."

Up close her face pierced him, it was so lovely. Soft angles in her cheekbones, slight fullness in her lips and nose that bespoke Hawai'ian blood. But in her slightly slanted eyes, straight black blunt-cut hair, he saw other blood as well.

"What's your name?"

"Sunny . . . Sun-ja Uanoe Sung."

Then he said a crazy thing. "You have very good posture."

Sometimes she came with friends from university. Then she came alone, and stood apart. He began to look for her. One night, wet and wrecked, he came off the stage and she was there. They spent nights walking by the sea, cautious, apprehensive. Keo spoke haphazardly, randomly, missing transitions. She described her life episodically, in reverse. As if their lives had not unfolded from prior events.

He learned her father was Korean. As they grew closer, he saw how her skin seemed to go darker in sunlight, her black hair turned slightly curly in rain. She confused him further when she relaxed, seeming almost playful. Her lips grew fuller and there was a lazy glide to her gestures. Like all mix-bloods, she was complex, sometimes seeming one way, then another, sometimes both bloods—Hawai'ian and Korean—struggling to dominate, giving her the benefit of neither.

One night, sitting on a bench, Sunny talked about her father, how he had never wanted her, how he abused her Hawai'ian mother. How being unloved sometimes made her feel invisible. She talked softly, wistfully, until she talked herself to sleep. Carefully, Keo put his arm round her. How defenseless she seemed. Yet he remembered how she looked when he first saw her—bold, casting her gaze at him recklessly, as if whatever he offered her would not be challenging enough. Now he pulled her close, and talked about a gnawing at his heart, dread of being mediocre. He talked about fox-trotting rich women, carrying their dishes, his fear that this would be his life.

"I'm more than that. I won't end up a should-have-been. I'll be the best—I just need a blueprint."

The moon on her face made her look extremely young. He shook her awake.

"Sunny. You don't belong with me. You're a college kid—"

She sat up slowly.

"—your father's a doctor, you live in the Heights."

"He's a lab technician. And we don't own our house."

"Still. What are you doing here? Slumming?"

She studied him. "I know what slumming is. That is not what this is."

"Then, what is it?"

". . . This is everything you told me. Everything we've said. I'm not afraid."

She bowed her head like a young animal drinking at a trough, and brought his fingers to her lips. Her hair fell forward, exposing her neck. He covered that place with his forehead.

SHE BROUGHT OMENS, EXHILARATIONS, SHE MADE HIM LOOK UP from his life. He learned that her good posture came from dread, the constant surge of adrenaline.

"I've known the taste of fear from birth. It was in my mother's milk."

And so she grew up testing her courage, lying in the road at night while cars raced up the hill, holding her breath as headlights stroked her.

"I'd wait until they hit the brakes, then I would roll away. Mama thought I was suicidal because Papa was so brutal. She didn't understand I wanted to live! I was toughening myself."

She told him how she had stood on cliffs in storms, fighting the wind, toes curled round the edges of her slippers.

"I was learning never to be afraid of things. I'd come home drenched, dazed, covered in mud, and Papa would hit me, thinking I'd been rolling in the fields with boys."

In summers she worked the canneries and clerked in stores. Her "proper" English and pale-honey skin should have smoothed the way for promotions, but Sunny kept putting herself on the line for darker girls.

"I watched how Hawai'ians and Filipinas were shoved around. It made me angry. I organized little strikes, wrote petitions, accusing bosses of favoritism." She laughed. "I've been fired from three jobs."

She mentioned a brother, an engineering student at Stanford University. Her father wanted her to study medicine.

"Is that what you want?" Keo asked.

"He doesn't care what I want. That's not the Korean way. Everything is *kongbu haera, kongbu haera!* Study, study!" Then she frowned, trying to be fair. "Papa says learning is a duty to our ancestors. He's not a bad man, just harsh and fatalistic."

"What about your mother?"

Sunny hesitated. "Mama's forgotten how to run, or even walk barefoot. I pull thorns from my heart watching how he treats her, wanting her to be a 'lady.' When she's too local, too *riff-raff*, or when she talks Pidgin, he hits her. Then I want to attack him. I have to leave the room he's in. Sometimes I do things to distract him, so he hits me instead. Other times he looks so sad I want to comfort him. I go as close as I think safe."

Keo shook his head. "My father did that, I would knock him down, much as I respect him."

"I've tried to take her back to her family in Waimanalo. But, you see, she loves him. His first wife died shortly after they arrived here from Korea. With Mama—Hawai'ian, uneducated—Papa feels he married beneath him. She was young and beautiful, and he was alone."

Sunny hugged herself and sighed. "Hard to explain. He couldn't live without her. Yet he treats her like most Koreans treat their wives, never calling her by name. It's always *Yobo!*—'Hey you!' "

Listening, Keo had the sense that he had walked into an empty room and there was this girl lit by desperation. Wanting to save her mother's life. He tried to translate that desperation, evolve it backwards to the girl herself. Make her pieces fit. Maybe it was *her* life that needed saving.

She kept a tiny rented studio up near the university in Manoa Valley, a campus so small and rural, cows still wandered into graduation ceremonies. The first time they made love, Keo felt he would do anything she asked. He would give her his trumpet, his lungs, his life, for more of her, for all of her he could get. Weeks passed in a kind of dementia. They moved on each other with a scratched-itch ecstasy. His kisses animal-mounting bites, him lathered and wetted in her vagina that felt like a slick rolled-up tongue sucking him to incandescence.

Breathing. It seemed an achievement, coming out of her. Coming back alive. Or half alive, nothing left but sweat, stunned marrow. Inflamed and semen-full, how beautifully she arched, how coming made her skin catch fire. Even when they slept, exhausted, their joints sought out each other's clefts, smooth and sly as water. Sometimes they woke up shy again, almost like strangers, until their hungers combined to focus them. Then how his lips sought out her nipples, how his teeth—oh, gently!—dented them. And she would shock him, coming at him in blind heat, mounting his penis, seeming to soar.

"Carnal," she whispered. "What we are."

He hoped it was a good word. What they did together seemed ordained long before they met. Everything fit. Organs, limbs, studs, and joists. Her perfect mouth accommodating him, his hardness, her jaw articulating. Even when she felt she was going into labor in reverse—a human bursting into, not out of, her, trying to grow deeper—everything fit.

She didn't say she loved him. She didn't understand the word. If what her parents shared was love, then it meant eagerness to punish. Be punished. It meant terrible deficits. Yet she moved into him. He breathed her, wore her like a tight midday shadow.

Even his mother, Leilani, was drawn to her, her beauty, her mixed-blood confusion, the toughness riding her fragile tremor. Only his sister, Malia, held back. Wearing a hat that looked like someone's bladder, she sat in the kitchen frosting a guava chiffon cake.

"That Sunny's no good for him. *High maka-maka* college girl. She'll break his heart."

Leilani stared at her. "What you know about dis girl? Keo say her papa mean, beat da wife. I t'ink Sunny carry plenny scars."

"Scars are contagious, Mama. Sometimes, hurt folks need to hurt."

"Maybe you jealous, you like go university like Sunny." She took her daughter's hand. "No need. I always say Malia going be somebody. You da one."

She smelled detergent on her mother's arms. Chinese parsley in her hair. She hugged her. "I must admit, sometimes I'm lonely. Everybody poking fun."

Leilani stroked Malia's cheek, touched her finger waves. "Dat's what I worry fo'. You so ambitious, got no time fo' men. How you going find one husband? You treat local boys like dey real trash."

Malia lit a cigarette, holding it just so. "Mama, everything takes time."

On the crowded bus to Waikiki, she imagined life with a "local." Shabby, bust-up rented house, kids in dirty diapers, beer cans on the floor. She would drink rat poison first. So what if now and then loneliness drove her to pick up a tourist? It was innocent, a drink, a conversation. In that way she got to study privileged whites—how they used silence, how they could summon waiters with a glance.

So what if sometimes she stole trinkets from hotel guests—

perfumes, designer labels cut from their dresses? Schiaparelli, Fortuny, Chanel. Resewn into hers. It made her feel expensive, worthwhile. Made life a little easier to bear. She thought of Sunny Sung, college girl who worked only in summers, never reduced to dancing *hapa-haole* hula in cellophane grass skirts. Who never had to endure strangers mauling her.

"TAKE DA 'BRELLA FO' DA RAIN."

Sunny heard her father's slap, then the aftermath.

"*Um-brella!* English, speak English!"

Her mother weeping. Sometimes when he slapped her, he wept too, hating himself, hating his inferiority in the eyes of the world, knowing it would outlast him. Unable to find work as a board-certified physician, he was reduced to testing blood and urine, tracking bacteria in dots of human excrement. Nights when immense fatigue blurred his perfect textbook English, he staggered round the house speaking garbled Konglish. When his wife answered him in Pidgin, he went berserk.

Sunny rubbed her mother's bruises with *kukui* oil. "Why, Mama? Why is he so violent?"

Her mother sighed. "Ovah-educated."

Keo found her in her studio. Eyes swollen, exhausted from a fugue of grief, she spoke in the stuffed-head tones of one who has wept long and copiously.

"If he hits her again, I will kill him."

He tried to comfort her. "Don't you see? He's really striking back at those *haole* and Chinese doctors who won't let him practise, who still think Koreans are medieval herbalists."

"Don't excuse him!" she cried. "I see Koreans working as garbage men. They serenade their wives, walk their daughters to dancing school."

She heard them at night—bed creaking, her father's moans, *forgive! forgive!*—trying to erase the bruises, destroy the evidence. Sunny vowed she would never enter into such a contract.

"So horrible, that Mama's happiness, her entire life, depends on what he will, or will not, do."

"I think it's the other way round," Keo said. "Your father depends on *her* to hide his humiliations. Pretty wife, nice house. Kids at university. You're his accomplishments in life."

Sunny laughed. "I'm his nightmare. Mama says I have his temper. But it's *mine*. All mine."

He sat back, studying canvases on her walls, images that seemed to leap at him, made him want to cringe. Human limbs metamorphosing into white vipers. A man on all fours wearing the dripping, bloody head of a deer.

"Scary stuff. What's it about?"

She looked at her paintings. "Anger, I guess. At Papa's obsession with his teas. He drinks them religiously. Albino-snake tea for longevity. Yellow-python tea for neuralgia. Deer-antler tea for potency . . . Unfortunately, there is no tea for compassion."

There was another painting—a faceless girl, repeated and repeated.

"Who is that?"

"The girl who my father—ohh, I'll tell you by and by."

While she slept he studied the walls again.

MONTH AFTER MONTH, SHE SAT WATCHING HIM PLAY, HIS DEEP concentration when other men soloed. Even his stillness was eloquent. She felt pride—yes, that was it. Such pride, she occasionally shivered watching the faces of the drummer, the bass, how they respected Keo. Not just his talent but the distance he left them when playing, the space each man deserved as his right. It gave them hot energy, a wire of electricity connecting them.

Yet she suspected the space Keo left them wasn't always out of courtesy, or manners, but the blind drive of someone groping, wondering how far he could push himself without going too far. Curious to know how *far* was too far. She was beginning to understand him, his ability to turn so easily from the world, to need no one but her. Maybe not even her, maybe no one but himself. And maybe not even himself, but someone he prayed he could become.

She was beginning to understand the word *love*, which really meant trust. An almost involuntary fusing. With it came fear of loss of the object loved. Of one's equilibrium. She thought somewhere in the future she would have to fight for him, for his attention, and that excited her.

Sometimes he waited until he thought she was asleep. Then he sat up in the dark and silently blew his trumpet, reaching for new combinations, new sounds, in his head. He played until sweat ran down his chest and back, until wetness spread across the sheet and touched her hips and shoulders, chilling her.

She lay still, imagining him searching, reaching, never satisfied. Sometimes she suspected he forgot she was with him, forgot, perhaps, she was even in the world. He would return and focus on her almost in shock. And she would be waiting, wondering what it was like to be so obsessed. When he reached for her, she felt frantic, eager to grip him and know he was real.

One day she played a record just released from France. Belgian jazz guitarist Django Reinhardt. As they listened, she carefully translated titles. "*La Tristesse de Saint Louis*—'St. Louis Blues.' *Le Thé pour Deux*—'Tea for Two.' *J'ai du Rhythme*—'I Got Rhythm.' "

Keo shook his head. "Man's a genius."

He'd heard of Reinhardt, a Gypsy with two paralyzed fingers, the most brilliant jazz guitarist known. He closed his eyes, imagining them playing together.

Turning the record over, Sunny nonchalantly asked, "Have you ever thought of Paris? The Hot Club. Club Saint Germain des Prés."

He smiled. "I hear they're breaking all the rules in jazz. It's absolutely wild. Sure, I've thought of Paris. I've thought of New Orleans. The moon."

She sat down facing him. "Few weeks on a ship, that's all. I'd go, if you wanted to. Once I knew Mama was safe."

He thought of the vast differences between them. He was just a guy from Kalihi. She was a college girl from the Heights, ready for anything, daring the world to call her bluff.

"Even if we could afford it, what could we do there? How would we talk to Frenchies?"

Sunny laughed. "Jazz is international. You wouldn't have to talk. They're all over there, all those guys you worship—Basie, Hawkins, Buddy Tate." She leaned forward, deadly earnest. "Keo. You've peaked here. You can't go any higher than dance halls. When big bands come to Honolulu, they don't hire locals. Even Ellington brings his own relief men. You've got to go where no one looks down on you. Where you can expand."

"And what would *you* do in Paris?"

"Find a job. And paint, which is all I've ever wanted. Imagine the museums! The galleries! Imagine seeing Titians and Rembrandts in *real* life, instead of tiny reproductions in books."

Her hunger for life scared him a little. "Your running off would shame your father, maybe destroy him. Do you hate him so much?"

"Yes, I hate him. And I love him. I hear him crying at night. But I can't stand what he does to Mama. What he has done to others." She took his hand, holding it tight. "It isn't all Papa's fault. He's a victim of his history."

She explained how, at the turn of the century, Japan and Russia fought for control of Korea. In 1905 Japan, the victor, annexed and enslaved the entire country.

"They burned Korean history books, forbade the Mother Tongue. Art and architecture were destroyed. They slaughtered villages, infants and elders. And there was mass rape, the most profound shame for Korean women. Thousands drank bowls of lye."

She told how Koreans were turned into second-class Japanese, fingerprinted like criminals. Children were made to take Japanese names.

"Papa's parents were fishmongers. Their childless landlord discovered Papa was intelligent, and sent him to university and medical school. When someone sponsored him to come to Honolulu and find a better life, he fled Korea, changing ships in Shanghai. But many nights I hear him praying for his parents. At such times there is throughout our house the smell of tidewater and raw fish. In the mornings, I smell his mother and father on his breath. . . ."

She lay in Keo's arms weeping like a child. "That is who he is, what he has suffered. Even though he's violent, and has never said he loves me, I cannot really hate him."

Keo wiped her face, thinking how her father's history paralleled her mother's. Hawai'ians invaded, their monarch crushed. Lands stolen, Mother Tongue forbidden.

"Yes," she whispered. "I am twice engraved."

Then she sat up, something in her eyes. "I will tell you one last thing. The wife Papa brought here from Korea didn't die of illness. But of broken heart. They had a daughter, Lili, born with a clubfoot. Not wanting to start a new life with a cripple, Papa abandoned her, forced her on relatives in Shanghai. His wife went mad, and died within a year of their arrival here. My brother found letters, this is how we know."

She hung her head. "*O Sister, Sister . . . one day I will find you.*"

Hele Wale

To Go Empty-Handed into the World

KEO'S FATHER, TIMOTEO, CIRCLED HIS TINY YARD, WATERING orchids from rusty Shoyu cans. *His only relaxation*, Sunny thought. *How he kills time between corpses*. She watched his eyes when he looked at his wife, sheer adoration. She felt safe here with this family. Such robust, handsome folks, it was like sitting in a grove of great dark trees, swaying and protective.

Sometimes she sat with Leilani in the garage, singing and eating crackseed while they cleaned *'ahi*, fish scales pelting their arms and legs.

"You like cook wit' yo' mama?" Leilani asked.

Sunny thought of her mother's house, kept so immaculate she asked permission to touch things.

"Mama doesn't relax like this. She's forgotten how." With her tongue she dislodged bits of salty crackseed from between her teeth. "The truth is, Papa treats her like a maid. Sometimes when she starts to talk, he snaps his fingers meaning *quiet*."

Leilani reared back, shocked.

"I know Papa suffers, too. Doctors at the clinic look down on him, they see him as merely an immigrant. I imagine them snapping their fingers when *he* starts to talk."

Sometimes she coaxed her mother from the house, took her shopping at Kress's for fabrics, eating ice-cream floats and trailing their hands across the store's black marble walls. Or they went to China-town for favorite *char siu* duck, joyriding the trolley down King Street, its noiseless rubber wheels making it seem a trip on air. Then her mother would look at her watch and panic, forgetting Sunny, forgetting everything, rushing home to her life of genuflection.

Sunny spent more and more time with Keo's folks, lulled by the steady seizure of laughter in this rollicking, feverish, high-strung clan, each member so restless and full of dreams, it seemed the walls of the house bulged. She brought dishes from her mother, stuffed squid sushi, jasmine-steamed *'ōpakapaka*.

Eventually she brought her mother and watching her with Leilani—their affection instant and mutual—Sunny felt envious. She had inherited that natural love of one Hawai'ian for another, but it was diluted by her father's blood. She wondered if that was why she had been drawn to Keo. Inside his dark exterior, she found light, strong and verifiable, a sense of who he was—congruous and proud.

Only Malia held back from her. The girl irritated her; she seemed to penetrate every room in their house.

"Do you find us so entertaining?" Malia asked.

Sunny studied her, her homemade dress, her earnest hat. She felt gathering affection for her. "In fact, I envy you."

"If you hurt Keo," Malia said, "I will come after you."

Hurt him? She wondered if she could ever mean that much to him, if any woman could. Yet because she was the type of woman she was, with a confidence that remained steadfast to its choice—without requiring self-justification, the approval of peers—Sunny's loyalty became unshakable. Her university friends laughed at him: professional waiter, fox-trotter. Onstage he was brilliant; in conversation they found him "dull." Without his horn he could be blinked away. Turning her back on them forever, she put herself entirely in his hands.

So little sheltered them, they seemed to live at the tips of their senses. He began to feel such a union with her, it didn't matter if they touched. He carried her touch with him. His feelings for her grew so intense, Keo felt tremors in his body, felt he could look at objects and raise them to their feet. He felt even if he failed, Sunny would still be there, urging him on, telling him to try again, that there was a future to live for, life ahead.

One night practising in the garage, moths swooping round a

naked lightbulb, something jolted him. Keo suddenly envisioned three people. He, and Sunny, joined by the single form they made together, a form of perfect symmetry that gave them human balance. In that moment he understood.

"I love her. I love Sunny Sung."

It made him cautious, careful of her well-being. It made him more considerate of others. Each time she brought up Paris, he brought up her father—how her leaving would demoralize him.

"He would be *relieved*," she said. "But I need to take care of Mama first, give her back her life."

"Sunny. She has a life. It's what she wants, or she would leave him."

"You don't understand."

"Maybe I would if I met him. Don't you think it's time?"

"I couldn't bear the shame."

Keo flinched, as if struck.

"I mean the shame of having *you* meet this man who threw a child away, who caused his first wife's death. I grew up lying in the dark waiting for him to come and hand me to a stranger. He wanted another son, not me."

"I want to meet this buggah," he said. "I want to look him in the eye."

She refused, exhausting all his arguments. He turned away.

One night she sat up in the dark. "All right," she said softly. "All right."

Approaching her father's house in Alewa Heights, he was so apprehensive, his shadow moved ahead of him. Meeting the man, Keo understood for the first time how inscrutability was a tactical skill. Samchok Sung experienced the shock of Keo with no discernible reaction other than mild glazing of the eyes, erasing from his vision that which was to him obscene. For Keo was sure that "obscene" was how the man saw him—unschooled, blasphemously dark, a sickness consuming his daughter.

Hair a helmet of smoky gray, his bronzed face rather handsome, he was almost Western-looking except for extremely wide cheekbones and long narrow eyes. Late fifties, lean and wiry, skilled in Tae Kwon Do. As Keo approached and tried to shake his hand, he heard the man's heart pounding much too hard for something that was human.

Keo had intentionally dressed loud, aloha shirt, bright linen pants, flaunting "bad taste" to escape the criticism of good taste. Yet he was so well dowered with quiet dignity, he achieved a composure that made Sunny's father detest him on sight. Still, he talked candidly about his life—waiting tables, playing trumpet—knowing the man hated jazz. During the meal Sunny's mother, Butterfly, chattered on about Keo's surfing skills, his family, as if he were an appliance she was trying to sell her husband. She talked until sweat ran down her forehead, until it pressed her eyes shut.

Not responding, Mr. Sung clicked chopsticks, brought food to his mouth, chewed in a way that was formidable. Keo leaned forward, addressing him, asking about his medical studies, his herbal teas. The man put down his chopsticks, placed his fists on either side of his plate like a man clutching prison bars. He studied his plate for long minutes, then took up his chopsticks again.

In the silence Sunny jumped to her feet, knocking back her chair. "Yes, Papa, he is *kanaka*! So am I. I love him. Though you taught me love means punishment. You've made me hate myself for all I lack. But Keo taught me I have *value*, I'm not *fated*, I can choose. I choose my own existence. One day I will leave this house and go where there is kindness. And I will live and live, until the last day of my life!"

Butterfly covered her face and rocked.

"Mama, I will never abandon you. I'll take you with me."

That night Keo dove into the sea, stroking with such fury, he felt sheared clean. Hours later when he struggled from the surf, she was there. He imagined the scene with her father.

"I've put it behind me." She grasped his hands like a child. "I'm going to be with you wherever you go. Maybe we'll suffer. I don't mind."

THE YEAR PASSED AND THEY ENTERED A KIND OF LIMBO, A PERIOD of waiting, looking for signs. Keo talked to shipping agents, asking the cost of passage to San Francisco, a train across the U.S. mainland, another ship to France. The cost was astounding—it would take years of saving. And now other things claimed his attention. Honolulu teemed with military men, swelling Hotel Street brothels. Clubs were jammed. Each night he raced from the Royal Hawai'ian to Rizal's Dance Hall with his horn.

In December 1937 Dew Baptiste wrote Keo asking him to come to New Orleans. Scrap-metal factories were booming down south. Folks had more money to spend, and Dew was forming a jazz band. He wanted his Hula Man on trumpet. Keo read the letter over and over. Cradle of blues and jazz. Home of Fats Waller. Armstrong. The possibility of playing in that town, walking streets those men had walked, became an obsession. Yet, he felt terror.

"You must go. You *must.*" Sunny shook the letter at him, the thought of his not going appalling to her. "As someone of small talents to someone truly gifted, I beg you."

He was shocked by her honesty. "I won't go without you."

"I'll follow you. As soon as I save some money, and take Mama home to her family. It will give you time to settle."

"What about Paris?"

"Keo. New Orleans is halfway there."

"Swear it. Swear you'll join me."

She handed him her life. "Can't you see, I *have* to be with you. If you don't take this chance, we'll perish here."

DeSoto arranged his working passage on a freighter through the Panama Canal. His friends from the Royal took up a collection. Keo lost his nerve, returned the money, canceled all his plans.

Malia sat beside him at the Steinway. "Sure, you can stay home. Grow old playing *lū'au* and weddings . . ."

He spread his hand across the keys. "Don't you see, I'm scared. Suppose I don't have it? I still can't read music like the pros."

"Our ancestors crossed *one third of this earth* with nothing to guide them but stars and tides. Don't shame their memory."

"Would you go?" he asked. "All the way to New Orleans?"

"I would give an arm, I swear, to get off this rock. But I don't have your talent. I'm not sure what I have." Her voice turned harsh. "Brother, if you don't do this—how will you live with it?"

One night his parents came to him, his mother weeping, his father so stricken, small movements in his throat made him a child again.

"Best friend fo' journeying is truth," Leilani said. "Time you know t'ings, Keo. Sixteen my babies went die before DeSoto, Malia, you. So much *pilikia* in dose days. Our queen t'rowed in prison. *Haole* steal our lands. No mo' food. Lungs coming *puka-puka* from tuberculosis . . .

"But Muddah God went breathe *mana* in forebirth and afterbirth inside my womb. DeSoto born wit' lungs like bull! Den Malia. Still we begging. Eating weed, mud, pebbles fo' make our stomachs full. We coming true *'ai pōhaku*, stone eaters! Dat da reason you born so dark, Keo. You full of earth. Lava. Born near-blind, eyes swimming mud and mucus from plenny dirt I eat. Later years, when sight come, you no believe, no trust yo' vision."

He lay quiet, remembering the coming of sight, how he didn't trust what his eyes beheld, how he kept his head turned sideways, ear thrust forward, relying on sound.

"People t'ink you simpleminded," Leilani said. "But I know you special. Somet'ing in you meant fo' greatness. I see folks wipe dere eyes when you blow horn. You touching somet'ing in dere pride. Now, you going far away, break my heart a little. But you going find dat greatness."

They held him in their arms, rocking him.

"One year," Timoteo said. "If you coming great, or not. One year, den you come home, son."

"One year, Papa, maybe two. I swear."

Much later he woke, hearing muffled sounds. He found Jonah sitting in the garage.

His brother looked up slowly. "Shit. I going miss you, Keo."

Keo leaned over, punching his arm affectionately. " 'Ey! Jonah-boy—remember plenny folks here love you, real proud of you. Athlete, good student. You going university, be one doctor, judge. You Mama's hope! You need advice, DeSoto's always here for you."

The boy shook his head. "DeSoto always shipping out. *You* da one I look fo'. When I competing—baseball, football—I always t'inking, *Be one winnah! Go fo' broke! Keo watching!*"

He looked away, embarrassed. "Aw, Jonah . . ."

His brother stood, bronzed and muscular, four inches taller than Keo. Physically daring, yet generous, large-hearted, he seemed born to be a champion.

He grabbed Keo, hugging him fiercely. "You going see da world. Important fo' you. But no fo'get. Come home!"

HIS LAST NIGHT WITH SUNNY. A CLARITY, AS IF HER TINY ROOM were floodlit. Her eyes like anthracite. Arms outstretched, pushing back the hours. At first, they were leisurely with their bodies, as if there would be time for rituals, a playing of nose flutes, clacking of stones, a pounding and staining of *kapa*. Then breath grew agitated. Skin slapped in soft emergencies. She bit his chest. His tongue probed a dark ear-y channel, making her swoon. Entering her, his entrance sheer.

Later they danced, steps mincing and effete. Run through with sadness, they danced themselves still. He carried her back to bed, holding her painfully tight, wanting to melt her skin down to oils. He would drink those oils, they would ride his blood. He licked her teeth, her eyes, chewed at her hair. He sucked her fingers as if trying to steal her fingerprints. He wanted to swallow her nerve ends, blood vessels in her neck, so he could feel them swell and pulse when he blew his distant horn. He wanted to take out his heart and leave it with her, buried in her, his hammering, hers.

He gentled down beside her. "I'm going to take care of you. We're going to see and hear and taste everything life has to offer."

She was very still.

"You want that, don't you?"

"Yes. But I can't turn my back on . . ." Her mother. The sister she was haunted by.

"Sunny, you've saved my life. You've rescued me into the world. You can't save *everyone*. Why do you need to?"

She sighed. "Maybe it's guilt. In many ways my life is good, even privileged. Then I think of my sister, a cripple. How does she live? Begging? Selling produce in the streets? Someday I'll find her, you'll help me, won't you? I'll bring her home. Surely Papa would love her. Surely, he would feel ashamed. . . ."

Keo shook her gently. "Listen to me. You can't fix everybody's life. Undoing what your father did. You can't fix *him*."

"No," she said thoughtfully. "I can't. Even as a child, I played a game. Setting my room in order, setting all my toys in order. Setting everything exactly right, so everyone was happy."

"Maybe you just need to prove you're not your father." He turned her on her side and held her. "From now on, promise me you'll be a little selfish."

"I promise."

At dawn he dressed, his face crumpled and sordid. She ran bleating down the hall, dragging him back. When he dressed again, she stood brave and formal. Only her lips moved.

DESOTO HAD FOUND HIM A BERTH AS GENERAL LABORER ON A freighter out of Singapore bound for New Orleans. Up the gangplank, legs rubbery with fear. Parents waving, then burying their faces in their hands. Malia stood apart, extremely proud. Slowly, as though engines were harnessed to elderly whales, the huge blunt-prowed freighter crept out of Honolulu Harbor.

The Koʻolau Mountains were still behind them on the horizon, his islands sinking fast, when the first officer laid down ship's rules. No gambling, no liquor. The ship's bridge and hold were off limits. His stomach rising and falling with the shift of the sea, he stumbled up and down greasy metal stairways, swabbing decks, oiling machinery, and when he could stand upright, scraping and painting filthy walls. Flung by the pitch and roll of the ship, through endless weeks he worked his way from bow to stern and back again, his body adopting the trembling of the freighter, his heart the drum-drumming of diesel engines.

Most of the crew spoke Malay and broken English, chattering about girlfriends, families, *kampongs*. Notorious gamblers, they flouted the rules, rattling mah-jongg tiles, playing fan-tan in the shadows. The food was execrable, tasting like garbage the ship had picked up in its travels—rancid oxtails from Penang, cabbage dredged up from a Bangkok *klong*, Kowloon pigeon drowned in motor oil. He gagged his way through meals, staring across the table at his cabin mates.

A wiry Tamil who trained slender snakes to slide into his mouth and out of his ear. A pink-eyed Javanese, pale as a candle, who claimed to have wings enabling him to fly forwards and backwards. Tattooed Brit, tattooed Australian, both silent and menacing. A tiny Hawaiʻian-Chinese named Hugh—pronounced Oogh—a human whirlwind of a dwarf who spoke a skewered island Pidgin/English/French and claimed to be clairvoyant. He told Keo he had seen him in a dream, in a city where pig-footed women with blue faces rode the backs of greyhounds.

Keo laughed, while Oogh continued. "Yes, *mon ami*. One day you will wake in such a godless place. You will wear a tuxedo and play roulette, and fondle a stranger's broken heart."

"And where is this godless place?"

"Ahh . . . Shanghai."

Keo had stepped off his island, stepped out of his life. Now the ocean was his home, it was all he was sure of. At night, legs spread on deck fighting for balance on the churning sea, Keo wiped his lips, lifted his trumpet, and blew. He played without hearing, feeling only vibrations in his fingers. Whales heard his cries and swam in close, responding, coursing alongside for miles. When they were gone—shadows diminishing like great thoughts dispelled—he felt an emptiness, a caving in.

Drenched from blowing in a storm, one night he stumbled into the cabin. In the dimness Oogh opened his left eye.

"Hula Man. I hear you playing in my sleep."

"No one can hear me playing. I can't even hear myself."

"*I* hear. I see."

Keo moved closer. "What do you see?"

"Life, anew."

He knelt, so they were eye to eye. "Do you see me playing? Do you see success?"

"In time. One day you will blow and it will be the sound of diamonds."

"If only . . ." Keo held his head between his hands.

"But you will pay. There will be grief. Ah, well—what is happiness? A coma."

"Tell me, how should I prepare?"

Oogh turned his head, so large it overwhelmed his body, yet his face was perfectly symmetrical, an Oriental coin.

"Allow time's passing. This is your rebirth. Everything began at sea, and so must you."

After that, Keo blew his trumpet relentlessly, pouring out all he knew and felt, all he remembered and imagined. He played in honor of a deaf Filipino at Kamaka 'Ukulele and Guitar Works, the man who had taught him how to hold each instrument like a human, to feel each tremor in the wood as it inhaled and exhaled. Now he held his horn that way, as if it were a child, a favorite pet. Weeks passed, he began to feel impatience, a longing to *hear* his horn, not just feel it in his nerve ends.

He was unclear about their course across the Pacific, and how they would finally reach New Orleans. One night while the Tamil lay in his bunk, a small emerald snake sliding into his mouth, then flicking its tongue and peeping from his ear, and while the albino from Java hung in the doorway flexing its furry shoulder blades that somewhat resembled a drake's wings, Oogh sat down with Keo and pointed to a map.

"When you are old and looking back, you must know where you have been. You see, we are sliding down the coast of Mexico, stopping here in Manzanillo for supplies. Then on to ports of call in Guatemala, El Salvador, Costa Rica. Then, we will pass through the great Panama Canal."

Keo stared at the map. The world was so large, so many weeks to reach one destination. And Panama. Here, it looked slender as the stem of a vanda orchid, yet it separated the great oceans of the Pacific and the Atlantic. What held those oceans back? What kept them from crushing Panama in their rush to flood into each other? He could not sleep, afraid he would miss the passage out of his birth-seas, afraid it would all pass in a dream. Yet his greatest fear was of arriving.

On cloudless nights he stood on deck wondering what lay ahead, how much it would change him. Longing washed over him. He thought of Sunny, hours melding their breath in sleep. He thought of his big handsome mother, arms damp from wrestling hairy tubers of taro. And younger brother Jonah, rubbing his surfboard with paraffin sealing wax from his mama's jelly jars. And DeSoto, smelling of the sea, bringing Waitaki tongues from Auckland, a jaguar tooth from Davao. And Malia, with her English airs, her clothes of false labels.

He thought of his childhood, kids calling him *hōhē*, coward, because he couldn't swim, and *keiki make*, corpse-boy, because his father was a mortuary man. He remembered deep shame for his fear of the sea, and for his father, who smelled of formaldehyde. For years Keo wouldn't kiss or hug him. Sometimes the man stared at him, a look so sad, Keo did not think he could bear to go on living. He thought if he did not hug his father, he would die. This man he did not want as a father touched something deep inside him. Yet there was the awful smell.

One night when he was ten, something woke him, took him by the throat. Keo rose and stood beside his sleeping father.

"Papa," shaking him awake. "Teach me to swim."

They walked down midnight lanes until they reached the sea. His father floated facedown, put Keo's hands on either shoulder, and struck out for the deep. He was so powerful a swimmer, Keo felt the bulging of his muscles. They swam through shallow blue, then black waters, out and out beyond the reef. Waves pummeled them, mammals brushed against their thighs.

Keo held on, gulping seawater. "Papa! No need fo' swim fo' China!"

Timoteo laughed so hard, he took them under. The boy sank, and his father sank with him, patting his chest, relaxing him. In time, air in their lungs took them slowly to the surface. His father held him for a while, so he could gather strength.

"No need fear nutting, son. De ocean yo' muddah. Listen what she say. Now . . . try move yo' arms, like dis."

And so they swam, side by side in darkness in a giving sea. They swam toward the beach and out again, waves smacking them, stunning their cheeks. There was moonlight. And meteors. They swam in circles, then floated on their backs. When Keo showed fatigue, his father took his small hand in a powerful one, squeezing it, pulling his body close so he rested his head on his father's chest. Hearing the thunder of the man's heart, Keo looked into his father's face. And it was *his* face. The hand holding him was *his* hand. It was *his* very heart he heard. He felt then that they could die out there, they were the only two who mattered.

In that moment Keo felt himself dive out of the world of the cowardly schoolboy, out of the world in which he felt shame for his father. They swam in secret every night for weeks. Keo would become a powerful swimmer, a man whose great escape would be the sea. And the sea would always bring him back to this night when he came to love his father wholly and completely, the two of them walking home hand in hand, the flap and drag of his father's rubber slippers echoing his own.

Again he thought of Sunny, who had never deep-dived with her father, never held her head against his chest to hear his beating heart. He thought of a young girl lying in the dark, waiting for her father to come and hand her to a stranger. He thought of their future, how she would lie beside him, how he would turn her on her side, and hold her, and hold her.

Rabaul

New Britain, 1943

She sits stroking this brown, hard thing, all jagged edges and corners like broken pottery.

Kim lifts her net, crawling in beside her. "What is it?"

Sunny holds it in her cupped hands like a prize. Then slowly presses it into a cup of filthy water. As it begins to soften, its half-rotten scent enters the air. Their mouths water. They bend their heads down, breathing in. When it is soft enough, Sunny tears it in two, gives half to Kim. Kim puts it to her nose, and moans with pleasure. Then, very carefully, they slide it between their broken teeth, and chew. They chew for hours, remembering. They chew until there is only saliva. Then they sit smelling their fingers, the half-forgotten scent of orange peel. For days they will not wash their hands.

Two Quonsets over are six English and Dutch women, taken when Japan captured Hong Kong. One woman, crazed from torture, bit a Japanese officer. At dawn, before the assembled women's camp, she was beheaded.

Now Sunny recalls wet, heavy air, flies lining her lids like sequins. She recalls the officer with the bandaged hand, Lieutenant Matsuharu, his uniform immaculate. She recalls the Englishwoman on her knees, arms tied behind her. Mad, half blind, she lifted her battered head and laughed. Life had already passed out of her, all that was left was a shell breathing out of habit. Sunny saw the lieutenant foaming at the mouth. It wasn't her body he wanted to destroy, but her superior laugh.

He looked near Sunny's age. There were rumors he was university-educated, a gentleman. But he had seen too much combat. He was believed insane. In one year he had already cut off the heads of nineteen girls. Guards said he was addicted. When too many weeks went by without taking a head, he grew depressed. Sometimes, strolling through Quonsets in the women's compound, he saw a certain neck and paused. Even when addressing superiors, it was said, he studied the slope and thickness of a neck.

Sunny remembers his eyes, the ebony gleam of their facets as he bent toward the neck of the mad Englishwoman. She remembers him pulling his sword from its scabbard almost casually, never quite raising or swinging it. He seemed to merely draw it across her shoulders.

Now, three weeks later, Matsuharu summons Sunny to his quarters. She sponges herself, combs thin hair, smooths her pathetic, ragged dress. She will go to her end with dignity. Girls sob, embracing her.

Kim doesn't cry, she hugs her almost formally. "If you go, I will follow."

Palms rustle in sunlight, she feels blinded by the sudden clarity of things. Escorted by guards, she walks out of the compound of Quonsets toward the lieutenant's quarters.

"I shall not beg. Above all, I shall be hanohano*." Dignified.*

Matsuharu greets her with lethal politeness. She looks left and right for the sword. There, in its scabbard. He seats her, offers tea, never looking at her neck.

She jumps to her feet, crying, "Gomen nasai! Gomen nasai!" *I'm sorry!*

On entering, she has forgotten the ritual bow. Now she goes through the formalities, head bowed, counting slowly one to five. He snaps his fingers, impatient. She sits again, as he passes a tray of porcelain bowls—tapioca chips, sago biscuits, sliced pineapple. Her tongue becomes her heart, taking up her whole mouth so she cannot swallow.

"What is your given name?" he asks. All girls are given Japanese names.

"Moriko."

"You are—?"

"... father Korean ... mother Hawai'ian ..."

She is terrified, but also distracted. This is the first time she has seen him up close, without his military cap. Something about him is eerily familiar.

Matsuharu speaks softly in a cultured voice. He has heard she is educated and once lived in Paris.

"I myself attended the Sorbonne." He smiles, begins to reminisce—Montmartre, surrealism, Dada. Bateaux mouches *on the Seine at dusk. A strange dance called the Java. Foreign women, foreign tongues. The vaunted rudeness of Frenchmen.*

He shakes his head. "And what is left of such faubourg *tyranny and pride?"*

While he talks, he tenderly pats his bandaged hand where the Englishwoman bit him. Then he brushes invisible dandruff from his shoulders. Patting, brushing, hands never still. She suspects he is nearing a breakdown. Night falls, he closes blackout curtains. He lights candles, staring into corners.

"... Fernet Branca in French cafés ... debating Trotsky, Freud, Ciné Liberté ..."

He forgets she is there, drones on and on for hours. Hearing bombs, he goes to a window, pinches back a curtain. Suddenly he turns to her.

"Why did you leave Paris? Were you called home as I was? Were you forced into combat, into filth, human carnage? Well?!"

She stutters, explaining how she left Paris to find her sister in Shanghai, to take her home to Honolulu.

"I wanted to know her. To reunite her with our father. I wanted to give her a decent life. ..."

Matsuharu leans forward, slaps her hard across the face.

"You *wanted.* You *wanted. You Western women. So free, so indulged."*

He slaps her again, knocking her backward from her chair. He leans down, slapping her and slapping her until she is unconscious. He sits in his chair, floats off again, remembering. French girls in Bugattis. Chestnuts marbled amber in the Tuileries at dusk. Then one day his uncle Yasunari Seiko telling him he must go home to Tokyo and fight for the emperor.

At dawn sirens wail. Allied planes, the whistling down of bombs. She has stayed on the floor all night, watching him, listening to his ramblings. Now he counts explosions. He strokes his sword. After a while he points her toward the door. Guards prod her with rifles, taking her back to her compound. Her face is ballooned with bruises, eyes almost swollen shut. Yet her mind is inflamed, her body sings. She's still alive.

Crossing the base, she sees giant plows leveling bombed installations, POWs shoveling dead bodies. In the distance, steel jaws gouge earth in the hills round Rabaul. Soon underground hospitals, bunkers, and barracks will form a huge subterranean fortress.

At night girls whisper back and forth. "It means the tide is turning! Guards say there will be miles of underground tunnels. Japs will hole up there for years, they'll never surrender."

In the dark Kim asks, "What of us? Will they take us into the tunnels? Will they set us free?"

The question haunts them, haunts their sleep and consciousness. Eating weeds, searching dead girls' mattresses for carrot skins, they wonder: What of us?

And always there is thirst, terrible thirst. Pipes are bombed, cutting off fresh water from mountain streams. Wells are guarded. One night in a thirst dream, Sunny moans. In the dream, Lieutenant Matsuharu slaps her face, then brings her water in a crystal glass. They are in a terraced park, and there is music. She wakes up haunted.

Still, at night girls emerge from behind mosquito nets, fluttering like half-dead moths round Sunny's bed.

"Please, Sunny—tell us again about your sweetheart. Why did he leave you behind?"

"And did you suffer?"

"And how, oh, how did you find him again, so very far from home?"

She shakes her head, wanting silence, to be left alone. But three of these girls will soon die, she hears the water in their lungs. Illusions, dreams, are all that is left them.

She turns on her side, facing them. She sighs. And, in a soft, mothering voice, begins.

"At home in Honolulu, I was hungry for a larger, richer life. But I was cowardly. That's why I loved Keo. He was brave. One day he

picked up his horn and walked into the world, like a scout, easing my way. Eventually I would follow. But first he went to a city that is sacred to musicians. He was poor, he went with very little, earning his passage on a ship. Through many weeks, stopping at many ports, he finally reached New Orleans. Imagine his terror! An island man, crossing the great Pacific. Entering his first real city . . ."

Kūnoni

To Progress Slowly

What would he remember of his entry? Delta mist. Sunlight on the heads of racing water moccasins. The smell of creosote and bait. Where the great Mississippi narrowed, from the levee dark bouquets of Negro children waved. Behind them mudflats, lopsided shanties on spidery stilts.

Then, the port of New Orleans—freighters suckling a vast harbor, Cajuns and Creoles hoisting cargo with savage-looking crate hooks. Beyond teeming docks he imagined the deception and glamour of a big city. But more forbidding, music halls full of jazzmen waiting to test him. Men who had altered the history of this place, whose lungs blew genius. Men who were born, and belonged, here. He picked up his battered bag and trumpet case and walked down the gangway.

Negroes washing down a shrimp boat pointed the way to Storyville, heart of jazzland. One of them called after him.

"Say, Jim, 'fore ya jazz it, or rag it, or any damn thing, better get some new threads! They'll laugh ya outta town."

He wore a flowered aloha shirt under a navy blue suit that, after weeks at sea, had turned a rusty, iridescent purple. Walking up Canal Street, he saw whites staring at his brown, damp face, his iridescent suit. He ducked down narrow streets overhung with iron balconies like black crochet, where folks bartered for crawfish and oysters and chicory. Scenes so familiar he stood paralyzed and homesick.

Through French doors he glimpsed rooms with wedding-cake ceilings. In choked jungle gardens moss hung like terrible blue hair. The lusty scent of jasmine, gardenia. He kept walking, afraid to stop. In alley shacks, walls were papered with ads for JAX. DR PEPPER. In every other window, hand-printed signs: HEXES. REMOVAL OF HEXES. Honey-colored whores with Spanish cheekbones beckoned.

What Keo wanted wasn't sex. He wanted to sit in someone's parlor, telling where he'd traveled, what he'd seen. He wanted to hold a cup of something warm, and say how lonely he was, and that he had fifteen dollars to his name. A handsome quadroon playing the combs told him he was in the Vieux Carré, the French Quarter. This was "front o'town," near the river. Storyville was north of Rampart, "back o'town."

"Watch it! Devil live up there. After dark, he cut you wif a knife."

The sun slid into the Mississippi, turning alleys a rosy hue, and somewhere a woman spoke in soft patois. The smell of oysters frying. He walked in circles while neon signs lit up the dusk, then curled up on a bench and slept. At dawn he walked the streets of Storyville, remembering its history, sons it had spawned—Buddy Bolden, King Oliver. He stood in front of places Dew had named as legends. Tuxedo Dance Hall, the Frenchman's. Look! Mahogany Hall and Lulu White's Bordello side by side on Basin Street. He sat down on a curb, taking it in.

Stale smells of beer and urine. Shutters creaked as faces peered out, yawning. Keo took out his trumpet, screwed in the mouthpiece, and cautiously began to play. This was what he came for. This was what he knew. He did scales at first, then simple tunes. Then he blew his journey crossing the Pacific.

A man with patent leather hair and pink spats dropped a coin in his horn case. "Tha's right, son. Tell it slow."

Then he blew louder, telling of his own town, his origins, the colors of dawn coming up over the Koʻolaus, neighbors snoring down Kalihi Lane. He told of taro fields, and groves of singing-jade bamboo. Of arcane seas, and ancient skylines of coral reef. Deep in reverie, he forgot the hour, the place. By noon the sun made everything look bleached. Maybe he hadn't sounded too bad; a small crowd lingered—delivery boy, a postman, a butcher in an apron who threw him a dime.

Keo stood and cased his horn. "I'm looking for someone on Perdido Street. Dew Baptiste—"

The postman laughed. "Oww! That one. Runs whores. He owe you money?"

"I'm here to join his band. Came all the way from Honolulu."

"Ho-no-loo-loo? What kind of voodoo place is that? You say you was a horn man—or a *hex* man?"

They laughed, pointing him up the street to a decrepit building. "Dew don't come alive till afternoon. You wake him now, he'll kill ya."

He bought a sandwich, sat across the street and dozed. When he woke, Dew was thumping his back, jumping up and down.

"Hula Man! I knew you'd come. I knew." Then he stepped back. "Who laid that purple joke on you? We got to get you off the street."

Up two flights of creaky stairs, smell of vomit, stale perfume. "You stay with me for now. We'll take turns sleeping in the bed."

He was still dashing and immaculate, pin-striped suit, Dubonnet tie, but Keo wondered how he could afford a band, living in this tiny room. Single bed, single chair, a plywood chest of drawers.

He sat Keo down and studied him, an edge, a calculating.

"Listen. Just you getting here tells me a lot. It proves you got it. Least, I hope you still do. 'It' is what will not be slicked down, or jived up. You dig?"

Keo thought he did, he wasn't sure.

"Too many guys with talent jumping on the 'big ride'—name bands, singing strings, all that college-swing shit. I want *jazz*. I want to make sounds that don't repeat, stuff that will vanish. Have crowds ripping their throats out for more. To get to that place, we gonna have to sacrifice a little."

Keo leaned close, following Dew's every word.

"What I'm saying is, forget where you sleep, or when you eat. All you got to know is your horn. I got plans, Hula Man. How much money do you have?"

". . . Around fourteen dollars."

Dew bent over laughing. "Anyway, let's burn that clown suit." He threw him a robe. "Then, I want to hear you blow."

They jammed all afternoon, Earl Hines playing background on the Victrola. When Keo blew too loud, started striding out, Dew lowered his sax and was on him.

"Boy, forget those screaming visions. When your turn comes, just cloud my mood a little—darken my tangible."

Keo hesitated. "You mean, you want restraint."

Dew smiled. "I want . . . poetry. Take the teeth out of your horn. Pretend the thing is your woman's cunt."

He grew depressed, fearing Dew had overestimated him.

"No, no," Dew said. "You just need oiling, more practise."

During a break, he explained who he'd gathered for his band. Honey Boy Lafitte, half blind but a maniac on piano. Slow Drag Madeira, making a comeback on bass after kicking heroin. Slamming Sonny Dunlow, who was tearing up drums all over Storyville. Dew on sax. And Keo. Maybe later a trombone or tuba.

"Thought I'd call us Dew Baptiste's Persuasion Jazz Band. Got a real nice flow."

Warming up again, they played round the opening bars of "Honeysuckle Rose," kicking the chorus back and forth. After ten minutes Keo tapered off, letting Dew slide in. Watching his African/Spanish/Creole blood step forth in high cheekbones, in sharp, dilating nostrils, he began to glimpse the real Dew Baptiste.

Dew had played big bands in Chicago, St. Louis, Kansas City. He could blow towns off the map with his saxophone, but he wasn't meant for that. His tone was deeply personal, his intonations subtle, too full of shadings to blend with other sax men. He quit every band because he didn't like the rules they set.

"Who says time always has to be the same?" he asked. "Who says if jazz starts slow, it has to stay slow? Or if it starts fast, it has to fly? Who says chords always have to jibe?"

Keo now saw him as a true jazzman who made his own rules, his own rhythms. Even if it meant playing alone in a tiny room, blowing notes so pure they were like needles driven into the skin.

Suddenly Dew moved to another mode, with slow excitement. He advanced on that theme, building a terrible anxiety, as if he'd never find his way back. But always he found an outlet in his improv and, almost by sleight of hand, came home, his notes still immaculate and pure. ". . . *you're confection, goodness knows, Honeysuckle Rose* . . ."

Later, in a tailored suit—a little long, for Dew was taller—shoes polished to mirrors, his curly hair slicked straight with Conkolene,

Keo strode out into Storyville. So many wondrous shades of skin: yellows, tea colors, rich mahoganies, reddish auburns, mink browns. Smooth blacks with bluish highlights, and then a true, majestic ebony—this one coming at them in white suit, white spats. Honey-colored women smiled, rocking their hips. Dew seemed to know them all. He guided Keo through tides of heat and musk, still pep-talking like a father.

"This town is seductive and sly. Some folks will try to get their hooks in you. Rule one: Heroin will kill you. A little reefer is okay. Rule two: Whores will disease you. Take the ones I bring."

"Dew . . . they said you were a pimp."

He stepped back, laughing. "Hell, even Satchmo started out cutting in on chicks."

Long past midnight, he took Keo to a club with a tiny stage, a shambling, ragtag band.

"They call the trumpet 'Buddha.' "

He was high yellow and bald, with penetrating, slanted eyes. Lips soft and depraved like injured petals, immense fatigue in his droopy cheeks. His body was enormous, the trumpet tiny in his hands. Before he even put it to his lips, Keo was afraid of him. The Buddha smiled, stuck out a rough, magenta tongue, flicked it obscenely at the crowd.

They were five—trumpet, tenor sax, guitar, bass, piano. An "ear band," no music sheets, no memorized arrangements. One of them called out a song, and they'd take off, sliding in and out of chorus, taking turns at improvisation, no one rushing the other. The Buddha ignored them, not joining in the first three songs. Then midst "Sweet and Lovely" he stepped forward, snapping his fingers, waiting his turn. Almost painfully, he dragged the trumpet to his lips, then blew nervous, jagged sounds making Keo's fillings hurt.

He watched him coming, watched him going, approaching the chorus, darting off. Keo understood the man wasn't playing the chorus, or the song. He was playing the ambush to the song, playing the colors of the camouflage he hid in while he plotted his ambush. Then he was playing the Mississippi River, couples dancing, riverboat sex, a young whore drowning, a girl whose face was sweet and lovely. There! The chorus again. But playing it tragic, blowing like he was the river. He was that girl.

"Tell it, Buddha! Tell!"

In that tiny room, people hammered tables, they stood and shouted. The huge man kept on blowing, igniting the place with accusatory madness, his horn almost disappearing in his huge, doughy gut. He darted and feinted, playing soft now, intimate, his sounds skimming the levees of the river, skimming white shoulders of magnolia, parting delta mist. Sweet and lovely, yes. When the crowd thought they were with him, that they'd caught up, could anticipate, he suddenly blew them ragtime—old, stiff, dotted eighth and sixteenth notes—then slid into "swing" smooth, linear rhythms.

He did it so brilliantly, they forgave him, drunk with his long extended solo. Then he tore the horn from his lips, weaving like a mountain collapsing, the band blowing round him, giving him rest. Someone pushed a chair under his backside. The Buddha ignored it, wiped his going-purple face, lifted massive arms, dragged in shredded nets of air, and blew again. His eyes flashing bright red as if his heart were exploding. He still had tremendous control, still had integrity in his rhythm. They still heard dregs of "Sweet and Lovely" hanging in his lungs. He was still telling a story, many stories, still building to a climax.

Keo sat paralyzed. Here was a jazzman of the first order, a physical miracle like a great athlete, one of almost superhuman control and range, a man of almost freakish shape who could soar and swing like an angel. Here was a musician who night after night risked killing himself because he couldn't, or wouldn't, stop. One day they would drag his lungs out of his trumpet. Finally the Buddha heaved himself from the stage, steaming, his body throwing off wild perfumes. Keo dropped his head, completely stunned.

Out on the street he wiped his face. "I'll never play like him."

"You don't *want* to play like him," Dew said. "He's fucking Lady Needle, dig? Besides, you got your own brand of wild. You just got to ease up—hypnotize yourself into stupidity."

"Oh man, talk straight, so I can understand you."

They sat down in another bar, Dew sipping pink gins like a dandy, his elegant fingers tipped with blue nails. His drawl was soft and smooth, extra slow so Keo could follow.

"Look, imagine you're an old man who spent his life reading books. Now you need to gather all those books and read them backwards until you reproduce your mind at the time of your birth. Empty. Clean. What we want to deal with is your pre-mind."

Keo leaned forward, trying to absorb it.

"Hula Man, you still think jazz is music. It's anything but music. Jazz is *jazz*, dig? When you're playing, lost in your own landscape, blowing sounds you never heard before, maybe sounds you won't ever duplicate, what's at issue is not whether those sounds are good jazz or bad jazz, but whether they should be heard at all. You got to start thinking of yourself as a sort of—sound warden."

He sipped his drink, thoughtful. "You mean . . . I have to ask myself, Are these sounds fit to be heard? Not fit to be heard? Are they just fit to be . . ."

"Surmised. Right. Split-second decisions." Dew slowed for emphasis. "Now—what if you're goofing off, experimenting, and you blow a sound that might lead to something maybe even brilliant? But it's something that could undermine your self-esteem, because you'll probably never be able to match it. What do you do then?"

Keo shook his head.

"See. That's what you got to figure out when you're playing. The moral dilemma. And you got to figure it out in advance. With jazz, what is, is under constant threat of extinction. You can't be sentimental. Can't repeat. Always got to be cold, distant, even from yourself."

Keo stared at him. "Man, how'd you get to be so smart?"

Dew thought a while, then answered softly. "My daddy and mama gave their lungs to cotton. Sharecropping. Before she died, Mama said, 'Don't never scrape. Don't never yield. Don't be the bottom of the pile.' So I went north and found some heroes who taught me how to think."

Keo looked so new and scared, Dew tried to comfort him.

"I'm not so smart. I make mistakes. There'll be nights you think you hate me. You'll want to kill me. And there'll be nights when I cream you with my sax. Or the drummer will, or the bass. But, there'll be nights you'll crap all over us. Nights when you'll drag music up from your balls. You got 'it,' Hula Man, just remember that."

Back on the street, Dew offered him a girl, a mustard-colored beauty. He declined and Dew went off with two of them. Keo tossed in bed, dreaming of a sea eerily still; now it was the land that surged beneath him. At noon Dew shook him, got him to his feet.

"OK. Let's blow some dogma at the walls."

IN THE LATE 1920S MOST AMBITIOUS JAZZMEN HAD LEFT NEW Orleans for Chicago, St. Louis, Kansas City. Now the late 1930s had brought a resurgence of interest in original, seminal New Orleans jazz, without the seductive smoothness of the big bands. It was the jazz of raw and ruthless men huffing, making mistakes, urged on by hunger, sometimes genius.

Dew Baptiste's Persuasion Jazz Band had that authentic sound. They caught on slowly, playing for drinks and meals in small bars on Perdido. Whores who knew him brought their johns. Fans of Slow Drag Madeira came. Some came out of curiosity, hearing the trumpet was a "hex man" from some place called Ho-no-loo-loo.

When they grew popular enough, they took a percentage of the door. Between engagements, they practised all day and then split up for night jobs. By the time they got a weekend gig at Moulin Rouge across the river in Algiers, crowds stood in line for them.

Sometimes dancers shimmying across a floor would stop, mesmerized by Honey Boy Lafitte, half blind but going wild on keyboard. Or they were lulled by the way Slow Drag enfolded his bass, picking out ripe, full-bodied chords shimmering like rubies. Dew and Keo played intricate ensembles, moving in and out of improvised counterpoint. Then Dew took off with his sax, his sounds elegant, profound, always leveling off, diminishing to a final moan.

Keo learned to be frugal on horn, but deep within was still that need to scream, and sometimes Dew allowed him. Some nights he brought the horn to his mouth and paused, filling the dance hall with anticipation akin to dread. Throwing back his head, trumpet riding over his face, he played half a dozen choruses, each with searing intensity. Sometimes what he blew wasn't sound, but just outside the realm of sound, maybe a new way of controlling his breathing. And sometimes what he blew was tragic and coherent.

Most folks had never heard of Honolulu. They only knew Keo

was from an island far away. But when he played like that, he blew Negroes the bitter rapture of their history, their present, still bowing to the white man, still shuffling in his eyes. He blew them truth: "back o'town" brothels, and street prostitutes, and Storyville cribs where twelve-year-old girls lay, and good-time mansions of octoroons where only rich men were allowed—because how else could a Negro girl make a living?

He blew them echoes of street parades, Dixieland bands, strutting marching bands, sounds of other eras—hurting tunes, and dirty tunes, the blues. And the "hot blues," the genesis of jazzing. He blew them wah-wah gutbucket sounds of King Oliver with his film-covered walleye. Mentor of Louis Armstrong, founding father of jazz, he had died toothless, a janitor in a pool hall. Keo blew and screamed to them of rampant pride, of the fact they had survived their history and given the world this unique and genius thing called jazz.

One night in the last sobbing notes of a solo, he staggered, blinded by sweat, his shirt and pants pouring water, shoes squishing like galoshes. He went out with a great soaring wail that climbed and climbed, so folks raised their arms as if surrendering. Then he finally took his dive, freezing them in attitudes of disbelief. When he was finished, head bowed, horn hanging at his side, the applause was deafening.

Exhausted, Keo stood there thinking, *It was not as good as the Buddha.*

MAKA KILO, MAKA KIHI

To Observe Closely, Out of the Corner of the Eyes

ONE WEEKEND DEW BORROWED A CAR AND THE BAND DROVE to Gulfport, Mississippi, playing at the Great Southern Hotel. They drew standing ovations from all-white crowds, but were forced to eat sitting on the roadside, forced to sleep squeezed together in the car. Hotels and restaurants did not allow "coloreds."

It was the same in Biloxi. Practically living in the car, washing in streams, tracking down "coloreds" who would press their clothes. In Mobile, Alabama, playing the Tick Tock Dance Hall, they rented an empty room in the Negro section. It was winter and they slept on the floor, five shivering men side by side, in overcoats and shoes and hats. For two nights Keo lay freezing, in shock.

The same whites who applauded them at night taunted them in daylight, walking the streets three abreast, forcing them into the gutter. Their last morning in Mobile, Keo entered a luncheonette, Karl's Kozy Korner. Exhausted, he slid onto a stool and smiled at the blonde behind the counter.

"Black coffee, jelly doughnut, please."

She leaned across the counter, flirting. "You sure are brave, boy. My daddy catch you here, he'll skin you alive."

Four white customers sat frozen on their stools. Then something moved behind the girl. Later Keo realized it was a reflection in the mirror behind her, of a large man coming at him, swinging something heavy. Stunning pain across his shoulders. Blackness, shouts. He woke in the street, his mouth full of gravel, the white man kicking him viciously.

"Dirty nigger . . . Walked right in, in broad daylight! Messing with my daughter."

Crowds gathered, the baseball bat swung again. Someone grabbed it in midair. "Not here, Jake. He's one of them niggers at the Tick Tock. Wait till they finish playing tonight."

A boot cracked his chest, he inhaled dirt and bits of glass. Dew pulled up in the car and, in the seething, shifting crowd, stood apologizing, "Yes suh, yes suh."

Lifting Keo, he slowly, carefully, drove away. ". . . out of your damned mind! I been saying watch out, watch out, since we left New Orleans. Are you deaf? Are you insane?"

Keo doubled up with pain. "I thought segregated . . . meant buses and hotels."

"It means *everything*. Karl's Kozy Korner. KKK! Don't you get it?"

He wheeled left and right, driving like a madman. In ten minutes the band had packed up the car. Quietly, they slid out of town, and out of Alabama. They stopped for gas in Mississippi, urinated in the woods, then drove straight through to New Orleans. Broken ribs, fractured shoulder. Dew told him he was lucky, told him what they *would* have done, had they caught him after dark.

Keo grew wary. Homesick, disenchanted, some nights he walked Jane Alley where Satchmo was born. He sat on the curb in front of his house. The great Louis Armstrong, whose mother had cooked him meals from things in garbage cans. Made him shoes from used rubber tires. A man with more soul and genius than any jazz musician alive, yet he was still called "nigger" in the South. His image fired Keo, made him more determined to press on.

He adopted Dew's style—tight-waisted suits, spectator shoes, stickpins in his ties—looking debonair, even handsome, when they played Lulu White's brothel, and Mahogany Hall on Basin Street. Each night he carefully dressed himself like a priest for High Mass, knife-pleating his pants, shooting his cuffs. Then he went onstage and tore himself to pieces, ending a shambles, shoes off, shirts ripped, suits soaking wet, his once conked hair standing up electrified. He spent his early paychecks on his wardrobe.

A scout from a record company up north arranged a recording session, standing Keo fifteen feet back from the mike. Still, his trumpet overwhelmed them. On "Body and Soul" he went into a trance, playing twenty choruses before Dew snapped him out of it.

The scout complained, "Guy's too wild. Can't tone him down, he doesn't blend." Record companies passed them by.

Feeling a failure, Keo walked the streets again and found himself in Chinatown. Tiny shops hung with skinned ducks, old men with peonies tattooed on their feet playing fan-tan and mah-jongg. He sat in a tea shop where a girl served him oolong. Smelling salt fish and *jook*, he closed his eyes, strolling down Kalihi Lane. Mama flirting with the *poi* man hugging bags of purple paste. Palama boys across the way singing in falsetto. Snores of Mr. Kimuro on the left answering Mr. Silva's on the right.

And out beyond the lane, Kalihi district. Lee Su's Bakery offering pink and green *mochi*, Kalana's Take-out selling fresh *laulau* and *limu* rice. Eels dancing in tanks at Yokio's Fish Place. And then beyond Kalihi, Honolulu's Chinatown—sewing machines chattering in doorways, barber clippers snip-snipping in the streets. In butcher stalls, necklaces of offal, bowls of pig's cheeks. Tripe singed pink.

And somewhere in the Heights was Sunny. He dropped his head, asleep in the dark lakes of her eyes. Taste of guava on her lips, her rope of body he had climbed. Sunny, pushing him out into the world. Charging him with her fierce ecstatic hum. Yet she was a terrible correspondent. He wrote her every week explaining how, moneywise, things were moving slow. He received maybe one letter a month, and in between, he tortured himself—she had changed her mind. Met someone rich and light-skinned.

When her letters did arrive, they gave him new momentum, he felt gears shift in the suave machinery of his neck and shoulders, he moved with urgency. She was boning up on French. She was selling her jewelry, saving every dime. Her letters made him want to touch someone, made solitude almost unbearable. Dew brought him girls of every hue, but he turned away.

Still, women loved how Keo blew his horn. They'd come into honky-tonks, stockings full of dollars, and listen all night. His name, Hula Man, his strange Pacific origins, the fact he seemed to desire no one, went with neither male nor female, intrigued them. Women turned when he passed, stared at his horn after his hands and mouth had been all over it. During a break, a woman walked up to the bandstand and bent down, smelling every inch of his trumpet. Another stole his mouthpiece.

The band pressed on, always hustling, always hungry. If record companies didn't want them, Dew said, Damn! they'd make their own recording. They rented a mike, recording machine, and acetates, and set up in an empty room. When they played back the record, everything was raw and brassy. They set up a second session, using two mikes.

With no record scouts yelling, no one in earphones waving at them like trained monkeys, Keo relaxed. He still wasn't that good at reading sheet music, not all his notes were right. But his lead was perfect in its supple variations on "Am I Blue," his attack direct and urgent. By the flick of an eye, a signal from Dew, he knew when to tone down, when to gracefully slide out of a chorus for the next man's solo. Each song came out so effortlessly, they ran straight through nine titles. When they finished, they knew they had a record. *The First of Persuasion.*

Weeks later, after begging, passing the hat, Dew set up another recording session in a wood-paneled dance hall ideal for sound. The first night was rehearsal, the second the real recording. But they blew with such control—"Tiger Rag," "I Should Care," "St. James Infirmary," "That's My Home," "Mahogany Hall Stomp," "Nobody's Sweetheart"—they didn't need a second night. Dew haunted radio stations, but local DJs were white, and when they played "colored jazz" they only wanted Louis Armstrong. He sent records to stations in New York, Chicago, Kansas City. After a few months, he stopped calling them.

Sometimes Dew saw sax men in the audience stealing his compositions, jotting down notes on their shirt cuffs. He started playing with a handkerchief over his valves so no one could follow his fingering. One night, Honey Boy aped him, playing with a white sheet over himself and the keyboard. Horn men began stalking Keo and Dew, jumping onstage, challenging them in "cutting" contests, trumpet against trumpet, sax against sax. Dew held his own; no tenor sax in New Orleans could match his beauty and inventiveness.

As for Keo, there were better players with more control, but his raw sounds, his searing altissimos, fantastic high notes, defeated challengers. He listened to a man's control, his lyricism, and grew angry. He would blow that anger through his horn. Sometimes he achieved high F, holding it so long word went out that here was a man with lungs like Satchmo, but without the control or patience to read music.

Dew defended him. "Well, yes, he's lousy at sight-reading, but his ear is perfect. Man can identify the pitch of a fart."

In fact, there were men Keo feared. Hearing the music of giants up north—"Red" Allen, Buck Clayton, Roy Eldridge—he knew he would never achieve such genius. Still, he possessed the ability to incorporate into his playing every sound he'd ever heard—Beethoven, Wagner, the growl and rasp of Bessie Smith, cereal jingles, ads for beer, the praying and cursing of Negroes squatting at their gambling games—cooncan, pitty-pat. He began to see where he was limited, where he borrowed from the genius of others. This knowledge became his dark secret, the careful note he never blew.

A PARTY OF TOUGH-LOOKING WHITES IN EVENING CLOTHES SAT close to the bandstand. After soloing twelve choruses, Keo slid out, giving Slamming Dunlow his turn on drums. One of the whites caught Keo's eye and rubbed his nose repeatedly. Keo looked away. Later the man's bodyguard nudged him at the bar.

"When Bateau Creole does this"—he rubbed his nose—"it means more. He wants more horn."

During the second set the man rubbed his nose again. The band ignored him. When Keo looked down, Bateau Creole had placed a revolver on the table before him. Dew flew into a solo, dancing his horn high over his head. When the man rubbed his nose again, Keo followed with eight choruses of "Just a Gigolo," blowing so hard his brass mute blew off his trumpet and flew across the room. The gun man loved it. At 3 A.M. when Dew and Keo left the club, his toughies guided them into the backseat of his Cadillac.

"To show my appreciation." Bateau Creole shook their hands, stuffed hundred-dollar bills in their pockets.

He was small and pale, his face all frontal like a rat. A ruby glittered in his tooth.

His drawl was slightly cultured. "You boys are verrry good. I love good jazz. I once studied violin, oh yes."

He said he would like to manage them.

"What does that mean?" Dew asked.

"Well, it will never mean I will tell you where, or what, to play. It *might* mean I will bring you crowds. I can make you famous."

"What do we have to do?"

"Just play. I will come and listen. Now and then"—he rubbed his nose—"you might play special solos just for me."

Dew leaned forward. "Do you know DJs?"

"Why, yes." He smiled. "Have you boys cut a record?"

"Cut two. DJs won't play them. The only 'colored' they want is Satchmo."

He smiled; his ruby twinkled. "Send me your records. Leave it to me."

After that, wherever he got them dates he always appeared, bringing men in tuxedos and beautiful mulatta girls, sending champagne up to the stage for "his boys." Sometimes they started to close down a set and Bateau rubbed his nose. They inhaled and started swinging again, playing until they passed out. One night he kept them playing for thirty hours, straight into the next night. Each time they collapsed, he sent up food and liquor. When it was over, he rushed the stage, stuffing bills in their pockets, in their sleeves, even their socks.

Dew began to worry. "This cat don't care about music. He's into *control.*"

No one listened, they were busy counting hundred-dollar bills. His Conkolened hair pressed down with a head rag, Keo sat on his bed rubber-banding piles of cash. A pile for Mama and Papa. One for Malia and his brothers. A pile for Sunny's passage to New Orleans. When the knock came, he reached from the bed and opened the door. Dew studied the little money piles, then bent down, sweeping them together.

"Don't even think of it, whatever you're planning. This here's going in the bank, like mine."

He stuffed it all in his pocket and turned to go. Keo threw him against the wall so violently, a mirror cracked.

"I love you, man, but I ain't your 'nigger.' That money's mine. I sweated for it since the day I got here."

"You'll blow it. You always do." Dew got slowly to his feet, drew the piles of money from his pocket. "What is this? You turning into a philanthropist?"

"I got family. Responsibilities. I got plans for Paris someday, like I told you. Nothing's happening for us, Dew. Our band's not going anywhere."

"It takes time. Bateau's got connections."

"Bateau's a gangster."

Dew slumped back against the wall. "Yeah, I thought of that. One wrong move, we end up in the river."

A year had passed. Keo was still living hand to mouth. And Malia's letters alarmed him.

> *. . . U.S. military building more barracks and runways . . . Sunny's father real tense, afraid he'll lose his job to defense workers coming in by the thousands. He takes it out on her mother. Sunny tries to intervene. . . ."*

He felt such guilt, he sent more money home. Then he started waking up at 3 and 4 A.M., his heart pounding, body covered with sweat. He thought of Sunny left defenseless with her father. Imagining the man striking her, he jumped up shouting, blinded by pain in his damaged shoulder. He stood in the dark in his tiny room until his body quit shaking, until his breath no longer came in gasps. He thought of her pale-honey skin, her lovely slanted eyes. Here, they would call her *mulatta.* Here, too, she would be endangered. He wrote her, explaining how things were not exactly happening in New Orleans. He mentioned racism—"much worse than Honolulu." He vaguely mentioned gangsters.

He changed the tone of his letters, hoping to sound like a man certain of what to do next. He already envisioned them in Paris. They would go, he wrote, as soon as they had the fare between them. He would be a waiter or busboy, anything, to find somewhere safe for her. He would blow his trumpet on the side.

One night he stepped down from the bandstand thinking he was dreaming. "Oogh!" His little Hawai'ian-Chinese cabin mate from the freighter.

Oogh smiled up at him, and took his hand. "*Mon ami*, are you well? You are going to play in Paris, no? Then you must be prepared."

Keo bent down, hugging him. "You rascal, you disappeared! We never said goodbye—"

"And why? We haven't parted. I come to hear you when I'm in port."

"I've never seen you."

"I listen. That is more important."

They sat down and Oogh began talking as if they were still aboard the ship crossing the Pacific, as if their conversation had not been interrupted.

"Hula Man, your ear is still miraculous. You can play anything. But now you must begin to know what you are playing, so you will know what rules you break. Europe will be different. Prepare. Listen to Bach, Stravinsky. Your friend Dew knows these names. They were revolutionaries, jazzmen of their day."

He talked for hours, recognizing Keo's fears: that he was not original, not a genius.

"And what is genius? They say it is the idea of a great principle growing into the promise of its logic. Who possesses such logic? Mozart? Beethoven? Sub-Saharan tribes with drums and gourds?"

Keo sighed. "You know, I'm still scared. Still an island boy. Paris is where brilliant jazzmen gather from round the world. They'll laugh me out of town."

Oogh shook his head. "Listen closely. Europeans don't play jazz, they play their *idea* of jazz. What is jazz, anyway, but longing, raging? And what is music but the rearrangement of eight notes on a scale? All that is important is that the next note be *indifferent*, but inevitable. You have that gift, my friend."

The next night, Oogh brought him a recording, a trumpet solo of the "Nessun dorma" aria from Puccini's *Turandot*. Keo had only vaguely heard of Puccini, but listening now, the horn—its tragic, haunting tones—astonished him. He wept.

Oogh patted his arm. "Yes, weep. *That* is genius. It captures the solitary longing, the triumph of the human heart."

He played it over and over, then jumped up on a chair, beating his little chest theatrically, translating from the aria.

" '*Vincirà!*—I shall win.' You will never compose such as this. Few do. But one day you will learn to play this aria just so. I believe it."

Keo drew closer. "Oogh, how should I prepare?"

He sat down, put his hands together. "You must digest everything you have seen and heard here, even the ugliness. It will enrich your playing. Later, when you throw away what you don't need, you'll be doing it from strength, not ignorance. And try to learn to carry conversation. Europeans value talk. You must understand even the word 'jazz,' many people have no knowledge of its genesis."

He continued talking softly, trancelike.

> *. . . Some hold that "jazz" has its roots in the jasmine scent of Storyville, its prostitutes. You see, Frenchmen brought the perfume industry with them to New Orleans. Oil of jasmine was a popular local ingredient. When perfumers added it to a scent, that was known as "jassing it up." And, also, there is the French word* jaser, *to chatter. . . .*
>
> *Often, jasmine-scented women asked potential customers if "jass" was on their mind, meaning more of course than chatter! Oh, yes. Since slang terms for semen were gism and jasm, "jass" came to mean—well,* l'amour. *It became a common word, also describing music played by little bands in honky-tonks and brothels. . . .*
>
> *It may be, in the languid Southern pronunciation, the word "jass" was dragged out, sounding more suggestive and erotic—jazzzzz. As New Orleans musicians worked the riverboats, migrating north to big cities, the sounds of jazz went with them. And with them went memories of family, genealogy, the pounding of ancestral drums in Congo Square. . . .*
>
> *And too, went Voodoo, gris-gris ceremonies. Nightmares of slavery, and running. And maybe too went love for Choctaw. Indians living in the swamps who hid slaves. So there is always a poignancy in jazz, a homesickness for what we leave behind. That is the real definition,* mon ami. *Jazz is the sound of loneliness, human need. Jazz is the tongue of the exile. . . .*

They listened again to the trumpet solo of the "Nessun dorma" aria. When Keo looked up, Oogh was gone.

OVERNIGHT, IT SEEMED, THE BAND'S TWO RECORDS WERE AIRED by local DJs. Calls came in, clubs wanted to book "Bateau Creole's Persuasion Band." He had changed their name, signifying he owned them. Dew tracked him down, took a sledgehammer to his Cadillac, crunching each fender, smashing the windshield to glittering beads.

While the others fled to Chicago, he and Keo grabbed their savings and caught the first train out for New York City. As the landscape flew past, Dew sat cracking his knuckles.

"No one's gonna *own* me. Least of all white gangsters."

All Keo would know of New York City was a room in Harlem where they hid for weeks, waiting for passports and berths on a ship to France.

One day Dew came running, waving documents. "We got passage! We got bookings!"

In fact, what they had was a job at a circus in Paris, playing with a broken-down band. A clerk in the passport office had warned Dew that, with Europe on the brink of war, most Americans were headed home.

Nonetheless, one July dawn in 1939, traveling in inverse direction to the rest of the world, Keo and Dew sailed third-class into days of unremitting seasickness. Days where they moved crablike across their cabin floor. They docked at Le Havre filthy and exhausted. There Dew spoke enough Creole French to find the boat train to Paris. A circus representative was waiting, and within a week they were playing in the band at Cirque Medrano.

France was miserably damp and gray. The band was ghastly, mostly amateurs and students. At night, smelling sawdust and manure, hellish roar of lions in the background, Keo fell asleep remembering Oogh's words.

Jazz is the sound of loneliness. It is the tongue of the exile.

KA WEHE'ANA O KE KAUA

Prelude to War

STEAMING PACHYDERMS. SIBERIAN WILDCATS SOARING THROUGH rings of fire. Aerialists like spangled moths traversing the heights in dazzling fugues. At first they viewed Paris through the warped prism of the Big Top. Then they began metroing in to the heart of the city, standing on boulevards mystified. So little of what they knew seemed to count here.

But bit by bit Paris's pulse, its tempo, seeped into them. They sat at cafés trying to fathom conversations. Frenchmen debated everything. Even their silences were full of teeth. Then they discovered *bals musettes*, where for a few sous they danced with French girls redolent of cheap *eau* and Gitanes. Bands were mediocre, still advancing the Java, the fox-trot. Nights dilated into dawn as they searched for the sounds of "hot" jazz.

On the Left Bank at Les Deux Magots they met a painter, Etienne Brême, who came to hear them play at Cirque Medrano. Listening to Keo's lonely apotheosis screaming through his trumpet, Dew's magisterial sax, the man was horrified, afraid their talents would be buried in this sawdust arena surrounded by eyes.

He found them cheap rooms and odd jobs in Montmartre, weddings, funerals, a ball for a famous transvestite—his head shaved, frosted with icing, thirty candles poised on his superb skull as he stepped from a giant birthday cake. Slowly Brême introduced them to jazz boîtes, and in time they began jamming at "hot" clubs—Can Can, Croix du Sud.

Caught up in the life, hungry for recognition, they were only vaguely aware that half of Europe was lining up for gas masks. Paris was mobilizing. In September, after Hitler invaded Poland, and France and England declared war, meat and petrol disappeared. From northern border towns, families bled into the city, turning parks into refugee camps. Lamplights were hooded; blue flames of curb lanterns turned streets into dreams.

"I go back to New Orleans, I'd be castrated," Dew said. "You haven't got the fare to Honolulu. We're here, that's it."

They registered as foreigners, carried *cartes d'identité*, and queued up for ration stamps. Keo wrote Sunny:

> *. . . foreigners evacuating . . . the government discouraging people from entering. Don't know how long before it's physically dangerous here. Don't worry. We'll be together . . . even if it's somewhere else. . . .*

Ironically it was war, the threat of impending invasion, that opened up cafés. Hot jazz was suddenly in demand, audiences wanting music that was anarchic, that cried out for freedom. One day a Jewish tenor sax fled to England; Dew replaced him at the Java Club. Keo was offered a job at nearby Club Can Can. As more jazz musicians went underground, "coloreds" moved in to replace them—Moroccans, South Africans, men from Guadeloupe, Tahiti, Fiji.

"Nazis say we're all one thing," the Guadeloupean shouted. " '*Jazz-loving jungle niggers.*' So, boys, let's swing!"

Off Rue Pigalle, at the studio of Etienne Brême, Keo met a drummer from Guam, another from Rarotonga, a Maori sax man from New Zealand. All Pacific islanders, they fell upon each other, speaking ragged phrases of their mother tongues. Brême, it turned out, was half French, half Rom Gypsy, a painter and jazz lover who had spent ten years traveling the South Seas.

His cavernous studio became their sanctuary, where they congregated, jamming to records from his huge collection—Maori funeral songs, "sing-sing" chants from Papua New Guinea, the *pitpitjuri* and kangaroo skin drums of Australian Aborigines. For the first time

Keo heard hot jazz recorded in Sydney, Tokyo, the Philippines. He heard the genesis of jazz in cross-rhythm Lakkas tribal bands of Africa.

Brême's walls were draped with fishnets, ancient warrior spears, shrunken heads from Borneo. In between were paintings, primitive and modern, some old and semivaluable. They could point to any painting, and he would launch into its history, its composition, the chemical makeup of the paints, the life of the artist, whether it was good art or mediocre. Keo sat listening, absorbing; it was like attending university.

The place became a beacon. Islanders dragged duffel bags up the narrow circular staircase winding up four flights like the dark, brooding newel of a snail's shell. Their fragrance, soft melodious voices, dark tattooed skin, recast the place into an ocean oasis. When the studio was full, they spilled out into the streets, renting rooms in nearby pensions, congregating at the Halo Bar. Drunk on warm beer, they performed dances of their islands, waved letters from home, singing out the news.

"Ta'a attacked by barracuda!"

"Apirana finally tattooed . . ."

Sunny's letters were troubled. Her father becoming more violent, her mother refusing to leave him. Keo pictured the two women facing each other, Sunny unable to grasp that her mother did not want saving. He brooded, seeing her face float up in a glass of rum, in light refracted from his horn. At night Parisians sat watching the sky for bombers. He had chosen another place where she would be endangered. He thought again of going home, but Dew resisted.

"This is *our* time. What we been practising and praying for. We can't leave now. To do so would be to fail our time."

"Suppose the Germans come?"

"Ask me then, man. All I know's right now."

One night they played a benefit for Polish war orphans. Seven "coloreds" dressed in white tuxedos, a white piano, all in a kind of gilded cage suspended high in the air over a ballroom. They played without sheet music, shouting songs one after the next, swinging, arching, and feinting, their sweat pouring down on rich couples below.

Sounds from that suspended cage—thumping, haunting drumbeats, sobbing horns, sliding glissandos of a trombone—enslaved the crowd, woke them to hot jazz at its zenith. It would never be that pure again. Afterward, however long the war took, would come another kind of sound. But right now, at this time, this was the ultimate, what the forefathers of jazz had been meaning all along. They played suspended in that cage all night, so drenched and wild when they finished near dawn, each man was a smaller size, his tuxedo, even his shoes, too big for him.

As more musicians fled Europe, club owners frantically sought out new jazzmen. Keo and Dew were now booked weeks in advance, sometimes with groups they knew, sometimes with strangers. At night Keo stared as couples danced in a kind of exhausted sensuality. He watched them on the avenues, their double shadow gliding along curbs, dropping down drains, their inseparability making Sunny's absence more severe. Longing made him play harder, putting such pressure on his tender top lip that little bleeding cracks appeared.

While they searched the neighborhood for lip salve, a carful of thugs sped by, flinging ammonia bombs, screaming, "*Retournez en Afrique!*"

Keo and Dew flung themselves through a doorway. The shopkeeper swore the bombers weren't French. "*Sales boches,*" he cried. Filthy krauts.

One night a gas bomb went off in a cabaret. Next night the audience collapsed when Dew and the band mounted the stage with women's panties on their faces as "gas masks." Signs appeared in windows. NO BLACK OR BROWN OR JEW MUSICIANS HIRED. Working a crossword puzzle, Keo felt his stomach turn. The answer to seven-across was "kike."

Still, Dew was seduced by the city, people begging his autograph, comparing him to Coleman Hawkins who had left for the States. His African and Spanish blood now bowed to the French Creole in him. He talked and gestured like a Frenchman. He lounged in cafés with beautiful women, running up bills for hand-tailored suits.

"Not bad for a sharecropper's son," he said, remembering the orphaning, the hardships. Then he scolded Keo. "Man, you forgetting how to dress! You just want to be remembered for your feet?"

Saving his paychecks, Keo was wearing thin his two good suits. It didn't matter. Even in smart cabarets, crowds had come to expect the barefoot Hula Man. No matter how immaculate he started a set, by the time it was over, he looked deranged and mangled, suit wringing wet, his big *kanaka* feet still leaping round the bandstand. Sometimes when he played, Keo felt his feet, his whole body, turn into his instrument, as if the horn were blowing *him*.

He carried his favorite mouthpiece like a talisman, blowing on it, keeping in touch. He treated his trumpet the same way, stroking it, cleaning it out with hot water. He felt he had to live with it, be loyal to it. Even in conversation, he would almost absentmindedly pick up the horn, fingering the valves, playing scales or long notes.

Watching other men with girls, Dew with a voluptuous Polish blonde, sometimes he feared his trumpet was all he had. Maybe it was all he would ever have. Maybe Sunny was beyond his means. At such times, he thought he would die from loneliness and sexual frustration. The soaring, scalding notes he played, the high Cs he blew for twelve or fifteen minutes, one after the next (crowds counting eighty-eight, eighty-nine, ninety!), the orgiastic F he sometimes achieved—maybe they were just a way of staying sane.

Another letter from Sunny:

> *. . . doctors at the clinic think Papa's sympathetic to Japan. Ironic, no? . . . He comes home and goes berserk, slapping Mama. I try to talk to him, to comfort him. . . . With what you sent I have over half the fare to France. Still saving every dime. Soon as Mama's safe, I'll figure out a way to come. . . .*

As if she had not read his letters, as if France were not on the brink of war.

Malia's latest news was brief. Shirashi Mortuary where his father worked was firebombed. DeSoto had had a fistfight with Mr. Chang for biting off part of Mr. Kimuro's ear. Chang had family in Nanking where Japanese armies had massacred hundreds of thousands. Everyone in shock that Keo was in Paris instead of coming home where he belonged.

Guilt. Sorrow. His eyes hung in their hollows.

THE BLONDE NAMED GILDA MOVED IN WITH DEW. SHE SAT IN cafés blowing him kisses, telling strangers she was going to have his babies. Some nights there were parties of "Dutchmen," known to be Germans and rumored to be Gestapo. But they were serious jazz lovers, record collectors, always begging for encores, for autographs. From the bandstand Keo watched them eye Gilda with contempt, even though she was big-breasted and beautiful, teeth sparkling, features pale and Aryan. Then they gazed at Dew, so elegant, so Negroid.

One night Dew stormed into the club. Gilda had disappeared, presumably with another man. Days later, he was called to a hospital where she lay in shock, looking nightmarish, as if she had chewed and swallowed half her face. She had been found unconscious in an alley, all of her teeth wrenched from her gums, leaving her mouth a gaping, bloody maw. Dew hung his head and sobbed, thinking this had been done because of him.

A nun guided him to a chapel where candles in red jars threw ruby stains on her pallid cheeks. She told him that when Gilda was found, scrawled across her dress was one word, JUIVE. Jew.

He looked up, he looked down.

"Did you not know? Her last name is Feibel." She bowed her head and crossed herself. "A witness said they did it with pliers. One tooth at a time."

The day Gilda was released, she wrote Dew a letter, then hanged herself in a rented room. He sat in the room for two days, not knowing where to take the body. Then Keo and Etienne Brême arrived with Gypsies in a van. They drove her to the countryside, where the Rom buried her under mounds of flowers even though she was *Gaje*, non-Gypsy. Brême stood at her grave, pouring a libation to her memory onto the ground.

"Remember her like this, under roses and lilies and warm sun, in the meadows of my people."

"She was so beautiful," Dew said. "So full of life."

Brême looked back at the Rom. "Beauty. Life. These are words for another age. For now, it is better to be mist."

NOW GERMAN HEADLINES SHOUTED JUDEN-NIGGERJAZZ SIND VERBOTEN and even Dew talked of going home to New Orleans. Creole gangsters seemed benign compared to Nazis. After Gilda's death he changed, his clothes less flamboyant, even his playing more subdued, which gave his sax a beautiful spare tone, rather like a clarinet. He drew closer to Keo, now and then touching his arm.

In the streets of Paris, thoughts vanished, conversations blurred. They were in the "*drôle de guerre*," that limbo period before France fell. Still, all over Europe, in little boîtes and smoky basements, jazz prevailed. Keo and Dew were invited to play in Holland and Belgium, where borders magically opened. In each city, Germans sat watching in the shadows, musicians reflected in the glossy convexities of their stares.

"No more dates outside Paris," Keo said.

Returning to the city, to a club engagement, they were informed the management no longer hired "coloreds."

Keo sat in cafés with foreign students from the Sorbonne, warning them they could be next. The Germans would sweep up everything but Aryans. Rich and privileged, the young men laughed. A few students were Japanese, dedicated jazz fiends who saw jazz as the symbol of anarchy, liberation from their bourgeois lives. They followed Keo from club to club, wherever he appeared. They took him to Japanese restaurants for *yosenabe* or sushi while he talked about Sunny, how he was trying to get her to France.

"I guess it's too late now. Maybe we should all go home."

One of them argued. "With my country and China at war, and the United States suspicious of all foreigners, Paris is probably the *safest* place to be."

Another student, a tall, graceful young man named Endo Matsuharu, leaned forward. "Hawai'i has become a huge U.S. military base. A sitting target. Keo, you must not go back!"

He mentioned his uncle, a Japanese diplomat. "He has many contacts here, he could help get your sweetheart an entry visa. He could help process her papers fast. Uncle will be in Paris soon. Please honor me by joining us for dinner."

A week later Keo sat with Yasunari Seiko, a small, dapper Japanese consul to Belgium. During the meal he politely asked about Keo's music, his politics.

Eventually he asked about Sunny. "Why Paris? These are dangerous times."

Keo answered carefully. "Her father, a Korean doctor, thinks of me as a lowlife. We have no future in Honolulu."

"There is jazz in the States," Seiko said. "You would be safer there."

Keo remembered the South. Would it be much better in the North? "I've got work here. And, well, we've dreamed of Paris."

The man looked down, thinking. Yes, he said, he could probably help Sunny with documents, entry visas.

Ignoring his family, their urgent need of him, Keo wrote Sunny that Seiko was willing to help her into France. They met again a few weeks later, after Seiko made some calls, and at that time he mentioned other work he was involved in—helping Jews flee Europe.

Keo looked at him, confused. "Why would Japan help Jewish refugees?"

Seiko quietly explained.

"During the Russo-Japanese War of 1904–05, a Jewish banking firm, Kuhn, Loeb, arranged huge loans to my country. It was, you see, a protest against the czar's persecution of Russian Jews. All other banks denied us loans. Those arranged by Kuhn, Loeb financed half the Japanese navy, which defeated Russia's Baltic fleet. After we won total victory, the head of the firm was awarded the Order of the Rising Sun by our emperor. Japan still feels indebted."

Keo studied him. "And with your victory . . . Japan enslaved Korea."

The man nodded slowly. "Not all of my country's history makes me proud. That is perhaps why I would like to help your sweetheart. And . . . maybe you would consider helping others if the opportunity should arise."

At that moment a French-Jewish couple were sleeping in Keo's bed, awaiting the night train to Marseilles. He thought of the girl named Gilda. He thought of what Brême had told him when they buried her: Gypsies were starting to disappear.

"Yes," he said. "I *would* help."

For weeks fog blanketed Paris, settling in the bones. Keo stumbled along, missing sunlight, ocean, his family. He felt helpless, caught in the here and now. As fog slowly lifted, he saw Paris mobilizing—skies full of barrage balloons, roofs sprouting antiaircraft guns. During blackout, people ran past with stolen meat, forged papers. Now and then, gunshots. A body flung from a bridge. After a vicious knife fight in the men's room of a bar, he found in the urinal, staring forlornly up at his penis, a human eye. He felt he was back at the circus—drum rolls, humans shot from cannons, death-defying acts.

Two months passed. As German armies advanced on Paris, luxuries disappeared. Everywhere, the smell of scorched fingers, as cigarettes were smoked down to extinction. Old folks sat at their windows inhaling from empty coffee jars, rubbing the residue into their gums. Bars closed early, some forever.

"Wait a bit, you'll see," Brême assured them. "Frenchmen are very cynical. A few weeks, a month, it will all go back to normal."

And it was so. After the first wave of hysteria, the fluster of mobilization died down. Nightlife resumed, more brilliant than ever, and what people craved most was jazz. One night Keo stood soloing at Club Hot Feet at 3 A.M. He was damned, torn out, exhausted. Then he felt a radiance, felt life's claws retract. He looked up, and she was there.

Nā Ka'a Kaua

War Maneuvers

A slow delirium of locomotion. Half carrying her down the street to his room, removing her damp, musky clothes. He tucked her into bed, then lay beside her, not wanting more than this, just this. Hours later when Sunny woke, he washed her face and fed her, afraid to do more, afraid he would consume her. Then he held her hands and listened.

"My brother, Parker, quit Stanford University. Enlisted in the army! Papa went insane, tore the house apart. Threw Mama down, and beat . . . and beat. I couldn't pull him off." She looked at him with blank detachment. ". . . the kitchen knife, cold in my hand . . . I put it in his back. I almost killed my father, trying to protect her. When doctors told her he would live, she looked at me and pointed. She was pointing to the sea."

He couldn't swallow, his mouth was like parchment.

"DeSoto found me in your garage, in shock."

"But . . . how did you get to Paris?"

"It was not how I imagined leaving home. The pain unbearable. I stood on deck wanting to die. And she is *still* not safe from him."

She shut her eyes. "DeSoto watched over me, slept outside my cabin on that groaning freighter. Somewhere near Yokohama, I pushed back pain. The sight of land . . . I was moving out into the world, I was on my way to you! We were in port two days, then sailed on to Shanghai."

She sat up, taking Keo's hand. "That's where she is, my sister who I've never seen. DeSoto helped me search, he took me to a silk mill. We found a girl named April Bao who thought she knew my sister. She remembered Lili's clubfoot. But in three days we sailed again. I gave April Bao this address."

He could hardly grasp what she had done. He felt, in her telling, she was somehow measuring him.

"DeSoto stayed with me till Bombay, when his ship turned back to Honolulu. I had left with only two hundred dollars. He paid for everything—passport, visas, passage on a connecting freighter. In times like these, people fleeing countries, trying to get home, it's not so difficult. All it takes is money."

"And from Bombay . . . ?"

"He entrusted me to the captain, a kind man who carried snapshots of his children. He locked me in my bunkroom for my safety, the first mate brought me meals. For weeks I was horribly seasick, I missed our journey through the Suez Canal. But every night strange men, the crew, sat outside my door, scratching with their nails, whispering what they would like to do to me. What they had done to others."

She closed her eyes.

". . . I had never imagined such physical things could be done to a woman. Each night while they whispered through the door, I could *feel* those things being done to me. It was a nightmare. . . . I don't remember much until the coast of Italy. It seemed a miracle that I survived."

He opened and closed his fists as if molding her pain, her degradation.

"DeSoto had cabled your Mr. Seiko. A couple met me in Trieste. My papers were dated wrong, police tried to detain me. The couple gave them money. Then riding in a butcher's truck, its vibrations like bullets hitting my teeth. Then France . . . the woman flirting with border guards so they overlooked my papers. Changing cars, an old man in a rusty Fiat . . . and after many hours, Paris. I stood outside your club, terrified." Her hand flew to her heart. "Then! Hearing your trumpet from the sidewalk . . ."

Keo undressed, slid in beside her, still afraid to touch her, afraid to breathe. They stared, like two animals caught in a trap. Then thoughtfully she kissed his forehead, his cheek, his curly hair. All was new and must be slow. She kissed his lips, her fingers stroked brown shoulders. She sighed, and slept again.

He backed off, feeling terrible constriction in his chest. He had remembered her face, her beauty, but had forgotten the impact of actual touch—how his brain quickened, how his skin pimpled from shocked roots. He cupped a pale, honey-colored shoulder, felt the bowl of bone beneath. He lifted a wrist, refined and imperturbable. Even her elbows were refined. Her skin, blushed silk.

He studied a breast, the textured nipple, like an object he had never seen. Why did such a soft formation make him want to weep? Make his erection seem vulgar? He cupped both breasts, the nipples hardened, yet she slept. He inhaled her hair, her ears, her underarms, smelling salt, and rust, and female. He pulled her close, letting her wash across his senses.

At noon she woke craving everything, a bath, a meal, him, mostly him. Covering his body with hers like a pelt. Hours later, wrapped in sheets, he sat her on his lap, pulling aside blackout drapes. White pollen dusted the city, Sunny's first sight of snow. She reached out, catching and tasting crystals as sunlight roared down the street in thunderous chords. Somewhere, the bronze agony of ringing bells, a child's cry muffled.

He knew that outside the city conscripts marched, awkward in new uniforms. Heavy-hearted farmers led horses off for requisitioning. In dark confessionals priests dispensed forged papers to Poles and Jews and Gypsies. But just now, just here, they were safe. Life suddenly had depth and edge, a clarity. It almost hurt to look at things.

"Our dream came true."

"I hope it won't be brutal," she whispered.

Now morning, evening, night were measured by the extreme luxury of waking, the slowness of animal activities merging each with each. The uselessness of clocks, the liquid motion of unplanned hours. Each dawn he made forays to black marketeers, returning with melons, cheeses, warm *croissants*, *tartes Tatins*. Packets of real coffee, cigarettes. Shivering, they took the food in under old eiderdown comforters, sipping and chewing, lying back in buttery crusts. Convulsing and fainting together again. Waking with hips stained from jams and crushed *tartes Tatins*.

Some days he dragged up his horn for her, his playing so heartfelt, so rich in vibratos, she felt it in her kneecaps, the back of her skull. His playing hung the room in jewels. As he warmed up, the room warmed up. All her life she would remember that place, five flights up a spiral staircase smelling of rancid butter. The room itself a sloping cube, a crumbling balcony leaning out from the tortured façade of the building. Clandestine gurgle of rusty pipes, walls sprouting estuaries of mold. And she would remember the extreme joy at finally being there with him, sure that the war would never come. Sure that these days, this city, even the sounds of his gleaming muscle of yellow horn, would go on forever, would never end.

Keo was so moved, he felt physical pain. Some days his heart couldn't seem to pump his blood, it couldn't bear to. Other times it danced in its cradle of ribs. Sometimes he woke and lit a candle just to stare at her. As if by mystical articulation, Sunny turned, opened her eyes, and drew him to her. He was as gentle, as refined as he could be.

But he was not always sure that was what she wanted. Sometimes he felt her pull aside, as if wanting to watch his ejaculation from a distance. As her own orgasm approached, Sunny looked terrified, like a woman about to be shot. Her eyes widened, her mouth hung open. Keo would start to slow, back off, and she would clutch him fiercely. Then spasms, clamor, her body fusing with his.

He took her dancing at smart cabarets, La Lune Rousse, Le Lapin Agile, haunts of black marketeers and the rich. Strangers stared, trying to make out what they were. Keo, sleek and dark in evening dress, lips scarred like a gangster. Sunny, vaguely Oriental in the eyes, the black hair cut in a pageboy, the fortuitous pale gold skin. But something else, something sensuous in her full lips, rounded breasts and hips, an indefinable mingling of bloods. They looked like no other couple, which made them somehow vulnerable.

Dew welcomed her like a sister. She brought back memories of a warm, gaudy island where he was still a raw recruit bursting with confidence. She hung Keo's walls with ti leaves, which she had carried for safe journey, and old prints of torch ginger and heliconia.

She made them jasmine tea with little floating petals. In bare feet she cooked them meals of tinned pineapple and black-market pork and rice. She taught them to say grace in Hawaiʻian.

"*Pule hoʻomaikaʻi i ka papa ʻaina. ʻAmene.*"

She took them for walks along the Seine just to be near water, any water. She stood at black-market fish stalls, bargaining, stroking the bellies of tuna. She corrected their Pidgin French, took them for pedicures and haircuts, and found churches still providing heat where they could sit for hours. She was like a sudden balm in those mad days advancing in hunger and blows.

Sometimes Sunny forgot what had happened. She would half wake, not knowing where she was. She would listen with dread for the sound of her father's voice, then come fully awake and remember. . . . *diving into Papa's back . . . his flesh unseaming . . .*

She wept, recalling the plunging blade, her father's Oh! as if he had forgotten something. Recalling his arms thrown up as if trying to fly. She remembered thinking it was the knife's, not her father's, blood. . . . *Metals age, become fatigued. Couldn't they bleed, as well?* She remembered her mother's mouth. Its silence. Her mother's finger pointing. Telling her to go *makai* and *makai* and *makai*. Far away, across the sea. She did not even hug her.

At such times Sunny felt not hate but horror. At what she had done to her father. What he had done, for so long, to her mother. Mostly, she was appalled at what men could do to women because they were physically stronger. She turned to Keo then, glimpsing his strong back, the muscled arms, and started to pull away. But in his sleep he reached for her, hands warm as if bringing her euphorias of sunlight. She chewed and swallowed her father's name.

NOW THE CITY PULSED WITH HUMANS ON PSYCHOPATHIC ERrands. Bankers buried gold bricks in coffins, lowering the coffins into graves. Fur merchants bartered ermines and sables for a wheel of Brie. Folks drank ersatz coffee made of acorns, then strolled public parks stalking the swans, dragging their strangled corpses home. Pigeon traps sat on rooftops next to antiaircraft guns.

In exchange for fresh produce, the concierge shared his wife with the greengrocer. Twice a week he stood in the hallway whistling while his wife and the grocer fornicated next to a cage where guinea pigs fattened. Sunny heard them squealing. Some days there was no motion, only eerie silence. Folks sat behind blackout drapes as reconnaissance planes flew over Paris. Bad weather, lack of equipment, held the Germans back.

At first she would not acknowledge what was coming. As if on holiday, she dragged Dew and Keo to galleries where they studied Velázquez, the light of Titian and Vermeer. She stood in front of Braques and Picassos, explaining how Cubism reduced natural forms to abstract geometric forms. They stood inside Notre Dame staring at the rose window of the north transept, a whirling, flaming kaleidoscope forty feet across.

"Jesus Christ," Keo whispered. "It's visual jazz."

In the Church of the Sorbonne they listened to Bach's "Toccata and Fugue." Deeply moved, Keo hugged himself, remembering Oogh saying Bach was the jazz genius of his day.

After a few weeks Sunny set up an easel and canvases, painting in early mornings while he slept and in the evenings while he played the clubs. She painted relentlessly hour after hour. Some mornings he watched her through half-closed eyes, her flowing brush-arm a dancer weaving color through his days.

Before she arrived, the room had seemed a crypt for his tired bones. Now it palpitated chaos—drooling palette, half-stretched canvases, rags mitred stiff with paint. In old kimono, hair pulled back in a knot, Sunny bent over paintings with a marksman's squint, executing hundreds of oblique strokes. As soon as she finished one, she turned it to the wall. Eventually, stacks of canvases edged the room, rounding off its corners.

"Don't look at them," she said. "They're awful."

One day he turned her paintings round, leaned close, and studied them. All painted in that geometric Cubist style. A flock of razor blades flying in formation. A head sliced up like a pie. Soaring wedges, shredded cubes. Pyramids of eyeballs. A man exploding into flesh squares, strangling a grinning child.

Keo sat back, exhaling slowly. "Ho, man!"

"Well . . . what did you expect?"

He struggled, trying to articulate. "Dew once told me never play a note head-on. Never give it all away. Always try to ambush myself."

He stroked the edge of a canvas. "Sunny, there's no ambush here. You paint your anger head-on. You pound your theme to death."

"I know I'm mediocre." She said it softly. "Everything boils down to rage."

He took her in his arms. "I'm sorry. I love you so much I don't know how to lie."

She kept painting, needing the chaos, the motion, the warding off of demons. And it was something she could control. The rest of their life seemed increasingly unreal. Paris kept changing day to day, like a city too quick for memory. In clubs and cabarets, crowds still drank themselves witless. But faces looked bland, as if made of wax. Some people looked featureless, trying not to call attention to themselves. In every crowd Gestapo sat quiet, posing as Danes, Norwegians.

"How can you play for them?" Sunny asked. "Knowing who they are?"

Keo shrugged. "We're not politicians. We just play for who digs jazz."

"You are politicians. Jazz celebrates freedom. Have you forgotten that girl Gilda? Don't you listen to the news?"

She had begun following Hitler's progress across Europe. During rehearsals she paced back and forth before the band, feeling faint revulsion at the maleness of it: men entertaining men who slaughtered.

Keo tried to reason. "There's no choice. We play or starve. Some of these Germans are okay. They bring us liquor, cigarettes, even get us bookings."

Sunny's voice turned soft. "Keo, in every country that Germany has invaded there are trains full of people pulling out of stations. No one knows where they take them."

"Rumors. Folks are hysterical—"

"What do *you* know of hysteria? Or terror? You're blind to everything but jazz."

He sat back as if she'd struck him.

"You men sit in clubs and blow your horns thinking you're safe because some Nazi loves your music. When Hitler's finished rounding up Poles and Jews and Gypsies, he'll start on what he calls 'mud races.' You. And me. Have you thought of that?"

She looked round the bar at black and brown faces—Guadeloupeans, Algerians, Rhodesians, Fijians.

"My God, you'll be sitting ducks when the tanks roll in."

When she talked like that, he backed away, seeing a trenchant side of her that frightened him—the side of her needing to challenge authority, set the world right. He thought of her father, and what she had committed defending her mother. He didn't believe Sunny saw herself as heroic. It was just that she did not know how to walk away.

She found work as assistant window dresser at Trois Quartiers department store. One day, dressing a dummy in a window, she watched a Gypsy girl in scarves and rags begging in the street. The girl approached, pointed to the bald, half-naked dummy, and laughed. Sunny tangoed it, cheek to cheek, round the window, then she pulled out a handful of francs, wondering how to give them to the girl. Two leather-coated men approached, backing the girl against the wall. Sunny watched their lips move. The girl shook her head back and forth, back and forth.

One of them held his hand out as if asking for her papers. She cringed, trying to hide behind herself. The man hit her in the face. The other grabbed a handful of hair, yanking her to her knees. They continued yelling, she continued shaking her head. As they dragged her away, Sunny shouted through the window. When they didn't hear, she banged on the window with the bald, wooden head of the dummy. Banging harder and harder until they turned.

One of them walked back to the window, curious. Sunny waved her arms, shook her head emphatically *no*, pointing to the girl. He could not hear her words. He watched her lips move, her face full of rage. He said something to his friend, nodding at Sunny. The other paused, then shook his head no. The man stepped closer to the window, wagging his finger at Sunny in a warning way, then both of them dragged the Gypsy girl off. By the time Sunny got out to the street, they had disappeared.

"I witnessed it," she said. "And there was nothing I could do."

Keo shook her by the arm. "*Never* interfere like that again. You could have been arrested."

She turned to Etienne, in shock. "How in God's name can we ignore what's happening?"

"There's no room for God," he said. "There's hardly room for life."

She was drawn to Brême, feeling a kinship because of his mixed blood. Sometimes she sat in his studio listening to records of old native chants while he studied her, trying to figure her out. At first she had seemed cool and catlike with her delicate movements, her slanted eyes. Then he saw flashes of quick temper, a tough, probing mind. An almost bitter intelligence. He wondered how long she could take Keo's life.

To anyone but jazzmen and their casual women, it seemed a life of sloth and repetition. Sunny struck him as a woman meant for more than that. Something in her needed to be doing, needed to be rescuing, redeeming. And that was what she couldn't see: how much Keo needed her, her nurturing. She thought of him as gifted, needing no one, driven by his horn. What Brême saw was a man born with a gift so rare and fragile it could expire quickly, because Keo lacked confidence.

She strolled Brême's studio, marveling at his collection. "Corot. Utrillo—is that an original? Gauguin, I never liked him. Renoir . . . Oh! Hiroshige."

He followed her, impressed. "You know a bit about art."

"I know a *lot* about art," she said. "I've studied books, I've *memorized* paintings. Unfortunately, that's what I do best."

"Have you *tried* painting?"

"Oh, I dabble. That means 'without serious intent.' Dabbling reduces it to a hobby, so no one expects excellence." She smiled philosophically. "I don't pity myself, Etienne. There are worse things than being not-gifted. If I could just discover what I was *meant* for, I would be content."

"You were preparing for . . . medicine?"

"That's over. My life is mine now. I want to do something worthwhile."

He turned thoughtful. "I have something that might interest you. Give me a little time."

One night the men's room of the Chat Noir Café was riddled with bullets: the burgeoning Underground Resistance had cornered a German spy. Then Dew learned two Negro jazz musicians playing in Copenhagen were now in prisoner-of-war camps. People were disappearing left and right. April now, Hitler predicting he would take Paris by May. Men sat in Brême's studio and talked of heading home.

"Go," he said. "Before you end up hiding in sewers."

"What about you? They're rounding up your people."

"I have errands here."

They had wondered if Brême were a Nazi sympathizer. German "Danes" drifted in and out of his studio, swapping Ella Fitzgerald for Sidney Bechet, playing Count Basie through the night. Keo had learned otherwise, that Brême was one of the Rom Gypsy partisans working against the coming Occupation. Rom knew the countryside, they trafficked in contraband, excelled in the art of invisibility.

One night at the Halo Bar, Brême sat down with Sunny.

"I've been thinking. My father is in restoration at the Louvre. I wonder . . . would you work for no pay, but maybe extra ration cards?"

She gave him her full attention.

"I'm asking if you would like to help save great art."

They talked in a corner for hours.

"You cannot discuss this," he said. "Ever. If you do, you will probably be shot. I'll explain to Keo what I can."

SINCE 1938 THE LOUVRE HAD MOVED ITS MOST VALUABLE TREASURES several times. The first had been after the Munich Agreement when Europe seemed on the brink of war. Paintings were moved downstairs to the museum's basement, and it was so well planned, it took only twenty minutes to pack the most important paintings behind bombproof walls once used as wine cellars for Henri II and Catherine de' Medici. It took another ten days to wrap the paintings. As soon as the threat of war receded, they were unwrapped, restored to their original places. The museum reopened in seven days.

The next crisis had come in 1939, as Hitler took Czechoslovakia in March and, in September, Poland. By then the Louvre had been quietly moving its masterpieces—Rembrandts, da Vincis, Delacroix—out of Paris to privately owned châteaux in the country. For the second alert, they had called on legendary packers of antiquities who had moved pharaohs' coffins from Egypt to the British Museum, who had moved emerald doors the width of rooms from Mayan jungles to the Prado. Men whose hands were delicate as eunuchs', others who had backs and shoulders like wrestlers.

Fifty such packers were chosen, along with half a dozen Chinese experts in bamboo scaffold rigging, the medieval art of lashing bamboo poles with flosslike strips of split bamboo, creating nailless scaffolds of strength and flexibility. For one long night, Chinese scaffolders sat in bare feet before a thirty-by-forty-foot Veronese weighing three tons, quietly debating how they would scale the thing, how to attach pulleys and delicately remove it from the wall.

Through the night, ten of the husky packers practised walking backwards through the Louvre, semaphoring directions to their colleagues with the three-ton burden in its frame, guiding them in slow motion through the highest, broadest exit portal. A large truck then moved into the night taking the master painting to safety in the country. The Chinese sat again meditating before another three-ton monster, retwisting their bamboo strips, strengthening their scaffoldings. Perhaps remembering their fathers' fathers' legends of the time before paper, two thousand years earlier, when ancestors wrote their literature and history on this talking jade-grass called bamboo.

Next, the massive Venus de Milo and the Winged Victory of Samothrace were moved from their pedestals with the help of the graceful, wiry Chinese and their bamboo scaffolds. In bare feet, they arabesqued and pliéed, seemingly climbing air round the sculptures, lowering levers and pulleys, hoisting ropes. The statues were wrapped and boxed, laid on their sides, and slid along corridors and down specially built ramps to trucks. In frigid dawns, the Chinese quietly dismantled their scaffolding, winding up flosslike strips of bamboo, laying the poles side by side. Then they sat studying bare walls, imagining, inside grimy outlines, the paintings they had rescued.

Now in the first months of 1940, with Hitler's invasion imminent, lesser masterpieces were being packed—Ingres, Corot, Chagall. Brême invited Sunny to join a skeletal staff, mostly wives of curators and restorers who had marched off with the army, in a desperate attempt to save them from the Nazis, with their mania for obliterating "decadent" art.

In gray overalls, gauze mask, and hair net, Sunny knelt in the basement of the Louvre with dozens of other women, supervised by experts. Smaller paintings were removed from their frames and rolled up, while canvases over three feet were wrapped intact. First, thick cloth was wrapped carefully round each canvas. Next came layers of excelsior, to cushion shock. Asbestos, a fire preventative, composed the third layer; then, to prevent water damage, came tar paper, the final layer. Now and then women interrupted their work, stepped aside and wiped their eyes, shaking with emotion. Each package was finally berthed in wooden cases, on wooden pegs preventing vibration as they were transported to the country.

Every night for weeks, Sunny bent over the wrapping crates, back aching, fingers swollen from the constant prick of excelsior. Rashes now circled her arms and wrists from the irritation of tar paper, reminding her of pineapple rash from summers in the canneries back home. She never complained. Each night she entered the Louvre with senses so heightened she felt drunk.

When she came home exhausted at dawn, Keo fed her and put her to bed. She fell asleep trying to tell him what she had held in her hands, the living flesh of paintings she had touched. She tried to explain what it meant, how she had never felt so necessary. So alive. She wondered what in her life would compare to this.

Now the Louvre was closed to the public. With all paintings safely gone, curators and workers began cleaning and polishing, scrubbing walls and marble floors not scrubbed in decades. Sunny moved slowly, concentrating on each marble square, each mosaicked tile, kneeling and scrubbing the grouting between them with tiny brushes. She scrubbed like a penitent, head truantly low, face so near the floor she felt cold exhalations from the stone.

Each day she moved slower, praying the war would not come, it would pass them by, so she could continue here forever. One day there was nothing left to scrub. The Louvre was closed to everyone. She stepped through its portals into soft rain, and backed away slowly until its shimmering façade could be held in her hand.

Nā Hoa Paio

The Enemy

Malia's letters from home kept him abreast.

> *... Folks tense, almost a quarter-million military men in Honolulu ... Jonah-boy wants to leave university, join the army. Which makes Mama go pupule ... Shirashi Mortuary still closed ... Papa with no job ...*

He hung his head, guilt mixed with longing. He closed his eyes, smelling coral furred with *limu*. He felt his hands rubbing the grain of old *koa* canoes. He was sick to death of stone. Buildings, streets, even the river seemed made of stone.

"I'm homesick too," Sunny whispered. "But this is what we chose."

He thought how pitiful they were, like weeds. He thought how dehydrated he felt, no sea, no humid air. He missed soft voices in his lane, the smell of ginger.

Sunny thought of her mother. "I didn't *save* her. Papa will make her pay ... for everything."

They wondered if they had traveled too far from their islands, if they would ever fit in again. For now, there was enough here to sustain them. Other jazzmen transplanted from the Pacific. Tahitian

Frenchmen with fabric shops off Rue Cordorcet. Polynesian dance troupes. And there were always foreign students at the Halo Bar.

Some days Sunny sat in a small park near Sacré Coeur, watching sunlight electrify the saxophone of Endo Matsuharu while Keo coached him on melodic structure. A handsome, sensitive young man, he talked of abandoning law studies, becoming a serious jazzman. At which point his uncle, Yasunari Seiko, blanched.

Men still converged on Etienne Brême's studio where they slept, practised, sat around cleaning their instruments. Sometimes Gypsies came, dark, silent men, oiling handguns and rifles while Brême spoke with numb discretion of how his people were being forced to flee. Women settled there, too—students, au pairs, starlets—who had come from Tahiti, Fiji, the Philippines. They took over Brême's studio and set to work barbering, laundering, cooking. The scent of strange spices wafted down halls and into the streets so that, just by lifting their heads and sniffing, folks knew where to find the "island crowd."

Seeking out corners and niches, women set up boundaries with hung sheets, like a steerage hold. They drank and danced and slept with their men in this cavern resembling a watery ballroom hung with marine life and nets. And in leisurely ways, they let Brême use them as cogs in his network.

"Don't be polite," he instructed them. "Parisians don't understand manners."

With their sinuous walk, their sloe-eyed gaze, women sat in offices of French bureaucrats, flirting and dickering over entry visas, exit visas, *cartes d'identité*, working papers, papers for non-French-speaking Gypsies. They crossed their legs asking innocently for black-market tips, more ration cards, introductions to border guides. Sometimes they slept with immigration clerks in order to get what Brême needed. They put themselves in danger, doing anything he asked; times were perilous, everyone a little mad.

One night Sunny delivered forged papers to a woman who paid her with an emerald brooch. The stone bought extra ration cards for three French families whose men had been mobilized to the Northern frontier. Walking two miles across Paris girdled with electrical wiring for an Underground radio to be set up in a church, she was struck by how she seemed to have entered Paris by the back door.

Before she had climbed the Tour Eiffel or seen the interior of the Madeleine, she had found herself wrapping masterpieces in the basement of the Louvre. She had barely glimpsed the white cupolas of Sacré Coeur before she was running errands for the Underground—bartering forged papers, stapling leaflets for clandestine printing presses. The raw energy of the city, people arguing communism and fascism in a dozen languages, even their underlying terror, galvanized her. She came in from the streets trembling with new schemes to beat back the Nazis.

Yet she had only to glance at Keo to know when he needed solitude. He would put his horn to his lips and step out of a frame into his private chaos. Sometimes he came back from that place and looked round their room, wanting more, more money, more acclaim.

"I work day and night, don't I deserve it?"

Such thoughts turned him morbid, even despotic. Often, while practising, he lowered his trumpet.

"Damn clock ticks too loud."

She put the clock away.

He still complained. "We're not supposed to *hear* time."

She went to a street where people bartered, trading the clock for an old brass-stemmed hourglass. Keo was pleased, liking how time was now under his control, how hours stood still until he turned the glass chamber over.

"Do you remember," Sunny asked, "our beautiful word for hourglass? *Anahola*. To measure the hour. Time set aside."

Still, there were days he ignored her, giving the best part of himself to the frightful lucidity of his talent.

"I don't feel you're with me anymore," she said. "Even when we make love. You're not even in the room!"

They would argue in deadly confrontation, Sunny smoking a Gauloise, one hand supporting with affected attitude the elbow of her smoking arm, her fury emptying itself in smoky exhalations. She would turn her back on him, high heels making her walk with excruciating elegance. And she would leave, leaving him empty. Later while he played she would show up at the club, looking miserable. He would smell her cologne across the room and close down the set, wanting her.

So caught up with his life, the lack of everything but jazz, Keo didn't see that something lovely and unrepeatable was being squandered. Something she kept offering him was being pushed aside.

PARIS STREETS GREW DESERTED, THE AIR UNBORN. A MAN HUNG by his neck from a lamppost.

"*Collabo,*" someone whispered. "Partisans strung him up."

Dew's voice suddenly had the cadence of a girl. "Spread the word. All my poker winnings for a berth, third, fourth, any class, on any ship heading to America. If you're smart, you'll come, too."

Then France surrendered and overnight Paris became a fugitive. Even the landscape disappeared. Boulevards blank, days unmodulated hours. Only jackboots marching in the streets, the crunch of tank treads. Night was not allowed. People lay holding each other fully dressed, wondering what came next. At 3 A.M. black-booted men in black sedans. Like harvesters amongst the human grain, sometimes they harvested all night. Dragging families into streets. Machine guns stitching. Syllables of human cries. And then it would be morning. A woman's corpse sitting in a doorway. A child's foot in its melancholy sock. In Brême's studio, men assembled homemade bombs.

Banners flying, red swastikas snapping in wind, each day, while German bands played "Deutschland über Alles," antennaed vans prowled streets, feeling the air for Morse encoders, radios. Posted handbills announced public executions of members of the Resistance, for blowing up railroads, for murdering German officers. In reprisal for one Nazi commander, forty civilians were tortured and shot. Brême walked the streets ripping down handbills, his face like something hardened in a kiln.

Even defeated, Paris resumed, nightlife resumed. Clubs and cabarets were packed. Behind blackout drapes, British agents wearing lime cologne sat at tables with gun-running Gypsies. Gestapo clapped their hands, keeping time with the Underground. All jazz maniacs, begging for more. At dawn, exhausted jazzmen shuffled home without after-curfew passes, hiding in doorways at the sound of marching boots.

That summer of 1940 the going was still good, though they thought it was bad. Cigarettes could be had on the black market. Watered-down Scotch and gin. Yet, each night he played, Keo felt something waiting in the shadows, something awful blinking its eyes. Even in dreams he glanced over his shoulder. In occupied Holland another musician, Freddy Johnson, the Negro pianist, had been arrested. Nazis found him too outspoken. His sax man and drummer had gone underground.

One day while the band practised in a borrowed studio, the door was splintered by men in black leather.

"*Jam sessions sind verboten!*" the leader screamed. He and his thugs broke every bit of furniture, though they didn't touch the musicians or their instruments.

"They're friends," Brême said. "It was a warning. The concierge of that building is a *collabo*."

Days later, the same Gestapo man showed up at Brême's, terribly excited, carrying a recording of Stan Getz smuggled in from Sweden. When Brême told him Getz was white, the German cursed, disgusted.

"Take it. I only collect Negroes."

Brême shook his head. "You people are *murdering* so-called inferior races, yet you worship Negro jazz. Where is your logic?"

The German looked down. "Logic? There is only madness." He stepped closer. "Be careful, my friend. You're drawing attention to yourself."

That night Brême asked Keo to join him for dinner. When he arrived, Brême was sitting with Yasunari Seiko, former Japanese consul in Belgium, now at the consulate in Paris. Keo was shocked that they knew each other.

"In these times, nothing is coincidence." Seiko smiled. "I hope you and your fiancée are well." A subtle reminder that he had eased Sunny's entry into France.

By now Goebbels had banned jazz from radio and was trying to ban jazz and "swing" altogether. Still, jazz-loving Germans—industrialists and the very rich—had grown insistent that more Negroes undertake a German tour.

"It would be very good," Seiko said, "if you could do a short tour. The Berlin Hot Club, for instance. There is someone there waiting for . . . documents."

Keo studied him. "Someone important?"

"Extremely," Brême said. "Fans are begging for Dew Baptiste. If you could persuade him to join you, we might find him passage home."

That night during an air raid Keo lay facedown in the metro, inhaling plaster and debris. At home, he woke Sunny.

"Tonight I found myself in a French subway being bombed by English planes. Earlier, I had dinner with a Japanese diplomat and a Gypsy spy who want me to go to Nazi Germany because someone needs papers." He took her hands. "This is not the life we planned."

"This is life," she said. "I'm going with you."

"No. You're staying here."

IN FRANKFURT AND HAMBURG, THE GERMANS WERE IMPECCABLE. Keo and Dew and their band were treated like royalty. The Lili Marlene Club in Frankfurt was packed three nights running, crowds begging for more, men and women in evening dress, drinking champagne, Armagnac. Their tastes sedate, more swing than hot jazz. "Sophisticated Lady." "Stardust."

Berlin was wild, crowds rushing headlong to destruction. Outside clubs, students listening from the streets drank hair cologne, cheap perfume. Some were anti-Nazi "swing kids" who shrieked when Dew and Keo chorused "Do You Know What It Means to Miss New Orleans." When the Guadeloupean drummer went berserk, they tore their clothes off.

Even older crowds were reckless. Glasses overflowed. They drank champagne and brandy straight from bottles. Keo had the sense of a crown glittering with jewels whose settings were rotting. Outside clubs, women in furs and gowns threw themselves at the band, beckoning from Daimlers and Mercedes. For the first time in his life, Dew demurred.

Seiko had had papers sewn into the shoulder pads of one of Keo's jackets. One night, returning to his dressing room, he found the shoulder seams ripped open, documents gone. Heading back toward the German-French border, they played one more night in Stuttgart. The next afternoon they were driven to the train, where the band split up into two compartments.

At a small town the train was stopped by troops of German soldiers. After an hour, black sedans pulled up with Nazi officers wearing the full insignia of the Totenkopf, the Death's Head Squadron of the SS. All passengers were ordered onto the platform. In that moment Keo resolved to admit his guilt if he were interrogated about the documents. He would give his life for Dew.

Soldiers lined up more than two hundred men, women, children, German and French, heading back over the border. They stood holding out their papers, their transit visas. The commandant, strolling the platform, moved to a young man and slapped his face repeatedly. The SS surrounded him. A popping sound: one of them collapsed. The young man had fired a pistol. His body leapt and jitterbugged as bullets hit him from all sides. Not one word was uttered by the SS.

As it grew dark, spotlights were lit, blinding them, while officers barked orders. Soldiers moved up and down the platform, machine guns poised, spotlights haloing helmets, reflecting off black, shiny boots. People cast their heads down. To make eye contact was to die. Randomly, rather casually, officers pulled individuals out of line, checked their papers, slapped or questioned them. Women fainted. Boots stepped over them.

Keo stood numb, fingers squeezing the handle of his trumpet case. The commandant paused before him, snapping his fingers; a soldier ripped the case from Keo's hand, dumping out his trumpet. They did the same with Dew's saxophone. The commandant stared silently at the brassy, flagrant instruments, then shone his flashlight in Keo's face.

"I am not a fan," he said in precise English, "of your *Hottentot* music." His voice turned soft. "But I am curious."

Almost gently he inserted his swagger stick between Keo's legs, lifting it until it pressed against his genitals.

"Tell me, when you make this noise, this so-called *jazz*, does it excite you?"

He moved the stick back and forth in a fondling way. The flashlight moved to Keo's groin. "Do you become . . . aroused?"

Keo concentrated on the stick, waiting for excruciating pain. The commandant laughed, snapped his fingers again. Behind him the soldier stiffened, pointing his gun at Keo's chest. He heard the ocean in his skull. . . . *I've shit in my pants*. How sad a dying thought it was.

A shadow suddenly leapt from the platform in front of the train and started running down the tracks. The rat-a-tat-tat of machine guns. An old German woman on Keo's left fell babbling to her knees. The commandant spoke to her in German, gently lifting her to her feet. People prayed out loud.

Beyond his own foul smell, Keo smelled Dew's sweat beside him, wild and rancid. He could hear Dew breathing like a running dog. The flashlight swept to Dew's face. Sweat poured down his cheeks, and stood like pearls in his frizzy hair.

The commandant leaned toward him, then recoiled. "God, you mud races . . . STINK!" He shoved a handkerchief to his nose.

A soldier prodded a child in a woman's arms. A dead infant, probably stuffed with bullets, a map. They wrenched the corpse from her, and hit her in the stomach. She spat in the face of a soldier. The rat-a-tat-tat again. An old man was pushed to his knees, then dragged by guards to a truck, his eyes huge, begging Keo to help him. A couple passed before them, prodded by guns. By daylight more than sixty people had been pushed aboard trucks. Refugees, saboteurs, the innocent.

At 8 A.M. the officers went away for breakfast, then returned, belching and bored. Passengers had been standing there for more than sixteen hours. A whistle blew. Soldiers barked, ordering the crowd to board. Dew and Keo knelt, gathering their instruments. Then they moved toward the train in little hesitating steps. They boarded, sat side by side, staring straight ahead.

The train coughed and snorted, jolted once or twice, then slowly moved forward, soldiers grinning in the windows, waving them good-bye. Even as the train accelerated, trees and meadows coming into view, they never moved, not an eye. Later, Keo heard Dew beside him, teeth chattering as he sobbed, both of them still staring straight ahead.

When he could move, when he finally dared to, Keo glanced out the window. A cloudy day. Yet the landscape almost blinded him. He saw life, the pure miracle of life—its ancient realms, its vast jeweled portals—wherein each human stood suspended in his moment. He saw it as if for the first time.

To be alive, he thought. *To be allowed to live!*

Mahuka

To Flee

He ran down his narrow Montmartre street as if he had never seen it, as if he must memorize it. He stood before the mildewed façade of his building wanting to embrace it, embrace each scalloped step of five warped flights. He bathed, took her in his arms.

"Oh, Sunny," he whispered. "How much I love you!"

Half awake, she turned to him.

"I want to marry you. *Today*. I want us to have children."

She sat up, instantly alert.

"We're going home. The hell with jazz, I'll drive a bus in Honolulu."

"Keo. What happened?"

He shook his head, unable to describe it.

"I can't go back," she said softly. "Remember?"

"Sunny, things are closing in."

". . . Couldn't we move to Switzerland?"

He smoothed his hand across her shoulder. "It's a desert for jazz."

"What about Spain?"

"The war is there. It's everywhere."

He spent days staring from his window, thinking of innocent old couples dragged to trucks. The swagger stick between his legs. The O of the mouth of the machine gun pointing at his chest.

Seiko kept his word and found Dew a berth on a ship out of

Marseilles. Dew begged them to leave with him and, after one sad, boisterous night at Brême's, he was gone. Keo was so depressed he didn't play for days.

"No more crossing borders," he told Seiko. "I'm no hero, I would have given them your name."

Seiko made it up to him, assigning simple errands. He spent time with Keo and Sunny, sensing they needed someone older to confide in. She told him about Lili, the sister she had never met. She wondered what her life was.

"If she's pretty, she's probably in a Shanghai brothel." His words like slaps across her face. "If she's crippled as you say, she's begging in the streets."

He took her hand. "Forgive me. You mustn't deceive yourself. To look for her would break your heart."

"One must have hope," Sunny cried. "To give up hope is greedy. It's dishonorable."

One bright, frigid day they found Brême's studio a mess, valuable paintings slashed in their frames, chairs gutted, spilling kapok. Musicians and their women gathered, waiting for him like children. After a week, near freezing, they started burning things in his fireplace, shredded journals, fishnets, wooden picture frames. One day two Rom Gypsies in the doorway in dark felt hats, profiles like hawks gliding on thermals. They pried floorboards aside, shoved firearms into canvas bags.

"Where is Brême!" Keo shouted.

They looked down. They shook their heads and crossed themselves.

The burning continued, gutted mattresses, wooden bed frames, ticky-tack souvenirs. They burned everything. All that was left were memories of a sheer, inviolable space. They spoke his name, he who had been their source of coherence, their unity. In mother tongues, they prayed. Then they headed for port towns, the Spanish border, anywhere that led to ships headed to their homelands.

Sunny began dreaming, a woman calling her for help. She woke crying for her mother. And she began to understand she and Keo could disappear in a minute.

Sometimes she watched him sleep, his lip bleeding and crusty from too much playing, from not knowing how to stop. She touched his dark, smooth cheeks, long black lashes, ran her hand along his stubbled chin. Except for Seiko's errands, she had no work now, no prospects. . . . *Our lives depend on a horn.* Some days she felt insane, jealous of the trumpet. She thought of crushing it flat, donating it as war metal. She thought of razoring Keo's lips while he slept. Then she would have to nurse him, she would have his full attention. Without him, she felt she had nothing to live for, no bright shining cause.

By Christmas 1940, Americans were being ordered out of France. They went to the American Embassy where there was a waiting list of weeks, and all ships sailed directly to the East Coast of the U.S. mainland. Yasunari Seiko said he could help them get out, but it would take time.

"Meanwhile, we have many projects."

They started running "errands" again, trading jewelry for black-market medicine. ID photos left in a cigarette pack at Café de Flore. Forged papers sewn into a beret. Sunny moved like a pro, never pausing, not looking back. Sometimes she thought about getting caught, being interrogated. *Then I would know what I am really made of.*

In early spring a package arrived, postmarked so many times, its stamps were almost illegible. German censors had sloppily retaped it, so half the contents were falling out. A smashed jar of plums. A Chinese doll with a shattered face. A stained and crumpled letter from the silk-mill girl, April Bao, who had found Sunny's sister in Shanghai. Her sister, Lili, knew some English but not enough to write. She had embroidered the silk doll-gown for Sunny. She prayed one day they would meet.

April Bao wrote how bad things were. Japanese and Chinese troops fighting just outside Shanghai. A whole block had been bombed, thousands dead. There were Germans there, and Russians, Jews, and many French. They called Shanghai the Paris of the Orient. She wondered, did they grow silkworms in Paris? Did chemists sell tiger hearts for cholera? Did people wear nosebags in the streets? What were the fashions? She asked if Sunny could send a tube of lip rouge, and for Lili a piece of lace. The rest of the letter was censored in blackout.

She sat holding the shattered doll against her chest. At night she tucked it in, like an infant. She kept the news from Keo, needing to absorb things, to decide. When she faced him, she wanted to be strong.

One night she handed him the doll. "I found my sister, Lili."

He shouted. His hand flew to his mouth. He put his arms round her, held her in his lap while she read him the letter.

"I've had dreams," she said. "I thought it was Mama. It's Lili, calling me for help! I need to get her out of Shanghai, to someplace safe. Even back to Honolulu."

He understood. He thought he understood. "Sunny. Shanghai's halfway round the world."

"I traveled halfway round the world to be with *you*."

Patiently, he tried to explain. "That was over a year ago. Now Italy's in the war, the Mediterranean's closed. We'd have to sail round Africa, five or six extra weeks—"

"People are doing it."

"It's very dangerous."

"*Life* is dangerous. Keo, I've been living for myself. Selfishness has to stop here."

He sat up thinking half the night, trying to be rational. By morning, he had made a resolution.

"There's only one right way to do this. We're going home as man and wife. That way your father can't hurt you. And it is what I've wanted. We go to the embassy, get on a waiting list, a ship to New York City. Then a train to the West Coast, another ship to Honolulu. Sure. It could take months. There's no other way. Once we're home, we start processing papers, get your sister out through proper channels."

She stared at him. "By then, she'll be dead."

They argued back and forth for days.

While he played in cabarets, Sunny walked the streets, ignoring curfew, thinking of her sister. One night she stood in the shadows in a club watching Keo perform, his face dark with the ecstasy of blowing, eyes gazing far beyond the crowd. Something kicked her ribs, something turned over. In that moment she understood he would never be able to give her as much as he gave his music. She could never compete with his horn.

For three nights running she watched him, watched over him, while he slept. Her lips moved as if she were praying. One day at dawn she unwrapped a Burmese ruby a woman had traded for ration stamps. She went to the steps of Sacré Coeur swarming with black marketeers, and sought one she had come to know. She went every dawn, bargaining, until she found the right offer. Paying exorbitant fees, she was registered near the top of a waiting list for passage on a ship. She put her documents in order.

One night she begged Keo, "Take me dancing. I just want to hold you, and dance."

Dressed in their smartest clothes, they danced—waltzes, tangos, paso dobles. He didn't even know what they were dancing: his feet seemed to follow hers. Her eyes were so big that night, her whole face seemed taken up with eyes. She gave off heat, her body glowed. He held her, thinking, *She has never looked so beautiful. Nothing more could be added, nothing subtracted.*

They closed every dance hall, dancing furiously, destructively. Later, when she came to him naked, her passion had that same furious desperation. At dawn, while he slept, she sat beside him weeping, then touched his face, picked up her China doll, and left. At Brest she boarded a freighter facing a long, circuitous journey to the South China Seas.

Keo woke in early afternoon, his arches painfully sore. A note was taped to the mirror. He approached it slowly.

CONTRAPUNTO OF GUNSHOTS. SEARCHLIGHTS TRIANGULATING. The WHOOMPH! of distant bombs. He walked streets where everyone looked like they needed an ambulance. Hungry whores working out of alleys took margarine for payment. Children lived on garbage. A city becoming a memory. Maybe Paris had never been real for him—just background while he blew his horn waiting for Sunny. She had driven him out into the world, saved him from the temptation of defeating himself. She had helped him ripen, define himself as a man.

Yet, he knew the measure of a man was his willingness to shoulder responsibility. His meagerness had let her down, and in that way Keo felt he had let himself down. In darker moments, he thought maybe there *was* no sister. Maybe Sunny had just wanted to be free of him. He lied to himself, so he wouldn't have to admit he had let loose in the world the one thing he had meant to protect.

He met with Seiko, offering all his money, even his horn, for passage on a ship, a freighter.

Seiko shook his head. "Shanghai? You will never find her there. You will not be prepared for such a place."

Still, Keo has been kind to his nephew Endo. Not everyone in Paris had been kind. Now the boy was gone, forced to return to Japan and train for the Imperial Japanese Army. To show gratitude, Seiko reluctantly agreed to help him.

"Though, waiting lists are endless. Thousands of Jews seeking refuge in Shanghai. All other countries have closed their doors."

He put Keo on a list. Meanwhile there were still errands.

". . . a family hiding out on Rue Margot, the child needs penicillin. And there is this gold watch needing to be sold. And this snapshot needing duplication . . ."

Now even the best cabarets were half empty. Fewer musicians, fewer instruments available. Drums were smashed by French Hitler Youth bullying their way through the city. Pianos broke down, the tuners in prison camps. Most clubs were lit by candlelight or generators fed by exhausted pedalers in basements. Some nights Keo took the stage alone, hoping a few sidemen would turn up. He blew like a man possessed, exerting such pressure that his lips were open and raw, sometimes bleeding down his chin. To blow less was deprivation.

One night, soloing "I Got a Right to Sing the Blues," he chased himself in chorus after chorus, long glissandos up and down the scale requiring seemingly superhuman wind and control. He felt so lonely, so bereft, he couldn't stop, or even slow down. He kept going, climbing the register to a C note, then, incredibly, an F.

He felt his chest stretched so tight, a lung was marked forever. He tried to climb higher. The note he was going for didn't exist. Women screamed as blue electricity shot out of his hair. Germans cheered. Momentarily blinded, he went down. When he came to, a German officer was wiping his face with scented linen. Pale, slender fingers covered with blond pollen.

Keo punched him away with his fists, and staggered to his feet. Insulted, the German returned to his table and gathered his friends. They raised their glasses, saluting Hitler. The crowd jumped to their feet, returning the salute. Keo lifted his glass and ceremoniously poured its contents on the floor. The Germans left, and in the silence someone laughed.

Keo turned on them. "You Frenchies fuck off, too! You smug bastards act like this war's got nothing to do with you."

His behavior grew more blatant and aggressive. Later that week, standing at the bar, he tripped a German officer and laughed. Club engagements dwindled, owners were afraid. He volunteered for more of Seiko's "errands," running maps, a razor, and a .38 to a downed British pilot hiding in a *boucherie*. He sat with the pilot all night, drinking bootleg brandy between sweating sides of hanging beef.

"I could be setting you up for the Gestapo," he said. "How do you know I'm the good guy?"

The pilot frowned. "Because you haven't killed me yet."

For seven hours he helped partisans take fingerprints of eighteen massacred Gypsies dug up from a shallow grave.

He played with whoever he could find, in bedrooms, a bakery, a chapel. Life was reduced to errands and pacing his room, waiting for passage to Shanghai. Some nights he sat up in the dark. If only he had known how to be equal to her. He had let their life flow past, had wasted it. What was it he lacked? He had wanted to experience everything, learn everything. Yet that was what was missing: he saw he had not learned enough, had not been quick enough.

Fatigue weighed heavily; it stemmed from the inability to know. *What should I have done to save her?* It haunted him. Sunny had surrendered everything to come to him. Then she had surrendered even the meager security of him, their life together, to go beyond, to another extreme. *I never understood. Something in her had to be expressed.*

He started collecting illegal ration cards, wolfing down black-market eggs and steaks to keep up his strength for the voyage. Not wanting to look fugitive or desperate, he washed his socks, underwear, shirts, in his sink, flattening them out wet on the top of the bureau in lieu of an iron. He polished his shoes with the back side of the sheet, remembering his mother's horror of top sheets, an old Hawai'ian phobia of being wound in a shroud like the dead. He pressed his trousers by folding them neatly under his mattress. His health and appearance became his obsession. But sometimes, seeing his reflection in windows, Keo saw someone looking half insane, a man caught in the maelstrom.

"You look frightful," Seiko told him. "Relax. Learn to be a blank-face."

He practised keeping his expression deceptively bland. When passing German officers, he looked down, slumped his shoulders docilely, while yearning to rip out one of their eyes, squash it underfoot until he heard it POP!

He bartered surplus cigarettes for a bar of good soap, then, heading home, found himself in front of the Louvre. He was still uneducated to the beauty of things—great operas, great paintings. But in that moment Keo hung his head for all the fragile beauty that was scattered from this place, some of it lost forever. He thought of Sunny packing treasures, of how one night he helped transport them across the countryside in trucks. He gave thanks then. For a short time, he had stood in the flow of history. He had been a fragment of that flow.

He grew extremely restless, wanting to be somewhere fighting, not sitting in a room. He wanted a weapon, not a horn, something he could assemble, aim, and fire. He gave himself another month. If Seiko hadn't found him passage, he would go over the Pyrenees to Spain, join up with the English or Dutch, fight with the Allies. He would get to Shanghai on a troopship. He would . . .

One night Seiko knocked on his door, switched off the light, and sat down. "I've been recalled to Tokyo."

He had managed passage for both of them, escorting one of the last groups of refugees to Shanghai. Keo clasped him by the shoulders. Before he could speak, Seiko gripped his arm.

"We must leave. Now. There's a night train to Bordeaux."

He bent for his suitcase beneath the bed. The man's grip tightened.

"*Now*. This moment. I have learned your name is on their list. Do you understand?"

One glance around the room, then he left, leaving everything. His clothes, his horn. At every street corner, every encounter with Germans, he weighted his features into a blank, looking almost bored. On his false passport, *visa de sortie*, a name that sounded Indonesian. With thick eyeglasses, battered briefcase, he passed for a rubber exporter returning home to Jakarta.

At Bordeaux, they pushed through mobs, presented their papers, and boarded the ship. Keo stood on deck clutching the rail—they could still come for him. He held his breath until land slowly receded. He felt breezes build, the ship settling into the Atlantic, shouldering its way south toward the coast of Spain. Then the long, long slide down Africa. *Probably the same route Sunny took.* At night he woke calling out her name.

Two weeks later, at Dakar, men from relief agencies boarded the ship with medications, lighter clothes, for refugees. As the climate changed, so did wardrobes and appearances. Keo saw how pale the refugees were, how emaciated. He began to listen, to understand what they had lived through in ghettos and camps. Some were so damaged, they never moved, just stared at the ocean. Others came to life as if for the first time.

A woman stood on deck cutting her hair, flinging it overboard. Cutting off the old life, she said. Folks rounded a corner, coming face-to-face with someone thought dead. They would live, because Shanghai had opened its doors for them. He thought of his Rom Gypsy friends, for whom no doors had opened.

Once more, Keo found himself sailing into the unknown, like a man trying to get to the core of things. Some nights he sat on deck for hours, thinking of Sunny who had taught him how to suffer. Before her, he had known nothing of real pain.

One night Seiko sat beside him. "If you find her, be prepared. A lovely girl, but . . . restless. Some women will always move on."

He wanted to tell Seiko he was wrong, that he knew nothing of Sunny. She may have taught him heartache and chagrin—her leaving had been like finding himself skinned, his flesh all raw and vivid—but she had also taught him to be a man. She had been his witness.

His lip was healing but he missed the pain, even missed the small scabs he was always wiping from his mouthpiece. Sometimes his fingers curled round the handle of his trumpet case. He looked down, shocked to see it gone. Nights, he fell asleep fingering imaginary valves, remembering the feel of the trumpet in his hands like a smart, stiff pet, missing the cool metal blossom of its bell. Without it he felt paralyzed. Playing was the only way he understood anything at all.

Weeks later at Capetown, relief agents boarded again with medical doctors, and supplies. People whose eyes and skin changed in the slow evolution eastward. Continents seeped into him, new tongues, new scents. The ship sailed into the Indian Ocean, stopping at Calcutta. Then the Malacca Straits, turning into the South China Sea.

Heading up the China coast, he stood on deck trembling. Ahead was Shanghai, and Sunny. And far to his right, nestled in the Pacific, his birthsands.

Pili Pū ka Hanu

To Hold the Breath in Fear

Shanghai, Autumn 1941

Seiko tried to prepare him for Shanghai, seething entrepôt of the Far East, the city foreigners called Whore of the Orient.

"Meretricious glamour," he warned. "Evil that will fascinate. Beware."

Keo shrugged. "All I want is to find her."

"Ah, yes. But sometimes life has other plans."

They turned up the great Yangtze River that brought commerce and trade to China's interior. But where the Yangtze was intersected by the Whangpoo River that fronted Shanghai, the waters became an abattoir. Acres of sewage rocketed by—bloated oxen, a human corpse. Near the docks, they passed Chinese junks, cargo freighters, British and American warships, so that the harbor seemed a city unto itself.

Within hours Seiko would sail on for Yokohama. Now he returned Keo's American passport, and they embraced.

"If war comes," Seiko whispered, "please, think well of me."

Outside customs clearance, armed Japanese soldiers in white leggings pushed crowds back behind barbed-wire barriers. In this city of millions, Keo looked up, stunned. The soaring architecture of Shanghai confused him, somewhat resembling Paris. Art Deco skyscrapers, neo-Gothic office blocks. Except that certain buildings listed eerily like ships. He would learn Shanghai was built on shifting silt, so nothing stayed put in the ground. Buried coffins drifted to sea. The weight of gold stacked in vaults caused banks to tilt dramatically.

He was shoved down the Bund, the main boulevard along the riverfront, and into the onslaught of strange, frightening faces. Wild-eyed Russians, Mongolians, and Finns. South Africans, Egyptians. Pompous "Shanghailander" Brits and Scots. Americans, Australians, Sikhs. And hordes of "under-races," Malaysians, Indonesians. Waves of yammering humanity that made Paris seem provincial.

Rolls-Royces pulled up before luxurious hotels two steps away from coolies thin as crucifixions, sleeping under rickshaws. Starving Chinese women held their infants up for sale. He saw food stands and barbershops flourishing in gutters, prostitutes stalking sailors. The air smelled of sewage and English cologne. Gangsters roamed, knocking people down for their money. Orators stood on soapboxes haranguing each other while a woman waving a pistol chased an armless man. Rounding a corner, Keo almost fell into a hole full of little corpses. He jumped back, screaming.

A White Russian shoveling lime laughed up at him.

"Hah! Another squeamish darkie. This here's the Girl-Child Pit for newborn females. In five-coat weather, you'll see their spirits frosting round."

He backed off, momentarily slowed by signs pointing to a stadium:

PUBLIC EXECUTIONS, BEHEADINGS, STRANGULATIONS
(For Criminals and Thieving Politicians)

Then he was swept into a giant souk—stalls of jade from Indochina, rubies from Burma, vermilion silks from Tashkent, lush rugs from Kashmir. A man in a raincape of seal intestines offered ermine pelts from Siberia. Everything looked tainted by odorous air. A sense of dreadful greed, dreadful suffering. Concubines passed in sedan chairs, rouging their lips, while sightless beggars fingered their pustules. Even rich whites passing in Bentleys looked sickly.

He bought cheap shirts and a secondhand suitcase with strange currency, piastres. A Chinese beggar followed on his heels, eyes bright with starvation. He snatched Keo's suitcase from his hands, pointed to his naked, bony chest. He would be his porter, his guide.

"Hotel!" Keo cried. "Cheap, cheap. You savvy?" He felt instantly ashamed, for this was how tourists spoke to native Hawai'ians.

The beggar nodded, chattering in singsong, his ribs glowing like glass rods. Jumping a corpse hit by a car, Keo followed him down Canton Road, passing two naked white men in leather gloves boxing in an alley. A man in a lurid red turban jumped rope. Farther on, three fat Turks sat playing *tric-trac*, spitting indigestible things at mangy dogs.

They stepped out on Avenue Foch, a tree-lined boulevard separating the International Settlement from the French Concession. Again, armed Japanese soldiers, and barbed-wire barriers holding back mobs of screaming Chinese. In broken English the beggar explained they were refugees trying to flood into the city from villages ravaged by fighting between Japanese and Chinese armies. Then the man stopped, this was as far as he would go. He pointed down the street, waving Keo's suitcase.

"Cheap, cheap. Hotel Jo-Jo! You pay me now."

Keo overtipped him, then, waving his documents at police, he was pushed through the checkpoint into the French Concession. Down the narrow Rue Ratard stood Hotel Jo-Jo. Hotel Double-Charming. A shabby place of fake Tudor run by an expat Frenchman and his delicate Indochinese wife.

"Amazing," the Frenchman said. "You left Paris for this madhouse?"

Accepting a cognac, Keo explained about Sunny, how he had come to find her.

The man shook his head. "Hundreds of thousands of girls here. You'll never find her."

Keo gulped his drink in a desperate way. "The sister, Lili—she limps. A clubfoot."

The Frenchman roared with laughter. "Forgive me, it's too *drôle*. To search for such a girl in a city of bound feet."

"She may be working in a silk mill."

He spat on the floor. "Hellholes, every one. Child slavery. Their little hands are needed to pull cocoons from boiling water. They're scalded, terrible infections—every week young corpses carted off in trucks." He hesitated. "Is your fiancée pretty?"

"Oh, yes," Keo said. "And very smart. She was at university."

"If she and her sister are trying to get out, they would be reckless, do reckless things. . . ."

Keo leaned forward, not understanding.

"Beautiful girls are in demand as . . . hostesses at sporting and gambling clubs. Posh *maisons tolérées* for whites and rich taipans."

Keo almost knocked him down. "Brothels? She would never sell herself."

The Frenchman smiled. "Then she is not in Shanghai. This is a city of desperation."

He walked the streets trying to get his bearings, dodging trams and limousines. Chauffeurs screamed from their cars, trying to penetrate wave upon wave of humans. In smothering humidity, crowds looked fanatic, faces lacquered with oily sweat. Clothes seemed to drip from their bodies. Then fog rolled in, and people turned into floating shrouds. Keo had never tried to envision hell; now he imagined it as something like this city. The Devil would thrive here.

Traversing avenues and alleys day into day, he began to see how Shanghai was divided into sections. The International Settlement with its neo-Grèque skyscrapers, fake Tudor houses, was made up of mostly Americans, Brits, and Western internationals. The French Concession was a little less chic with its French and honorary Western population. Then the old Chinese City, where most Orientals lived, a place of medieval filth and squalor. Here several million Chinese huddled in tiny windowless row-huts like furnaces, no electricity, no running water. Thousands slept in the streets, hugging their rice bowls.

He haunted the Chinese City, knowing that would be where Lili lived. He pressed through crowds wearing nosebags against cholera, floating debris. He stared at faces, walked in and out of a hundred tea parlors and laundries, describing Sunny and the sister with the clubfoot. Old men in cheongsams stared at him: a dark man looking for two girls. They dragged their daughters from the shadows and offered them.

At night Keo tossed and shouted in his dreams, feeling her slip through his fingers. Some nights he heard armies fighting outside the city, the distant BOOM of naval guns striking at shore batteries. He wondered how long before skirmishes became full-fledged war. Only the privileged seemed oblivious. In warm, sticky mornings after the rains, Keo saw Englishmen in tennis whites, talking through speaking tubes to chauffeurs. Walking down Theodore Road he heard orchestras from garden parties, saw blond children diving into pools, their amahs holding clean towels.

One day he paused before a pawnshop. In the window a cat gnawed what looked like the skull of a rat. To the left of the cat, a trumpet. Keo walked out with the glowing horn under his arm. Shanghai was alive with jazz bands; he lingered in several clubs until he heard the right sounds. At a place called Ciro's he approached the bandstand, asking the Japanese sax man who seemed to be the leader why they had no trumpet.

"Called home to Tokyo. The army."

Keo waved his horn, offering to sit in.

"Where you from?" the Filipino drummer asked.

When he said Honolulu, the man looked instantly amused.

"Sure you don't play 'ukulele, pal?"

"I can do that, too," he said.

He screwed in his mouthpiece and started to play, not smooth, not Continental, the way bands played for Shanghai crowds. He stood there plumbing the heart of jazz, inspired by work songs and field hollers, spirituals, the blues. Then, for twelve minutes straight, he blew chorus after chorus of Duke Ellington's "Diminuendo and Crescendo in Blue." When he finished, the band was very still.

Within a week his name was in the showcase outside the club. Each night after every set, just before the band broke, Keo stepped up to the mike.

"I'm looking for my sweetheart. Anybody come across a girl named Sunny Sung from Honolulu, tell her Hula Man is playing here at Ciro's."

Audiences loved it. Whether it was true or not, it gave him a poignancy that nicely balanced his cool, controlled demeanor. One night he sat with the sax player, telling his story.

The man shook his head. "No address? No photograph? Not even a private eye could help you." He hesitated. "Although, I know a place, House of Sighs. Very high class . . ."

Keo tensed. "She won't be in a brothel."

"Then the only way to search is street by street."

He went to the American Embassy where he learned that, since Korea was a Japanese colony, the sister, Lili, would be classified as Japanese. They were now prohibited from entering the U.S. or its territories such as Hawai'i. Keo sat down, utterly depressed. If Sunny had found her sister, she would never leave without her.

One day he stood in an alley of silk shops. Over each doorway hung banners of German swastikas beside flags of the United States and Great Britain. Tourists bought small replicas of them in souvenir sets of three. He walked in and out of shops, asking the names of silk mills. Most were in the factory section called Pootung.

Outside a factory surrounded by fences Keo approached a Chinese security guard. Holding out money, he tried to question him. The guard grunted and Keo moved closer, not understanding. In one motion, the man slashed his shirt from shoulder to waist with razor-tipped brass knuckles. Others came running, waving rifles.

The Hotel Jo-Jo owner explained the guards were part of "protection" gangs.

"Mills pay them. Otherwise they'd burn them down. Gangs own the mill girls, they bring many of them in from villages as laborers. They thought you wanted to buy a girl. I'm amazed they didn't kill you."

Each mill he went to was "protected" by gangs. Chain-link fences, armed guards. He learned to stand some distance from the mills. When women changed shifts, he approached, asking if they knew Sunny or Lili Sung, a cripple. Women ran, afraid he was a kidnapper, a slave trader. He haunted bars and ballrooms. He studied dress clerks at Wing On and Sincere department stores.

At Ciro's he met White Russian bodyguards who spent their days balanced on the running boards of limousines, guns slung over their shoulders. They moved though the city's strata, knew members of the Green Gang, Red Gang, the underworld societies. They had an eye for beautiful women, but no one had heard of Sunny Sung from Honolulu.

Keo pressed on, through a city he felt was sinking, whose very air made him sick. In early dawn after finishing at Ciro's, he leaned against buildings retching as "honey carts" passed by. Night soil was used for manure, which made fresh produce a death trap. His chest and groin were raw with rash. He suffered eye infections from floating bacteria, and learned to wear a nosebag, a gauze muzzle with straps fastened behind his ears. Raw sewage leaked from the ground into the city's water supply. He was forced to sterilize everything, even coins, even his horn.

Death seemed to stalk the city. Syphilis, typhus, rabies. Children died like flies; each day trucks hauled off the dead. One night a bouncer at the club walked home through a flood with a sing-song girl, both drunk and barefoot. Something entered the soles of their feet. Within weeks they died in each other's arms, legs blown up like watery balloons.

Yet midst depravity there was paradoxical beauty, too. One day Keo came upon a Chinese prostitute, a little girl of nine or ten. Rouged and costumed, she sat on a pier at sunrise, singing her heart out. With the tiny voice of a child—exhausted, besotted, beyond shock or dreams—she sang and sang. Swinging her feet over the edge of the pier, her embroidered slippers catching the light, she sang until the sun rose, until she was a flickering dot in its center.

In that city of tilting skyscrapers, a camel driver and his herd appeared magically at dusk. Twilight made the camels seem aquatic. The streets they traversed looked suddenly submarine, their silhouettes antediluvian. Keo stood thinking how, long ago, their saurian necks might have thrust above waves, legs paddling left and right like fins. Now the sea had disappeared for them, they had turned into steeds, preserving rhythms of ocean waves. They made him long for his own warm seas, slow adagio of his islands. He sat down and finally wrote his family.

One day, in the Old City, on a street where scribes wrote letters and marriage contracts for illiterates, he followed crowds to a bridge built in nine zigzags which led to an ancient pavilion on its own little island in the heart of a lake—Wuxing Ting Teahouse. On the seventh zigzag, unaccountably he looked up. Ahead, two women sitting in the teahouse, profiles in a window. One of them was Sunny. Keo stood as if struck, then shouted her name, climbing over crowds on the rickety bridge. People laughed, watching him fall, shouting as he struggled to his feet. Between the eighth and ninth zigzag, he looked again. The window was empty.

He exploded into the teahouse, upsetting trays, nearly sobbing as he ran from table to table. An old waiter approached, speaking broken English. Keo embraced him.

"Two women here." He pounded a table. "Five minutes ago."

The waiter nodded yes.

"One spoke English? Very pretty?"

"Ah. Pretty!" The man touched his cheek. "Other not so good. Bad leg." He aped a limp.

"Where did they go? Which way?" Keo thrust bills into his hand. "Oh, help me. Please."

The man shrugged, turned slowly in a circle, pointing to three tiny doors exiting onto a wraparound porch leading customers back to the entrance of the Bridge of Nine Windings. Hundreds of people flowed back and forth. Insane, Keo circled the porch several times, then pushed through crowds, calling out her name.

He traversed the bridge for hours, haunting nearby streets and alleys. At dark, a monk with an iron hook through his chest trailed a chain ten feet long. Behind him a brother monk beat a drum and clashed a cymbal. They stood over the dark man slumped in the street looking hopeless and lost. They chanted over him until Keo gave them money to go away.

He placed notices in English-language papers. He waited outside fences of silk and cotton mills, searching haggard faces of women whose fingers were white from fungus growths. Some held bloody kerchiefs to their mouths, signing tuberculosis. Their children limped beside them carrying the pungent stench of dead cocoons, their hands clawed, arms horribly scarred, boiled as penance for not working faster.

He began to pray. *Dear God, let her be in a brothel, let her not be in this hell.*

He followed every lead, went to cabarets, taxi dance halls, bordellos. He went to scissors factories, which paid more than silk mills because the work was more dangerous. Lead poisoning from metal dust of machines turned faces and gumlines blue. Chromium ate weeping holes into arms and legs. Workers went blind. Still they chanced it—the wages enabled them to buy steerage passage out of Shanghai. There was coolie work in the poppy fields of Burma, or the rubber plantations of Sumatra where, when they died, their coffins stayed buried and did not float to sea.

Near the Bund a dog-meat shop was bombed, the owner said to be Communist. Cages were airborne, animals howled. People ran through the streets snatching up succulent rice-fed puppies and poodles, even greyhounds stolen from the dog track. Keo saw tiny old women with bound feet—blue-faced workers from scissors factories—leap onto the backs of terrified greyhounds, trying to bring them down. He stood very still, remembering his friend Oogh on the ship to New Orleans. He had seen Keo in a vision. ". . . *in a city where blue-faced, pig-footed women ride on the backs of greyhounds* . . ." He remembered the rest of Oogh's prophecy. ". . . *One day you will blow and it will be the sound of diamonds. But you will pay. There will be grief*. . . ."

November now. Japanese armies surrounded Shanghai. Though the International Settlement was still under foreign jurisdiction, soldiers continued erecting barbed-wire fences and checkpoints. Amongst burnt-out blocks and flattened buildings, skyscrapers glittered like mirages, and on the Yangtze River trade and commerce died as Westerners evacuated.

One night Keo sat in for a horn man at the rooftop café of a large hotel. The band wore tuxedos and, in between sets, gambled at the roulette wheel. Guests relaxed with pink gins and brandies watching the "night show"—shells from the Japanese Army arcing across the sky to land on Chinese troops. A bomber droned in from the river, lazily veering toward the hotel. People pointed casually, noting that the Chinese fighter seemed off course.

A waiter screamed. "Fly-fly egg! Look now!"

Keo took his trumpet from his lips, looked up in time to see the bomb falling like a pod. Diners, jazzmen, couples on the dance floor froze, that's all he would remember. Then something wet, a human arm, hit him in the face. Flying concrete, black smoke, the shuddering building sheared in half lengthwise. Dragging themselves down eight flights of stairs, wounded dancers and waiters saw people staring horrified from the untouched half of the building. Offices, apartments, shops intact, only the wall missing. A barber stared down at his lathered customer, a hunk of metal piercing his head. Beside the dead customer, a girl in shock continued his manicure.

On the street, Keo coughed up someone else's blood. Unnameable things stuck to his jacket, sliding into its creases. He sat down on a curb, watching fire engines, ambulances, the wailing mobs. Sanitation men were already clearing the streets, sweeping bodies into alleys. Rickshaw coolies quietly combed limbs for jewelry, shoes, shredded clothes.

He heard thumping hooves, saw horses gallop from burning stables toward the outskirts of the city. Running beside them, coolies tried to carve out meat from their flanks. In the suburbs, bandits and gangsters would have shootouts over the horseflesh.

Keo reached into his pocket, feeling something sharp. He pulled out rib fragments, an organ nestled in a web of fat. He stared, imagined it still pulsing.

"*. . . You will wear a tuxedo and play roulette, and fondle a stranger's broken heart. . . .*" Where had he heard that? Who said it? Flinging the wet human organ away, he screamed, rocking like a madman.

HE WOKE IN THE MIDDLE OF A LECTURE. AN ELDERLY CHINESE woman, arms ringed with jade, was scolding a tiny white elephant. Insulted, the little creature lay down and sobbed.

"Petulant! He will not do his trick. . . ." Her voice was the voice of a Chinese bird speaking English brush-stroked with a hint of French.

Keo was lying on a divan at the end of what looked like a ballroom. Out on the floor, two sing-song girls in cheongsams split to the thigh were dancing a fox-trot. Tommy Dorsey's "Night and Day." They moved together like lovers, lascivious and sly.

The old woman soothed her sobbing albino pet, then turned to Keo.

"My son gone to fetch you nightingale broth. You suffering from shock. Nuns brought you from the street."

Her voice dropped, sounding conspiratorial. "They live next door, tend syphilitic infants. And too, they smuggle virgins out of Shanghai in coffins. Clever! No?"

He saw he had been bathed, swaddled like a child. He imagined himself borne to safety by wimpled angels. When he woke again, Oogh held a steaming bowl before his face.

"So, *mon ami*, you are finally arrived."

"Oogh! What are you doing here?"

"Shanghai is my home. Where else would a *kanaka-pākē* dwarf fit in, if not in Sodom?" He nodded toward the ancient woman. "*Ma mère*. She owns this ballroom, and many brothels. I put to sea when she exhausts me, for she is mercantile as a pharaoh."

He spooned broth into Keo's mouth. It tasted like gardenias, feathers, and sewage, yet made him strangely languorous.

"Yes. The nightingale's sadness is left in its juices. They will generate old memories, make you forget the terrible present. Buildings split like loaves of bread, bodies like burst figs. Tell me, have you found your sweetheart?"

Keo gasped, then remembered Oogh was gifted, a seer. He grabbed his arm. "I saw her! Was it Sunny? Is she still in Shanghai?"

He closed his eyes. "Perhaps."

"Oogh. Please, help me find her."

Oogh concentrated very hard. When he opened his eyes, they were sad. "Life will find her."

Keo lay back, defeated. "I've seen so much since we first met. I still don't know anything. Every day, I think: Turn left? Turn right? How do I know what is wise?"

Oogh laughed softly. "Haven't you learned? Wisdom isn't necessary. You can be a cretin and still get by."

"But you are wise. You see the future."

"The wounds of tomorrow dripping at my side . . . It doesn't make me happy."

Keo studied him, as if for the first time. "What would make you happy, my friend?"

"To be eye-level with the world. To make folks physically look up." Oogh pumped out his little chest. "I would like to be a judge. Oh, yes! Induce anxiety with a gavel."

He turned to Keo, serious again. "As for you—don't expect to return alive from what you've given your soul to. Happiness will only come from your trumpet."

Keo sat up, slowly. "What about Sunny?"

Oogh's words were sly and wounding. "Your horn was eating her alive. But women are soldiers, they survive. She will be in your life. She will gather round you. In her time."

He gestured to little Chinese boys laboring in a circle, embroidering silk underwear. "Another industry of *ma mère*. What a savage. Her greed is my penance. Sleep now. When you wake, the boys will guide you home."

Keo's lids drooped with the weight of nightingales. "Oogh . . . don't go. . . ."

Oogh smiled. "It is you who come and go. You are the searcher."

He turned to a phonograph, placed the needle on a record. " 'Toccata and Fugue.' Bach is excellent for embroidering. Sewing-boys say it makes their silk tremble, longing for cocoons. Now, I shall talk you into dreams. Let's see . . . shall I tell you of the Rickshaw Man?"

His voice took on a tenderness:

. . . Why do they call him "coolie"? Such a mean name when, in fact, the Rickshaw Man is legend, a fragile wonder. He came to China from Japan introduced by, yes, the English. He is the only contact most whites have with Shanghai poverty. Did you know, each day and night there are eighty thousand Rickshaw Men dashing through these streets? He knows each street by heart. And why? The street is his home, his cradle, his mattress, his grave. . . .

Riots, many-flag festivals, weddings, killings—these are the Rickshaw Man's daily theatre. Life limitless in its horror. And, food! It is his happiness. Some days he counts his grains of rice, tiptoeing on the cusp of starvation. He was originally a farmer, did you know? Driven off his land by warlords. He comes to the city in thousands, like ants. Wifeless, childless, as such things are luxuries. He sleeps in mud, straw, back to back, in sheds for livestock owned by rickshaw owners.

Have you seen him drinking from the creek running through the city? On Yao Shui Lane there are four thousand Rickshaw Men, no candles, no light, no water but the filthy creek. Which is also his latrine. Each day he dies many times, in floods, fires, disease. He is thought to laugh in winter, because he is often found frozen with a grin. What strange names we give to pain. . . .

The Rickshaw Man loves spring and summer. Heat! Humidity! Midst garbage, filth and flies, he finds a woman. He sees his baby crawl. That is his happiness. Sunshine. A little rice. His family round him, huddling on the street. 'Auwē! *Now and then he eats himself to death. His shrunken stomach not prepared for full-to-neck meals—bean curd, noodles, congee rice.*

Do you know? It costs the Rickshaw Man one American dollar to pull his rickshaw for one day. Oh, no, he does not own his own. He shares his rickshaw with another man in shifts of twelve work-to-death hours. Have you seen how he runs and runs? To stop is to be robbed and beaten. Most days, after paying the owner for his daily rickshaw, he has not enough coppers left to eat. He drinks a bamboo dipper of dirty water, eats soil and dreams it is a bowl of rice. Sometimes he cheats, he steals. He stalks rich white drunk folks falling out of nightclubs. He strikes them down for coppers. He steals their clothes, leaves them naked in the street. Sometimes he pauses, smelling their pomaded hair, their lime cologne, he runs his nose across their skin. Sometimes he takes their fingers, or their ears. Can you understand? Do you know the depths of hunger?

The Rickshaw Man is like a moth, a shadow. In sunlight he is less and less. His flesh so thin, his ribs are burnt by sunlight. His lungs so frail, he can only run two days out of three. Do you wonder how he sleeps so many hours, in gutters, sidewalks, standing up? Do you understand dying on your feet? I knew a Rickshaw Man, one with great imagination. He sold his daughter for a pot of tea. His heart burst with the joy of drinking. Imagine. They say he smiled in death. Not a frozen smile, for it was summer. He smiled for he was happy. He had never tasted jasmine tea. The wonder! The Rickshaw Man, father of ma mère . . .

Oogh's cheeks were wet. He sighed, patted Keo's sleeping head.

"So, *mon ami*, that is my *pākē*, Chinese, side. One day I will tell you how the daughter of the Rickshaw Man fled the Jasmine Tea Man and sailed to Honolulu, a picture bride. And how, instead, she married a Hawai'ian, who taught her love. And desperation. Sleep now . . . when you wake, the sewing-boys will clean your ears, trim your nails, guide you back to Hotel Jo-Jo."

Huli Pau

To Search Everywhere

Another accidental bombing. Bodies hung from buildings like rags. He searched the wreckage for her face. He searched the docks, departing crowds, hoping she and Lili had found passage to Hong Kong, Manila, anywhere.

Sometimes he let himself be swept up in the city's life. Embassies held what seemed a weekly competition, Brits showing newsreels of Allied victories in Europe, Axis clubs showing Hitler's devastation. Audiences cheered, then rushed into the streets, beating up their enemies. Keo dragged a belligerent German to an alley and punched him in the face. He thought of Etienne Brême, and hit him in the face again.

Sometimes, exhausted from his search, he sat with an old Chinese scholar near Hotel Jo-Jo while the man aired his Buddhist texts in sunlight. Rippling humid pages, he popped silver fish into his mouth, so his teeth were furred and gray. A frail, elegant man in long coarse robes and pointed slippers, his movements were leisurely and learned. One day he turned to Keo, speaking near-perfect English.

"You wait. Chinese are four hundred million strong. Our strength, the strength of ants. We do not win battles. But we absorb our conquerors every time."

Keo thought how not just Japanese but all the nations of the world had converged on Shanghai, growing rich on its silk, opium, tea, turning its children into slaves. Now the Yangtze River was closed, trade with China was in its death throes. He pondered the fate of Shanghai's four million people when the rest of the world had abandoned it.

"Yes. Japan will overrun us," the scholar said. "But we will turn them into Chinese. Give us five hundred years. You wait."

He suspected the old man was right. Westerners thought in days and months, Chinese in generations.

Now, with war imminent, clubs and cabarets thrived, just as they had in Paris. Nazis, Italian fascists, officials of the Vichy government arrived, aligning themselves with their Axis partner, Japan. Among them, as always, were jazz fanatics. Once again, Keo blew his horn with the energy of pure hate. He stayed because someone he loved was here, and he played because this was his life and, if he didn't play, his life had no purpose. It seemed every musician in Shanghai had his own reasons for staying.

"Where else can I go?" the Japanese sax man asked. "They've closed all dance halls in Japan. I would be killed anywhere else in Asia, after what our armies have done."

One day the drummer left for Manila, replaced by a Polish Jew from Warsaw. The Polish bass man was replaced by an Austrian, reportedly an Axis spy. When his throat was slashed behind Ciro's, he was replaced by a black South African run out of Peking as a Communist. The turnover kept audiences intrigued.

Suddenly musical instruments became *bo gum*. Precious gold. Saxophones and trumpets disappeared as Japanese confiscated them, shipping them back to Japan as scrap metal for bombs. A horn was spared only if its owner was excellent. Jobless musicians buried their instruments between tombstones with special markers. Now Keo was never without his trumpet. He slept with it, walked it down the street like a pet.

Some nights before he played, he walked back to the teahouse in the heart of the lake, over the Bridge of Nine Windings. He went week after week, looking for the face in the window, though the old waiter said she had never returned. He haunted streets and shops. He prayed.

One day a speeding Mercedes with swastika banners rounded a corner and hit a child. The chauffeur jumped out, lashing the unconscious boy with a crop, then drove the car up to the entrance of Ciro's. The man who stepped out looked eerily familiar. During the second set, Keo recognized his cologne. The German officer who, one night in Paris, had wiped Keo's face with a linen handkerchief. Now he lowered his horn and walked off the stage. The others joined him in the alley.

"Gestapo," the drummer said. "As long as he applauds, we're safe."

Keo stared at him. "You, a Jew, would play for that bastard?"

The man laughed. "Half the audience are Nazis. You play for them every night."

The bassist nodded. "Other half are sympathizers, a few British spies thrown in. If they didn't dig jazz, we'd be playing in the Pootung stockade for lepers and syphilitics."

Keo dragged viciously on a cigarette. "I had friends murdered in Paris. Almost lost my balls to an SS swagger stick."

The bandleader touched his arm. "Forget Nazi, Axis, Allies. Our aim is just to stay alive. Please. They are waiting."

Audiences began to look alike and sound alike—Germans, Americans, Brits, even Japanese officers. They all had a formal code of manners, a distinctly intense way of leaning forward, listening. Their gaze like thrown knives. Yet they were offering a truce: jazz was their condition. He began to move in a world of repetition, everything known, predictable. On certain nights he knew what the audience would wear, how they would smell, what songs they would request. After a while he left them behind, left the city behind, blowing his trumpet for himself. Imagining one night Sunny would hear it, it would lead her to him.

So involved in his playing again, sometimes Keo lost all sense of place. Walking home before dawn—no light save those from swaying rickshaw lanterns—he felt beneath him the pavements of Montmartre. Other nights he imagined the Seine flowing past like rollicking eels. He saw sleek couples at *bals musettes* lost in the hesitating, dragging rhythms of the tango. He smelled the salt of rotting fishnets in Brême's studio, heard the haunting tremor of Dew's saxophone.

Or, he heard guitars, violins, Rom Gypsies dancing in lime green fields, celebrating life. *Alegría!* Men of ferocious courage, women of fire, people who lived with divine address, loving deep and inchoate things. He saw their caravans on fire, paint blistering their wagons. He heard machine guns, saw children bursting from fields like pheasants.

ONE NIGHT, RETURNING FROM CIRO'S AT 3 A.M., HE FOUND THE owner of Hotel Jo-Jo looking apprehensive.

"She's been waiting in your room all night. . . ."

Asleep in his bed, the sheet severing her legs. Shadows tearing scoops of flesh from her shoulders. He flung himself across the room, burying his head against her breasts. She woke, taking him in her arms.

"Forgive me!" she whispered. "I didn't know. . . ."

He crawled in beside her and held her, their bodies shaking, both sobbing like children. When they finally calmed down he switched on a lamp so he could see her.

"When you left I died. I swear, I died! I've searched these streets for months."

Dark crescents under her eyes, her beautiful face haunted. Fear and hopelessness, and something else.

"Sunny. You're so thin. . . ."

"Filth," she whispered. "It kills appetite."

"You should have waited. You should have let me come with you."

Then he remembered she *had* waited. In Paris, she had begged him for weeks.

She sat up now in weary exhalation. "Keo, I found Lili. I found her—but I can't get her out. The U.S. won't let her come home with me." She clung to him. "Help us. Help us, please. I can't leave without her."

"I've been to the embassy," he said. "She's considered Japanese. Forbidden to enter the U.S. or its territories. It's hopeless. One day soon, they'll evacuate Americans. You *have* to leave with me. We'll try to get her out later."

"I can't. I can't desert her." She began to sob again. "I am *not* my father."

Holding her, he felt bone, all her softness gone. Everything seemed corners. Even her breasts under her slip seemed flatter, as if this city, so covertly cruel, had pressed her into one dimension.

"What has happened to you? How are you living?"

At first she couldn't answer. She hugged herself, her body trembling with emotion. Finally, her eyes met his. "Forgive me. I didn't know. I never would have left you if I knew. . . ."

He felt a chill, felt his brain crank a little tighter.

"Knew what? What is it?"

In the silence, mosquitoes whined in their blood quest. The ceiling fan shuddered like something hurt.

"It took seven weeks to reach Shanghai. I was ill, day and night. The ship's doctor examined me." She hid her face in her hands. "I was . . . carrying our child . . ."

Keo sat very still.

". . . almost three months pregnant when I left you. I didn't know! She was born here, in August. So tiny and frail, but she's alive."

"Where is she?" He shook her by the shoulders. "My God, she'll die in this filthy place. Where . . ." It was all too much. He wept again.

"She's with Lili and her aunty, near the Bridge of Nine Windings. I couldn't bring her, the air so full of bacteria. I wanted to tell you first. Keo, you *must* take our daughter home, safe to Honolulu. I'll come with Lili after."

He shook her violently again. "After? After *what*!"

He was not listening. He could not listen. He could not believe that they were living lives already so exhausted. When he quieted down, Sunny pulled him back into her arms.

"One day at dawn I gave birth to our daughter, with Lili and a midwife. Lili took her from my thighs. I brought life to my poor sister, whose only life has been the mills."

She smiled, giving him clarity, and hope.

"She looks just like you. Her eyes, her perfect little mouth. I named her . . . *Anahola*. Time in a glass. I remembered your hands turning the hours while you practised your horn."

He dropped his head against her chest. "Oh, Sunny. Take me to her. We're a family now. We must go home."

He heard the old intransigence again. The part of her that would not walk away. "I *want* to go home. To be with you. Live long, quiet days and quiet years. I've had enough of the world. But I can't leave my sister. Please. Help me get her out."

He held her tight, hatching impossible schemes. "A guy at Ciro's knows someone who makes passports. They'd make one up for Lili. I know a Brit who's sleeping with a woman at our embassy. Maybe she would help us. . . ."

At dawn they were still whispering, scheming, wondering how to save their lives, how to regain control of them. They made love frantically, desperately; it seemed even their bodies were beyond their control. While Sunny dozed, he tried to comprehend all she had told him, to comprehend that she was even there beside him, it was not a dream . . . a dream. . . .

When he woke at noon she was gone. He ran up and down the halls, his face screaming back at him from mirrors. His nerves disintegrating into salt.

The owner tried to reassure him. "She'll be back. She said she's bringing you the child. My friend, whatever you are planning, be quick about it. All who can afford to leave are clearing out."

For three days and nights Keo sat in his room, waiting. Each hour moved across his flesh. Maybe she feared if she returned to Hotel Jo-Jo, he would force her on a ship with the child. Maybe the sister refused to give up the child, afraid Sunny would desert her. Maybe the child had died. *Was* there a child? By the fourth day he was crazed, running the streets like a madman. At the Bridge of Nine Windings, he searched, and searched, then sat babbling in an alley, telling beggars how he had lost her. He had let her go again.

After a week, he went back to Ciro's. But every free moment, he searched, each fruitless search a horror. Now there was a child, and not to find her meant her death. He lived in the roar of his heartbeats, watching bare-bottomed men and women squat beside streams, uncoiling their excrement into the waters. Waters that bathed his infant daughter. He prayed, he bargained with God. He would give up everything, his horn, his *life*, if he could save Sunny and his child.

KŪĀ'INO

To Turn from Good to Evil

ONE MORNING, A MONDAY, HIS BED COLLAPSED, THE WALLS FELL in upon him. He grabbed his horn, covered his face, and staggered to the street. Tanks rode abreast, flattening everything in sight. Keo flung himself out of their path, watching battalions of Japanese marines with fixed bayonets running in formation. A motorcycle braked in front of him; a young Japanese officer stepped from the sidecar.

"You. Report to checkpoint for red armband."

Keo stood dumb. "What is it? What's happened?"

He slapped Keo hard across the face. "No obey, I kill you. Your thoughts and my thoughts now enemies."

Retrieving his documents, he struggled through debris, making his way to Ciro's where security guards kept a shortwave radio. Crowds were gathered, listening to the broadcast, and Keo watched in disbelief as folks attacked each other. A pattern emerged: people striking back at their oppressors.

A Chinese amah reached up, slapping a White Russian au pair. White Russians in turn seemed to be slapping Frenchmen. A sing-song girl pounded the chest of a red-turbaned Sikh policeman. The Sikh beat her off, then struck a shouting Englishman in golf pantaloons. The Englishman gasped, then slapped his sobbing wife. Mothers struck their children. Rickshaw coolies dragged uniformed chauffeurs from Buicks and Bentleys, beating their heads with metal pipes. An old woman with empty eye sockets sat in the dirt strangling a chicken.

In the madness, Keo heard static from the shortwave, voices fading in and out. ". . . PEARL HARBOR . . . PEARL HARBOR . . ."

He started running toward the Old City where Sunny lived. Crowds overwhelmed him, carrying him backward toward the Bund on Shanghai's waterfront, where British and American warships were anchored. All around, enormous explosions. A building sat down. People surged in thousands, wave upon wave, not knowing where they were running.

In the harbor Japanese naval officers stood at attention on cruisers surrounding what was left of American and British warships. Flags of the Rising Sun now replaced the Allied flags. Keo pointed helplessly at sailors bobbing in flaming oil. An Englishman in a tailored suit cried out at the burning men, then turned and cursed a Japanese soldier. The soldier thrust a bayonet straight through his neck.

Down every street, he saw them taking over the city, marching in long columns of troops and light tanks, the same Prussian military goose step he had seen in France. In between troop columns, teeming mobs—whites and Orientals—ran frantically toward the Bund, looking for safety.

It was then, in the rushing assault of thousands of bodies tumbling over each other, that he saw her. An infant in her arms, dragging a limping girl beside her. He screamed her name. He scrambled up on the shoulders of strangers, and screamed her name. Over and over. Sunny turned, looked up, incredulous. He would always remember that moment, an inhalation, like a great intake of breath before the rapids. She beheld him, a tender radiance in her eyes. She reached her arms out with the child. She spoke his name. Shoulders collapsed beneath him, he went down.

HE WOKE IN A WARD SO CROWDED, PEOPLE DIED SQUATTING IN corners. His head hurt terribly, his vision was off, but one day he hobbled to a window. Shanghai was now a combat zone under Japanese domain. Troops, tanks, lookout posts manned by soldiers with machine guns. They busted up rickshaws, beating coolies so they exploded like bags of dust. Out in the harbor, lugubrious clouds of black smoke, half-sunken ships and sampans. The harbor paved with broken bodies.

A Swiss doctor with the stooped grace of a tired bird told him the United States had declared war. "Cheer up, a few weeks, you'll be headed home on a repat ship."

Mosquitoes swarmed, bringing malarial chills, malaise. He slipped in and out of fever. One day he woke smelling mandarins.

"Hula Man. This is becoming a habit."

"Oogh. I found her. Then I lost her, and our *child*."

"This is no place for a child." He doled out sections of the fruit. "In the streets they're eating rust off wheelbarrows. It is going to get very bad."

The sweetness of the mandarin made his cheeks ache, his tongue shiver in shock. "How did you find me?"

Oogh sighed. "Don't be sentimental. You needed to be found. Here is the news. They want you at Club Argentina, that fascistic haunt next door to *ma mère*'s."

"They?"

"The usual. Axis. Spies. Ciro's is *kaput*."

"I can't play. I've got to find her—"

"You *must* play. If not, you'll wind up in an internment camp. Or worse." Oogh moved closer. "Last week nine people died during surgery. Doctors here are under instructions from the Gestapo. Do you want to disappear?"

Keo sat up, suddenly alert. "I need to know what happened to my family. They live near Pearl Harbor."

Oogh moved closer. "A shortwave in *ma mère*'s loo. Few casualties in Honolulu outside Pearl Harbor. Japs weren't targeting civilians."

He gripped Keo's arm with amazing strength. "Come. Each day you remain in this sinkhole you're courting death."

They made their way down stairwells until they found an exit. On the street, six young girls were being forced into a truck. Soldiers with fixed bayonets stood on the running boards guarding them.

"Where are they taking them?" Keo asked.

"Stockades." Oogh shook his head. "For soldiers' pleasure."

PLAYING AT CLUB ARGENTINA, HE WORE AN "A" AMERICAN armband. The Jewish drummer wore a "J" for Jew. British spies in the crowd, posing as Netherlanders, wore "H" for Holland. The city was now draped in flags of the Rising Sun and fluttering swastikas. As each day more Allied nationals were arrested, trucked to internment camps outside the city, Keo understood his freedom depended on how well he blew his horn. And tracking Sunny down depended on his being free. Life carried on, not as before, but as a parody of what it had been.

The band was housed at Hunan Mansions, near the Club, a drab hotel seething with arms dealers, black marketeers, intelligence gatherers. Weeks dragged into months as each day Keo walked the streets, searching, and each night sat on the bandstand feigning apathy. In Paris, Sunny had accused him of not thinking, not observing. Saying all he did was blow his horn. But now it was another time, another place. He saw the mindless brutality of the Japanese, and of the Nazis, masquerading as Japan's allies while dismissing them as "little yellow monkeys."

He watched them with their sleek heads, meticulous dress, their posture strenuously correct. Even the cars they stepped from, suave dark pods. Remembering Brême, remembering three women of the Resistance publicly hanged, Keo shook with rage. He studied his reflection in a mirror. His face was flying off its hinges.

Night after night he lay sleepless, knowing it wasn't grief that killed a man, but impotence. He thought of their child, longing to hold her, longing for Sunny so much that he couldn't think of touching other women, couldn't bear to. He couldn't even look. Sing-song girls swayed daintily before him, cheongsams slit to their thighs. High-class concubines peered from sedan chairs, pursing wet lips. White Russian whores in silver fox winked while they danced with Germans. He looked away.

The details of living began to elude him. He forgot certain rituals, bathed and shaved sporadically, stopped oiling his hair so it grew rough and kinky. It was through Sunny he had come to love his skin, his compact body. In loving him, she had extolled his dark elegance. Now he understood how beauty exists only when one exists in someone else's eyes, how in the existence of another human, we find our human dignity.

One night the German stalked him, the Nazi with cologne and linen handkerchiefs. Pale, whippet-thin, his suit impeccable. Each time Keo blew a note, he wriggled in his chair, applauding feverishly.

The bass man whispered, "He's got eyes for you."

He followed Keo down the street, his dark Mercedes purring. The car pulled up alongside, the back door opened.

"Hula Man." The voice soft, but somehow acid.

Keo climbed in so naturally it seemed congruous. They sat silent while the driver maneuvered slowly through checkpoints, bombed-out streets. The man barked through the speaking tube. The driver stopped and stepped out beside a park, leaving them alone. A hand drifted round Keo's shoulder. Lips brushed his lips, the taste of schnapps. The other hand pried at his crotch, unzipping his pants, taking hold of his penis. The German whimpering and squirming. In one fluid motion, Keo dragged him from the car and slammed him up against the door. Mashing the German's windpipe with his fist, he thrust his face at him.

"You Nazis are so *pale*. What is it, does the sun go round you?" Then he smiled, zipping up his pants. "Relax, man. I'm not going to hit you. What I hate about you isn't physical."

He turned and walked away, then changed his mind, retraced his steps, pulled back his fist, and smashed the German's nose. "I lied."

It seemed an honorable act, one of valor. As if coming to the end of a long charade. Almost languidly, he walked home through crags and spires of mortared streets. He slept deeply, dreaming of Oogh, who lectured him.

"Hula Man, you go too far. The day comes when you add one more soupçon to what's already too much."

At dawn, sirens whined down in front of his hotel.

Half asleep, he asked, "Am I going to prison?"

Oogh sighed. "Oh, yes."

"Am I going to die?"

". . . a little."

Hearing the naked percussion of boots on stairs, he rose from his bed and dressed. They slashed his clothes from his body with bayonets, until he stood running red.

Streets glided into undifferentiated scenes of horror. Off to the west a sky of furnace colors matching his arms and legs, already beginning to fester. Squeezed against him in a puddle of waste, a Scotsman tortured to death or unconsciousness. Packed in the back of the rumbling truck, Brits, Dutch, Americans huddled against bedrolls and suitcases, tearing their eyes from Keo's blood-covered body to the half-dead man beside him. Japanese guards on the running boards poked at them with bayonets.

Headed to Woosung Internment Camp three hours north of Shanghai, they passed through wealthy suburbs where estates had been commandeered by Japanese troops. Empty swimming pools full of excrement and bottles, Daimlers gutted in driveways. An officer in a white kimono lying on a pillow atop a Rolls, smoking a cigar.

And farther out across a cratered wasteland, they saw platoons entrenched in what had once been villages, as defeated Chinese armies withdrew into the interior. Now hordes of homeless refugees roamed the countryside. The truck moved fast, the driver and guards pissing in bottles rather than stopping. Bandit groups of refugees had formed, ambushing trucks en route to internment camps.

The truck stopped at a water station heavily guarded by Japanese troops. Prisoners stood dumb in sunlight. Some had been held for weeks in transit camps in the city, so they were already half starved. They sipped water, then crawled toward deep grass, needing privacy. From flooded paddy fields, rotting corpses seemed to watch. Inside the truck were also camp supplies, mildewed potatoes, rice full of weevils. Bandits lying outside the guarded perimeter watched and waited.

A mile after they left the water station, Keo heard the driver curse. He crawled up on his knees, saw piles of coffins blocking the road. Across bomb-cratered fields he saw something that would haunt him all his days. Hundreds of running yellow skeletons in rags, red gaping holes instead of eyes. Starving refugees—men, children, old women—swarming toward the truck like locusts, waving tennis racquets, golf clubs, cricket bats—booty stolen from bombed-out houses near the city.

Guards shot wildly, unable to find them in their sights, some so thin bullets seemed to pass through them. The driver braked while soldiers jumped down, dragging coffins from the road. Bandits gained, climbing the back of the truck, dragging sacks of potatoes and rice past terrified prisoners. Then, ripping their clothes from them, they attacked the prisoners with golf clubs, cricket bats, beating them with the equipment of their pleasure sports.

Another military truck sped up behind them, full of soldiers firing guns. In the chaos of tumbling bodies, a Dutch woman shrieked as her infant was wrenched from her arms. She kept shrieking as refugees melted back across the land, dragging rice and potatoes, waving bats and clubs. Machine guns sprayed dozens to the ground, missing the skinny yellow form clutching the infant like a succulent white puppy.

Would her shrieking never stop? A soldier crawled into the truck and hit the woman in the face. In the silence, Keo thought of the fate of her infant, but something in him turned away. The man beside him gurgled. He spat on his hand, moistening the man's lips, lips so foul with fungus Keo gagged. He wiped himself with a rag, the pain of his bayonet cuts intense. He felt such thirst, he bit down on the inside of his cheek, sucking blood.

Under the tarpaulin cover, heat was stifling. People packed so close, they sobbed trying to breathe. A man with broken glasses viciously scratched his arms and chest. People backed away. Body lice, carrier of typhus. They knew it would come. It would all come. Keo looked down at his body, his skin white-gray from dust. Cuts throbbing, infection setting in. He knew they had reached Woosung Camp by the smell of sewage.

Gates opened. Guards literally threw them from the truck. On his knees, he looked up, astonished. There were hundreds, maybe a thousand, Allied nationals already interned. Some looked relatively healthy, others near death. Japanese guards yanked him to his feet, threw a filthy shirt and pants at him reeking of stale urine.

One of them spoke broken English. "You dress. Commandant want see you."

They pushed him up flights of steps to an office overlooking the camp.

Lieutenant Tokugawa was young, sporting a mustache. He looked up cordially and smiled.

"Ah. Hula Man. Yes, word travels fast." He pointed to a chair. "Please. Sit?"

He paced the room importantly, then frowned. "You no like

homosexual. Good punch! Ha ha. Next time . . . 'Feint East, Strike West. Hide Sword Within Deep Smile.' "

Keo shook his head, understanding nothing.

The man's voice softened, becoming almost fluid. "*Art of the Advantage*, old Japanese text. Many strategies more subtle than smashing nose."

Keo mumbled, "I guess I lost my head."

"For sure, almost lost your head!" Tokugawa laughed. "I no like homosexual, too. But right now Nazis much like anus-plug for corpse. Japan need them for holding insides *in*."

He spread his legs, stood with hands on hips in front of Keo. "Listen. You behave. I behave to you. I know Benny Goodman, Count Basie. . . ."

He pulled out dusty record albums stolen from plundered houses. "Before war, I know tango, fox-trot. Real swing-kid jazz fiend."

Keo swayed, on the verge of fainting. "I think . . . I need to lie down."

"Okay. Be patient. This German chase many boys. Embarrassment to Nazis. Soon he smothered in his sleep. You have big fans. Can go back Club Argentina. If *behave*."

Two husky Dutchmen half carried him down a cinder path to makeshift barracks. Inside, beds were curtained off for privacy with hanging cloths, patched linens. Within each space a human moved, the brackish odor of unwashed flesh, clothes stained from dysentery. He passed a weeping group covering a child's face with a sheet.

Arms were still supporting him, as Keo shouted, "Don't give up! *Never* give up."

They laid him on a cot, partitioned from his neighbors by dirty rags on one side, a bloodstained sheet on the other. The stain seemed to spread before his eyes, forming a huge five-petaled flower. He thought he even smelled hibiscus giving off its scent. Sweat poured down his face. Delirium. And he was home in Honolulu. Good grease of *laulau* dripping down his chin. Smell of *limu* and *'opihi*. Starch of sea salt on his legs, hands blistered from paddling canoe.

"Mama." He sat up crying, reaching out.

A murmuring, and she was there. Golden, sweet-smelling, touching his cheeks with Chinese parsley–scented hands.

"*Pehea 'oe, pehea 'oe?*" she whispered. "How you doing, son?"

She waved flies from his face. Spooned seawater and fresh kelp between his lips.

"Swallow. Swallow. Seawater same as human blood. Ninety-seven elements. Kelp give you iron. You grow strong bumbye. Sleep now . . . Mama going sing down yo' fevah."

While his body rattled with escalating fever, Leilani bathed his limbs, rubbed them with oil of *kukui*. She sang. Her voice so soft, so lilting, inmates in the barracks turned and listened, seeing no one but the feverish brown man.

Rabaul

New Britain, 1944–45

Hair a matted woolly rush, skin like bark. How long since *she has bathed? Sometimes she rears up from her cot, glimpsing something. Something she should remember. Life. Youth.*

Each day the gravelly roar as Allied planes rush in, emptying bomb bays over Rabaul. Airfields are reduced to dust. Ships in the harbor obliterated. Wounded soldiers mount up so fast, surgical theatres resemble slaughterhouses. As military nurses die from typhoid, girls from the Quonsets are forced to replace them. Mouths covered with rags, they stitch up limbs and stomachs while guards stand behind them with fixed bayonets.

After victories at Guadalcanal, Bougainville, and Buna, Allied forces bypass Rabaul, their sights now set on Saipan, Tinian, Okinawa. Instead of landing troops, they bomb Rabaul's harbor and airfields, "softening" the base for Australia's mop-up forces. Still, Rabaul's commander in chief orders its air force and navy to persevere. In the evenings after rice, young pilots studiously discuss collision tactics and Kaiten, the suicide submarine corps.

Knowing all is lost, that there is only honorable death, officers begin to show a human side, sharing food with favorite girls, those not yet wasted by disease. Lieutenant Matsuharu summons Sunny to his quarters, commanding that first she bathe. Sometimes he talks again of student days in Paris. Or, he falls silent, staring at her neck.

He forgets she's starving, that only officers eat decently. He plays with his food. He sees how she watches him eat, by not watching, not begging. One night he offers her steamed eel. The first mouthful is so succulent, so shocking, she almost loses consciousness. She steadies herself, inhales deeply, chews so slowly there is nothing left to swallow. As hunger is appeased, she takes the time to savor. The eel tastes so fresh, she imagines the moment it was killed, how it must have screamed. She remembers how long-beaked eelfish go awww, awww, awwww when speared, as if crying. She remembers spearfishing with her brother, and in a dreamy way begins to tell.

". . . Once my brother speared a great moray eel. The spear lodged in one eye. Trying to thrash free of it, the moray half crushed itself against a rock. Its lower jaw was torn off, its flesh hung in shreds. Yet it was indestructible, its muscles locked in a horrible spasm, its good eye fixed on my brother, the enemy. It got away. For years spearfishers came across it, darting in and out of reefs, the spear like a stalk growing from its eye. . . ."

Matsuharu studies her. "Where is your brother now?"

"He was at Stanford University, when I . . . left home."

Sometimes it's safe to talk. Sometimes dangerous. He might begin to rave. He might begin to slap her. Until he cannot stop. He has never molested her. Others girls, yes, even rape. But he wants something else from Sunny. He's saving her for something.

Another night he sends for her, and faces her, bewildered. "Minister Tojo has resigned. Now your planes bomb Tokyo. How is it we miscalculated?" He shakes his head. "Our emperors were descended from gods. We are much cleaner than Chinese. Much wiser. We have accomplished more. Our cities, our warships. Why does your government defend China? What can China give you?"

He looks right through her.

"Yes, we are diffident, proud to the verge of hysteria. Bound by a thousand laws and conventions. Do you know . . . a man who commits hara-kiri is not permitted to fall sideways. He is bound by rule to fall on his face."

Each visit he seems more insane, yet still comports himself as an officer, immaculate, boots highly polished. He speaks perfect English, quietly, with courtesy, never displaying the crudeness of other officers. When they part, he always bows, even after he has slapped her to unconsciousness. Now he stands, civilized and deadly, dreamily examining his sword.

"No one understands. Japan meant to win back Asia. To free millions of peasants in China and India from slavery under colonialist whites . . ."

Somehow, she summons the courage to ask him, "If you love Asians, how can you continue slaughtering millions of Chinese?"

He strokes the sword absentmindedly.

"We had great respect for Old China. What exists now is appalling. Beyond the Great Wall only famine, corruption."

Sunny thinks of her father, of his homeland, Korea. "And so, you exterminate whole villages. Wipe them from history . . ."

"It is war. We need land. Our islands are so small. Even Communists do not love China. They want to make it a second Russia! Nothing there but starving millions."

"To starve is a tragedy, not a sin," she whispers. "My father is Korean, a people descended from Chinese. I have been taught they were worshiped for their wisdom. An ancient and inventive people."

Matsuharu turns to her as if to a child. "What do they do with their inventions? They invented gunpowder—and? Made little rockets! Shot off fireworks for thousands of years. Never dreaming it was useful for conquering people. The invention of printing. For generations they printed nothing but poems. Sentimental discourse. They failed to use the printed word for propaganda. Look at Shanghai—four million Chinese, opium-addicted whores, rickshaw coolies living in filth. Only a few thousand whites there, and yet they live in mansions, skyscrapers. Tell me, which of these people is superior?"

He points to a Japanese landscape on the wall.

"And Japan. Our land is beautiful. Our people industrious. We have no debts, beg of no one. We are tolerant of all religions. We are honorable. What has the world against us?"

Sunny thinks again of her father, what his homeland suffered under Japan. Not caring if she lives or dies, she speaks with anger.

"The sword is your religion. You are invaders, barbarians. You

would wipe out whole countries. You train your young men to die before they've even lived."

He waves his arms like a madman. "If you're looking for evil, look to the white man first!"

He sits down again, eyes rolling, out of control.

"What can you know, what can anyone know of us? We have too much feeling. We are people of the soul. Yes, Japan lives by Bushido, the samurai code of honor. Yes, we are complex. The fear of life and the courage to die dwell side by side in our hearts. Yet there is also love of beauty. Nature."

His voice grows distant, a young boy calling from a dream.

". . . Ah, September. I hear the threshing of rice sheaves. Fields are flooded with water preparing the soil for plowing. Pine trees rise sharply through mist, and I hear temple bells across the hills where shaven-headed monks meditate in Buddhist monasteries. Carp swim in sun-dappled ponds. Girls stand in tea fields in large bonnets. My father writes proverbs in the last rays of sunset. Such bold sweeps of his brush. O Father!"

Sunny reels. She closes her eyes. She has finally recognized him. Endo Matsuharu, the young man who played such sweet saxophone with Keo in Montmartre. The student who argued Schopenhauer and Poincaré, who wept over Albinoni and Bach. Now he rapes. Decapitates. Who did this to him? Was the evil always there?

This night before he dismisses her, Matsuharu steps close, strokes her cheek, slowly unbuttons her tattered dress. She knows by the agility of his eyes, the speed of his lowering gaze, it is not her breasts he seeks. His fingers touch her glowing ribs. He seems to count them.

BOMBS DEVASTATE JAPAN. NAPALM FIRES CAUGHT BY HIGH WINDS roll like carpets through entire cities. Tokyo gutted, two hundred thousand people dead. Nagoya, ash. Osaka. Kobe.

One night Kim crawls into Sunny's bed, cheeks so bony, her eyes appear to grow on stalks.

"They say the streets of Tokyo are impassable because of human corpses." She weeps with so little energy it comes out as barks. "Why doesn't such news make me happy? Why?"

Sunny holds her in her arms. "Because you are still human, you still have a conscience."

"I want to hate. I need to hate. I need to feel something!"

Spring 1945. Allies reclaim the Philippines, they win at Iwo Jima. Okinawa. One night there is shouting in the men's POW compound. Germany has surrendered. By now, three hundred miles of tunnels surrounding Rabaul are completed, making it an almost impregnable underground fortress: barracks, hospitals, bunkers, antiaircraft guns.

Summer heat unbearable, a furnace door flung wide. Dust coats their faces like white masks. Salt becomes precious as water. It must be replaced in the body; in the tropics, its absence means death. In the officers' mess, girls watch men grow drunk on sake. They serve them meals, wash their dishes, are forced into their beds. When the officers have finally passed out, girls swarm through the kitchen, stealing scraps and salt, as much salt as they can carry.

Knowing Allies are approaching through the jungle, girls fight over bits of metal used as mirrors. Some see their reflections for the first time in months. They stare. How, after this, can they return to ordinary humans? The sickest, the near insane, talk of tomorrow, after Rabaul—parties, flirtations, marriage—as if they will scream normalcy back into their lives. Sunny watches them mend ragged dresses, rouge scabby lips with plant roots. They haven't bathed in more than a year. They cannot grasp their squalor, that youth and health are finished.

After three years, Sunny's clothes have worn to yeasty rags. Her leather shoes are green with fungus, crumbling with decay. When she walks, they feel like dank mushrooms. A bit of shrapnel lodged in her leg has worked its way out after months. It leaves a large infected hole which maggots feed on. She grows used to the sensation, her body as a living host.

She suspects they will all die before the Allies arrive. Girls weakened by disease are marched outside and shot, or herded into boats blown up in the harbor. Yet something in her won't give up. With a pointed bamboo pole flung over the fence by Papuan natives, she walks through her Quonset, smacking the sides of beds, threatening girls who use drains outside the hut as toilets. At each new outbreak of dysentery, she makes girls dig pits in which contaminated rags and refuse are buried. She begs guards for quicklime.

Finding lice matted in someone's hair, Sunny shaves the girl's head, then shaves her own, forcing others to do likewise, knowing how fast body lice spread typhus. She nurses girls dying of beriberi, and one whose infected gums have poisoned her starved body.

One night Sunny approaches a doctor injecting a girl with steroids meant to treat syphilis. It also affects their minds, turning them to zombies. She has sharpened her pole to a brutal point and lifts it, aiming at his back. He turns, offering her a cup of clear water. Pipes have been bombed. She has drunk polluted water for so long her tongue is cracked and swollen. If she contracts cholera again, there is no hope for surviving. She takes the cup from the doctor, forgetting to kill him.

Now, each time she is summoned by Matsuharu, Sunny remembers her father, why he was so full of hate. In that way, her father gives her strength; hate usurps her crippling fear. Some nights the lieutenant is kind, rather vague and distant. Other nights he slaps her, as if trying to forget. That there is a war, and he has lost it. That he has lost all innocence, and honor. One night he takes her in his arms. He sobs against her bony shoulder. She holds her breath, held by the executioner.

POWs in the military compound pass word to the women. Hiroshima. Nagasaki. Gone. Hysteria mounts amongst commanding officers. More girls are marched out to their deaths. Sunny vows if soldiers come for her, she will go down fighting and screaming, until their cartridges are finished, until their swords are bent. They pass her by. At night she shows girls how to sharpen ends of sugarcane, how to roast them in fires until the tips are spearlike, hard as flint. The sticks are hidden beneath their beds. She makes each girl vow to die ripping and slashing, not mewling and bowing her head.

Now all underground tunnels are reinforced. All food is gathered and transported. Soldiers are prepared for hand-to-hand combat with the Allies. One night soldiers march through the Quonset. One of them drags Kim from her bed. She is so weak, she merely moans.

Sunny wrestles with the soldier, begging him, "Take me. Take me! I'm older."

He hits her with his rifle. "You! You saved for Matsuharu." He mimics the slash of a sword across a neck.

Kim calls back almost dreamily. "Sunny, it is over. Now only . . . blessed death . . ."

Things rise up inside her. The mother she can never be, the soon-dead girl she has mothered. They take up residence along her spine, little skulls that will never stop screaming.

One day, rumors. A murmuration. The war in the Pacific is over. The silence of sixty thousand men. Refusing to surrender, some rebel officers begin moving troops underground to wait for the enemy. Fewer than ten girls are left in Sunny's Quonset.

That night Matsuharu summons her. She prepares herself, washing her neck. Pushed from behind by a bayonet, she crosses the base to his quarters. She sits in a corner of the room. He strokes his sword, studies his reflection in the blade. His flat, rather handsome face is gone. Defeat, horror have left his face eerily lean and frontal. His eyes are vacant. His head swivels like a bat.

" 'The potter takes clay to make a pitcher / Whose usefulness lies in the hollow where the clay is not . . .'

"A quote from Lao Tzu," he whispers. "Do you understand it?"

Sunny waits.

"One day soon, I will explain."

OCTOBER 15, 1942

Beloved Brother,

Thank Mother God you're alive! May she have mercy on us all. Your 25-word letter from Woosung (April) took three months to reach us through the Red Cross in Tokyo. The Japs had censored out five words. (Can't believe I'm calling them Japs. I can't believe what's happened to us.) When we got your letter, Papa sobbed. We thought you were dead.

This is my third letter, did you receive the others? We're only supposed to write 25 words, but I've got so much to tell! I'm mailing this to Club Argentina. Maybe your friends will get this to you. Since Pearl Harbor, nothing's real. Jonah-boy enlisted. He's in army training somewhere in Minnesota. Then they'll ship him overseas to Europe. I think Mama's died a couple times. . . .

DeSoto's freighter was captured by the Japs somewhere near Java or Sumatra. Australian soldiers rescued him. We got a card. By the time you get this your pal, Krash Kapakahi, will be long gone. He's combat-training now in Utah.

Can you believe? The night before Pearl Harbor, the band was playing at the Royal, Krash on 'ukulele. Between sets he stepped out on the beach for a smoke. In the distance he saw what looked like a periscope, then he watched a Jap submarine surface! He said it just sat there on the water. He yelled and folks came running. The thing had disappeared. Folks said he'd been drinking too much rum. Who could believe a Jap sub got through navy minesweepers and was cruising Waikiki? Weeks later it was in the papers—a captured Jap seaman said while they were waiting to attack Pearl Harbor, the sub had surfaced the night before, saw the lights of Waikiki, even heard music from the Royal!

Krash came to Kalihi Lane that night, told us what he'd seen. What he thought he'd seen. He visits now and then. I like his humor, his ambition. Imagine a beachboy going to night school, planning to study law! But we always seem to end up fighting. We hadn't talked for months, since our last argument. For some reason KGMB was playing music through the night instead of signing off at 12 A.M. We sat in the garage gabbing away. Everything my fault, his fault, and why did we always fight. We stayed up all night, dancing almost every song.

Well, next morning, Sunday, Mama cooked us shoyu eggs, fried rice, her toasted taro bread. Krash peeled a mango, handed me a slice. I was sucking on that sweet, sticky pulp, admiring his hands, when I heard them droning in. I remember Mama turning in slow motion. . . .

We ran out in the lane. Mother God, they flew close enough to see the Rising Sun painted on their sides. Then, oh baby, I never saw such hell. Pearl Harbor turned into fireballs. Mountains of black smoke rising up like giant devils. A million pounds of gunpowder going up on ships. All those boys, those haole boys . . .

Then a second wave of Japs flew in, so low their landing gear ripped down telephone wires. Papa went berserk, shooting at them with his pig-hunting rifle. Mr. Kimuro stood in his undershorts, trying to bring them down with his bow and arrows. Me? I ran inside and changed my clothes. If we were going to die, I guess I wanted to go out in style, best dress, my Lily Daché hat. These things aren't planned. I'll never hear the end of it from Mama.

Krash pushed Mama and Papa inside, walked back and forth in front of the house with a carving knife. I don't know what came over me. I took his hand and walked beside him. A plane dived straight at us. This is it, I thought. I looked at him and said, "I love you." But it passed. . . .

Afterwards, we hitchhiked to Queen's Hospital. Blood-donor lines for miles. I still dream of burnt flesh, wake up smelling it. Sailors covered with black oil. Legs missing, eyes destroyed. They brought them in in trucks, poured them out like pineapples. This captain, he didn't have a stomach anymore, he thought doctors and nurses were his crew. Still giving orders when he died.

I spent fourteen hours putting "M" (for morphine) on sailors' foreheads so we wouldn't double-dose. Some begged for a smoke, going while they inhaled. Hardest thing was peeling cigarettes off dead boys' lips. Soon I was soaking red from head to toe. Blood flowed up and down the halls—folks were sliding in it. My good dress dried stuck to me like plaster. Nurses had to cut it off me, had to cut off my hat. My hair so blood-starched it stood out like wings. I threw my shoes away, walked up the lane that night in half a sheet, followed by red footprints. That's why I call them Japs. . . .

Folks say not one antiaircraft gun was ready, not one fighter plane airborne to greet them. Pearl Harbor laid out for them like plate-lunch . . . You wouldn't know Honolulu. Streets zigzagged with trenches in case of more attacks. Martial law. FBI. Folks arrested in pajamas. We carry ID cards with fingerprints. Everybody vaccinated, gas masks strapped across our backs. Of course, all food is rationed. (What I wouldn't do for a hunk of pork! A sip of real-kine coffee . . .)

Well, Brother, we're now an official combat zone. Tanks guarding 'Iolani Palace. Waikiki Beach a mass of barbed wire, tourists long gone. The Moana and the Royal Hawai'ian converted to hospitals for the army and navy boys. More shipyard and defense workers brought in from the mainland. There's such a housing shortage, they're sleeping in their cars.

Blackout is hated like the plague. Each block has a warden. We get fined for leaving lights on, even headlights. Mama's calabash cousin out near Haliewa was crushed to death when two buses collided in the dark. He was walking his dog without a flashlight, got slammed in between. Oh, baby, what a mess . . .

Now soldiers walk into our houses. Search and seize. Arrest. Trial without jury. The army tried to shoot Mr. Cruz's rooster, that crazy Tacky. Said his midnight crowing might be some kind of spy code. He pecked off half a soldier's ear and chased another down the lane. He got away, but Mr. Cruz was put in jail. Just an excuse to arrest him. He's got a lot of Jap friends. . . . Hundreds of them arrested in Kalihi, Palama, Chinatown. Buddhist priests, language-school teachers. All now at Sand Island Internment Camp. Like your *camp, probably. Do they let you blow your trumpet? Do you have enough to eat?*

Just heard from baby brother Jonah. Army's teaching him to handle bayonets, strangulation ropes. He's learned how to turn baseball bats into war clubs with barbed wire and spikes. Also had instructions in chemical warfare, machine guns, mortar firing. My heart breaks. I tore the letter up so Mama wouldn't see it. Whatever happens, even if this war ends tomorrow, Jonah will come back different. I'll tell you something. We're all going to come back different.

. . . Real shortage of girls here. One for every hundred or every thousand men, depends on who you talk to. Brothels booming on Hotel Street. The army and navy even had to put their wounded up in brothels, till they expanded hospitals. For a while, Hotel Street looked like a Red Cross camp! You got to give those hookers credit, they helped nurse those boys like babies. We all pitched in. . . .

With the Moana closed, I got on the dawn shift at Dole cannery. That old pineapple drag. But too many workers, shifts too short. I hired on for maintenance crew at the downtown police station. Then they handed me a bucket to clean toilets (again)! So much for that job!

Mama and Papa got to keep the mortgage up, but Papa can't get work now. Military has him listed as Jap sympathizer, because he won't bad-mouth his old boss, Shirashi. (Now interned at Sand Island.) Mama's still mending uniforms for Palama Women's Prison, paid in nickels practically. I found part-time sewing here in Kalihi. Plus, three nights a week, same old hapa-haole hula at an enlisted men's nightclub. Oh, who am I kidding? It's not a nightclub, not even a bar. It's a lowdown joint on Hotel Street.

. . . Also wrapping bandages for the Red Cross, and volunteering for USO dances. Some military snothead with a row of medals saw me at an army/navy dance. Thought I looked part Jap. He said I couldn't volunteer if I had more than a quarter Jap blood. I told him my eyes were swollen from crying myself to sleep at night. Why? Because I've got a brother in a Japanese prison camp, and a second brother whose ship was captured by the Japs, and a kid brother who's training to fight Germans in Europe. Well, the snothead apologized. . . .

'Ey! Do they think Hawai'ians are just sitting back, sucking poi, watching from the sidelines? I see the wounded, and think of you. Nothing matters but that you, Jonah, DeSoto come home safe. And Krash. Mother God, I will stitch, and starve, and dance my feet down to the bone if that will bring you home.

Soldiers coming back from combat see Oriental faces here and go berserk. Plenty street fights, even killings. Locals get confused. I feel real sorry for our Japanese neighbors. They have to surrender all heirloom weapons, even ancient family books where there might be invisible writing. All Japanese language signs are down, no one wears kimonos.

. . . Chinese neighbors put signs in their yards: WE ARE NOT JAPANESE. FBI arrest-teams race through the streets in military cars. Even arresting Germans and Italians. Last night at the enlisted men's, a soldier back from Guadalcanal pulled out a Jap scalp, waving it around. I went outside to vomit. So, who is right and who is wrong?

Forgive me, Brother. You're in prison, and I ramble. I will die if anything happens to you. It's not a military POW camp. They can't cut off heads. Or torture you. We hear the worst things in those camps is lack of food, and typhus. Be careful, try not to show your temper with the guards.

We also hear repatriation ships are coming out of Shanghai. Papa called the navy, asking if your name is on a list. Well, that's classified. They told him go to hell, there's a war on. We won at Midway. Maybe Mother God is on our side. . . . Hope you get the package. All we could spare from ration-stamps. Spam, cigarettes, powdered milk. Soap. Sugar. Salt. Also a rosary. Snapshots of us all . . .

'Auwē! *Each time we hear air-raid sirens, have to run to bombshell bunkers, stand knee-deep in rainwater till we hear all clear. Helmeted guards in every lane, bullhorns yelling,* "TURN OUT ALL LIGHTS. STAY INSIDE. DON'T COME OUT TILL SUNUP." *Some nights we take turns sitting in the closet, reading with a flashlight.*

Mama got fed up, tarpapered the bathroom window for total blackout. So the bathroom's now our living room. Newspapers stacked on toilet, portable radio on the hamper for latest news. Sometimes we get that slut, Tokyo Rose, trying to lure our boys from battle. . . . Papa is block warden! When he's pau at night he drags a futon into the tub and neighbors squeeze in, "talking story," playing 'ukulele after supper. Good fun! Some nights we even drag in that dopey rooster, Tacky Cruz. Sure as hell, at midnight, he crows his head off!

Remember Rosie Perez, down the lane? She went "got chubby all a sudden!" One night, sitting in the tub she feels bad cramps, starts screaming. Next thing we know there's a little head between her legs. She's pushing, pushing, Mama playing midwife, grabbing its tiny, slippery body. Me holding while Mama cuts the cord. Then everybody crying. Oh, baby, what a night! Papa comes in from warden duty and I shout "Look what popped out of Rosie!" He fell down, and laughed and cried. Up and down the lane, folks took turns visiting, holding the little keiki. Rosie's husband in training somewhere in S. Carolina. Brother, how can I tell you of the sweetness, a newborn infant's cry in wartime. Our best night so far.

. . . Swing bands coming here in droves, playing for servicemen. Artie Shaw, Dorsey Brothers, even Louis Armstrong. For me, no one compares with that Duke Ellington. I pushed my way backstage and told him all about you, said you played with Dew Baptiste. Well, we sat in his dressing room, talking for hours. New Orleans, Paris . . .

Goodness, what a flirt. He said I was a "luscious miss," my "beauty dignified his countenance." He said if he were stay-

ing longer, he would make me his favorite sundae. Did that mean feed me? Or devour me? Brother, I will never be the same. The man is physically exquisite. That pretty smile, those high-heeled shoes. His suit, his shirt, his tie. Well, there'll be lots of jazz dates when you come home. Folks know you've been out in the world. So much aloha being sent you. Everybody missing you ...

I went to Sunny's house, her mother wouldn't let me in. Said there's been no more word from her. If she's alive, which she is because she's too clever to die, she's off on some adventure. Probably making bombs in basements with those Communist silk-factory women, and that poor crippled sister. That girl always had too much energy and nerve. Forget her. Come home. Where you belong.

O Brother, look! The moon is full. Even as I send you our prayers and alohas, a perfect vivid rainbow—Hawai'ian omen of victory—arches over Kalihi Lane. . . .

Love from your sister,
Malia

Nā Kūlana Pō'ino

The Ill-Fated

Woosung Camp, February 1943

HOPE NURSED THE FICTION OF NORMALCY. THEN, AS PEOPLE starved, the fiction died. Nothing but bowls of tainted rice, a rotting carrot. He lay on his cot recalling great meals with wrenching clarity, dissolving and synthesizing them infinite times. The flavors, the aromas!

He retreated to the past. Sunny's face in blue lozenges of morning light. Her insurrections and her calms, her riddles rising up like riffs from his horn. Paris suffocating them with its ashes and embers. Their dream had turned on them, turning them to fugitives. Now they were caught in a new history but an old, old time.

In spite of hunger and fatigue, Keo was afraid to sleep. Then he became prey. Of foul, fat flies whose bites were often fatal, of mosquitoes bringing malaria. Lice left him scratching like a madman. Centipedes wriggled remorselessly across his scalp, setting his head ablaze.

Camp population had swollen to almost two thousand. Beaten down to a perpetual nightmare existence, people retreated to a privileged time, disbelieving rumors that Chinese chauffeurs had sabotaged their cars, stealing carburetors, draining gas tanks. That Japanese soldiers had ransacked their palatial homes, defecating in their beds.

Refusing to accept that camp life was now the reality, they considered it only a momentary horror. Soon they would wake to luxury again.

When Malia's letter arrived, Keo lay on his cot trembling. It had taken four months to reach him through Club Argentina. Her package of food never arrived. But just reading the words—salt, Spam—made him light-headed. He closed his eyes, held the letter to his nose, smelling ginger and mildew in his father's garage. The scent of Malia's heavy perfume, his mother's wrists fragrant with spices. He could smell starch on his father's collar, Jonah's leather baseball mitt, even the rough maritime smell of brother DeSoto.

He lay quiet, thinking of Krash and Jonah en route to war in Europe, DeSoto detained somewhere in Malaysia. He thought of Sunny and their child, glimpsed once in her mother's arms. He turned on his side and, with openhearted and despairing passion, he mourned. For all of them, for a life that was over.

Mostly, he was shocked by Malia's views on Sunny.

". . . she's too clever to die, she's off on some adventure."

He read those words over and over, feeling such rage, he staggered across the campgrounds, screaming into the latrines. Screaming that Sunny loved him, that that love was now sustaining him.

Each day his rice bowl seemed heavier with rat shit. His teeth broke from biting down on lime. Yet each time Japan lost another battle, Tokugawa called him to his quarters, offering cigarettes, stolen jazz records.

"I'd rather have rice for our children," Keo said. "They're dying like flies."

Tokugawa shook his head. "Not enough rice even for my men." His voice grew softer. "Even for my family in Osaka."

Typhoon weather, and one day Keo stood up to his ankles in mud, emptying latrine buckets. In the guard tower, drunken soldiers fought over a woman. He heard her laugh. Some women volunteered to clean guardhouses, offering themselves to soldiers for an extra scoop of rice, a strip of cloth to bind crumbling shoes, avoiding hookworm.

Who can blame them? he thought. *If it keeps them from the Death Hut.* The place for terminals, those in the last stage of starvation and disease.

In pouring rain he gazed outside beyond the camp fence. Mobs of Chinese refugees struggled to their feet, as if his image raised the dead. Near-skeletons, many would die trying to unravel the puzzle: If Japan was fighting to save Asia for Asians, why was the enemy locked *inside* the fence, with food? Why were the Chinese locked *out*? They screamed at Keo, begging for garbage, a rotting potato. An infant.

"Yes," Tokugawa said, "they would eat human flesh. You ever know real hunger, kind make you insane? Anything keep you alive, fair game."

They sat in his office, Tokugawa explaining that Keo had finally been pardoned for hitting the Nazi homosexual, who had died of "smotheration." He was being "guaranteed out" of Woosung by the owner of Club Argentina. The man had signed documents promising Keo would not work against the Japanese, that his expenses would be met in Shanghai, that his music was indispensable for the entertainment of Japanese officers.

Tokugawa's smile was mischievous and sly. "When you return Shanghai, I send you to special shop where human parts for sale. Liver, finger, cheek. When fought in China, starve for months. I myself ate someone's smile."

Keo studied him. "And now you may have to die because you don't believe in surrender."

The man reared back. "Not my fault. We not taught how to be prisoner." He slapped his scabbard at his side. "Listen me. We no hate Yanks. We attack you because you interfere."

"How interfere?"

"Embargo. U.S. stop deliveries of oil, iron to Japan. Should mind own business. Our fight not with you."

Keo was stunned by his arrogance, by the fact that he was blind to it. "Listen, this whole war started because of your aggression toward China."

Tokugawa's voice turned soft, almost apologetic. "Japan too many people. Need to expand."

Through the window, Keo watched a small, thin boy struggling to carry three large rotting potatoes. He thought how much there was to covet in this world, yet how little each man could really handle.

" 'Ey!" Tokugawa smacked his arm. "Even U.S. guilty of invasion. Look your islands. They knock down your queen, make you colony so can own Pearl Harbor. Same thing!"

Keo sighed. "Yeah. Same thing. But, tell me, Lieutenant. If Japan won the war tomorrow, what would victory mean to you?"

Tokugawa smiled and looked out at the boy. ". . . Wife. Child. Garden. Full meal. Good sleep." He paused, thinking what more he could want. "Few jazz records . . . Koichi Okawa, Benny Goodman of Tokyo. Funny. Same things I had *before*."

REENTERING THE CITY, HE SAW THE HYSTERICAL ENERGY OF Shanghai still thrived, people continuing to deny a world at war. Whole blocks had been obliterated by bombs. Yet in the old Chinese section dentists still pulled teeth in the streets, nightingales still sang in bamboo cages. Wealthy brides still passed concealed in red lacquer sedan chairs. On side streets, bamboo poles still leaned out of eaves, dripping diapers and foot-binding bandages. Professional letter writers still sat with brushes and rice paper, their chattering monkeys still grinding ink with tiny ebony fingers.

Refusing to see the city sinking beneath them, folks still thronged Blood Alley bars and brothels. Restaurants thrived, and Chinese opera. Jai alai matches continued on Bubbling Well Road. Axis powers and neutrals—Swiss and Dutch—still fox-trotted at the Majestic, drank absinthe at the French Club. Jazz lovers still crowded Club Argentina.

Laughter, the scent of healthy people in clean clothes talking in horizontal languages, seemed to him a miracle. A bath at Hunan Mansions, a bed with clean linens, sleep lasting for days. He spent his first week bent solemnly over plates of food, then joined a group at the Argentina, wearing his "A," for American, armband. The other musicians were strangers, two "J" armbands, and two "I's." At first he played cautiously; touching the new trumpet made him shy. But soon he was blowing with the same breathless drive, though he noticed he tired faster.

He began again searching for Sunny and the child. He questioned people in the streets, in dance halls, even gangsters in bulletproof sedans. He queried pederasts in shantung suits entering the House of Small Boys on Avenue Edward VII, and patrons of the Blind Executioner where naked men were pilloried and whipped with wire brushes by nude little blind girls with sequined eyes. He even queried bystanders as the Guild for Night-Soil Coolie Carriers marched for higher wages, shorter hours, honey carts that didn't tip.

He asked creatures passing in fog, "Have you heard of Sunny Sung from Honolulu?"

After a few weeks the guttural sounds of German accents began grating on his spine. The laughter of White Russian whores fox-trotting with Japanese generals. He listened to Frenchmen discussing ten-year-old "pig-footed" Chinese girls, how the more bound and broken and twisted their feet, the more folds in their vagina. Which made them more pleasurable. Such words struck Keo in the face.

His playing slowed. He turned crude and ugly, cursing couples on the dance floor, loosing aeolian belches in their faces. Crowds laughed, amused by his dark, sweaty perversity. Watching well-fed people drinking Scotch, sliding round the floor like skaters, he thought of the horrors at Woosung. At such times he would go back to Hunan Mansions and tear his room apart. Then he behaved for a while, holding everything in.

One night a Frenchman asked for Louis Armstrong, ". . . his scat vocal on 'Tiger Rag.' "

A German shouted up at him, "Yah! Give us real *nigger* music!"

Something deep within him turned. Keo leapt from the stage, landing with both feet on the German's chest, trying to flatten the man's head with his trumpet. Felled by the club of a bouncer, when he came to, they were dragging him out of the Argentina.

Keo's head dripped blood, he shouted at the crowd. "You whores—don't you know you've lost the war!"

AT WOOSUNG CAMP THEY HUDDLED IN WINTRY CEMENT BARracks. Bare walls, bare floors, dim electric bulbs. Ragged sheets originally hung to separate them were now used as blankets or shrouds. People simply ceased to see each other. Nudity now passed unremarked, so that in some perverse way they achieved privacy. The only thing that bound them together was knowledge that they would probably die.

That year, typhoons never ceased. Rain fell in sheets, flooding the makeshift hospital where patients floated from their beds. A barracks collapsed, killing six. Electricity failed. Finally, cesspools overflowed. Stalled in filth, people surrendered. They stopped dodging it, stopped holding their breath, they slept and lived with it. And typhus spread.

One day the sickly camp doctor weighed Keo's neighbor. In the morning he was 130 pounds. Midday he weighed close to 150. By evening, horribly bloated, he weighed 187. "Wet" beriberi. His yellow-gray face so blown up he could not look down the mountains of his cheeks. Each night as the doctor tapped him, drawing off fluids, folks watched horrified as this human balloon deflated to nothing.

Starvation brought incipient madness. Men knocked each other down in fistfights. Women went at each other with ragged nails, rusty hairpins. Children bit each other like dogs. Yet somehow they understood fighting was good, distracting them from the horror and, for a moment, from hunger. By March, even guards began to starve. Who was winning the war no longer seemed to matter.

One day Simmons, a big Canadian working for the Germans, was struck down by malaria. Parasites in his red blood cells multiplied. Fever rampaged, bathing him in cold tremors, then heat, delirium. Ravaged cells clogged the lining of his arteries. His urine turned brown from the broken cells. If his urine turned black, he was finished.

People lingered near his cot. "Let the bastard die."

For the past eight months the man had hung round torture cells in a special compound at Woosung where Japs kept downed Allied pilots, most of them injured and half dead. Simmons prodded them for military information, offering morphine, cigarettes. When they refused to talk, he beat them. He had kicked a burned American pilot to death while guards laughed, egging him on.

Now, with fever rampant, Simmons's face was almost unrecognizable, like raw animal skin stretched over sticks and left in the sun. His whole body looked like that. Keo stared at his shrunken head. His eyes stuck out of it, enormous.

He grabbed Keo's arm. "Water. Help me. They're sending quinine from Shanghai. . . ."

Keo heard his chest bones rattle. He leaned down, shaking his head. "No one's sending you *shit*."

Simmons tried to sit up. "I'll pay you. Get you out . . ."

Afraid they were indeed sending quinine, and that he might pull through, Keo viciously pushed him down, yanking a filthy pillow from beneath his head.

"You bastard. This is for the air boys you murdered."

He shoved the pillow over his face, then sat down on it, watching Simmons's hands claw air. He felt the tremor of the man's muscles pass through his haunches. He clenched his teeth until the tremors stopped. Folks watched from the doorway. That night he shoveled the body into a pit of excrement, then crossed himself, praying for the air boys. He found gifts on his cot—a new potato, four cigarettes, clean socks.

One night after curfew, a pale blond woman stood beside him. "Please. Let me lie here. I'm so cold."

She had a distinctly pungent, female smell. Most of the women had it from their monthly bleeding. He wondered when she had last bathed, when she had held a piece of soap. He pulled her to the cot, put his arms round her. She began to cry.

"Simmons was my husband. . . ."

When Keo tried to respond, she covered his mouth.

"We met in Shanghai. He married me because he needed a cover. I didn't know. When I found out he worked for the Germans, I cursed him, wished him dead. He said he would kill me if I told." She found Keo's hand in the dark. "I moved to the single women's barracks."

Her name was Ruth. She was irredeemably thin and plain, her fingers constantly rubbing bleeding gums. But she was a woman, and she was warm. He found himself terrified, wanting to drop his head between her breasts and sob. They slept like children, side by side. Warmth seemed to be all they were after. Then one night she told him:

"The guard, Suga—he forces me. When he finishes, he sticks a sweet potato in my mouth. I'm too weak to fight him."

Suga was a big, husky guard who had gone a little crazy. Keo could tell when he was near because he smelled so bad. The man boasted how he hated whites, hated Chinese, even hated his superiors. Since being conscripted for war, he'd come to hate everything. He had killed two Brits with his fists, then stolen their shoes and bartered them. He stalked women in the dark.

"When a woman's starving," Ruth asked, "is rape so bad if afterwards she's fed? If I accept food in return, is it rape? Or barter?"

Keo sat up slowly. "How often does he do this?"

"Several times a week. I don't scream because he'll strangle me. And . . . I'm so hungry I think of the potato. Am I a whore?"

He held her like a child. "No. You're just trying not to die."

One night Suga heaved himself upon her, knocking her down, smacking her legs apart. Keo came up from behind holding a length of wire. Wrapping it round his neck, he yanked with such ferocity he heard something crack. Suga rolled off her, gasping and blinking, his penis hanging from his pants. Furious that it wasn't over, Keo cursed, condensed everything inside him, and threw his body forward, slamming a rock down on the guard's head. He died clutching his penis. It was still erect when they slung him into a mudhole.

Keo led Ruth back to his cot, both of them shuddering and dumb. At dawn she was gone, but the next night she came with a sliver of bartered soap. Behind the makeshift camp kitchen they boiled water, bathing each other, laughing and crying while their lashes froze. That night they became lovers, half starved, half mad.

"Don't mention love," she begged. "Or God, or any of it."

After that, whenever possible, they were at each other's side. He told her everything—his music, his travels, the search for Sunny and their child. They never talked of Simmons or the guard. Death was an everyday occurrence, and now so was killing. Keo would do it again in a minute. And in a minute it could be done to him. There were rumors that all camp prisoners would soon be marched farther into China's interior. As Allied forces defeated the Japanese, prisoners would be mass-executed.

They ignored the future, making sure each day had its errand, that there was a point to every day. And each night they held each other, not out of love, but out of a need to signify they were alive, of human flesh, connecting the way humans did. One morning during muster, Ruth bent over, sick. Her legs became swollen, so she couldn't walk. Her lungs wheezed, full of water.

He buried her in her own small grave, feeling immense fatigue, so immense that nothing mattered. Everything was far away. He hung his tattered sheets again for privacy, staring at the mildewed wall, Malia's letter damp and ragged on his chest. He knew it by heart, its contents mattered less and less. Nothing moved, not in his head and not in his body. He couldn't think of a reason for moving.

By then he was down to skin and bones, his color a sickly, scaly gray. He woke feverish, fluid round his joints had turned to needles. Horrendous pain, then chills and shivers. Neighbors examined his urine, relieved when they saw it was still yellow—low-grade malaria, not yet advanced to blackwater fever. Quinine was smuggled in.

One day guards stormed the barracks, punching men with rifle butts, ripping at hanging sheets. They headed for Keo. One of them stood over him yelling outlandishly, slapping his head like a bully. Then he leaned down and spat on him, great gobs of mucus. Dazed, Keo watched them kick his piss-bucket down the aisle as they left. Neighbors came with a rag, wiping the filth from his chest. That was when they discovered, in a gob of mucus, a small pellet-size vial of white powder.

"Heroin! Just enough for a good night's sleep."

And buried in the powder, a tiny rag of silk upon which miniature words were printed. COURAGE. OOGH.

Keo found the strength to smile.

HE BEGAN TO RALLY. HEARING FOOD CARTS CLATTER ALONG cinder paths—a litany of pots of rotting rice—he sat up feeling suddenly charged. He caught a whiff of something, not rice but the *wheels* of the carts as they struck sparks from flinty stones. The sparks gave off the smell of firecrackers, the same smell given off when *pōhaku*, stones, were filed to make old-time Hawai'ian bowling balls. His papa had shown him how. For the first time in weeks, Keo dragged himself outside and stood in line, just to smell the sparks that momentarily flew him home.

One day the tempo changed, the camp was swept and set in order. Guards brushed their uniforms. A black Mercedes entered the gates, flanked by trucks with soldiers pointing machine guns from the running boards. Tokugawa bowed repeatedly as a Japanese colonel stepped from the car, consulting a list with his aide. Soldiers marched into a barracks, dragged out an American mother, father, and child. Others pushed two American women and two men from the singles barracks. The colonel frowned and tapped his list, grunting at Tokugawa.

"One more from this camp—Meahuna, Keo."

Soldiers dragged him from his barracks and pushed him to a truck. The whole camp stared, no one brave enough to wave. For the next three hours Keo studied the barrel of a machine gun, knowing he would soon be dead. They were taking him to Shanghai where he would be shot for smothering Simmons, the informer. Or beheaded for killing the guard. Or for beating up the Nazi homosexual.

A curious gnawing in his gut, terror snapping his senses alive. The guard sitting nearest him stank. The man's breath, his sweat, even his clothes smelled of stale, pungent grease like pork. For months Keo had not let himself think of food, afraid it would drive him completely mad. Now, believing he was about to die, he allowed himself that luxury.

Roasted, dripping hunks of pork. Succulent *kālua* pig. Thick strips of crisp-fried bacon. He could taste it, feel it crackling between his teeth, drawing saliva from his cheeks. He began to chew, his chewing like praying, like prayers answered. He drooled on himself, and on the soldier. He drooled on the barrel of the machine gun. Guards backed away laughing, thinking he had gone insane.

He would not remember arriving in Shanghai. Red Cross nurses helped him to his feet. And he stood ready for the bullet, the truncheon, the bayonet. An Indian-looking doctor came toward him, brandishing a syringe, and wiped his skinny arm with alcohol.

"This is glucose. Nourishment. Just now, solid food would lacerate your stomach."

"Am I going to be shot?"

The doctor stepped back, then sighed and patted his shoulder. "Dear man. You're being repatriated."

Keo shook his head, confused.

"Do you understand? You're going home."

White sheets. Beds full of humans so skeletal he seemed robust beside them. He thought of those left behind at Woosung, at camps all over Asia—typhus children, men weighing eighty pounds. *Why me? Why was I chosen to go free?* Riven with guilt and great fatigue, thinking of Sunny and the child, he wept. Red Cross people asked his name and nationality, asked about his time in camp. He wept. A glass of water, the cool, clean bedpan, made him weep.

"Yes, cry," they said. "It will help you heal."

Doctors gave him sedatives so his body could relax, begin to mend itself. Malaria fevers returned, then slowly dissipated. Ulcers on arms and legs began to heal. The horrible pain from salt deprivation gradually subsided from bones and muscles. He hadn't understood what a broken mess he was. He gained a pound. Then another. The man beside him died from overeating. After two weeks he was moved to the ambulatory ward. He now digested solid food. He smoked a cigarette. His skin turned from gray to dullish brown.

He compared his sores, his digestion, his bony behind with other men's. He took three-hour baths, and had a haircut. He watched movies, tried to read *Life* magazine. War raging all over the world, millions massacred. He learned of the aftermath of Bataan, seven thousand Allied soldiers marched to death. Volunteers brought him civilian clothes but he refused. Until he could get into uniform and serve his country, he would wear GI fatigues.

He searched for her name on internee lists, repatriation lists. Not finding her name meant she had fled, she and their child had gotten out. He couldn't face the possibility that they were dead. Negotiations for exchange of captured Japanese soldiers and Allied prisoners took weeks. Then, one night, military officials stood before them.

"You're no longer prisoners. Now, you're evacuees. You'll wear life jackets at all times."

At dawn, nearly twelve hundred people were ferried from the docks to a huge steamer waiting in the harbor to take them to Tokyo. There a converted troopship would transport them to Honolulu. Slowly, laboriously, they climbed its gangways, and stood at the rail as Shanghai receded. Within hours of sailing down the Whangpoo into the great Yangtze River, dozens were in sick bay, too weak to stand or hold down food. Others sobbed because they'd forgotten how to use plumbing and utensils.

Sailors gently assisted them, picking them up when they collapsed. Some people were hysterical, afraid it was a joke: at any minute a Jap ship would bear down on them, forcing them back to the camps. Or they imagined the steamer hitting a mine, being blown to splinters.

"That's why families are assigned to cabins, so they can die together when we're hit."

Singles were issued mattresses or hammocks up on deck.

Keo sat for hours catching up on the news: attempted assassination of Hitler, Admiral Yamamoto shot down in the Pacific. Camp stories—sadistic commandants, atrocities. Some days he sat on a toilet just to be alone. Nights were best, lying wrapped in army blankets, the ocean foaming at his side.

One night while he dozed, something tapped his cheek ever so lightly. He smiled, knowing it was Oogh.

"So, Hula Man. You have had enough adventure?"

"I should have known. How did you get me out of Woosung?"

Oogh snapped open a gold cigarette lighter, lit it with cavalier flourish. "Observe."

"The gold."

"The *flame*. What causes it? Simple flints. They do not perish, and are now much sought after. Weight for weight, flints bring a higher price than gold. *Ma mère* hoarded them, a hedge against inflation. She now has a monopoly in Shanghai. Japs are mad for cigarette lighters. So they must have their flints, no?"

"But, why me? There were so many others needing help. . . ."

Oogh stamped his little foot. "Always questions. Your life out in the world is over, don't you see? Take your knowledge home, use what you have learned."

He appeared to be in uniform, a miniature soldier in GI fatigues.

"Yes. I, too, am evacuating. *Ma mère* exhausts me, still mercantile as a pharaoh. I never forgave her for Shanghai-ing me from Honolulu when I was a boy. She ran back to China saying my papa was too *moloā*, lazy. She wanted to make me 'pure Chinese,' bleed Hawai'ian out of me. Now I'm going home to my *kanaka* papa!"

"You'll break your mother's heart."

Oogh threw back his head and laughed. "She has Tsih-Tsih! Scram-Scram! That boring little pachyderm. A perfect son, who does clever tricks, and weeps on command."

"But, how can you . . ."

Oogh pushed him back into his hammock, breaking into island Pidgin. "No mattah! Now time fo' *moe moe*. Maybe when we wake, da war be *pau*."

For the first time in months, he slept. Such a long, deep sleep, he would only half remember the harbor in Tokyo, Red Cross nurses leading them up a gangplank to a huge converted troopship. A band playing maudlin songs.

His hammock slung across an open deck, Keo swayed in moonlight, calm seas turning nights into balmy fiction. With minesweepers testing the waters ahead, each day was a spiraling infinity of meals, endless conversations. He was already tired of people.

He thanked God for night when he was alone, blood recombining in his veins, his veins paralleling the ocean's tides. The ocean that had carried him out into the world was bringing him home. He was coming home without her.

Part II

E Hulihuli Ho'i Mai

Turn and Come Back

HO'OWAHINE

To Grow into Womanhood

HONOLULU, SPRING 1943

A TOWN OF WAR NERVES. THE NIGHTLY WHIP OF SIRENS. EVERY-thing rationed, beyond their means. Reduced to Chinatown's Hotel Street, Malia swayed her cellophaned hips, dancing for enlisted men. Off-hours, she helped a woman three fields and five lanes over in Kalihi, sewing cheongsams for street girls and *haole* prostitutes at brothels like the Bronx Rooms, the Senator, the Beach Hotel.

When she discovered Malia was low-class dancing for servicemen, the seamstress, a stately Hawai'ian named Pono, scolded her, said she could smell *haole* on her. It tainted her fabrics, even her thread. She lifted her ancient sewing machine, its underside orange and scabrous. She pointed her finger at Malia.

"Your *haole* smell even rusting my Singer. Shame!"

Malia threw her eyes at her. "Don't speak to me of shame. I feed my mama and papa. I pay the mortgage on their house."

"With bar-girl money? Same as eating dirty rice."

"No choice." Her shoulders stooped. "Papa lost his job. Brothers overseas, at war."

Pono sighed, glanced at two of her four daughters hanging laundry in the yard. She handed Malia seven folded dollar bills.

"Go. Come back when you finished smearing yourself with sailors' breath. I'll teach you secrets of design. You're plenty *akamai* at sewing."

Malia pocketed the bills. "Meanwhile, how am I supposed to live?"

"Like all *kānaka*. The cannery." Pono pointed at her girls. "For them I work twelve-hour shifts. Come home, cook, iron, sew."

"Where's their father? Overseas?"

Pono's body seemed to retract. She closed her face like a door.

She was a beautiful woman with the stature and grace that harkened back to Polynesian ancestors, fearless Vikings of the Pacific. Over six feet tall, black hair cascading down her back, there was something forbidding about her, the strength of a woman who had suffered, who had committed every conceivable act, for the father of her daughters, a man cursed with *ma'i pākē*. Leprosy.

Years back, they had hidden in rain forests, running from bounty hunters rounding up lepers. After a year, Pono's lover had been caught, banished to an island where lepers were left to suffer and die. Pono continued running, his seed flowering in her womb while bounty hunters pursued her. Medical doctors wanted to quarantine and study her, see if she would erupt with sores from her lover. Immune to the disease, alone in the jungle Pono had birthed a healthy daughter, then found laundry work on a sugar plantation.

For months she had suffered the nightly abuse of the *haole luna*, the foreman, who threatened to turn her in to the bounty hunters. One night, rage-full, she plunged a sharpened chopstick straight through his heart while he lay on her. Then she picked up her daughter and ran. She ran for years, island to island.

But each month she left her child behind, making her way to the island of Moloka'i to be with her beloved, Duke Kealoha, at the leper colony, the Place of the Living Dead. Through the years a second daughter was born, a third, and then a fourth. Each month when the interisland supply steamer sailed for Moloka'i, Pono left her girls with neighbors, strangers, anyone, piling them up like sacrifices offered to the world.

When they grew old enough to ask about their father, she told them he worked the gold mines of Alaska. When the oldest asked if he would ever come home, Pono answered, "By and by." She let them grow up fatherless rather than admit to them he was *ma'i pākē*. It was Duke's wish, for he could not face the shame of their knowing what he was. Pono was not by nature maternal, her senses seemed tuned to something more distant. Yet she endured, sacrificing youth and beauty to nourish, protect, educate the daughters of this man. Loving her girls, she cursed them, too. But for them, she could join him in his banishment.

Duke Kealoha was a man who loved music, books, and conversation. He came from educated people, all wiped out by the leprosy that had devastated Hawai'ians in the second half of the nineteenth century. Even into the present, it was still killing off whole families. Until he had found her—a wild thing living alone—Pono had not known who she was, how much she could be.

As a child she had had such strange visions, she was rumored to be *kahuna*, a seer. As she grew into young womanhood, it was said she could transfer pain from one human to another, that she was endowed with double *mana*. She could look someone to death. There were even rumors she was part *manō*, shark. Nights when she swam in the sea, folks swore they saw her skin turn gray, her jaw deform into a snout. Terrified, her family had cast her out forever.

Honoring her double *mana*, Duke had patiently nourished her, drawing the best of her to the surface. Through the years he had taught her the verities of living, of the heart—pity and pride, compassion, sacrifice—lacking which a human life was doomed. No matter how terribly *ma'i pākē* ravaged him, how badly it mutilated his face and limbs, Pono would love him. He had rebirthed her, he was still the heart of her.

Now, often in her solitude she wept. Love had made her impotent. Her *kahuna* powers did not extend to Duke. She was not able to cure him of *ma'i pākē*. Year into year, she watched his face slowly collapse, his limbs turn to artifacts.

MALIA LASTED FIVE DAYS AT THE CANNERY. CLOYING STENCH of pineapple. Rashes growing down her arms. The forelady behind her screaming, "*Pick up your pine! Pick up your pine!*" The click and slash of knife blades. The whispered history of chopped-off fingers, chopped-off hands. After that, she found work mopping floors at the downtown police station. Until they handed her a rag and bucket, pointing to the toilets.

She spent a month at Pearl Harbor, training for welding work, before the crude remarks began. Shipyard and salvage workers, electrical and mechanic crews, had come from the mainland in thousands. Decent ones seemed outnumbered by the brutes. A mechanic with a yellow beard called her Java. Java Hips. Said he'd like to stir her coffee with his dick. Malia turned, approached him almost languidly, and opened his nose from bridge to tip with the claw end of a hammer.

How to live? How to make a living? One night, staring at their rationed meals, her jobless father, Malia pulled a cheongsam on, insinuating herself into the slots and fissures of Hotel Street, calling herself Colette. With a soft, sibilant sway, she glided along, pulling the eyes of servicemen. Army khakis, navy whites. The colors of boy scouts and virgins. *God, they make my blood laugh.* Skim the cream, white skin off *haole*, and underneath was male, ordinary male. No different from *kānaka*, *pākē*, *Flips*, all grinding with the same old rhythms: fainting in a woman's hips, leaving seed and hoofprints.

Yet even with soldiers and sailors who she charged too much so they would think she was worth something—even in cheap hotels making hit-and-run love—she thought of Krash Kapakahi, remembering the first time they had made love. The night before Pearl Harbor.

They were lovers for only five weeks when he enlisted. But in that time, she and this man had entered each other, sculpted each other's bones. They had worn each other to near transparency until all they were was held breath. They never made promises, always approached each other with a Sunday-slow deliberation, with the covertness of nocturnal animals. She began to understand that this love was not passing, it was spine-deep, intractable.

When he went off to war, she knew by a tightening—a small blithe crepitation—that she was carrying his child. As it grew and stirred inside her, his absence became so powerful Malia wondered how, if Krash survived, she could bear his actual presence again. Now she bore his presence every day, in the face of the child, in the way folks looked sly-eyed when she said the child was *hānai*. Adopted. She bore it in dread of the future.

For months she kept her "Colette" life outside her, nothing to do with her. Each night after leaving Hotel Street, she removed the cheongsam before turning up Kalihi Lane. In her father's tiny garage, she showered with the rubber hose, watching the sweat of strangers guttering the yard. Still, she couldn't bear herself until she bathed a second time—scouring her skin with detergent soap and scrub brush in the tub where one night Rosie Perez gave fictional birth during blackout, only Malia and Leilani in attendance.

Some nights she sat in the dark, remembering. Nine months sliding through a tunnel of unbleeding. Then birth, unhinging, orchidings of blood. She recalled biting down on a bar of soap to muffle her screams. Her body sizzling, suddenly deflated. Skin the soft beige-white of eggshell, eyes the faltering blue of plums. The tiny face, Krash's features in duplicate. A quiet infant, dangling beside Malia's life, hardly noticed, her story untold. But something in her watchfulness began reaching out to Malia, her infant's look almost a begging. One night she removed her cheongsam, turned her back on "Colette" forever.

She went back to *hapa-haole* hula dancing in Hotel Street dives. But no man touched her, there was something in her eyes, and no man dared. Some nights she stood beside the infant in her crib in Jonah's room. She gazed down at the sleeping face, wondering if her brothers would believe this child was *hānai* from Rosie Perez who already had a yardful of kids. Rosie and her husband, both Hawai'ian-Portuguese, had spawned all-kine colored children, one golden-skinned, one pale as tofu, a redhead with freckles, and one real *kanaka* dark.

Even Timoteo believed the child was Rosie's. Dear woman. She had smeared Malia's birth-blood on her thighs and crawled into the tub, onto the bloody towel, swaddling the infant just as Timoteo came home from warden duty in the lane. Now Malia touched the lashes of the sleeping child, smelling talcum, diaper soak. A smell that made her gag. It had less to do with the infant than with motherhood, what it represented.

I won't be slowed down. A mistake must not become an obstacle.

Some nights she surveyed her own small room, dresses hung like soldiers, shoes petrified in rows. She remembered Keo telling her to grab life, be clever and daring. In five years what had she become? How could she face him, he who had been out in the world, seen and done everything? While she could fit her whole life in a spoon.

Now late at night, after hosing, showering and scrubbing, she picked up her face where she had left it in the mirror. She lay down, remembering him. A trajectory through her consciousness, raising her temperature, adding to her secretions like sugar and insulin. In such moments she felt every nerve in her body focused and erect. Krash had given her dignity. With him she felt she had a future beyond dancing for tourists, beyond maid work—changing sheets, staring into strangers' suitcases wondering, *What can I steal? What won't be missed?*

At first she had wanted to love his child, to nurture it. Then, discovering the infinite, witless patience motherhood required, Malia decided it was *not* Krash's child. That way, she could put it aside and get on with her life. Still, he haunted her; in sleep he kept touching the small of her back. Waking thoughts of him slowed her down, as if the gods understood she needed traction.

Well, let him come home, let them all come home. Let the war be over.

Then she would show them ambition.

EARLIER IT HAD RAINED, THEN RAIN HAD TURNED TO LIQUID sun, the Koʻolaus diademed in triple rainbows. Good news in Kalihi Lane. Dodie Manlapit's boy had been transferred to Iceland, far from the fighting in Europe. He wrote home asking for twenty cans of Spam. And Walter Palama's boy, Noah, had been assigned to teaching judo stateside. The army didn't trust him in combat with six fingers on each hand.

Walter shook his head. "Noah feel real *hilahila*, fo' no can fight wit' oddah boys."

Timoteo nodded sympathetically. "You folks evah see Noah wit' rifle? All dem fingahs! He dis-semble, re-semble dat damn t'ing fastah dan you blink one eye. U.S. Army plenny *hūpō*!"

But in their darkened bedrooms, each parent had got down on their knees in thanks. To celebrate, folks gathered in Timoteo's garage with folding chairs, guitars, and ʻukuleles. Behind hanging blackout sheets, they broke out jugs of *ʻōkolehao*, ti-root wine, and beer. Then four men with ti leaves hanging from their shorts danced *mele kahiko*, ancient chants, for their sons overseas. Fierce slapping of arms, chests, thighs, heels kicking up dirt and gravel. Such vibrant singing, such soul-depth chanting, neighboring streets fell silent as people stopped and listened.

Hours later, Malia trudged slowly up the lane, a full moon making her forget long, punishing hours. Kicking off her sandals, she felt the stickiness of *liliko'i* webbing her toes. Stars blanketed the sky, turning the lane into an Oriental wash-drawing, so everything looked blue, the blue of ice, of shadows, just-remembered dreams. The blue of rotting hoses in deep grass, of footprints, old tattoos. Up ahead she heard voices singing old-time songs—"E Ku'u Morning Dew" and "Nani Ho'omana'o" and "Pua Sadinia."

In that moment it seemed the moon fired a million silver drops into prismatic lights that showered her, showered this narrow lane foaming with human rhythms. A lane so narrow that, when someone sliced a Maui onion, across the road someone cried. It seemed suddenly a mythic place, known only to a favored few, a tiny kingdom whose people were given to dreaming, fabulating, where white trumpet flowers hung like choruses of upside-down angels blowing jasmine and ginger across their lives.

Folks drifted in and out of yards, recalling ancient tribes going forth to borrow fire. Geckos, like little green consumptives, skittered and coughed. Malia leaned against a fence, watching young lovers dart through shadows like reef fish. She smiled, thinking how walking up the lane each day was like strolling through a bazaar.

Each yard, each garage was a merchant's stall wherein something was offered, someone performed. Elders with teeth like yellow tusks sat scraping scales from *aku*. Sororities of porcelain wives—delicate-boned Chinese and Filipinas—bent scrubbing at washboards. A child held up a rabbit. Warriors with tattooed shoulders polished golden carapaces of upturned canoes. And darting in and out of bushes, caravans of kids with green/purple Kool-Aid tongues, playing "ting a ling" or flying homemade Kleenex-tissue kites. There a rat-whiskered dog named God who only ran backwards, here a rooster who only crowed at midnight.

Until Pearl Harbor, until she saw their world in flames, Malia had never understood that this narrow lane, so precious and ephemeral, could disappear in a minute. Now she saw how each night was a homecoming, like touching the roots of feeling. Here at dusk, folks stepped from the working world into a kind of genesis. They who had seldom heard of unions, Sundays off, or equal wages, put down lunch pails, took off slippers and shoes, and stretched bare feet against soil that was regenerative and giving. Something existed here so primordial, all that was human in Malia now responded.

Songs drifted from her father's garage, and somewhere among the neighbors she heard Kiko Shirashi's birdlike voice joining in the singing. Timoteo had defended her husband, now interned, and so he could not find a job. Each week the woman brought Leilani sacks of rice, kegs of *shoyu*, half a pig, her big black car shining up the lane. She always wore a tiny American flag and her Red Cross volunteer pin, and always asked after Timoteo's boys. Some neighbors gave her the stink-eye, wondering how she got past gas rationing. Most folks were kind.

Malia stepped into the garage, behind blackout sheets, feeling shy as Kiko waved and made room for her. The woman was always dressed exquisitely, black with touches of gold, or jade, bringing to mind an elegant small spider. They sat watching Aunty Moa Kalani dance hula to "Hanohano Hanalei," except that where the dance called for *'ulī 'ulī*, seeded rattle gourds, and bamboos, she used empty beer cans. Then she broke into naughty hula with Uncle Pahu.

Aunty was well past seventy, with big, luscious arms and thighs. Uncle Pahu, a handsome part-Filipino, was slim as a reed, bald as a drum. When they danced "Princess Pupule," Aunty Moa swung her behind wildly, going "round de island in a lewd-kine way." Convulsed with laughter, folks wiped their faces with towels, reaching for more homemade wine. Half drunk, Timoteo leaned sideways and blew his nose on the orchids from whose petals he emerged with perfect self-possession.

Songs slowed, Kiko Shirashi turned to study Malia, smiling approvingly. Malia had lost her chubbiness, so her Polynesian bones stepped forth. She would never be a great beauty, but she was extremely handsome. Kiko had always felt compassion for the young woman, thought she might like to help her, but Malia did not encourage help. Her self-conscious speech and manners led her away to dark corners, made her seem quirky rather than refined. It filled Kiko with inquietude, yet the girl's only sin was trying to improve herself, her aspirations lavish.

The first time they met, Malia was wearing a secondhand dress, probably from a hotel guest. It was faded but expensive, with set-in shoulders, exquisite seams. Visiting Shirashi Funeral Home, she was also wearing toe-pinch high heels, much too small, surely Goodwill. Attempting an elegant stride, she had skidded across varnished floors, making sounds like the screech of coffin screws. Kiko had felt sorry for her, fearing her ambitions and natural attributes would never jell.

But now Malia seemed more polished. She had abandoned the quick electric flirtation of gestures, no longer nervously striking a pose. She had traded outlandish hats for snoods and upswept hair-dos. Her dresses were simpler, wide-shouldered, and seemed to fit the shape of her still-voluptuous body.

"With the Moana closed," Malia confided, "no more hand-me-downs. I make my own dresses now."

There was something relaxed about her, maybe it was fatigue, the war pressing everything close so there was no room for extras. Still, there was a desperation in the eyes, as if something's claws were sunk in her back. Kiko had heard rumors—Leilani's new "*hānai*" daughter, the lovely child now petaling round their ankles.

"So, now you have a little sister," Kiko said, stroking the head of the child.

". . . Yes."

Kiko turned, and took her hand. "You look wonderful, Malia. A little slimmer?"

She smiled. "Food rationing. And sadness does things, doesn't it? Poor Mama, all three sons gone." Her hands flew to her face. "Oh. Kiko. I'm sorry. How is your husband? Can he write you?"

She nodded sadly. "But, his dignity—he won't let me join him. He's now at Tule Lake Camp in California."

She spoke in a well-meaning, obtuse way, as only the rich and leisured could, so that at first it was hard to feel sympathy.

". . . twenty thousand American-Japanese interned with him. Some take their own lives out of shame."

"Sad! So sad."

Kiko's shoulders slumped. "No one calls. The grass has grown across my door. I must coif my own hair. Lacquer my own nails. I cannot get appointments. Hard not to feel alone, and shamed. But then, tonight. Your parents. This!"

Her hand flew out, encompassing the music, the neighbors. She tapped Malia's hand. "Everything you seek is here."

Malia smiled impatiently. "You've traveled, haven't you?"

"Oh, everywhere. Paris, Athens. Peking. I spent four years in London. Fabulous."

"But you came home."

"We all come home. Go out and look around, dear. After that, you'll understand."

"What is it I will understand?"

"How we come back to the beginning. For instance, in my youth, for years, I only wore Guerlain, 'L'Heure Bleu,' costly French perfume. One day, I was fifty, I picked a ginger blossom. It smelled more costly, more precious than any scent." She offered the inside of her wrist. "Eau de fresh ginger, straight from my yard."

Malia bent to her arm, breathing in, already eyeing her father's yard for blossoms. For months after, she would drag ginger across her arms like yellow emergencies.

That night before she left, Kiko took her aside. "Come visit. We'll gossip away the hours. And hearing that you sew, I have yards and yards of fabric I would like to give you. Bought in Paris, Rome."

That night sleep was impossible. She lay awake, taking Kiko's offer as a sign. The woman would school her, guide her into position for the next phase of her life. She imagined Paris, Rome. Imagined herself poised on great boulevards. *Her dress. Her shoes. Her walk. Her talk.*

Yet, even then, something mocked her, suspicion that drastic change was not what she was after. That her destiny would always be this island, that it would always be *hunger* that drove her, not geography.

At 2 A.M. she slipped from her bed, running through fields and lanes to Pono. Malia watched through the window as the woman hunched over, ironing uniforms of a Catholic girl's school. She was huge and beautiful, tears on her cheeks sizzled in steam. Malia watched her for almost an hour. She watched because she could not look away. Something in this woman called to her. She approached the screen door and tapped lightly, in her hands nine dollar bills.

"Pono! I didn't forget. Your seven dollars, plus interest."

She unlatched the screen, perspiring and exhausted. "What you doing out so late? Still 'Colette-ing' on Hotel Street?"

"*Pau* Colette. That life gave me nightmares."

Pono eyed her skeptically. "So, what you do for work?"

She sighed. "Still *hapa-haole* hula, part-time selling war bonds, part-time nurse's aid. Rolling bandages. This, that." She was impatient. There was something on her mind.

"Still too good for the cannery?" Pono asked. "Well, stick to nursing. Get a certificate. Respect."

Malia stepped back, appalled. Bagging blood in rubber-soled shoes was not her goal. Neither was tending near-adolescent soldiers. She remembered their eyes, could still feel their dying down in her coils and crucibles.

"Pono. I have an important thing to discuss." She sat down, folding her hands. "I want to practise on your Singer. Two-three days a week, while you're at the cannery. In return I'll watch your girls."

The woman studied her, suspicious.

"I swear. I want to learn real dress design. Make elegant clothes. You see, I plan to travel."

"Ho! The war is getting to you. Such *lōlō* plans. While boys are coming home in boxes."

"Listen to me. I've got to have a *dream* for when the war is over. You give me lessons, let me practise on your Singer, I'll pay you back with yards of rare material—from Paris."

Pono waved her arm. "You see my life? Wash, iron, cook. Cannery ten-twelve hours so can feed four girls. What am I to do with high-tone fabrics?"

"Make something special. There must be someone you want to be beautiful for? A secret someone? The father of your girls?"

Pono checked herself. Mention of the man she loved seemed so blasphemous, it made her want to strike Malia. Instead she leaned back, thoughtful.

"Maybe. Maybe. Come next week for tryout. Bring material. In return, I show you what I know, secret journeys of the Singer. Ways to twist, and turn, and double-sew while guiding thread in-out the fabric. Ways that make a dress look seamless as a glove."

It was nearing 4 A.M. when Malia stood, exhausted with their talk, their plans.

Watching her melt into fog, Pono vaguely smiled. In a dream she had seen her own dressmaking fade and vanish. She would move into another, a more urgent life. Her sewing talents would seep into the fluids and flesh of Malia, enriching her. The black-lacquered, prehistoric-looking Singer would become so much a part of Malia's life, it would become another limb.

Seams would be stitched so fine they'd disappear. Human veins and silken threads would intertwine. Wool tweed turning into hair, linen turning into sun-starched skin. A heart-shaped pincushion would palpitate; Malia would feel the pinch of just-stuck pins. When she pulled thread through a needle, she would feel a humming in her brain.

My legacy to you, Pono thought. For she believed any woman wanting life so much, with all its blows, its quick electrocutions, should be endowed with gifts as well as weapons. Then as she stood ironing, Pono suddenly cried out. A horror reared up through the steam. The face of a young warrior, Malia's brother, wearing the treadmarks of a Panzer.

SHE WALKED DOWN KING STREET, DISTANT, SERENE. HER DRESS, her posture, even her gas mask slung across her back looked chic. Her hair upswept with a flower.

"Dorothy Lamour. Hey, Dorothy Lamour!" Servicemen still followed, wanting her, wanting more than what they found in brothels. She threw them dead glances, having left them behind. Kiko Shirashi had opened a door.

Suavely Malia took her place behind the counter at McInerny Department Store, smiling until her eyes took on a deathly gloss. Within weeks she felt herself failing miserably and convulsively. She came to hate the obtuse faces of customers, her cloying compliments.

Standing poised behind a sales counter made her feel like something in a barnyard at a trough, her head bent low, dipping into merchandise repeatedly while customers pointed and grunted and changed their minds. The voices of certain rich women came at her like whining bullets. She answered them in kind, granting them no grace or absolution. In her heart, Malia kept waiting for elegant customers like Kiko, so she could show them she had class. But women like Kiko didn't shop, maids ran all their errands.

The day she was fired, she sat demoralized at Kiko's.

"Nothing suits me. I don't fit in."

"You have a special nature, Malia." Kiko patted her hand while they sipped Tom and Jerrys.

In the silence Malia looked round the marble living room. "Your house is so beautiful. Every house on this street is huge. I've often wondered what people do in all these rooms."

"They suffer, dear. Now, let's look at fabrics."

Kiko brought out linens from Belgium, damask and silks from France, light tweeds from Italy. Yards upon yards. Malia gasped, studying the threads of the fabrics as if she would find written therein the formula for elegance, irrefutable class. Kiko wrapped them in tissue paper, gave them all to her.

"Make yourself splendid. Make something happen in your life."

Short of giving her money, she had no idea how else to help Malia. The largest hope she had for her was that a man with taste would find, and marry, her.

Malia took her hand. "I'm going to make you a splendid dress. What do you like, linen? It will be sleeveless, very simple like a sheath. Very elegant."

Kiko smiled. "Yes, make it simple. I must get used to the unadorned."

She turned, staring at tall glass-doored teak cabinets, each intricately inlaid with jade and rosewood. There were four, antique and priceless. Each stood absolutely empty. Malia's eyes followed her gaze.

"They were searching for seditious material," Kiko whispered. "We were forced to burn everything. Antique fans, scrolls, volumes of poetry. Miniature pastels with kanji lettering."

Calmly she sipped her Tom and Jerry. "We burned our entire Japanese library. Then the house shrine. Then, my *obāsan's* kimonos. I was grateful we have no children. They did not see our shame."

Malia put down her drink and took her in her arms.

"Oh, Kiko. Forgive me. I have been selfish. My problems are so small."

The older woman wiped her eyes. "Nothing in life is small. It becomes full. It becomes empty. It is never small. But I will tell you this, Malia. Always stay a little selfish. Give everything to others, you become an empty gourd."

ONE DAY A MILITARY CHAPLAIN IN THE LANE, ASKING FOR THE Meahunas. Neighbors pointed the way, then watched, mouths slack, hands diffident behind their backs. He knocked on the door, looking through the screen. Seeing a *haole* in uniform, Leilani screamed. Refusing to invite him in—who wanted death dripping on their carpet?—Malia kept the screen door between them.

The chaplain spoke, and then again. What he said, what he was telling her, had the slow force of the ocean dragging everything back to its center. He was delivering *them* back to the center, his voice earnest and gravelly, saying they were bringing Keo home. Malia turned to her parents, unable to speak. She pressed them to the screen door, making him repeat it yet again.

Timoteo's voice came out dreamy like a child's, his words stirred by the ceiling fan, echo and echo and echo.

"Keo . . . Keo . . ."

Leilani's was a vocal soaring, rebirthing of her favorite son. She dragged the chaplain outside where neighbors waited, terrified.

"Tell!" she cried, shaking his arm, then turning to the neighbors. "He coming home! My boy, Keo. True!" She shook his arm again.

The chaplain smiled, nodding toward a military car backed up in the lane, then he patted a document.

"Yes. I'm here to inform his family that, by the grace of God, Keo . . . Mea . . . huna . . . is on a transport ship en route to Honolulu."

That night rains came, a cleansing eucalyptus smell washed down from the Ko'olaus. Malia stood outside letting it beat on her eyelids, her breasts and ribs. A stinging, prickly sensation as if she were shedding skin, as if she would slide out slick and new. As if, like a snake, she were tranced.

She spun in circles. "Keo. Keo . . ."

The sky rumbled back old parables. She remembered the chaplain with the news. Remembered his voice, like a boy reciting rhymes. Remembered the military car that brought him, how its bloodred taillights lit up as they pulled away, leaving behind her brother. Giving her back his blood-ripe life.

Nā Pali o nā Ko'olau

Cliffs of the Ko'olau Mountains

The fear of vision. Sight could be so dangerous. It had been a long, long sleep wherein he groped for exits, but everything was night, spherical and doorless. He ransacked dreams for keys and clues. *Maybe I will wake up in Woosung.* Better to remain unconscious.

His ship rounded Ka'ena Point just after sunrise, O'ahu still in shadow, but sunlit vessels offshore sparkling like jewels. Keo struggled in his hammock. By then the decks were lined with passengers, some so frail others held them up.

Someone cried, "Honolulu Harbor!"

Half conscious, he pushed his way to a rail and looked out at his island.

The blurred image in his brain, the dream he'd held within him for so long, suddenly came into focus. His sea, his blue-green turf, was there, before him, all around him. Sunrise, wrinkling in the *pali* of the Ko'olaus, stained his cheeks. Things rushed at him, geometry of his boyhood, physics of his youth.

. . . The Royal Hawai'ian Band playing, hula troupes dancing on the dock. Ocean liners pulling into berths beside Aloha Tower. Where is Krash? Where are the boys? Time to dive for tourist coins . . .

People said he called out first, or maybe it was chanting. Then he climbed up on the rail, and dived.

. . . Oiled and naked, shooting the reef in my canoe. Diving deep

and deep to coral canyons . . . lagoons of unforgetting. Look, look, a shark tooth. . . . Our 'aumākua, *whose teeth don't sink in water. Let me sink. Let my hands web, my back scale. Let me settle where my cells remember lime. . . .* O *let the sea corrode me, scatter me to coral. Let it whisper* Mother Tongue *to me. . . . Let me be dispersed clicking, clattering, drumming to ancestral rhythms, those old ocean jazz bands. Let me never know again such thirst. . . .*

Lifeboats hit the waves, sailors dived in after him. While U.S. carriers saluted ships of liberated prisoners, he entered a naval hospital bound and tranquilized. The problem was, he didn't want to wake up in Woosung. If it was a dream, he wanted to keep dreaming. Each time he felt his mind reckoning toward consciousness, he thrashed and screamed, fighting it.

One day a nurse shook him impatiently. "Snap out of it. It's not like you saw *real* combat."

He came awake in one blow. Down the ward, gaunt faces, devoid of expression. Some would never make it back. Full awakening came as a series of small torches, intervals between them gradually diminishing, until whole squares of light were formed. Entering life a second time, everything seemed new, an eerie incognito. Looking back, Keo would think how small the cosmos, how paltry and stingy compared to human emotions, the soaring sense he felt seeing his sister, Malia.

He was dozing when she reached his bed. A gutted shell, his skull drawn back, his teeth protruding like a carnivore's. Charcoal blue moons circling his eyes. He woke, felt some subtle change in his surroundings, a new form brush-stroked into the environment. He felt a tugging at his toe. She was tenderly pulling it, an old Hawai'ian ritual for calling back the dead.

He would always recall her standing there, a quivering kind of poise, reverberant and cool in white. Big-shouldered dress, matching snood, her golden face trembling, trying not to cry. She moved close, took his hand against her heart, then laid her cheek against his cheek. He had even lost his scent. He smelled unknown, a machinery part. But he was there; somewhere under all the layers, he lay brooding. She crawled into bed beside him, sobbing like a calf.

"Brother! *Aloha au iā'oe!*" I love you.

When he looked up again his mother was rubbing his hands with *kukui* oil, his father babbling beside her.

". . . an so we nevah tell you, son, yo' mama birthed by midwife Victoria Na'ai, also lady-in-waiting for Queen Lili'uokalani. Fingahs dat touch royal shoulders, royal hair, also pull yo' mama to dis world. Give her special *mana*. She da one chant you home . . ."

He seemed to have walked into the middle of his father's recitation. Timoteo could not stop.

". . . and plenny *'ōkolehao* we make fo' you . . . one-fingah poi and *laulau* when you coming home. And real fresh *aku*. . . . Remembah when I teach you swim? Ho, man! Da nites we near went drown! . . ."

They brought his yearbook from Farrington High. He pointed at snapshots, asking which boys were fighting overseas. Asking how soon he could join them. His mother collapsed. His father led her sobbing from the ward.

Malia looked down like she would suck his eyes out. "You already fought your war. And it's not over."

A doctor sat down, trying to explain.

"Starvation turns the body into a cannibal. Refusing to die, it feeds on itself, first fat, then muscle. In final stages, organs. You're lucky, Keo. Your organs are intact. You'll build muscle again, and with rest, good food, thiamine shots, you'll recover almost a hundred percent. There'll always be recurring fevers from malaria. That never goes away. Vitamins will cure what's left of beriberi. Yes, it will take time."

He looked along the ward filled with repats from prison camps.

"Dysentery, typhus, cholera . . . You have to realize you people were closer to death than soldiers who might die instantly from a bullet. Their bodies are young and healthy until that moment of impact, whereas, for months and years, you folks were walking microbes, hosts to swarming bacteria. You need to start all over, like infants."

He was slow in comprehending. "You mean, I can't enlist. I can't join up and fight."

"Not this war. Not any war."

Keo turned his head away.

"They tell me you're a musician. That's what these guys need, entertainment. USO clubs, dance halls, where men are R and R. They come in from Midway, Guadalcanal, they don't know they're human anymore. Give them something to assure them."

One day he shuffled down a corridor and walked into a burn ward. Shock registered through the skin round his testicles. His anus clenched. Sailors off incinerated ships burnt black. Young pilots without arms or faces. He sat down in a chair, touching his arms, his legs, his fingers, holding them like gifts.

He started eating everything they brought him, like a dog knowing only the pleasure of fullness. Afterwards, he licked his plates. His gums hurt, his muscles hurt. He welcomed pain, it meant he was alive, coming back to living. He hounded nurses, asking about a little man named Oogh. He asked about repatriation ships arriving from Japan. Tides had turned; Japan was losing the war, their armies killing off whole camps of Allied prisoners. They blew up Red Cross ships at sea.

He sat on a *lānai*, watching planes patrol the skies. "I lost her. She slipped right through my fingers."

Malia looked away, impatient. "She was never yours to lose. She was out to save the world. You never understood that."

He hung his head. "She found her sister in Shanghai. I couldn't get them out. They're probably dead."

"Women like Sunny don't die. She's somewhere else, that's all."

"She loved me. She even had my child. Yes! A daughter, who's probably dead, too." He gazed at his sister. "Your problem, Malia, is that you've never loved. You only love ambition."

Moments passed. She hung her head, so full of things.

"How is Sunny's mother, Butterfly?" he asked. "Does she visit Mama?"

"All *pau*. Too much bad feelings. You and Sunny running off. Each mother pointing the finger at the other. Her father is a shell. Sunny's brother left Stanford for the army. Now, intelligence work in Okinawa." She shook her head. "My God. This life."

He was almost afraid to ask. "And Jonah?"

"Last letter, going into France. I can't bear to think about it. All I do is pray."

"Mama says DeSoto's safe."

"Australia. Defense work on Allied ships limping into Perth."

So many silences. Sometimes he wept with no sense of it, his whole face wept, his mouth, his nose. She saw him jump awake from sleep, eyes terrified. Each time she left the ward, she took something, a sock, his comb, small totems of his existence proving he was home.

"Mama told you about the baby? *Hānai* from Rosie Perez."

He smiled, glad there was something added to their lives midst so many subtractions. "And Krash? Any word?"

She shrugged, feigning nonchalance. "In France, or Italy. They don't let them say much."

HIS ENTRY INTO THE LANE WAS QUIET, UNSALUTED.

"Slow. Slow." Timoteo helped him from the cab.

He moved with a peculiar grace, Malia supporting him, remembering he had always moved that way. Now it was a different grace, of a man both blessed and cursed, lifeswept and slightly fragile. His mother stood laughing and sobbing, holding a child in her arms. He limped into the house and sat, exhausted. They put the child on his lap; she burst into a salvo of chirping and saliva.

Keo dropped his face against her hair. "She smells so clean, so *'ono!*" He hugged her, holding on.

Yards were empty, curtains drawn. Behind the curtains, neighbors clutching rosaries, little Buddhas. An exhalation down the lane. One of their boys had made it home.

He moved like someone who had slept for centuries in a city buried in sand. He roamed the house at odd hours, staring at clean water running from a faucet, weeping at the waste. He stared at the toilet, not knowing how to flush. He watched the eye on the back of a dollar bill. The eye watched him. He had forgotten the meaning of certain words. Deodorant. Mayonnaise.

Someone said, "Shampoo!" He jumped. It sounded like a command.

Cars backfired, he flew under a table. Sitting in the dim-lit bathroom during blackout made him shriek. But sitting alone in the dark, he cried. Meals were hardest. Everyone talked, so as not to stare. He studied forks and knives, confused, and ate with his fingers. He poured copious mounds of salt and sugar, together, on his food. He ate everything but meat—the sight of it took him back to an awful landscape, unspeakable things turning on spits. Sometimes, entering the kitchen, he was so swept by the *surplus* of food, he blacked out. Late at night Malia heard him digging in the garbage. She found half-eaten things stored beneath his bed.

Sometimes he locked the door to his room, privacy such a novel thing. Then he threw the door wide open, terrified. Neighbors came slowly, one at a time, bringing covered dishes, holding back tears at the shock of what he looked like, what he had been reduced to.

"So glad you home. Take time, Keo, boy—take plenny time."

The smell of fresh coffee took up whole mornings. The shock of toothpaste on his tongue. The scent of rain. Sounds of people laughing. The silken skin of the child nestled in his lap. Just *being* took up the whole day. He sat in the tiny yard, in the rich profusion of greens. The schizophrenia of flowers. He could eat a mango, he could sleep. He could do anything. Which paralyzed him. Sometimes he clutched the sleeping child, carrying her like a talisman, holding her up against his nightmares as people hold up crucifixes against vampires.

He stood in Jonah's room touching his football pads, his surfing gear. He studied snapshots, his big athletic body, a handsome face meant to break hearts. The smart son, destined to make the family proud. He remembered their last night together, Jonah hugging him, saying Keo was his hero.

Then he sat on his bunk, missing older brother DeSoto, ignored in the early years, belatedly admired. The man with many layers, tier upon tier of truths difficult to reach. Each brother had always been almost superhumanly brave, indifferent to danger, not knowing how to back away. In these nights, the void of their absence was so vast, Keo went numb with terror. He thought of the odds, wondering which brother would not come home. As if, in surviving, he had sacrificed one of them.

News came of Butchie Santiago's son, killed in France. All day a stillness, sun turning shadows to stone. At night a wailing, like someone searching for his torn-out eyes. One night Butchie climbed the hill up past Kalihi Heights into the rain forests of the Ko'olaus. He hanged his prize fighting-cock, then hanged himself. A little and a large corpse swinging like peculiar fruit.

AUTUMN NOW. ONE DAY THE TAILGATE OF A TRUCK CRASHED open, spilling ripe pineapples down King Street two blocks from Kalihi Lane. With wartime rationing, pines had become so precious, locals could not afford to buy. Now, while cars spun and skidded, folks rushed out in the streets with barrels, wagons, net bags.

"'*Ono loa!* The best!" they cried. "Ripe to perfection."

Traffic slowed to a crawl as drivers squished their way through twenty thousand pounds of spoiled pines. Leilani and Timoteo bent down, grabbing and sucking smashed pieces, ravenous for their juices, then dragged their fruit-full wagon home. Turning into the lane, Leilani saw the car and sat down in gravel. She would always remember sitting there, her hand landing on a wad of gum. She would remember holding the gum in her palm like a freaky pearl, its grayness the color of hardened wax—the corpse of a candle in a shack when she was a girl. She would remember people in the lane coming at her, Timoteo pleading. Air, she needed air.

The army chaplain. The things he had to say. She clutched the wad of gum, felt it softening in her palm.

. . . A wooden shack. Mama, Papa working fields of sugarcane. Even sweating sugar. Cane pushing through rotting windows, growing in cracks and corners of her mind. . . . Into her teens, the poverty, the sugar shack. She grew into young womanhood smoke-blackened from cane fires, wondering would she ever get beyond that life. Even now in dreams, she walks forever through burnt sugar air. . . .

Keo was sitting on the steps, the chaplain's hand on his shoulder, the child drooling on the chaplain's shoe. He looked out at his parents. They seemed so small, so childlike. He felt a grinding of teeth, a clenching of fists, wondering how he was going to get from where he sat to his parents. He stood slowly, took careful, intermediate steps. He had to get to them and save them.

Leilani watched his lips move. Then almost in slow motion, she lay down in the road. Her boy was dead. Her Jonah-boy.

Entering the lane that night, everything blacked out, Malia heard muffled sobs.

Her father weeping in the bathroom, Keo holding him like a woman. "Jonah . . . nevah see no mo'. Not possible!"

She slid down the wall, remembering all the nights she had prayed on her knees. Mother God had heard, but not agreed.

Keo looked up, gray and ghostly. "Go to Mama. She just lies there."

She went to her mother's room, lay down beside her, and took her in her arms. "Mama. Why Jonah? Why?"

Leilani sighed. " *'Oia nō*. So it goes. Always de innocent."

"Cry, Mama. Cry. Let go."

"No mo' can," she said. "Nutting left . . ."

"I would have died for him," Malia whispered. "I even prayed—take me, take me. Not Jonah."

In the dark, her mother gripped her arms. "Nevah say such t'ing again! You my life, my baby girl, my only . . . you my mama, *tita*, friend."

Malia lay still in shock. She had never known these things. Carefully she lit a candle, placed it near the bed.

"Mama? True?"

"True. I pray plenny hard fo' you, asking fo' one baby girl dat live. You my joy. You nevah know?"

Malia shook her head in wonder.

"And den *you* give me baby, girl of my girl, make me double happy. Even if we have to say *hānai*."

Still, she had fed sixteen babies to the soil. And now the soil had claimed her youngest, Jonah.

"When life take so much from you, bumbye you *pau* grieving. Somet'ing in you stop remembering how. You love what left a little mo'. Oh, my beautiful, brave Jonah . . ."

Finally she yielded, giving in to fierce dry sobs. Malia held her tightly, rocking her like an infant, the motion soothing, womanful, and ageless. Rocking her so, she thought of what she withheld from the child, the one she hardly touched.

In time the sobbing slowed and, calming down, Leilani whispered, "Bring baby . . . from Jonah room . . ."

She said it so softly what Malia heard was, ". . . bring baby . . . Jonah. . . ."

She slipped away, picking the child up from her crib, and brought her to Leilani. "Here, Mama. Baby Jonah."

"Yes!"

And so, for many years, that's what she was called.

HOʻOLOHI IĀ NĀ MEA NUI

To Go Slowly, toward Things that Matter

CHRISTMAS PASSED QUIETLY, FEW CELEBRATIONS IN THE LANE. Storms bred in the Aleutians lashed the North Pacific into wintry furies, driving monstrous swells southward to Hawaiʻi. Every day storm clouds stalked the coastlines, thundering like giants. Waves built to cathedrals thirty feet high.

Tired of war, of being cautious, surfers used black-market gas to sneak across the Pali. Loading up their trucks with surfboards, passing Keo in his yard—"*E hele mai!*" Come, have fun!—neighbors took him surfing with them. Driving the road across the jagged green teeth of Nuʻuanu Pali, a dizzying escarpment of the Koʻolau Range, they headed for the north shore's grizzled winter beaches.

Keo watched big, husky Hawaiʻians paddle their boards through the shallows, then sit waiting for waves like looming walls. They stood poised on their boards. The strongest surfers stayed the course, riding dramatically on each wave's crest, gliding down its face as though they were weightless.

Standing ashore, his face sprayed with mist, Keo felt his lungs shiver. Three months since his return. Still frail and underweight, he stood thinking how, after this war, everything would be minor in comparison. Everything but the sea. How small humans seemed, going up against its waves.

He listened to symphonic clashes, the slow excursions into fugues as waves fell down exhausted, lounging into ballads. Then preaching, bluesy ruminations of the tide receding. In that moment something in him reached out to his broken self, that searcher looking for the perfect note, the magic combination. The young man who had once breathed music, swam it like an amphibian.

Sometimes his fingers tapped imaginary valves. He stared at an old trumpet in his closet. He thought of playing again, but couldn't act upon it. How could he play when she was gone? Music and Sunny so connected, so merged in his mind. When he mentioned her, or his child, Malia grew sad. Yet she wished for proof of Sunny's death, so Keo could mourn her properly once and for all, and get on with his life.

"We've all suffered," she consoled. "Try to heal and go forward."

"You have to help me," he said. "I need to learn how to talk to folks again. I still think of other humans as competition for food."

He pressed his fingers to his temples. "I'm not even sure I understand that Jonah's dead. I keep thinking he's out for a swim. With DeSoto, and Krash . . ."

The mention of Krash's name sucked her mouth dry.

"Brother. Do you think it's possible to really know another human being?"

Keo shook his head. "I don't think we can bear to."

"Then, how do you know . . . when you love someone?"

He looked away. "Maybe, when they make us forget we're going to die. When, for a while, we act out of goodness, not greed."

He sat at the old Steinway in the garage, its lid now furred with mildew, keys so warped it sounded prehistoric. Still, on quiet nights in blackout, Keo walked the keys, feeling the longing in his fingers. Feeling his lip tense in sleep, pressed against the memory of brass. Sometimes when he passed the closet where the horn stood, his whole body swerved. Folks read about his homecoming, his slow recuperation. Some remembered him as Hula Man. Fan letters came, long-playing records. Ellington, Fitzgerald, Bechet.

Enlisted men, Negro soldiers on their way to combat on Tinian or Guam, tracked him down in Kalihi. They saw how frail he was, how haunted-looking. They were merciful, not asking questions, not really talking. Content to sit listening to records, commenting on an artist, an arrangement. He sensed these young men needed to sit there, touch his piano, stroke the keys, not so much because of music, but because he had been there. To the enemy.

A youngster came from New Orleans, sent by Dew Baptiste, now entertaining troops at Fort Bragg. Keo took him by the shoulders, hugging him. They talked for hours, it didn't matter what they said.

When he left for combat, Keo told him, "Don't be a hero. It's not about heroes. You come back and see me."

One day the leader of the eight-piece band and hula dance troupe at Lau Yee Chai came to visit him. He had been a teenager in those long, lost nights of Keo's trumpeting at Rizal's Filipino Dance Hall. Seeing how frail he was, the man looked away, watching Timoteo rake rotting mangoes.

"You were my hero," he finally said. "Anytime you're ready, you come play at Lau Yee Chai."

One of the best restaurants in wartime Honolulu. The best menu, best clientele. The band wore white dinner jackets.

"Every night, entertainment in our beautiful back gardens." He paused. "It isn't really jazz we play. More *hapa-haole* tourist stuff. But everything real tasteful. Might help you get in shape."

Keo smiled. "Don't know when I'll have the strength to blow again."

The man tapped his arm, lapsing into Pidgin. "Den . . . come be numbah one on 'ukulele!"

He fingered the trumpet in the dark, holding it, feeling sounds waiting deep inside. They were there, he just didn't know if he could pull them out, if he still had what it took. The lungs. The guts. He hummed a few notes, his fingers pressing valves, imagining the sound, clandestine, furtive, quickening the dead sea of heartache. He put the horn back in the closet. It recalled too many things—his world was too crowded with absences.

One night he took a bus and stood in front of Sunny's house. Through the window he saw her parents sitting, unmoving. They sat like that for hours. Two stuffed dolls, faces absent of expression. He spoke her name. Saw it linger in the mist and float away. He couldn't accept that she was gone, couldn't imagine this world not containing her. He stood lost again in reverie.

. . . Driving French roads in an open car, Sunny singing at my side . . . Sun and shadow running over us in waves, her throat, her

shoulders swimming through their tracery. We were driving through a sea of air. . . .

With Sunny gone, he suddenly knew that in the time he had left to be alive, and know it—in the precious, loaned time he was allotted to contemplate, earn wisdom, be decent—he had to find her. Had to earn her back again.

Very gradually, he ventured from the lane, into the streets of Kalihi, onto the main thoroughfare of King Street. Past ʻAʻala Park where they once watched puppet shows and *kinipōpō*, baseball. Past honky-tonks, jukeboxes hurling out wartime hits. Moving through crowds of servicemen, their youth and pent-up tension made him feel ancient, as if he were approaching senility and they were wind-up toys.

He passed food stalls in Chinatown where he and Sunny had stroked silver pyramids of cabbages, limbs of dancing ginger-men. Shops where they had bought cherries from tiny women who tied knots in the stems with their tongues. But then he saw hanging pigeon and duck carcasses, and thought of skinned dogs in Shanghai, a human corpse in an alley, fervid flies teeming at its anus. Sweat runneled his face as he struggled home.

Another night in pouring rain Keo knocked on the door of Sunny's house. Her mother, Butterfly, answered, pointing a flashlight in his face. His skin was soaked, reflective like mahogany. He tried to smile, which made his face look cruel. She screamed and dropped the light, and in the glow he saw the beached seaweed of stockings puddled round her ankles. Retrieving the flashlight, he traveled up her shaking limbs, her ragged dress. She looked like a derelict; all her beauty had come apart. *Did I do this?* he wondered.

"Sunny . . . I tried to find her in Shanghai. Is there any word?"

Shuddering, she closed the door, leaving him in the rain.

HE WASN'T READY FOR TRUMPET, HE DIDN'T HAVE THE STRENGTH. He started as relief man on ʻukulele. That first night, when he mounted the small stage in Lau Yee Chai's back garden, folks stood, applauding. A few remembered him as Hula Man, wild trumpet player from Honolulu's prewar years. Others heard he had been liberated from a camp.

Between sets he sat talking jazz with the horn men, and sometimes after curfew he sat outside in darkness "talking story" with chanters from the hula troupe. One night the old gourd player looked up at the stars, speaking eloquently of the ancient music of Hawai'ians.

"You been gone long time, Keo. Maybe you forget where *kānaka* get this urge to cry, make song. Remember, ancient Hawai'ians were poets and chanters. There was formal chanting, telling of religious life, genealogies, and battles. And there were joyful chants, passion poems of love. These were joined with dance, and sounds of skin drums, rattle gourds, clacking stones. This chanting form was *mele hula.* There was impromptu chanting, too, for laughter, entertainment. . . .

"Then came missionaries, who forbade our ancient sounds. *Kāhuna* of old chant forms had to pass their knowledge on in secret! Chants faded, Hawai'ians grew silent. In 1898, our kingdom stolen, we turned back to old songs to keep our hearts from breaking. . . .

"Then came ragtime, and ugly mainland songs chop-sueyed with hula, that made our music silly. Then came jazz and blues, the big bands. . . ."

The old man leaned back, sighing. "Sometimes I fear our music died, then I hear real haunting beauty of falsetto singing, slack-key guitar. I get a chilly feel, go all 'chicken skin,' sounds so Hawai'ian, so aloha-full.

"There's going come a renaissance. Folks going rediscover pure hula, chant forms of our ancients. You know why coming back? Hawai'ian music has real innocence, real purity and magic. Sounds that open up the human heart . . ."

Now he turned to Keo in the dark.

"Soon, boy, you going pick up your horn. I feel your lips grown thirsty. When you blow, always remember original wet rhythms in your blood. What you blowing come from chants you suckled from your mama and her mama's mama, and back and back. Chants of poetry, and lineage, and war chants . . ."

ONE NIGHT IT STARTED POURING DURING THE SHOW IN THE back gardens. Band, dancers, customers dashed crazily inside Lau Yee Chai's. After a while the pouring slowed to gentle rain. Feeling claustrophobic, Keo stepped outside. At a table in the rain a soldier sat, oblivious, fresh from combat on Saipan. Keo crossed the lawn, picked up a trumpet left onstage, and wiped it dry. Almost absentmindedly he fingered the valves, wiped the mouthpiece, brought it to his lips. He would not remember doing this. He would remember only a young soldier in the rain, head hanging, eyes entirely blank and lost.

He hadn't played in two years. He was weak. Yet in that moment what Keo wanted, more than anything, was to play for that young soldier. Help him explore loss, inexplicable horror, whether anything was left in him to save. He wanted to help him recover, move on. He blew a few stuttering choruses of "Its Been a Long, Long Time," feeling his lungs shudder, then slowly expand. Cautiously he segued into a chorus of "I Got a Right to Sing the Blues," the Armstrong oldie from his New Orleans days. He blew another chorus, half a dozen more.

Crowds moved out to the *lānai.* Sheltered from the rain, they stood like herds at feeding time, eyes moving from Keo to the soldier. As if an invisible wire connected them, one man's brooding solitude inspiring the other. His lips hurt. He wasn't playing excellently, the wind was taking it out of him. But he wasn't playing too badly. He could almost feel wheels begin to turn, something melting, oiling up his joints.

He paused, took a deep breath, played "Ain't Misbehavin' " slowly, very slowly, like someone yawning, waking up. Then more forcefully, flexing his muscles and his lungs. Across the lawn the soldier nodded, rocking slightly, almost imperceptibly, enough of him alive to listen.

Feet firmly planted, rain gentle on his cheeks, Keo felt a strange process begin. For the first time in a long time he felt a quiet, robust joy. He felt on a high wire of consciousness, as if for a moment he could peer from the heights without fear. In truth, he was still afraid, he was terrified. But at least he had finally opened his eyes.

Rain stopped, the crowd surged toward him, the soldier disappeared. But other servicemen came up, begging him to play enlisted men's clubs where they were starved for entertainment. On his next night off from Lau Yee Chai, he sat in on trumpet at the army's Club Maluhia. The dance floor was huge, thousands of men, only thirty or forty women. He started playing regularly afternoons, sitting in with the army band, relieving the trumpet, sometimes sitting in with guest bands.

He didn't strain or push himself. These boys didn't want brooding, searching jazz. With only two minutes to a girl before a whistle blew for cutting in, they wanted jitterbugs, love songs, anything that beat back death. Men about to ship out looked extra young, extra pale and big-eyed. He could pick them out of every crowd. Those just back from combat in Guam, the Philippines, brought violence and rage. From battered, weary bodies came a scorched smell like burning wires.

Late spring 1944. Folks said the war was essentially over. But there was still Iwo Jima. Okinawa. Soldiers and sailors back on leave dived into fistfights, full-scale brawls, throwing each other from balconies and rooftops. Men were killed. MPs were forced to turn on fire hoses with eighty pounds of pressure. Keo watched as bodies swept past like surfers.

Some nights in blackout, he walked down the beach to the Royal Hawai'ian, now full of servicemen back from combat, sunburnt and haunted-looking. Keo stood there remembering his friends. The "golden men." He remembered their dark, robust beauty, their innocence, strolling the sands like laughing bronzed gods. Tiger Punu, Turkey Love, Surf Hanohano. Krash Kapakahi, who had once saved his life, pulling him from a riptide. All fighting in Europe, the Pacific. Some already dead.

LEINA A KA ʻUHANE

Leaping Place of Ghosts

NINETEEN FORTY-FOUR. HAWAIʻI NO LONGER DESIGNATED A COMBAT zone. Nights were balmy, folks sat on their steps gossiping, a little more relaxed. Even the *manapua* man returned, the tiny wizened Japanese who every day for years had shuffled up the lane selling minced-pork buns from empty lard cans balanced on a pole across his shoulders.

"*Mana . . . pua . . . ! Mana . . . pua . . . !*" His cry made the world seem safe again.

Though the Allies were rumored to be winning, rationing grew worse, shortages of everything—meat, sugar, clothes. Demands for dresses and cheongsams increased. Prostitutes sent Malia black-market dress material, paying whatever she charged. She grew confident, began designing backless dresses, bolero jackets with matching belts.

Pono came home late from double shifts and found her laboring at the Singer, cast-iron treadle rocking, flywheel humming as the needle danced. She paid Pono extra money for wear and tear on the machine, even tried to talk her into setting up two machines, so they would both get rich off prostitutes.

One night Pono sat with folded arms, staring at Malia. She held up her hand; most of one finger was missing.

"Yes, I once sewed cheongsams for those women. But shame sent me to the cannery. Then I lost this finger on the slicing line. On sick leave, desperate, I sewed cheongsams again. Then I saw my daughters growing. I wondered how I could tell them their food and clothes were paid for by women lying on their backs. I went back to the cannery."

She leaned toward Malia. "But you, you sewing up a storm. You coming like the middleman."

Malia sat up. "What do you mean?"

"Your fancy dresses make *haole* whores look good. Men pay them more. Whores pay you more. Same as pimp work. You don't feel *hilahila*, shame?"

Malia stood up slowly. "I don't see you refusing my money. Do *you* feel *hilahila*?"

She was glad Pono was sitting. The woman was so tall, it was the only time Malia could look down at her. She continued:

"Listen. I rip and shred my fingers every night. Half these dresses have my blood on them. What I make keeps my folks alive. You know the kind of money these prostitutes are making? Buying houses, real estate. When the war's over, half of Honolulu will be owned by hookers."

Malia tapped the Singer for emphasis. "Do I feel shame? No. I admire them. Smart businesswomen."

Pono raised her eyes, almost lazily. "And your child? The one you call *hānai*. When she's grown, will you tell her how you made a living off the backs of whores?"

Malia reared back.

"Will you tell this to her one-lunged father, wounded in the war?"

"Krash, wounded? . . . Mother God, don't let him die."

In slow motion, Malia dropped to her knees. She closed her eyes, praying fervently for the father of her child.

"He will not die," Pono said. "But you will wound him many times."

After a while Malia opened her eyes. "I know you are *kahuna*. So look into your herbs and leaves, and you will see I love this man. You will also see I have a future. I won't whore-sew all my life. I practise even in my sleep, memorizing everything you teach me, so scissors and thread will cut and join in new and different ways. One day rich folks will wear my designs. I'm going to accomplish things. If that wounds Krash, then he does not deserve me."

Pono looked at her, amused. "Besides whore clothes . . . what is it you 'design'?"

"The tuxedo my brother wore his first night at Lau Yee Chai, the jacket with new formfitting torso rather than draped. He was too thin for that. I designed his pants straighter than old styles, which now look prewar and tired." She paused. "And I have something new in mind for beachwear. Matching 'cabana sets,' for men and women. They will be the rage."

Malia unfolded a dress of rich, deep green brocade, a flowing, light-refracting skirt, made from one of Kiko's fabrics. "I am designing this for you."

Pono stared. It was like a radiance waiting to surround her.

"I thought of red," Malia said. "The color of passion. But green is softer, and will complement your beauty."

Pono hung her head, astonished. "I am not used to kindness. Life has made me harsh."

Malia thought of the four girls sleeping in the next room. The unknown father. She thought of life waiting for this woman just outside the door. What it took to go through that door each day.

"I hope," she said, "there will be a witness to your beauty, someone special when you wear this dress."

Pono looked off dreamily. "Maybe. When the war ends."

"Will it ever end?"

Pono closed her eyes, and when she opened them, their blackness—black as the red-black heart of *aku*—faded to brown, then white, so that her eyeballs seemed turned inward studying her brain.

"In one more year. There will be swiftness. Spectacle. War as we know it will become extinct."

IN OCTOBER, AS MARTIAL LAW WAS LIFTED, DESOTO CAME HOME on a U.S. carrier, bringing his briny sea smell. Keo walked into the house and it was there. That old familiar form asleep, one arm hanging squidlike from his bunk. He sniffed the big bronze-colored hand, the callused palm. Staccato of brother-blood thrumming in those veins. His soul rose up, ecstatic.

In bays safe from military patrols, they spent hours fishing in DeSoto's canoe, baiting hooks with sweet potato, so loved by surgeonfish. They chewed *kukui* nut, spitting out the oil so it spread and quieted a place amongst the waves where they looked down, watching fish take the bait. They tried to catch up on the years, but it took time, each man a little shy. Patience was called for. Like watching seawater evaporate in salt canoes made out of ti leaves. Minutes dripping into crystals.

"I never thanked you," Keo said, "for sending her to me."

DeSoto nodded solemnly. "Sunny love you more dan anyt'ing. I t'ink she wen' little crazy widdout you. You find out where she is, what happen . . . ?"

He shook his head. "I check Red Cross manifests every week. Write letters to hospitals. Brother . . . Sunny and I, we had a child. Born in Shanghai. I never even held her."

DeSoto hung his head. "Dis fucking war!"

Keo reached out, shyly touching his brother's arm. They hugged each other fiercely.

"Keo, listen me. Sunny stay alive. I know. I *feel*! Yo' little girl. You going find again . . . somehow. You want search, I search fo' you. You need talk, try come talk wit' me."

"I've been afraid to." He looked out at the sea. "So many things I did . . . was forced to do . . ."

DeSoto nodded. "I did t'ings, too . . . I nevah going fo'get. Nevah going repeat, not even fo' priest. Now I talk to mirror fo' confession."

They fell silent for a while, then Keo asked, " 'Ey. You think our *hānai* baby sister, really . . . *hānai*?"

DeSoto grinned. "I t'ink she look exactly like Malia."

"And . . . little bit like Krash?"

"Lot like Krash! Light skin like his mama. She got some *haole* on her side."

"Going be plenny interesting when Krash come home."

One day DeSoto took him fishing in waters off Ka'ena Point, northwest tip of O'ahu. A desolate place, a point of land where, in winter, forty-foot waves exploded on beaches. Reaching the waters off Ka'ena, the brothers fell silent.

Elders called the point Leina a ka 'Uhane, "Leaping Place of Ghosts." Hawai'ians believed souls of the dead departed from here for the afterlife, sailing out from thousand-foot cliffs. *Ka'ena* meant "red hot." This jagged finger of land pointing boldly westward was worthy of its name. At sunset its waters boiled orange, coral beaches sizzled, shrubs burst into flame.

Along its shoreline were lava caves, spouting-horns—huge volcanic rocks through which water shot skyward. Now, as the sea slammed into these formations, they heard moans, cries, chanting. The sea scraping across crushed-coral dunes was like the barking of a thousand dogs.

Keo shivered. "I feel real sleepy."

DeSoto whispered, "Time fo' *moe moe*. Close eyes. Relax."

Afterwards Keo knew he had slept, because he dreamed. In the dream someone sat between them in the canoe. And in that haunted place, three brothers fished, and laughed, "talking story" for rich hours. Much later, waves almost swamped them and they woke, working their paddles feverishly.

When it was calm, Desoto asked, "You see him?"

Tears streaked Keo's cheeks. "Brother Jonah! He was here. Laughing. Joking. Like old times . . ."

"I know dat boy. Know his soul been waiting fo' us here, so we share aloha befo' his long voyage to *Kahiki*, true Polynesian home."

As they gazed ashore, DeSoto suddenly stood and shouted. An '*iwa* bird with enormous wingspan had appeared from nowhere, perching on a great white rock above the cliffs. Now it flapped its wings and slowly lifted. Flying in concentric circles that lazily expanded, it headed straight for Keo and DeSoto, its cry heartrending, wingspan so wide it overshadowed them.

Keo reached up, shouting Jonah's name. The great bird hovered for so long, Keo swooned as if in its possession. It moved in close and hung suspended, so close, each man saw his reflection in its huge, forgiving eyes. The mirror of each brother's mind trembled in its clarity. Then the '*iwa* dipped its wings, crying out again, a long soprano solo. It lifted, flew up and up following the call its body cast ahead.

"Fly, Jonah-boy," DeSoto cried. "Fly high! You going home."

They watched until he was a speck caught in each brother's eye. They dropped their heads, engraved forever.

IN SPRING 1945 A LETTER CAME FROM KRASH KAPAKAHI, WOUNDED in a "minor way," recovering in Italy. Then, in the mail, strange souvenirs. Two long, curved, narrow bones, each inscribed with his name. Malia stared at them, then wrapped them up and carried them to Pono. The woman stroked them, pressing one against her ear.

"You hear the thumping? Bones remembering a beating heart."

"I don't understand," Malia said.

"They had to remove them, to cut out the lung shredded by a bullet. These are your lover's ribs. He is courting you."

Malia pressed his ribs against her cheeks. "Let him heal! I will do anything. Don't let him be an invalid."

"He will be well. One lung is enough. But he will sometimes make the sound of one digesting pearls."

She stroked the ribs, like totems. "Pono, I'm afraid. I don't know what is coming."

"Yours will be a twisted love. You will both live forward, looking backwards."

GERMANY'S SURRENDER, DANCING IN THE LANE. IN JUNE, WHEN the Allies took Okinawa, Keo kicked off his shoes at Club Maluhia. He hadn't played barefoot in years. Now he stepped up his stride. Boogying across the stage, he played seventeen choruses of "Birth of the Blues" while servicemen kept count. Afterwards they mobbed him.

Even the young blond drummer gushed. "I gotta tell you, you got high-note ability that makes me damn near cry."

He had gained weight. He was swimming again, his muscles acquiring density. Some nights he felt so good, he walked all the way home to Kalihi, then slept straight through till afternoon. One day in August when he woke, the neighborhood was still. No *manapua* man singing up the lane. No tofu man. His mother and father sitting quiet, staring at their hands. He went back to sleep. In early evening he saw neighbors in the lane, whole families dressed in white, carrying paper lanterns in procession. Sometimes they paused, as if allowing the shadow of someone absent to precede them.

"Mama? Papa?" He looked from one to the other.

They shook their heads.

Baby Jonah ran in from the lane. "Uncle Papa! Everybody whispering, '*Kulikuli. Kulikuli.*' Be quiet! I say, 'Fo' why *kulikuli*?' Dey say '*hir-osh-i-ma.*' What dat word mean?"

Storefronts darkened. Traffic stilled. Somewhere in small coves, on hidden beaches, families in white robes floated paper lanterns out to sea. Ribbons of softly glowing lights floated on the tide, returning spirits of the dead to the Buddhist paradise.

Days later, Japanese neighbors who worked the cane fields—coming home smoky and singed, sticking together like taffy—rowed sixty yards off the north shore to a tiny isle, Mokoli'i. There they knelt on pillows, taking their lives. Hearing the story, Keo tried to imagine the delicate old couple embracing, saying their goodbyes. Then the sharp point of a blade pressed against each belly.

Finally, the sirens. The echoing BONNNG of peace bells. For years, folks would link the atom bomb to the end of war, surrender. They would say that's what it took.

Rabaul

New Britain, 1945

She scratches her legs, gathering fossils, whole colonies of cells. She studies her scrawny arms, as if they are microbes of huge proportions. She inhales. And exhales. She concentrates on grains of rice, each grain a textured world. She holds each world in her mouth until it is indistinguishable from saliva.

She imagines raw savannahs, rice paddies, humans with bent backs plowing fields. Imagines arabesqued horns of languid oxen trampling harvested sheaves. She imagines each grain freed from straw and chaff and dust, leaving its "rice spirit" in the soil. She weighs almost nothing, she can hardly lift her bones.

Fleeing from Allied ground forces who have taken the west coast of the island, Japanese troops arrive at Rabaul dying from starvation, typhoid, gangrene, many minus an arm, a leg. Those sane enough to talk tell girls the Allies will skin them alive, melt down their body fats for aircraft and bomb lubrication.

Sunny listens, feeling nothing, wondering, "When will I feel outrage? When will I scream this is all I can bear?"

She no longer sleeps. She stands outside herself and watches. Perhaps she is curious—how will it end? Water is now so precious, hands and faces are caked with mud. Bathing is a memory.

One night she is summoned to Matsuharu's quarters.

"What now?" she asks, so weak her words drag in the groove of her thoughts.

He studies her, his eyes deranged.

"We are going underground. We will survive in our fortress until instructions from our emperor. We will fight the Allies to the death!"

She thinks he means the troops are going underground. She thinks he means the time has come for her to die. She touches her neck, picturing the graceful arc of his sword in flight.

"Who is going underground?" she asks.

"You. Me. Now."

Hoʻokaumaha

To Cause Deep Sorrow

Honolulu, 1945–46

With magical abruptness, the lane came to life again. Folks strolled arm in arm, greeting the poi man, the tofu man. They sat up late with lights ablaze, celebrating *pau* blackout. Still later, others haunted the lane, war vets with the tired sway of somnambulists, squatting furtively in bushes, aiming imaginary rifles at people-shaped laundry flapping on lines.

Even parents of dead boys came to life, saving their grief for darkened bedrooms. At the National Memorial Cemetery up in Punchbowl Crater, boys were buried as they had fallen in battle, regardless of rank or race. Some days Keo stood over the memorial plaque to Jonah, and those of friends killed in Belgium, Normandy, a sniper the day the Allies took Berlin.

He thought of Hawaiʻian boys with dark, brooding faces that were also beautiful. He remembered their husky, seaworthy bodies, and skin that was brown but with golden undertones. He remembered how, surfing in moonlight, the goldenness came out, as if the glare of sunlight made it dark. Now four of his friends were gone. Two bruisers from Farrington High, and two of the beachboys from the Royal.

They were part of the forty percent of fighting soldiers from

Hawai'i—Chinese, Portuguese, Filipino, Koreans, Puerto Ricans, even Samoans and *haole*—that no one had cheered when they came home, that no one celebrated. No waving banners, no parades at 'Iolani Palace like the "Welcome Home 442nd" celebration for fierce-fighting Japanese-American local boys who had banded as a regiment.

He came to Punchbowl regularly to "talk story" with the unaclaimed, to honor them, sometimes clearing weeds away from their markers. One day, sitting near Jonah's plaque, he saw in the distance what looked like a child being choked by a giant snake, the thing twisting and thrashing in his arms. He blinked, and looked again: a dwarf wrestling a long hose.

"Oogh?"

Recognition like a whiff of ammonia firing his nostrils, the sharp insistence of the past. Oogh telling his future on a freighter, playing him Puccini in New Orleans. Oogh feeding him nightingale broth in Shanghai. Keo ran forward, lifting and spinning him.

"Hula Man. You make me plenny tired, coming here so often. . . ."

"What? How long have you worked here?"

"Three, four months now."

Keo sat down on the grass, amazed. "But, why a cemetery?"

"Dead folks plenny tactful. Dey no stare."

Oogh sat down beside him, wiping the brow of his massive head, his argot still a blend of English, French, and Pidgin.

"I worked Halekulani several months. *Très* posh hotel, no? They put me in uniform, paging folks, like that Philip Morris guy. Then these tourists try pick me up! 'Oh, so cute. Is he fo' real?' Dis big Texan, try buy me. BUY ME. Wan' take me home fo' souvenir."

Keo bit his lip, trying not to laugh.

"OK. Maybe funny, dat. But next time he try pick me up, what I do, I *head-butt* him real hard in da balls. Big Texan moaning on his knees. Now he suing Halekulani. No mo' *'Call for Philip Morrrrrrrisssss!'* "

They lay laughing on the grass amongst the dead boys.

Then Keo scolded him. "I searched for you for months when I got back."

"Hula Man. I always turn up. Guarantee."

"But, where you living now?"

"With *kanaka* papa. Over Wai'anae way. Whatta guy, whatta guy! No can read, or write, but can spearfish, surf, weave fishnet, plant taro like one pro. *Aku* every day fo' lunch."

Keo moved closer. "You don't miss your mama in Shanghai?"

His voice and posture changed. "Sometimes."

He lit a cigarette, blowing a series of perfect, progressively smaller smoke rings that snuggled inside each other like sets of Chinese boxes.

"Maybe I'll always be torn. Something of an exile. Much like you."

"Me? I'm back where I belong."

"No, Hula Man. You'll never quite belong. That's why I look out for you."

"What do you mean?"

Oogh shook his head. "Always explanations. Exile is not just physical. It's deep inside you. The truth—didn't you feel little bit of exile even with your sweetheart?"

Keo looked down. "I don't remember."

"On your happiest day in Paris, weren't you always little bit alone?"

"I thought that was fear that I was mediocre. That's still my nightmare."

Oogh jumped to his feet, lapsing into Pidgin.

" 'Ey! What wrong with mediocre? It mean ordinary, what most folks are. Ordinariness best kine quality. Look how mediocre man live—quiet, lazy, no bother others. T'ink 'bout digestion, making love, lying on beach. What better dan dat? Mediocre man understand life short, live while can. All dat other stuff—genius, originality, work, work, work—fo' da birds! Breed ugliness! Everybody come suspicious, competitive. 'Who da best? Who da best?' Who care who da best?"

"Dew Baptiste always said if it's mediocre, it isn't jazz."

Oogh dropped his large head to his chest, staring at his bandy legs. "Ho, man. How I pray fo' be mediocre. Keo, you no understand real nightmares."

Keo gazed at this little man who seemed to have witnessed much of his life, to have influenced it. He felt great and deep affection.

"Why? Do you have nightmares? What are yours?"

Oogh looked away. "To wake up on a leash, or in a cage. Somebody's souvenir."

PEACE BROUGHT AN END TO HOARDING. LEILANI STOPPED SQUIRreling away crates of Spam and huge bags of rice in bedroom closets. When she could bear to, she packed Jonah's things away until the room was empty but for Baby Jonah's bed.

Now bolts of fabric took up residence against the walls. Cutting table. Dressmaker's dummy. The child fell asleep to the gasp and snip of scissors, pinking shears. Sometimes while she slept, Malia lifted her, pressing a pattern to her back, winding material round her limbs. For years, she would remember being swaddled in fabric while she lolled half conscious. She would remember finding her little body chalked, as if she were a target, Malia's face looming large, mouth dripping cobwebs of needles and thread. She would remember rows of little dresses in her closet, how they hung like perfect children with their tongues cut out.

One day Malia handed Pono a wad of bills, tying the Singer to a wagon, trundling it five lanes over.

"Time you owned it," Pono said. "I'm *pau* sewing. Starting life anew."

She stood epic in the green dress Malia had designed. Oceans and currents of her long black hair upswept. She wore smart toe-pinch high heels that gave her a terrible, majestic height. Nothing about her lingered, everything rushed the light—full lips luminous, eyes dense as bullets. Cheeks so flushed and prominent she looked feverish, a woman prepared to beat back life. A woman who would outlive her daughters.

Malia stared up at her. "My God, I hope this man deserves you."

For the first time in their wary friendship, Pono let her guard down. "He is the reason I exist."

Years later, Malia would learn Pono's destination that day after the war, when peace had been declared. She had gone to fetch a man hidden away for most of his life, a victim of *ma'i pākē*. War had brought the miracle of sulfa drugs, and somehow Pono thought the drugs would cure him, that she could bring him home. What she found was a man whose flesh had horribly outpaced the medication. Damage could not be undone.

THROUGH THE WAR, KRASH'S LETTERS HAD BEEN BRIEF. BASIC training in boot camp where they thought he was Mexican, then vague, tissue-thin letters from overseas. Then brief letters from a hospital where he had recovered. He referred to his missing lung and ribs just once, as if he had misplaced them and they would turn up again. Yet each rib, when she received them, had been so thoughtfully inscribed—KRASH KAPAKAHI in old-fashioned script—so carefully padded and packaged. Malia still took them nightly to her bed, stroking them like an archer with miniature bows, her silent cries the arrows.

Finally, he was coming home. His letters grew even shorter, no hint of joy, anticipation. As if he had been wounded in his hand, and writing letters was mere exercise, a way to keep intact the nerve ends in his fingers. She held his last letter to her chest, watching it tremble.

"I don't expect things," she lied. "We never had that much in common."

"He going be different," Leilani said. "Dey all coming back different."

Soft-spoken boys had come home full-throated men. And there was something in the eyes, as if they'd stood knee-deep in fire. Even young boys with sweetheart faces. Even the toughest "Go-For-Brokers"—the 442nd Regiment of Japanese-Americans who had earned ten thousand Purple Hearts, four thousand Bronze Stars, six hundred Silver Stars. Even the ones who never saw combat. All came back different.

Malia was there the day his troopship docked, massive as a city block. Men, thousands, leaned at its rails while troupes danced hula dockside. A military band played; stretchers were carried off to ambulances. Then, men ambled down gangplanks. Strangers in khaki. Leaner, quieter.

Krash's family enfolded him. Then Keo grabbed him, weeping and not caring. Malia stood paralyzed, so close she smelled his aftershave. She had forgotten his impact, how his nearness made her tongue feel thick and raw. She had forgotten his bronze skin was rough, slightly pitted in the cheeks, but his features were still handsome. He was immensely graceful, even standing still. Modestly she shook his hand.

Days later, at a *lūʻau* honoring returning boys, they strolled the beach together. Up close, she saw he was the same, but different. Still muscular, but in a leaner way, face thinner, even his lips less full. There were deep creases in his forehead. He had a certain edge now, like someone looking for a showdown, yet his voice beside her was so soft, she could hardly bear it.

"I prayed for you." She kept her head down. "Thank God you're home."

"It seems . . . different now," he said.

"Different?"

"People chatter a lot."

"Your families don't know how to thank you for surviving. They just need to talk. That's all."

She wanted to mention his ribs, how carefully she had kept them. But that would make them too important.

Then, cautiously, he took her arm. "Did *you* make it through all right?"

For a minute, all she wanted was to lie down in the dark beside him, speak softly for a time, their heads together on a pillow. She wanted to take his face in her hands, promise never again to be selfish. Wanted to tell him she had learned how to be delicate and generous with feelings, and that she would always be quick and strong in coming to defend him. She wanted to ask him to walk her through life, keep her on her feet, keep her alive. She looked into his eyes. They darted, not quite focused, and she lost her nerve.

"*Did* you?" he repeated.

"I'm fine," she said. "I still know where I'm going."

"Still hooked on *haole* ways?"

She winced as if he'd hit her in the stomach.

"I understand. I learned things over there. Some *haole* are good, some bad. Like everything. A white guy saved my life, kept me from bleeding to death. I learned they cry, and hurt. Have feelings, just like us."

For a while he looked out at the sea. "I've got serious plans, Malia. I'm going to make it. In their world."

"Their world. How?"

"G.I. Bill. I'm going back to university. Not night school, either. Full-time. I'm getting a degree on Uncle Sam." He inhaled. "Then . . . law school. Maybe California."

Something in her sat down. He had come home too ambitious. They all had. He was headed for the bright lights, taking off again.

She turned, wanting to strike him. "Law? I hope you've got what it takes."

She walked back to the campfire and music, tables of greasy food, spilled beer, and sat apart, running sand through her fingers. She thought of their child, wondering how he would take it, how much he could handle. She had the feeling he was beyond surprise, of any kind. Well, she had known combat, too.

But somewhere in that endless war, in years of nightly blackout, Malia had made herself a vow. She would always *hurt* a little, deprive herself a little. After a while she would get used to the hurt, the pain, would almost forget it. Then she mostly wouldn't notice it, because she would have forgotten what *lack* of pain, not hurting, was.

She glanced at Krash across the sand. Just then he looked at her with all his heart. She saw his agony, he seemed to shimmer with it. As if he, too, had made a pact. To always hurt a little. To not give up that pain.

ONE DAY KRASH SAT WITH KEO AND DESOTO IN THEIR OLD hangout, Smile Café, telling of his plans to study law, then set up a practise, help native Hawai'ians get back on their feet.

"You know, in Europe I met a Negro professor. And an Inuit Eskimo who plans to be a judge. I fought beside Guamanians who want to become doctors on the G.I. Bill. I thought, 'Hell, I'm as smart as they are.' My mama told me all my life, 'Krash, you plenny *akamai*, real clever! Go university, get degree, den tell *haole* what and what!' So—that's what I'm gonna do."

He studied Keo, who was quiet. "What you think? Think I'm too *ho'okano*, vain?"

Keo squeezed his shoulder to show pride. "I think, Osborn Kuahi Kapakahi . . . you going be one tough son-of-a-bitch lawyer. You da future, bruddah."

Krash grinned, looking from one to the other. But he saw the emptiness in Keo's eyes, as if the hours of each day passed at a far distance from him.

"Keo, I'm real sorry about Sunny. But, listen—you got to have hope. Thousands of displaced folks still coming home from hospitals all over Asia."

Keo flinched, as if trying to throw this aggravation off his back. Then he remembered Krash was his best friend.

"He got plenny hope," DeSoto said. "He give up hope, I break his legs fo' real."

Krash laughed and sipped his beer, so full of plans, his thoughts were having thoughts.

"Your sister always wanted to travel, yeah? Maybe she'll come with me to the mainland. After I get my degree, I'm going to try for law school. California."

DeSoto frowned. "How you mean, come wit' you?"

"Well . . . tell you the truth, there were a few girls in Europe. Just fool-around types, meant nothing. Malia, she was always on my mind. Even though that's one stubborn *wahine*. Damn, one day I realized I love her. I want to *marry* her, take her with me as my wife."

Keo looked down at his beer, then looked at Krash.

"You haven't been up the lane since you came back. Let's go 'talk story' with Papa, old time sake. Maybe you'll catch Malia there."

Krash swaggered up the lane between them. Since the *lū'au*, he had been distracted, the shock of being home. Now he wanted to see Malia, spend quiet time with her. He knew Leilani had a *hānai* baby girl, almost four years old now. Nearing the house, he heard the child's laughter. They were all sitting outside in the garage.

Baby Jonah threw herself at Keo. "Uncle Papa!"

Leilani stood, a little frightened, giving Krash a hug.

" 'Ey, Krash, how you doing? Look! Here our little *hānai* girl. Pretty, yeah? Name after Jonah."

Malia sat on a folding chair, avoiding his eyes while her mother nervously kept up her chatter.

"Rosie Perez already tired wit' four kids, hubby fighting overseas.

One night she say me, 'Leilani, you like *hānai* dis numbah five? I say, too good! Why not? All my kids gone far and wide. Except for Malia, who t'ank God take care of us while everybody gone. Yeah. T'ank God fo' Malia."

Keo looked from Krash to his sister, to the child. A perfect composite of both of them. It was so obvious, only a blind man could have missed it. In that moment, even Timoteo understood. He gazed at the child, at Krash, at Malia, and tears ran down his cheeks. Same high forehead as her father. Identical wide-set eyes. Same dimpled chin, and something dear in the shape of her earlobes, like little pointed hearts exactly like her father's.

From Malia, high cheeks, the small, slightly flat nose, full, beautifully shaped lips. The proud way she carried herself. An endearing huskiness—like her mother she would be voluptuous. Yet again from Krash, the long legs, large feet a little pigeon-toed. And, too, there was her age. Born exactly nine months from the night before Pearl Harbor.

Seeing the mirror image of himself, he stood dumb. His mouth worked silently. Malia rose, and stared at him. Defying him. Refusing him knowledge of his child. *Let him go out into the world. Let him be a sensation.*

With no sense of it, Krash held his arms out to Baby Jonah. The beautiful, round child hid behind Leilani's skirts, peeping out flirtatiously.

He stood there for what seemed ages, then slowly turned, reeling down the lane. Seven years later when he came home to set up practise, he came back married to a *haole*.

Hili Pō

To Wander in the Dark

Honolulu, late 1940s

Each day had its errand, his trumpet gave each day a point. Sometimes his horn was a soaring hawk, his body's winds and currents holding it in equilibrium. The hawk's tension held his world together. He stalked it, ruffled its feathers, until his arms felt heavy as mercury, his throat all dust and broken glass.

Mornings when he woke, his lip was a scabby crater. Yet the next night and the next, and each night of every week, he blew his horn, dragging his lungs home like old balloons. Some nights he found himself in aimless exhalations of a predawn trance, staring down at Baby Jonah, wanting her to be his child. Some nights the dressmaker's dummy called to him.

He stood in the dark, face-to-face with the headless, armless woman. "Sunny."

He placed his hands on her shoulders, wanting to tear off his skin for having come home without her. He wanted to tear a hole in the world and find her. What was the point of living? How could life have meaning? He thought of the war-torn cities of Asia, survivors still crawling from debris. She was there, somewhere, she and their child. He knew she was there because Oogh said life would find her. He didn't want to wait for life. He wanted to outrun it, outsmart it, find her and get on with living. Six years. She could be dead. He refused to believe it, unappalled and unimpressed by the odds.

One day, Leilani pulled the bedsheet over her head, howling. Timoteo tried to comfort her, saying no one could hurt Keo now, the war was *pau*. Saying Keo had to do this—search for Sunny Sung.

"Why?" Leilani cried. "He almost die in camp because of her. Now he going back dere."

He stood on the deck of an ocean liner, feeling the engines' vibrations, the trembling of a thousand lives on the brink of other lives. Through cataracts of paper streamers Malia looked up at him. That he was going back there again seemed madness. She waved goodbye, as if scribbling curses on the air.

He watched the ocean rise and grope, falling heavily on its face. At night, playing with the cruise band, he blew with everything he had, screamed it out of him like a man pleading for redemption. When he wasn't playing, he dragged the decks, feeling time like whips across his back. The day they reached Shanghai, his face looked like someone else's.

Sailing up the Whangpoo River, approaching the harbor, Keo felt terror blow through him, as if there were only seconds to survive in. On the tender to the docks, memories of feudal madness sucked him in. Coolies dying in gutters. Infant-girl corpses stacked in alleys. Concentration camps. Still, he had been too tough to kill. After all, he had survived.

He stood dockside, and nothing happened. He saw the sad humanness of Shanghai, the sooty traffic of postwar crowds. There was nothing in it now of mystery. Except for bombed-out buildings, it thrived again, noisy, almost amiable. American sailors swarmed the streets, pimps following like wolves trailing herds. Europeans barked at liveried chauffeurs, gambling houses thrived. In mild shock, he saw Japanese soldiers directing traffic, the victors now the vanquished.

He checked into a modest hotel and took a cab as close as he could get to the old Chinese City. Much of it had been bombed. Where there had been hutments were now only filthy sewers, mounds of dust. . . . *Her face at tea.* He crossed the Bridge of Nine Windings, the old teahouse still intact. Now there were different waiters, the crowd mostly European.

He went back to the silk mills. One day at Dez Hen Number Two Mill, a woman stopped and spoke in halting English.

"I remember you. Always ask for two sisters."

He smiled, in shock. "Sun-ja Sung. Her sister, Lili . . ."

"Ever find?"

He shook his head.

"Plenty girls lost. Maybe they come sing-song girls. Maybe kidnapped. Jap soldiers come in trucks, take girls to pompon houses."

"Pompon houses?"

"For sex! Soldiers use girls plenty."

"I—I don't understand."

"Sure, sure you understand! Pompon girls like prostitutes. But *forced*. Pompon houses like prisons."

"Why didn't they use real prostitutes? There were thousands in the city."

"Disease," she whispered. "Soldiers want clean, young virgins. One day Japs take me in truck, then find out I diseased, throw me back. War end, doctors fix me up. Syphilis save my life."

Keo hesitated. "What happened to girls kept in those places?"

She shook her head. "Many died, exhaustion. Soldiers climbing on top them all day. Many suicide. Some just children, ten-eleven years old when kidnapped."

He quietly thanked her, gave her dollar bills, and walked away.

He went to Club Argentina. Different owner, mediocre band, but the manager remembered him. Keo sat in with the band for several weeks, asking regularly about pompon houses during the war. No one could help him. One night a U.S. Army colonel sat down at his table.

"I heard you play once. Honolulu. You want information on a comfort girl."

Keo looked at him, puzzled.

"Pompon house, comfort station, same thing."

His hand shot forward. He gripped the colonel's sleeve.

"There isn't much. Girls used for sex in war, what else is new? We've got war trials still going on. POW stuff. *Real* atrocities. What Japs did to our boys would make you puke. So no one's paying much attention to these kidnapped girls."

The man leaned closer, attempting to explain. "Japs officially called them *ianfu*, comfort women. They were shipped to frontline bases with foodstuffs, ammunition—comfort supplies. Unofficially, they called them P-girls, short for *p'i*, Chinese slang for vagina. So, coupled with their nationality they were known as Chom-P, Korean vagina, or Chan-P, Chinese vagina. Their huts and barracks were called P-houses, or simply 'toilet.' "

Keo closed his eyes, trying to absorb it. "My fiancée might have been one of those women. Kidnapped off the streets of Shanghai."

"Was she Chinese?"

"Hawaiian-Korean American."

"How in the world did she—"

"She was trying to get her sister out of Shanghai. Right around Pearl Harbor. I was here. . . . I lost her. Japs might have picked them up."

The man whistled, shook his head. "American women *were* held in some of those places. Dutch, Australians, captured missionaries, nurses. Information's still coming in. But most comfort girls were Asian."

"I need records," Keo said. "They must have kept files on them."

"No files. You see, it was covert. Wasn't supposed to be happening. Those girls were *kidnapped*, virtually enslaved. Many were kids taken right out of grade schools. Especially Koreans. It was condoned all the way up to the emperor."

Keo looked at him, appalled. "Why haven't the leaders been dragged into court and sentenced?"

The colonel frowned. "Well . . . now we got Russian Communism. Japan could be an asset in a confrontation. Look, I know there were half a dozen comfort stations here in Shanghai. Mostly for the Japanese navy, who were a helluva lot more civilized than the army. Three or four hundred women in all . . ."

He drew lines on a slip of paper. "Most of the really young ones, the prettiest, were taken here." One line moved along the Whangpoo River, south of the city past Longhua Airfield.

"You should know—a lot of those girls were later put on troopships, sent as sex slaves wherever there were Jap bases. Java, Borneo, Pacific Islands. That's where the real hell was. They were right there at the battlefronts. Tens of thousands of girls massacred. Some even forced to carry arms, fighting and dying beside the soldiers who had raped them."

Keo looked down, wanting to be ill.

The colonel tapped his arm. "I can get a military jeep and driver for you, run you out there. You won't see much. It was very primitive." He hesitated. "Tell you something else. The girls who managed to survive . . . most are disfigured. Aged beyond belief. Some were in those camps three-four years. Tortured. Diseased. Raped thirty-forty times a day. If you find your sweetheart, you might not even recognize her."

That night Keo walked in the rubble of what had been Hotel Jo-Jo. He picked at bits of mortar, an inch of filthy rag, ghost moltings of their night together. Sunny near reduced to bone, yet her beauty somehow radianced, skin and limb and milk of her now mothering. Breasts nourishing his child. His *child.* He staggered with the weight of it.

Days later he passed beside the Whangpoo River, his driver dodging potholes, an MP in the backseat of the jeep. They sped through the city's outskirts past miles of cardboard hovels, beside each one a small campfire. As if refugees were marking the place where suffering had become unendurable.

A compound now deserted—eight long barracks surrounded by barbed-wire fences, empty guard towers. Inside, tiny rooms, single cots, each "room" separated by plywood walls. Not knowing Keo's purpose here, the driver repeated what he had heard.

"Some of them girls was kept here two years. You believe it? Forced to do fifty-sixty guys a day. When fleets were in, they didn't even feed them. Just shoved rice balls in their mouth while men climbed on and off them."

The MP added what he knew. "Hell, I heard they weren't even whores—just kids, tied up like dogs."

Keo held on to a flaking door, his bowels jerking, a visceral urge to defecate.

He haunted nightclubs, cabarets, still searching. One night he woke, knowing she was not in Shanghai, she had not been there for a long time. He felt suddenly compelled to get out of there, it was still a place of nightmares.

He lit a cigarette in the dark, smoke conjuring parables of what he had done in order to live. To live with his conscience. Killing someone because he was a traitor. Killing someone else for raping hungry women. Making love to a woman he didn't love because she was dying.

Maybe that was the lesson of war, of life: that knowing too much, and seeing too much, could damage us. Experiences too profound could break us in pieces. He left Shanghai, too late to save a part of himself, hoping another part was salvaged.

AT HOME IN HONOLULU HE PLAYED A FEW CLUBS, MADE A RECORDING, then after six months, a year, felt the whirl of chaos pulling him again. He drifted, aimless with a diligence. Hong Kong, Bangkok, Manila—wherever there were cafés, nightclubs, that booked him for a week, a month. Any city touched by war, where people remembered. Where he might find her.

He would arrive in a city, find work playing horn or piano, usually in small watering holes for expat jazz lovers left over from the war. He would enter each place with hope, even blow his trumpet full of expectation, as if he were entering new time. There would be timidity, mystification, which after he got his bearings would evaporate. In time he would come to believe that this feeling of remoteness and mystery lay closest to the truth. The truth of anything.

At first, he would feel the way he felt when he first sat down at a piano, or picked up a horn. Alone and ignorant. Knowing humility was the only way to ever understand anything at all. If Sunny was in the town where he was playing, he had to wait for her to come to him. But first she had to know he was there. He took small salaries, asking instead that clubs advertise his engagements: KEO MEAHUNA, INTERNATIONAL JAZZMAN, APPEARING NIGHTLY. . . .

Wherever he appeared, whatever he played—trumpet or piano—he spent every hour watching the door. Sometimes he couldn't help himself: he went where damaged women went. Brothels. Opium dens. Clinics he heard of where disfigured women were still being rehabilitated. Hospitals where comfort women who were "healed" worked as nurse's aides. He talked to doctors, asked to see records. Afterwards he shook their hands.

In each city he sat on park benches, waiting. Because maybe she was searching, too. Sometimes he sat all night under the ghostly yellow clarity of streetlights. Maybe she was damaged, and only tested the airs of night. Another year passed. Keo went home, then left again, melting in and out of cities, up and down the Asian coast.

On an island in the South China Sea, he traveled to a Buddhist monastery called Po Lin—Precious Lotus. He heard there were female monks and acolytes, some who had been Japanese sex slaves in the war. He sat in their temple while they chanted. He studied each face. He peeled a mandarin in winter.

Once in northern Thailand, in the city of Chiang Mai, he watched a woman enter water. Her shoulders were Sunny's and her hair spreading round her, floating like black algae on a river of time. Afterwards she stood in sunlight throwing back her hair. One hand on her hip, she smiled at him. Through the triangle formed by her slender arm he saw the next town, and the next, pulling him on. Women approached him. He backed away, desiring no one he could see or touch.

In different cities, in whiskey-ridden conversations, people relived the war. Listening, he learned what had been done to hundreds of thousands of women. Kidnapped, tortured, sacrificed. Whites, Asians, nuns, missionaries, nurses. Children, and wives. Wherever they invaded, Japs had rounded up sex slaves, *jugun ianfu*. Or what Koreans called *chongshindae*, conscripted worker, a euphemism for P-girls. Most had been kidnapped from Korea. But one night in Jakarta, Keo learned that many girls, maybe thousands, had been kidnapped from the silk and cotton mills of Shanghai.

He reeled into the streets, wandering aimlessly. He stood in a garbage-strewn alley, helplessly sobbing. He slid down to his haunches, rocking. After a while he opened his trumpet case and removed the horn, placing his palm against cool brass. This thing that had become his voice, his conscience. He tapped the trumpet's golden bell, thinking how, through the years, he and his horn had become a separate creature apart from the world. Apart from her.

He thought of her standing alone in Paris nightclubs, watching while he gave everything—his heart, his soul, his juices—to this horn. This *thing*. He raised his arm and brought it down, slamming the trumpet against the street. He staggered to his feet and slammed the horn against a wall, then backed up and swung again. Reverberations made his arm feel shattered.

He reeled back and forth across the alley, leaning against walls for leverage, viciously slamming the horn over and over until he lost count, until boundaries blurred and he was the thing being slammed. Fingers torn, wrists scraped raw, he felt etched in metal. Nothing left. He collapsed, unseeing and unhearing. Beside him, a freaky configuration of flattened brass.

ANOTHER TOWN, KOWLOON, ACROSS VICTORIA HARBOR FROM Hong Kong. One day Sunny's face darted out at him in traffic. He followed her to a dingy building on Nathan Road, a place called Chungking Mansion. He haunted Chungking, riding elevators, tripping over cats vomiting in stairwells. One day from an adjacent alley he saw her on a tiny balcony hanging laundry. Insane, Keo shouted out her name.

Eight floors up, her features were slightly blurred, yet when she looked down, something in him buckled. It wasn't Sunny. But it *could* have been her, older, ravaged. It could have been her at sixty or seventy. . . . *After years in those camps, many are not recognizable.* Day after day he stood outside the building, asking merchants in the alley about the woman on the eighth floor. Thinking him mad, they shooed him away.

He was playing piano at Pimm's then, a small, dark club on Victoria Street whose customers wanted to be lulled. He gave them Gershwin, Cole Porter, Broadway show tunes. It didn't matter what he played, he wasn't in that town to play. One day he entered a jade shop. After an hour he purchased a small netsuke, then invited the owner to tea.

The man was Chinese, middle-aged and gracious. "It is not necessary. Although . . . I feel there is something on your mind."

They stepped outside and Keo pointed to Chungking Mansion, a huge building shaped like an H.

"Do you know anyone who lives there?"

The jade man nodded. "Chungking is made up of hundreds of apartments. Each day tenants let rooms to tourists of modest means. Traffic to and fro is madness."

They drank tea at a small café in the alley of merchants. To their left was a tiny park for their eyes to rest upon. To their right, balconies climbing a wall.

Keo glanced up. "There's a woman on the eighth floor—" As he said it, she stepped out and hung up dishcloths "There! I need to talk to her."

The jade man gazed upwards, holding a cigarette between his third and fourth finger like a mandarin. He exhaled slowly. A wreath of smoke trembled and lingered.

He studied Keo. "You are . . . a spy?"

"A spy! I'm from the islands of Hawai'i, a U.S. territory."

"Ah. American spy. Just now there is much tension in Kowloon. Important people here have fled Red China. Communist agents follow them. Maybe you follow the agents? Maybe she is hiding an agent in her room. Why else would you want a poor old Chinese woman?"

The woman disappeared; Keo stirred his oolong tea and brooded. "You see, I think I know her."

The jade man saw his sorrow and looked away. There was so much wretchedness in the world, it made him weary. He wanted the well-dressed brown stranger to make him laugh, tell him a tale about caprice.

He leaned forward languidly. "You have stood in this alley many times, neh? She has seen you. If she wanted to speak to you, she would make a sign."

"She may be running . . . out of shame."

The jade man smiled. "No one runs in Kowloon. No one is that free. Perhaps if she talks to you, she will die."

"No! I came to help her."

"Many things begin in charity . . . and end in death."

Keo rubbed his eyes, trying to be patient. "I'm not a spy. I'm looking for my fiancée, she may have been taken in the war, imprisoned. . . ."

He mentioned the sex-slave camps.

The jade man shredded the corpse of his cigarette.

"I know of these women. Many are dead." He blinked slowly. "What do you want, if this woman is your sweetheart? To assume her suffering?"

"No matter what happened, I love her."

"And do you think that, after this, she could love *you*, or any man? Be near a man? Think, my friend, only think. Is it love you feel? Or is your pride too great to adjust itself to a normal woman? Must you have your martyr?"

Keo gazed at him, remembering what war had done to his people. "How indulgent I must seem. Forgive me. I just can't accept that she is dead. I don't know how to live without her."

The jade man rose, bowing slightly. Then unaccountably he smiled. "I avoid sentiment as a rule. Ahhh, perhaps we Chinese are too fatalistic. Romantic love is a novelty to people of arranged marriages. Come and see me in a week."

That night Keo rode Star Ferry back and forth across Victoria Harbor. Fog hung like broth, yet he could see the lanterns of thousands of Chinese junks swaying in the wake of Coast Guard gunboats. Along the docks under street lamps woolly with moths, coolies lay sprawled and snoring in postures of death. Signs hung from their chests upon which were written the Chinese character for HUNGER. Smelling their wasted bodies, he was thrown back to Shanghai. A different city. Yet the same.

He leaned from the ferry, the smell of sewage and petrol burning his nostrils. A bloated sheepdog floated by, glowing like phosphorus. Around it ragged strands of garbage formed a bouncing, watery calligraphy. The letters seemed to spell DEFEAT. DEFEAT. In that moment terror pressed against his loins. If Sunny had survived, and if he found her, could she bear him?

That night in his modest hotel, he lay back on sheets smelling of cinnamon, letting a quietness come into him. He was tired, there was too much of the sooty world invading him. He turned on his side, remembering how she slept that way, her spine so vulnerable.

. . . Is she sleeping now? Does she know peace? Is there somewhere a quiet room? And in that room, does she lie watching light touch partly open shutters? Do the hours console her? Does she recall that Paris winter, how we softly lashed each other in snow, and sweat, and sorrow. . . .

HE SAT IN KING'S PARK WHERE THE JADE MAN HAD DIRECTED him, smelling the ripe smells of Kowloon. He heard the human din of uphill ladder-streets—tiny alleys where beggar-masters measured stubs, where men and pliers made dentist shops out of thin air, where blind hair-collectors dragged their fingers following itinerant barbers. In the distance, ten-foot sheets of noodles hung drying on lines between shanties. The clack of mah-jongg tiles on stone tables, hiss of fish frying in woks.

A large bleeding pig with human legs floated past him. Keo looked again. A delivery man wearing the disemboweled pig over his head, so its body dripped blood down his churning legs. Nearby, an old man on a bench rocked something squidlike in a baby carriage. The thing sat up, bulbous head glowing, its long-lashed slit eyes blinking slowly. A slithery tentacle suckered the air. Keo thought it waved. A woman passed with wooden legs whose shoes were pointed backwards. He felt he was sitting in a nightmare.

A ghost sat down beside him, asking for a cigarette. The man was white from head to foot. Eyebrows, hair, fingernails, clothes, sandals, even the crevices of his ears, the hairs in his nose. Only the whites of his eyes were yellow. He blew his nose in his hand, expelling white powder.

Keo had heard of the Flour Ghosts, refugees fleeing Red China. Kept as prisoners in Walled City kennels by greedy Kowloon landlords, they earned rice meals by making white-flour noodles day and night. Half-starved and diseased when they reached Kowloon, within weeks their lungs were mildewed, hung with flour. Most suffocated to death. Keo gave the Flour Ghost his cigarettes and several dollars. The man bowed repeatedly and tottered off, leaving the smell of incipient rot.

Then all receded. Keo froze as the woman from Chungking Mansion sat down beside him.

She spoke in cautious English. "Mr. Ten, the jade man, asked me to come."

"Forgive me," he said. "You looked so much like . . ."

"I'm sorry," she whispered. "I am not your sweetheart. But I find it interesting. I was . . . one of them."

He was silent, wanting to lie down at her feet. Then he said, "I know what happened. To all of you."

"You can *never* know. But how did you select me from all of Kowloon?"

"I was searching. I . . . saw something in your face. There's so much I don't understand."

She sighed. "... I was sixteen and very poor. Japanese scouts came to my school in South Korea, 1941. I volunteered to go with them to Osaka, to work in a steel factory and send money home. I never saw Osaka. They shipped forty of us to Okinawa, then Saipan. We were used as sex slaves until Japan surrendered. After two years in hospital for syphilis, and tuberculosis, I finally went home. People spat on me. Father locked the door. Now, I am here in Kowloon."

"How do you live?"

"Military assistance from your government. I brew my nightly potions on a hot plate. I crush my powders, mix my ointments. Without medication I will die."

In the sun's surgical glare, her hair was like white spiders, her skin entirely bleached of color. She wore dark glasses. Her dress and shoes extremely neat. There were her hands, and there were her feet, all in their proper locations. Yet she moved cautiously, like a mechanical doll carefully reconstructed. Not so much a woman as the memory of a woman.

"And, are you all alone? No husband? No companion?"

Her face hardened into fissured rock. Something went through her like fire.

She inhaled, moving away from him. "I came to see you for your sweetheart. I hope she is at peace."

Carefully he pulled out a wrinkled snapshot. Sunny, in loafers and bobby socks.

"Did you ever hear the name Sun-ja Sung?"

She looked at the snapshot and shook her head. "They erased our names, gave us Japanese names. They erased everything. In that way we were left alive, yet perfectly disposed of."

Keo leaned forward slightly. "I don't think I understand."

"Shame is more deadly than a bullet. A soldier rapes. The woman won't speak of it. Ever. That's why we do not talk about P-girl prisons, 'comfort stations.' There were hundreds of thousands of women used, maybe millions. Who will ever know the number? Yet Jap soldiers got off free. Not one convicted of rape during the war trials. Where were the victims? The witnesses? We were too ashamed. That's what was so brilliant about it, you see."

"I am so sorry. Is there something I can do?"

"Leave us. Leave us alone. We have nothing left for you."

She walked into the day, a woman not thirty, looking sixty. He wanted to call after her to be brave, to not lose heart. He wanted to promise that in time she would mend. All he could do was sit there, praying God would grant her the precious ability to forget.

That night he stared at the snapshot, imagining Sunny prematurely old. Or dead. If she had died, somewhere there must have been a singing out, for she had been so out of the ordinary, so filled with wonderment at living. She had been the bright torch of a burning match glowing in his hand. And when the hand began to close, dimming the brightness, choking the flame, she had reeled away from him into chaos.

KE KĀNE JACARANDA

Jacaranda Man

HE CAME BACK RAW. HE SAT ALONE IN DESOTO'S CANOE, THINKing of ways to kill himself. Weeks passed, a month of nightmares, of jumping awake in oily sweats. And then, a midnight humming, his fingers tapping, restless. A phantom trumpet like a smart, stiff pet. He went back to blowing horn. The only way he understood anything at all.

By the early 1950s he was sitting in with big-name bands passing through Honolulu en route to Asia—the Dorsey Brothers, Ellington, Count Basie. Listening to trumpeters like Harry "Sweets" Edison and Roy Eldridge reminded Keo he wasn't genius, he was only very good. But folks still called him Hula Man, he was still worldly in their eyes. There were rumors he had lost his sweetheart in the war. Some said he had been a spy.

He was forty-two, though he looked younger. But he *seemed* older—slowed down in person, in conversation. Yet when he blew his horn, folks closed their eyes and listened. The war was still fresh within them, everyone knew pain. Keo still knew how to ride that pain in ways they connected to, in spite of critics who said his trumpeting had gone soft, he had gone soft, his jazz wasn't pioneering anymore.

Bebop was becoming the new jazz, advanced by musicians who loved contrast and paradox, even if it sounded ugly. Bebop was mental and jagged, a dizzying alchemy of shock and clamor. Those who followed it looked on Keo and his generation as men to be respected but not imitated. Listening to the new sounds, sometimes he was tempted to stride over the boundary into bop, but it wasn't in him. His trumpet was a diving board, the thing he sprang off of in order to soar, transcend the given formulas. He wasn't built to snarl and rage, blowing desperate, gritty measures of what Oogh called *jazz du jour*.

Sometimes when he played, he let go in a way that was magisterial. He didn't have to take huge chances, didn't have to reach that far. There was sorrow and lostness in his trumpeting, crowds grew quiet, looking down. He kept on blowing, bleeding up the scales into the highest registers. One night, playing "There Are Such Things," his sound was so pure, it erased the audience. It was like a blade of light lifting him until he hung suspended.

Though he was older now, he was still larger than anyone playing in Honolulu at that time. Young horn men still came, wanting secrets, shortcuts. All he gave them was riddles.

"Be careful who you give your music to. There are things you can't take back."

Some nights he stared into mirrors, gauging the years, the wear and tear. He was still an enigmatic man, full lips and nose distinctly Polynesian, not quite handsome, not quite plain. He had fleshed out again, but swimming kept his body fit, so that he was muscular in a slender way. Dark skin unlined, curly black hair now faintly threaded gray.

And he was still a gentle man, courteous to the point of old-fashionedness. Still an impeccable dresser, his suits and shirts custom-made by Malia Designs. Women were drawn to him because there was something intensely physical about him. Not just the callused, slightly gangsterish lip, but also a suggestion of barely reined-in temper, seductive and menacing. A potent energy, a bottled storm, that exploded only when he played.

Malia felt women were attracted to his aloofness, his distance. The only time he relaxed and showed his softer side was with her child.

"Except for family, you're not really attached to anyone," she said.

"I try to be."

"You *pretend* to be. But you're not."

Now and then he went with women from the clubs, even women he paid. But sometimes when he lay down with them, within minutes he had to get up, get dressed, get out of there. He wanted to scream, to strike the woman because she wasn't Sunny. Then he would take off, traveling again, not even sure what country he was passing through. He wasn't searching anymore, he was just going.

ONE NIGHT IN 1954 A STRANGER ENTERED THE SWING CLUB and sat in the back, in shadow. At first no one noticed him, but eventually people turned, for the man had a distinctly bluish tint to his face and hands. He looked out at the crowd defiantly, flushed patches on his cheeks like ink stains, lips faintly violet.

Though he was tall, he had the expression of an aging jockey, his gaze extremely concentrated. And there was something about the eyes, round when they should have been slanted. An Asian trying to look Caucasian? Rather, the eyes were square, box-shaped, pinched back by scars. The man moved carefully, like someone surgically rearranged.

He listened, attentive, to the band, wincing when the sax man stumbled on "Thou Swell," smiling when Keo stood to solo. When he took off with a thumping, skidding version of "Muskrat Ramble," the crowd woke up. Keo kept at it, bursting into improvisations until, on his nineteenth chorus, he ran out of gas. The band settled into "Georgia," gentling down the roaring crowd. The blue-faced man just smiled.

Afterwards, lights up, crowds moving toward the exits, he made his way to the dressing rooms. Keo looked up, startled: in bright light, the man's face frightened him.

"Hula Man . . ." Yet the voice was familiar.

Keo slowly stood up. "I know that voice."

The man stepped forward almost shyly. "Endo Matsuharu. Paris, 1939. You coached me on saxophone."

He couldn't place him. He shook his head.

"I was at the Sorbonne. My uncle was the consul, Yasunari Seiko. He helped you get out of Paris."

Keo shouted, then threw his arms round Matsuharu, clapping him on the back repeatedly.

"Oh, man, he saved my life! He . . ." Keo pulled him to a chair and sat him down. "I remember now. You and I, we used to practise near Sacré Coeur at dawn."

He pumped Matsuharu's hands, then opened a bottle of rum and poured them shots. "To Paris."

Matsuharu drank, then sat there.

Keo filled his glass again. "What happened to you after that?"

"The war. Uncle could have fixed it so I sat behind a desk. But . . . it was a matter of honor. Anyway, we lost."

"Everybody lost," Keo said.

Matsuharu smiled. "You haven't changed much, Keo."

"Fifteen years? I changed. But you, where were you all these years? Do you still play?"

"Sax is my life. It's all I do, though not very well. I've played small clubs in Portland, San Francisco. Kind of rough—folks still sensitive to Japanese."

His voice was so well modulated, Keo felt if he closed his eyes, he could be talking to a college professor. He remembered Endo had been a serious student at the Sorbonne. Studying to be a lawyer.

". . . So I thought I'd try Honolulu. Look you up. You're pretty famous now."

Keo laughed softly. "Only in Honolulu. Although I seem to need to drift—Hong Kong, Bangkok—playing second-rate clubs. Did you hear that guy on sax tonight? He's tone deaf, I swear. I need to form my own group. Maybe that will keep me home."

Matsuharu's eyes wandered, taking in the room.

Keo apologized. "Man, I'm running at the mouth. I can't believe it's you. Say, look, are you hungry? Let's get some chow, start catching up."

On the way down Bishop Street, he pointed out landmarks, Aloha Tower finally whitewashed of camouflage, 'Iolani Palace minus the tanks. They settled in at Chico's, where night folks gathered, and ordered kimchee and beer and big steaming bowls of saimin. Keo stirred *shoyu* and mustard in small circles, felt his pores open from broth clouds. Through steam and floating *char siu*, the man's blue face came at him in a dream.

"How did *you* do?" Matsuharu asked. "I mean, the war?"

He sighed, put down his chopsticks. "I survived. Your uncle got me to Shanghai a few months before Pearl Harbor. I was looking for my sweetheart. Do you remember Sunny?"

The name meant nothing to him. He shook his head.

"Sun-ja Uanoe Sung. Hawaiian-Korean, from Honolulu. She left Paris looking for her sister in Shanghai. I found her there, but couldn't get them out in time."

He looked down for a while. "I played clubs there, Ciro's, the Argentina. Got arrested, interned in a camp. Red Cross brought me home a skeleton. Malaria, this, that. I spent the war entertaining troops at home. Same thing with Korea."

"Your family?" Matsuharu asked.

"We lost my younger brother. Italy."

"I'm sorry."

"What about you, *your* family?" Keo asked.

He went away for a while, gazing out at nothing. "All dead. Even Uncle Yasunari. The firebombs in Tokyo . . . fifteen miles of dust."

Keo hung his head. "God damn all wars."

"God? If he exists, he must be an angry child."

"But you." Keo studied him. "You made it through all right?"

Matsuharu plunged ahead, wanting it over with. "I served in the South Pacific. Lieutenant at a huge supply base for the army, navy, air force. Then came surrender, the war trials. I was sentenced to six years. Two on Manus Island. Four in Tokyo Prison . . ."

Keo didn't know what to ask. He was afraid to ask.

"It was war. There were times I was kind. Times I was sadistic, I suppose. Long periods I can't recall. We had a large POW camp. An Australian captain said I gave him food, saved his life. I don't remember. A Yank soldier said I kicked him in the head. I have no memory. Usually when other officers turned cruel, I walked away. That, too, is a crime against humanity."

"When did you know you were losing the war?"

Matsuharu closed his eyes. "Midway . . . maybe Guadalcanal. After that, no one was really sane. Officers went berserk, committed terrible atrocities, even on our own conscripts. At the war trials, many were sentenced to death and executed. I was convicted only of small brutalities. Yet I remember blood, my sword. . . ."

He sat up and audibly sighed. "After Japan surrendered, Allies swept our base, pulling us from underground tunnels that went on for miles. They say we lived hidden and submerged down there for fourteen months! I remember nothing. Somewhere in my head, in 1942, everything closed down."

Keo leaned forward, asking softly, "Endo, do you know how your skin turned blue?"

He smiled faintly. "Extreme hunger. And madness, I suppose. In prison, I began eating paint from the walls. In time I ate my way around my cell. They made me repaint it. Then I would eat it off again completely. I did that for six long years. Guards used to watch and laugh, I was their entertainment. No one told me what lead paint could do to a human body."

He touched his cheek, and then his forehead. "My nervous system's damaged. Medics say my brain cells are galloping to extinction. I forget what simple words mean. Map. Sock. Fork. Sometimes there are seizures."

". . . What happened to your eyes?"

"After a while, guards grew bored. They used our faces as punching bags. Probably they had seen too much war. For months my eyes were cut and swollen. The eyelids closed and festered. Finally they took me to a military surgeon, who did a lot of cutting and patching. He said I was a phenomenon. By rights, I should be blind."

Keo looked away, remembering Woosung, the many kinds of dying. Lights played on Endo's jacaranda hues. Even his black hair had a bluish, lunar glow.

"Who would ever believe, after the Pacific, there could be another war? Now, three million dead in Korea. Tell me, Keo. After all, what do you believe in?"

He thought for a long time. "Maybe . . . only music."

They began jamming together at night in a small studio Keo rented off Hotel Street. It had been fifteen years since Paris, when Endo was just a student warming up on tenor sax. Now they strolled cautiously through arrangements with record backup, Keo listening as Endo sailed into delicate, stiletto-sharp arpeggios. Then unaccountably he swerved into wailing contradictions.

He would start out clean and elegant with almost no vibrato. Even the way he held his saxophone was elegant, his blue fingers barely touching valves, merely hovering, it seemed, as if the instrument were all he had left in the world. But invariably he would lose his sense of timing, nearly lose control. His entrance into every song was like a prayer that suddenly combusted.

He put his horn down. "I start out OK, then something goes haywire."

"Nerves," Keo said. "You just need practise."

"I practise every day."

"Listen. After prison camp, I didn't touch a trumpet for a year. It was like putting the barrel of a rifle to my mouth."

Endo smiled. "You recovered. I won't have that luxury."

"What do you mean?"

"Organic deterioration. Like I said, even my brain cells are dying off."

Keo tossed it aside. "We're going to practise till you're genius on sax."

But something was missing from Endo's playing, an intuitive reckoning so vital to jazz. The naked ache and wonder. When he blew his horn, what Keo heard was someone fighting for control, someone beating back frenzy.

Keo slowly gathered a new bass player, a drummer, pianist, and saxophonist, using Endo as occasional relief man. Endo changed his name to Arito, honoring his dead father, and Keo called his new quintet Hana Hou! One More Time! They opened at the Swing Club, to standing room only. Apart from the band, Keo and Endo practised daily, Keo watching him struggle for precision, but hearing mostly infinite regress.

HONOLULU

Sheltered Harbor

HONOLULU, 1956

AZURE PEAKS OF HOME, INEFFABLE AND TENDER. AIR A BALM. *Folks carry luggage down gangplanks where small herds of families wave from the docks, chattering like monkeys. She stands still, observing. Just now, it is all she has strength for. She limps slightly, leaning on a cane, her pace so measured, she seems not so much a woman passing as a shadow following the cane's progress. There is about her a serenity, the otherworldliness of one who lives with constant pain.*

She stares out at the harbor, the waves going makai *and* makai *and* makai. *She gazes inland at the Ko'olaus in the distance, with the blank detachment of one who is not sure where she is, or, knowing where she is, is not sure it matters. That anything matters. Except that, breathing in soft, floral scents, something frenzied tumbles down. Echo of innocence, youth, bright random laughter.*

She carries her solitary suitcase down the dock, crosses a street, and sits on a bench. Seventeen years. She cannot comprehend the changes. So many tourists, blistered and peeling, like refugees from torched cities. Tall, parched buildings inching their way up to the light, like strange gigantic growths trying to connect. Yet somewhere, she knows, in dark humid valleys, in moist green groves, things remain primordial. Somewhere things still drip and sprout from mist and mold. She smells it in dank soil, in water-haunted air. There is so much wet, sunlight will always be defeated. This mildly excites her.

After the tunnels of Rabaul, all that was left of her was thirst. Through weeks of quarantine, all she wanted was water. Then priests came with Holy Water, asking for confessions. She confessed her sin—surviving—grabbed a vial of Holy Water and drank it down.

Crowds slowly pass, men glance fleetingly at her. She looks down, terrified. As if they will swallow her raw heart. Even now, she still feels sacrificial. Something to be sacrificed. When men pass too close, her spine hums, a string of little skulls bite down. She moans and people move away.

Somewhere in the long-lost past a U.S. Army officer, an interrogator, had asked her to talk about Rabaul, and what was done to them. He was white, well fed. He had spent the war behind a desk. She told what she could bear to tell, and when she finished, the man quietly suggested that P-girls had been too passive, too accepting. Sunny shook with rage.

"We were never meek, or passive! We were women with bamboo sticks. They were soldiers with machine guns."

She never spoke of it again. After that, she was still. She was no one. Between that past and the present, a crevice opened, she stepped in. Now life is no longer living. Time is no longer time.

Some days it's possible to recover for an hour. Part the curtains at the window. Anoint arthritic knobs with oils. Indulge in the harmless ecstasy of root of morning-glory tea. Or ʻawa*, the tea for curing grief, which she takes in measured sips. For several years now, days when she is strong enough, she has walked to the ocean wherever she is, slowly submerging herself, letting the sea sluice its way through her mortal threads. Sometimes intelligence of that great, wet mind addresses her.*

"E hulihuli hoʻi mai." *Turn around, come back.*

At such times, for fleeting moments, she is whole. She curls up like a child and thinks of home, archipelago of her beginnings. For an instant, she believes what doctors said.

"The worst is over."

Yet even as they said that, women had shed infected organs, shed gangrened fingers and toes. She gave up her womb. The hearts of some girls, grown huge in their emaciation, had burst, like overgrown babies bursting from cribs.

"The worst is over."

The human heart does not have bones.

Now she sits in Honolulu, wondering what she is doing here. What is the point. She sits for hours, wondering if she will just die here on a bench. Some wet intelligence had said "come home." Now she waits for further instructions. A paper on the bench beside her flutters. STATEHOOD: THOUSANDS MASS IN FAVOR. *The words mean nothing. She has done away with printed words. Books, newspapers, are to her like medieval documents, belonging to a world long past.*

She dozes, imagines she is a figure embroidered on an old kimono that has been sewn the ancient way, with the splintered breastbone of a crane. On the ship headed home to Honolulu, she dreamed she was part of someone else's dream, in which she was inching, like slow embroidery, toward a place from which all would be understood. She wakes sitting on this bench, in this sheltered harbor, Honolulu.

She stands, picks up her suitcase, her lips moving slowly. She always practises before she speaks.

"How much is a comb? A slip? How far is the clinic?"

Because she looks old and frail, folks assume she's deaf, and answer her by yelling back. Their words like bullets. All that shelters her from other humans is her skin. She flags a cab, and then a bus. They pass as if she is transparent. She walks with her head truantly bent, so thin that sunlight seems to knock her sideways. She finds herself in Chinatown, the lobby of Jade Hare Hotel, its furnishings neat but maculate and greasy. In a bleak, monastic room she opens creaking shutters.

It is almost twilight, time of heavy draperies an unseen hand will draw out of the depths of the east. Day is always repulsive to her—the knife of waking, the chasm of high noon, hours repeating and repeating like broken glass. She prefers night, a dark promontory where she stands calling out to armies of dead women.

Yet sometimes at dusk she becomes ill. Twilight excites madmen. The hour when they appeared at the Quonset huts in droves. Now she lies down, walled by the lunar green of jade hares. Her spine hums and buzzes, the tiny skulls a chorus. The past curls in and out of her, she drifts. Girls starving, strung up by their ankles. Girls shot for sport. Breasts lopped off. A grenade shoved into a vagina.

She remembers that even as Allies advanced on Rabaul, even as he dragged her to the tunnels, that honeycomb of nightmares, Matsuharu promised, "All will pass. This will be a dream, not dreamed."

. . . And in the tunnels of red clay, he finally took her, opened her like a tired eye. He wasn't harsh or brutal, by then she didn't exist for him. Nothing existed. He passed right through her. Only his sword existed, always near, gleaming in the background. Matsuharu mistook her terror for passion, and matched her, insanely riding her day and night, trying to kill both of them with exhaustion.

She grew used to him. Ceased to flinch or feel defiled. She only dreamed of killing him.

Sometimes he went away, deeper into the tunnels, into larger, more elaborate clay chambers reinforced with sandbags, walls lined with parachute silk, where demented officers gathered, drunk on sake, planning their suicides. For days she lay in dimness in a chamber like a red clay cell. Hearing cries of hunger. The smell of fungus.

Up and down zigzag passages, the smell of air exhausted from gas lamps, cooking stoves, human waste. Air exhausted from smoke-filled ducts. Gas leaked regularly in the caves, soldiers and P-girls were asphyxiated, blown up. Matsuharu brought her delicacies, grilled rat from the officers' quarters where they ate by generator-powered lights. Where they watched films, read poetry like scholars. Where they prepared for seppuku . . .

In that subterranean nightmare there were hospital chambers, kitchen chambers, barracklike chambers holding thousands of men. Chambers the size of playing fields for tanks, planes, antiaircraft guns. Chambers for P-girls, for latrines. Even temporary graveyards. When chambers of the dead grew full, they buried them upright in fetuslike positions along tunnel walls, covering them with clay or wattle. When waste jars were exhausted, full of excrement and plugged, people began to squat, dig holes with their hands, kick clay over their filth like animals.

Allied bombings increased, tunnel sections collapsed, soldiers and women buried alive. Incessant bombing overhead rained down debris that slowly blocked their air vents. People began to suffocate in droves. And in underground dampness, the drawn-out triumph of infection. P-girls died and died. . . .

He always returned, taking her like a madman, drunk on sake or drugs. But in times of fever, when she begged him to kill her, Do it, with the sword! he nursed her, fed her, shot her with stolen morphine.

One night he planted his seed in her. A warped thing, budding and tenacious. He went away again. There was no keeping track of time, they lived by oil lamps, matches, body rhythms. Months passed, maybe years? She thought she was dying, bloated with rot. Then something fell out of her, half formed, soft-skulled and blind. She spat upon it, then held it close.

"Anahola? Little Anahola."

When Matsuharu saw her stomach flat, he lifted filthy mats, looking for their child. She held her hands out, as if from deep within the muddy seams and creases, he could retrieve the infant's breath. She wiped her neck, waiting for the sword. He sat down and studied her.

"Moriko"—for that was the Japanese name he had given her—"perhaps you did not smother our child? Perhaps it is lost in a tunnel, taking its first steps alone."

She lunged at him. "You are insane!"

"It was our child. *Born of love. Of passion." His body shook constantly. His eyes no longer focused.*

"Why would you want a child? For sport?" She gestured to his sword, its shining tip. "It wasn't human. It was something else. Why don't you kill me now? I am so tired."

With great effort to be calm, he put his arms round her. "Take me to our child. Then, we shall sleep. Everything will be a dream."

Grateful that she would finally be allowed to die, she showed him the place along the tunnel wall. With bare hands, once again she clawed hard clay, sharp splinters ripping her fingers, until she unearthed the child-sized niche. It stood in its grave wrapped in filthy cloth, a little icon.

Matsuharu unwrapped the thing and held it to his chest, laughing and weeping, seeing it as dear and perfect, except for blind eyes, unformed limbs, a soft, pepper-shaped head. He returned it gently to its niche, repacked the clay, pressed his lips against the wall. Then he took Sunny's arm like a cavalier, walking her back to their chamber. He laid her down. She waited. The chamber seemed to wait. . . .

He moved inside her on the filthy mat, laughing without sound. When he finished he collapsed, exhausted. She took his sword, rattling out of its scabbard. She wanted so badly to be dead. She didn't have the strength to lift it. In the distance, up and down zigzag tunnels, echoes of mercy killings. Suicides. Allied forces pressing in . . .

Something stank, a new, heavy foulness, numbing her, turning her matchstick limbs to stone. Soldiers crawled past their chamber, rags soaked in urine pressed against their noses. Bombs had hit a pipe, gas was flooding the tunnels. Their shouts awakened Matsuharu. He had the strength to draw her close, making her breathe very slowly, sucking in air remaining in a shallow layer on the floor beneath the creeping gas.

"Death will be slow"—his voice was very far away—". . . asphyxiation."

Far in the distance, she heard men retching. Then there was only the stinking blackness of damp clay. . . .

By the time Allies penetrated the deepest tunnels, moving inch by cautious inch—setting off mines, chain explosions—they were both unconscious. A Papuan native in a fruit-dyed sarong, wearing a gas mask, tapped her shoulder with a spear. An Australian soldier in a mask waved a rifle.

"Bloody 'ell! Is she alive? She don't look human. Hey, you speakee English?"

Just bones and bound dust, so scabbed and filthy she was black. She crossed over then, from death to life, stumbling down passages whose clay walls were deeply licked with bayonets. MOTHER, *I* AM HUNGRY. MOTHER, PRAY FOR ME. *I* DIED WITH HONOR FOR THE EMPEROR. *Epitaphs for silent sons. Some chambers had become starvation rooms. Defecation rooms. A room of gnawed corpses with human teeth marks. Australian soldiers removed their masks, leaned against the walls, and puked.*

They inched along for miles, negotiating that fetid vastness at a snail's pace—native guides, Allied soldiers carrying rags of half-dead girls. Behind them, more soldiers prodding Japs with bayonets. When she could no longer walk, a native lifted her, not even flexing his muscles. She would always remember his healthy panther smell, sweat on kinky hair standing up like pearls, a diadem dripping down her shoulders. . . .

For hours, tunnels wound and climbed and circled, like cure-chants repeated and repeated. Then she felt wind, the sacrament of air. Then broken poles of moonlight. Magnificent and ruined stars. When she woke—sky red, runny in the east—rubber-gloved hands were cutting her lice-ridden hair. Masked nurses scraping at scabbed flesh. Masked doctors inspecting their microbes, their parasites. As if they were cattle.

X rays, injections, vaccinations. Periods of numbness, then violence, rage. Because she had lived enough. Because she wanted it over, and they would not listen. One day someone handed her a mirror. Eyes lashless, teeth decayed. Her facial bones like glowing knobs breaking yellow parchment. Childlike arms peppered with syringe marks. Bruises as if she'd been slapped. Her wrists red rings, a trace of straps. They had had to restrain her. They could not understand why grief was flooding out in madness. Stabbings in the wards. Suicides.

"One day," a doctor promised, "the scars will heal. You will forget."

Why did they think she wanted to forget? That any P-girl wanted to forget?

Afterwards, after what doctors called "recovery," all she learned was this. It was all the same. Only different faces. Now it was occupying forces of Allied troops who needed dance halls, nightclubs, sex. . . .

SHE HAS BEEN IN HONOLULU SEVERAL WEEKS. NOW SHE SITS IN *'A'ala Park, just west of downtown Honolulu.*

"You see, Lili, in our islands, trees are filled with Pidgin-speaking birds. We call them mynahs."

She listens with the stillness of the blind. Even folks who speak English here speak with a soft, quick Pidgin mouth. It is so comforting, she smiles, then squints against the red-hot shock of flowers.

"This is torch ginger, Lili. And this, hibiscus."

Seventeen years. She feels in her body's slightest adumbrations, its slimmest quakings, a lying back, melting recognition.

She looks down at her hands. They used to carry books, and touch the shoulders of young men. She knows they are her hands because they're attached to the ends of her arms. But she suddenly knows nothing about them, what they've done, what they've touched. She can't understand how they've grown so veined and liverish, how life has wrecked them so. For a minute she's amnesiac, marooned. Then she touches her cane, sees on her feet ugly orthopedic shoes, sees how folks look at her. She remembers who she is, and what she is.

She lifts her head, smells the air, explaining to her sister, "That is smoke of hulihuli *chicken from a barbecue stand. And there, brooding in the heights, are the majestic Ko'olaus."*

And just behind her, behind Iwilei, is the sea, a view beautiful to the verge of tears. Here is a place where, if one were ready, life could come clean. All around are promises, consolation. Children kneeling, laughing, playing ini quatro. *Flower women stringing leis. Delicate old Chinese and Japanese ladies sitting in warm sororities of chatter. Husky, dark construction men with metal hats eating* bento *lunches, white tusks jutting out from their lips in laughter.*

"And, Lili, do you hear women talking in Hawai'ian Mother Tongue? The language I thought in, and slept in as a child, the tongue of half my genealogy."

Now, trying to remember, she has to search for ordinary words. Grandmother . . . tūtū. *Mother . . .* makuahine. *Teacher . . . she cannot remember. Talking with her sister makes her think of family she no longer has. Sometimes at night she stands outside her father's house up in Alewa Heights.*

"Mama. I am tired. Papa. Now I understand. Let me sit and talk with you. O, take me in."

She sees them through the windows, orphaned by their children. She sees how gently her father touches her mother. How tenderly he combs her hair. Grief has made him human. Like her, they have grown frail and old. Seeing her would strike them dead.

ONE DAY NEAR DOWNTOWN HONOLULU SHE SEES FOLKS PARADING, *a kind of demonstration. She moves closer. Hundreds are marching and shouting. She does not see their banners:* STATEHOOD FOR HAWAI'I. *Fear, instinct, go beyond logic. She imagines these crowds marching to throw her out of Honolulu. To keep her out. They know what she is, what she has been. Know her unspeakable, foul, and filthy past.*

Soon police will come and shackle her. She stands rooted to the spot. Then, terrified, she turns away before they can catch her, whacking leaves and bushes with her cane, limping so fast, she stumbles. A woman broken into many women. After a while she slows down, breathless. No one has followed her. She leans against a doorway, wiping her face with a handkerchief, wiping perspiration from the knob of her cane.

Looking up, she sees, but does not see, a poster on a wall. She wipes her face again. Then it seems the poster looks *at her, it draws her eyes. Sweat streams from his cheeks down the sides of his neck. A spotlight doubles the depth of the surface of his mahogany skin, so that his face, his hands, even his shining trumpet leap at her. She reaches out, touching the face. Her hand seems to pass through his face and through the poster, through the doorway and the wall, stretching back and back into the vapors of the past.*

"Keo."

His name moves softly through her, reminding her of innocence, ordinary riches. Life still unprobed, unknown.

She studies the poster again. The shape of the body, the bend of dark arms. A memory of nights when he sat in a canoe, blasting his trumpet at the sea like a madman, not knowing she watched him. She leans her head against the wall, remembering a sea flight of dolphins rising and rising, bodies shimmering with salty jewels. Keo standing and playing for them. The blistering sound of longing. She remembers the dolphins attentive as humans uplifted by his horn.

FOR WEEKS SHE PASSES BACK AND FORTH ACROSS THE STREET. *She watches humans exit and enter, hearing their laughter. It has been so many years, she wonders what it is like to laugh out loud. How does one stop? One night she enters the Swing Club when it is very late and crowded. Braving the sargasso of bodies, she finds a place against the wall.*

Glancing at her, half amused, folks see an old woman in cardigan and leather tie-shoes. Someone of pedantic cleanliness. Gray hair cut in a short pageboy, eyes bespectacled, pupils magnified. Perhaps a once-lovely face—impeccable shape of chin and cheekbones—now ravaged by wrinkles, scars, exploded veins. Lips set in a sideways smile of paralytic contour.

In the dimness, a waiter offers a chair. She shakes her head, wanting to be a featureless, standing shape. At first she is numbed by the onslaught to her senses—distillate of rum, tobacco, tropical colognes. The caustic sweat of humans, the crowd's feverish anticipation. But she has learned to shut everything out, to be invisible and observe.

She does not faint when he appears. Her breathing does not change. And when he starts to play she is not nauseous with remembering. She shuts her eyes, flipping backward through the years. Life stacked before her as a folio. She does not grieve. She merely looks with wonder. She goes away and comes another night, returning and returning, always very late. And always she stands against the wall.

Sometimes she does not come for weeks. Sometimes Keo changes clubs. But Honolulu is a small town, and always she finds him. Some nights when he soloes, kicking off his shoes, he stands at the edge of a stage leaning into the audience, discerning shapes of heads at the back of the room. Occasionally in the dark, their eyes meet but never seize. His glance passes, his horn blazes on, adding little styptic touches when the group joins in, threatening to overdo things, go commercial or sentimental. From their names, she knows the drum man is Filipino, bass and piano men Hawai'ian-Portuguese. The strange-hued relief saxophonist is, by his name, Arito, Japanese.

Listening, she still hears that sorrowing in Keo, always threatening to engulf him, a fiery grieving from his horn. Some nights his blowing is the execution of secret demons, each one of whom is valiantly resisting. He charms them, disembowels them, or lulls them into acquiescent ballads. His body folding round his horn, boneless as a glove.

She sees he's still dapper and fit, but somewhere he has been used up. She hears in his music that he has peaked. Yet he is still possessed of excellence, for when he plays, he imitates no one, no one else's sound.

Sometimes she wants to shout, "Slow down. Slow down."

She remembers a man named Dew Baptiste, remembers how he once explained jazz. It was not calligraphy, the essence of which was speed. Jazz was about loitering. It was about soloing and journeying and coming home, embracing echoes of other horns and drums and strings and keys, so that audiences had the impression of being inside a great timepiece swung on a chain across the monumental girth of some dark god, and inside that timepiece were wheels that ratcheted and shrieked and purred at different rates though they were all related, all working to a common purpose, to touch the core of a human soul.

Sometimes she feels a resurrection, feels heard by Keo's trumpet, as though it understands and sings out all she cannot tell. If she remains, if she stays in this town long enough, maybe it will sing out everything. She will be purged, she will forget. But scars have an ingenuity all their own. When she looks round the city, she sees crowds of tourists, military. There are still too many men. Which always starts the humming in her spine, the little skulls biting down. For a while she avoids the jazz clubs, retreats to her bleak hotel room, wondering why she remains. There is nothing for her here. Nothing for her anywhere. Who she was is dead.

She begins to feel stalked, feels something shambling after her. A slow invisible thing that, once let loose, will have its way. She becomes breathless. Something swallows her oxygen, her every gasp, something gnaws her throbbing cells. She rakes her nails down skinny arms, whispers to her sister.

"Lili, I'm afraid."

Each morning, she looks at the depression in her pillow to see if it has filled with brains. She waits for Satan, for his footstep. For surely he is in this town.

She will leave this place. Each lane, each street reminds her of what she was, what she lost. What clearly happened to her. Whatever called her back is not strong enough to hold her. She packs her solitary suitcase, goes to hear Keo one last time. In a future stained with fevers, medications, he will be her balm, her indoor sea.

That night his playing is off. His lip is festering, he broods in the shadows. Perhaps it's the crowd, the smoke, the lighting, that turns her attention to the relief man on saxophone. His performance is usually mediocre. When he stands to play, Sunny always concentrates on his fingers on the keys, the blue bluntness of their tips. She has never quite discerned his features. Light bouncing off his jacaranda skin always leaves a glare, blurring his face.

But now, as he segues into "I Wished on the Moon," head bouncing up and down, the spotlight catches in his ear, locked in a blue puzzle of cartilage. He turns in profile. She moves closer to the stage. A nerve vibrates at the juncture of his neck and jaw, with the flapping motion of a frog's gullet. A nerve that pulsed before her eye all the months of red-clay nights he forced himself inside her. Riding her, and riding her. She turns, stumbles outside. She bends and vomits on her cane.

She moves down dehydrated streets, all her little skulls a-chatter, making her spinal cord snap and curl. In the glow of jade hare walls, she sits shuddering so violently her chair advances across the room. She wads tissue in her mouth, so chattering teeth won't break in bits. She buries her face and screams. After a time, she lifts her head and smooths her hair. She straightens her dress and cardigan. She reaches for her suitcase and slowly, meticulously, unpacks.

KA ʻUMEKE KĀʻEO

The Gourd Is Full, and So the Mind

IN HER SMALL SHOP OFF MERCHANT STREET, MALIA FITTED A dress on a middle-aged redhead wearing emeralds. Fifteen years ago, she had changed this woman's sheets at the Moana Hotel.

I cut Schiaparelli labels from your dresses. I stole your Guerlain perfume.

The woman studied her reflection in a mirror, then smiled with equine teeth and wrote a check, complimenting Malia on her shop.

Alone, Malia sat at her Singer, furious, whipping the motor into a frenzy so the needle snapped, chewing up good linen. Different hairdo, a few pounds less, but Malia looked exactly as she had fifteen years earlier.

She didn't recognize me. Because I'm not in uniform! Doesn't know she wears dresses made by hands that scrubbed her toilet.

Eventually she calmed down, soothed by the knowledge that within each hem, each dart, each shoulder pad of the woman's dress—of every dress she sewed for tourists—were scribbled curses, little war cries. "*E Poko ke Ola.*" May your life be short. "*Hoʻopī ka ʻAmo.*" May your anus snort and sputter. "*E Hele ʻEku ʻEku.*" Go and root as a pig.

They had appeared like little phantoms. One day the Singer took off on its own, the needle stitching madly while she watched. Malia had jumped back, the machine suddenly so hot it smoked. Its black enameled body gleamed. She thought of Pono, whose fingerprints still roamed the Singer, whose perspiration oiled its joints and screws. She felt her presence in the jerky dance of thread spools, the needle spitting oaths from Pono's brain.

Through the years, Malia's designs had become remarkable, clothes upon which folks remarked. She drew patterns with calligraphic speed, cut without measuring, sewed without basting. Her signature welted seams gave clothes a richer look. She perfected the cabana set, matching bathing trunks and shirts for men. Headscarves converting to halter tops for women. She created the pocket bra for falsies. Pocket panties for sachets. But she preferred dresses, jackets, anything with darts and hems where little curses were inscribed.

One night Malia sat cutting up old kimonos for cummerbunds and vests. Her scissors rasped and snipped, and something tapped her rib cage. Something caught her eye. A design in an antique kimono hanging in the window, an embroidered figure—an old woman with a cane. The eyes seemed to step out at her, the face gripped her, eerily familiar. She stood, stroking the kimono, trying to remember where it came from, and why the figure haunted her.

She turned up the radio, hearing the broadcast from the Reef Hotel. Johnny Almeida, blind mandolinist, singing "Pua Sadinia." Gardenia flower. Then Lena Machado, that old Hawai'ian songbird. Malia shook her head, wishing Keo would see how jazz was dying in the islands, something called rock and roll was moving in. She wanted to tell him that maybe it was time to turn around, come back, play music of his people.

She saw how his face softened when he heard ancient, haunting chants accompanied by gourds and clack-sticks. Or even when he heard folk music of 'ukulele, slack-key guitar. But each time she discussed it with him, she understood jazz was for him like breathing. To give it up would be to die.

"It would be," he said, "like burying the memory of Sunny Sung."

Hearing that, Malia almost slapped him.

"You know, for years I thought of you as a pure artist, not much caring for the things of the world. Now I see you don't much care for people either."

Keo looked at her, shocked. "What do you mean?"

"I mean, you're selfish. You dream of finding Sunny because you need her in order to be happy. It's still about *you.* What about Mama and Papa? What about DeSoto? He's got a wife and kids now. You never ask about them. Never lift your head and look around."

"That's not true," Keo argued. "I love all of you. I worry about you plenty."

Her words were venomed. "No. You worry about you. You drag your grief round like a sickness, letting it bleed from your horn. We *all* suffered in the war. Everyone has scars."

That night he studied his parents. "Mama? Papa? You OK?"

Timoteo nodded. "Yeah, son. Everyt'ing pretty good. How's about you?"

Leilani sighed. "He need find one wife. Been too long alone."

"Brother misses Sunny Sung. You folks know that." Feeling guilty, Malia continued, "You know, today I thought of Pono. She's got *mana pālua,* double mana. Folks say she's part *kahuna.* Keo, maybe she could tell you what happened to Sunny."

Leilani shook her head. "Maybe she look him to death, dat's what. No fool round wit' dis *wahine.*"

Next day, Malia walked through fields and lanes to Pono's, and discovered she was gone. Neighbors said there had been tragedy. All four daughters had deserted her, running off with strangers. She had moved to the Big Island where the *ma'i pākē* man, father of those girls, had left her a broken-down coffee plantation.

SHE TOOK A STEAMER TO THE BIG ISLAND, AND BEFORE THEY sighted land, her nostrils burned with vog—volcanic ash and fog. This was the island of seething volcanoes, of moody Pele, volcano goddess, whose boiling exhalations consumed forests, entire villages. Malia traveled up into misty mountains through little coffee-smelling towns—Holualoa, Kainali'u, Kealakekua—surrounded by miles of lush coffee-cherry trees. In the town of Captain Cook she asked for the woman named Pono. Folks stepped back, then pointed down Napo'opo'o Road, leading to a hidden driveway, a big white haunted-looking house.

She stood on the lawn, feeling the house look back at her. A peacock spread its shimmering tail and sobbed. Then a little bandy-legged woman with snaggled teeth came out onto the *lānai.* "Yeah. Whatchoo want?"

She hesitated. "Do you know the woman named . . . Pono?"

She bent over laughing. "Oooh, funny dat. I stand all day in kitchen, cleaning *pilau* fish fo' her. Scraping bloody pig cheeks. Cooking, scrubbing just fo' her. Why? She save my life. Pono like my *tita.*" She looked Malia up and down. "My name Run Run. What you want wit' Pono?"

"It's . . . personal."

She put her hands on her hips, squinting like a sharpshooter. "Well, I da 'personnel directah' here. You got message? I da message-man!"

"My name is Malia Meahuna. Pono taught me how to sew. . . ."

Run Run studied her, then pointed to the front steps. "Sit. Wait."

Malia sat on steps so worn they were scalloped and toe-printed. She seemed to doze. Then she felt all the air of the fields sucked onto that porch behind her. She felt wind on her shoulders like hot hands. She was afraid to turn, knowing that tree of a woman stood there smelling of eucalyptus, earth, and ocean. She heard Pono magisterially lower herself into a great, deep chair. She heard her sigh.

When Malia finally turned, she saw the familiar perfect face, golden-skinned and full-lipped, hair slick as lava braided down her back. She had changed somewhat. Black, slanted eyes now seemed to hold more pain and more intelligence than one human should possess. Yet she was still beautiful in the voluptuous, exhausted way of women who have done everything to survive.

The slight suggestion of a smile. "How are you, Malia? Do you still have airs?"

She laughed softly. "Yes. I'm still guilty of daring beyond my means."

"One *must* dare. Or live in imitation. And, you are well?"

"Very well. Designing clothes, and prospering."

She climbed the steps, presenting Pono with a soft, square package, wrapped in delicate rice paper, within which was an old and beautiful kimono.

"This comes with much *aloha.* I have often thought of you."

"And your child? How is she?"

"... Baby Jonah. She's beautiful. Twelve years old now."

Pono gazed into the distance. "The father has become a lawyer. He knows the child is his. Their features are identical."

Malia's legs began to shake.

"The man is haunted. He has only ever loved one woman. But he is dark, and you are proud. You still imitate the *haole*. In time you will be disgusted into wisdom. You will un-*haole*-fy your dreams."

She turned back to Malia. "Now, enough of you. Your brother Keo—each night he crosses a bridge of nine windings."

Malia nodded. "Someone he can't forget. He's searched and searched. Pono, can you tell me? Is the girl alive?"

Pono ceremoniously sat back. Her eyes snapped shut, and she was still. Then her lips moved rapidly, calling up a face. Her intake of breath was a roar.

"Sun-ja Uanoe Sung. The wild thread weaving through the tapestry. He has lost the design."

"I would do anything you ask if you could help him," Malia whispered. "He's still so lost without her."

Pono rocked, as if in prayer. Her arms ran with sweat, her breathing extremely labored. Her moans were knives scarring the soft, pale belly of the day. When she opened her eyes, they were white marble. Malia gasped. The marble slowly veined, bled into tan, then brown, then black as the red-black heart of *aku*.

What Pono saw so appalled her, she spoke with caution. "Sometimes we do not understand the implications of the search."

"What does that mean? Is she alive?"

She lied because she had to. "Nothing is clear."

"Then she is dead."

Pono shook her head. "She is somewhere . . . confessing."

"What should Keo do? What should I tell him?"

"Continue searching."

"But, how? Where?"

"In his music. It will keep his playing pure."

Malia felt as if she'd run a mile. She was utterly exhausted. "Will you let me come again? One day you might see Sunny in a vision. Hope will keep my brother sane."

Pono nodded thoughtfully. "One day, when the vision holds, I will send for you."

THE WOMAN STOOD AMONG CUSTOMERS, QUIETLY SURVEYING Malia's shop. Expensive rug, walls covered with *kapa*. Handsome *koa* chairs with wide armrests. Gilt-edge mirrors, potted palms. A small shop, but each thing understated, tasteful. Even the dressmaker's dummies wore elegant robes. She studied bolts of fabric until the customers left. Then, almost casually, she turned to Malia.

The woman's face was lovely, eyes dark, a little slanted, lips slightly full. She was not slender but rather what folks called voluptuous, wearing a simple linen dress, spectator heels of good leather. Malia could have been looking at her own reflection, except that the woman was white.

"My name is Vivian," she said. "I'm Krash's wife."

Instinctively, Malia backed away.

"I came to tell you I'm leaving him. You can have him."

"What? How dare you . . ."

She sat down slowly, hugging herself. "Take him, please. He's still in love with you."

Malia shook her head, frightened. "I don't *want* him."

"Yes. You do. You've got his ribs. That is so . . . primitive. I don't understand you people."

"How could you understand us?" Malia's whole body shook. "Understanding has to be *earned*."

Vivian nodded, looked about helplessly. "I knew I got him on the rebound after you. But he was so handsome, so ambitious. Seven years. Now I realize I never knew him. Never had a clue."

"What did you expect?" Malia asked. "Someone predictable? A man you could control?"

She shook her head. "Krash is smart, he could go places. But he only wants to succeed *here*, in Honolulu!"

Malia stood straighter, her English accent a little more pronounced. "Yes. We speak English here, we even practise law. Did you think he would give up his identity? Live on the mainland as a change-face?"

Vivian sat up, half defiant. "My father has connections, he would have helped set him up in practise."

Folding her arms, Malia exhaled, almost sorry for this Vivian. She seemed decent, even a little tragic. Then she remembered Krash had slept with her for seven years, his lips had been all over her. She suddenly wanted to strike her, suck out her eyes.

"I know I'm ignorant about your culture," Vivian said. "I'm just not meant for the islands. Your local talk. The food you eat. I have no friends. All his friends talk about is *'āina, 'āina.*"

"Land is what Hawai'ians are about."

"But, you're not forward-thinking. Don't you see? You people can't waste precious land on farming, planting taro. You need developments. Hotels. That's what progress is."

"Hotels! So my nephews can be busboys?" Malia turned away, afraid she would hurt the woman. "Please. Get out of here."

Vivian slowly stood. "I've followed you down streets, wondering what you have that I don't have. Maybe it's pride. I never had to struggle."

Malia turned back and stared at her, her voice growing soft, almost weary. "You privileged women, so naive. Struggle doesn't teach you pride. It teaches you to *take what comes.*"

She stretched her arms out, turning them. Tattooed and pitted from too-strong disinfectants—her years as chambermaid. She held her hands up closer. Palms and fingertips deeply trenched, crisscrossed and bunched with needle scars.

"Would you have pride in *these*? Would you want to even look at them?"

She looked, then her eyes met Malia's. "He doesn't want you for your hands. He loves *you.*" She pointed at their reflection in a mirror, their resemblance remarkable. "Why do you think he married me?"

"Please, leave," Malia insisted. "I don't want any part of this."

"You are part of it. You're *all* of it. I'm going back where I belong." In the doorway, Vivian turned to her. "You know, it's your child I think about."

Watching her walk down the street, Malia felt numb. She swallowed slowly, calling forth familiar things. There was her throat, and there was her tongue. Then someone moved behind her, Keo, bringing lunch through the back entrance.

He didn't skirt the edges, didn't negotiate. "I heard everything."

She set out plates and napkins. "Good. Then we can eat."

They sat on folding chairs, chopsticks waving like antennae. The sushi and pickled ginger tasted like chalk.

"When are you going to tell her?"

"Tell her what?"

"Who her father is."

She threw her lunch into the trash. "Imagine that hillbilly coming to my shop. Telling me her problems."

"Even a stranger is sorry for your kid. Malia, do you think anyone believes she's Rosie's girl? That she's *hānai*? She looks so much like you and Krash it's tragic. It's a joke."

"That bastard. How *dare* he bring a white wife back to Honolulu."

Keo laughed. "You threw him away. You *denied* him his child."

"She's not his child."

He stared at her. "Whose is she, then?"

"How do I know! It was the war. I had to support Mama and Papa, while you and Desoto were off having your adventures."

"What are you saying?"

"I'm saying we made choices." Her voice turned bitter. "You chose Paris. I chose . . . Hotel Street. And all that that implies."

Keo slowly stood, and took her in his arms. "My God. I never stopped to think what you had to do to keep things going."

She hung her head, then pulled away. "I had dreams. Remember? I would have given anything to live in Paris, like you. Then Pearl Harbor came, and everything got crazy. Don't ask me any more."

He sat down, not letting go of her hand. "I will always honor you. Because of you our parents never had to beg. But don't tell me Baby Jonah isn't Krash's kid. You thought you were too good for him."

Malia sat down beside him, trying to be honest. "Keo, I always felt he was lying in ambush. Him and his cousins from Wai'anae. Real low-class country jacks. Crime. Welfare. If I had stayed with him, I would have ended up out there."

"You loved him. Your letters were full of him."

"Having a child does that. I softened. I thought I would take whatever he offered. Then, he came home full of plans. Degrees. Law school. He never mentioned where I fit in."

Keo sighed. "He wanted to marry you, I swear. He wanted to take you to the mainland as his wife."

"He never asked. Ah, well . . ."

She was over forty now, still firm and lovely, still so possessed of Hawai'ian grace—a fluidness in gestures, in her movements—she could have had almost any man, of any color. But now she had the confidence of moderate success; she had achieved that alone, without compromise or loss of pride.

". . . now I'm too busy for such foolishness."

Keo shook his head. "I'll tell you what happened. You realized after all was said and done, you love a man with brown skin. You've watched Baby Jonah grow, and every day you look at her, you see her father's features. Everybody knows but her. And maybe even her."

"What do you mean?"

"I mean even though she calls you *tita*, sister, she says it with sarcasm. Malia, what are you doing to this girl?"

She rubbed her forehead, weary. "Trying to save her. Don't you see, if I admit I'm her mother, then I have to tell her who her father is."

"You would wreck a young girl's life out of vanity? You already stole twelve years from her." He stood, looking down at her. "You make me feel real shame, Malia. If you don't tell her . . . one day I will. *Everything*."

ONE MORNING IN HER SHOP, PINNING A DRESS ON BABY JO, Malia saw slight swelling, the beginning of breasts.

"You're getting buds," she said softly.

The girl blushed so deeply, Malia felt her heat. Breathing in her young-girl sweat, fragrant hair, luminous shoulders smelling like damp ginger, she sat back in shock. *This child is the one thing I will never regret.* She wanted to tell her then, begin to tell her, who she was, who she came from. But the habit of not telling was too fixed between them.

Does she know? Malia wondered. *Does she hate me?* Sometimes she felt all she really knew of this girl was her dress size. Her chest and waist measurements. She rarely confided in Malia.

"You should talk more," Malia said. "Ask me more important things."

Baby Jo turned away. Her thoughts were not Malia's to claim.

Even when they sat alone at the kitchen table, she looked away from Malia, focusing on something safe. She chewed as slowly as possible, knowing she wasn't expected to talk with her mouth full.

Sometimes Malia ambushed her in the bathroom, or the garage. "How is school?"

"OK . . . boring."

"It isn't boring if you use your brain."

"What you t'ink I use? My feet?"

It was sarcastic, but Malia laughed. Baby Jo backed away, thinking she was laughing at her.

One day she stood beside Malia, listening to the metal gasp and snip of pinking shears.

"How's come Uncle Papa get nightmares?" She had heard Keo crying out in his sleep.

"The war," Malia said softly. "A girl he loved disappeared."

"She died?"

"Not sure. Don't know what really happened."

Baby Jo turned slowly, looked her in the eye. "Not knowing truth give plenny heartache. Yeah?"

Malia wanted to shake her then. Tell her she should be grateful for having been born, for Malia hiding her in her stomach, for bearing her at all. Theirs was a silent, cadenced dance where they carefully skirted each other, most tense when they actually touched. She seldom entered the girl's room. She couldn't remember Baby Jo ever entering hers. Sometimes she pretended to talk on the phone in the hallway, just so she could watch Jo in her little room moving amongst her things, watch how delicately she touched them.

Now and then she stood in that room, hearing her daughter's soft inhalations. She picked up snapshots, touched her clothes, her talismans. Just now she was in the chubby stage, her features extra round. But she was growing into a beautiful girl, pale but clearly Hawai'ian in her big bone structure, large *kanaka* hands and feet. And she was especially smart. Except round Malia, where she became clumsy and sullen, retreating into chop-suey Pidgin: Hawai'ian and "Portagee" Pidgin mixed with Flip and *Pākē* Pidgin, so at times she was almost incomprehensible to Malia. Everything was *da kine, da kine. W'addat? W'addat?*

Watching Baby Jo fawn over Keo while ignoring her, Malia began to bully her, force her into conversation.

"Any of your girlfriends going out with boys?"

Baby Jo tensed. ". . . Two. Mebbe."

"Any of them menstruating yet?"

The girl cringed, mortified.

"Soon happen to you, Jo."

"Ugh. Mo' bettah I been born one boy."

"Boys are what you have to stay away from now."

"Fo' why?"

"That's how you make a baby, lying with a boy. By and by I will explain it."

She leveled her eyes at Malia. "What you t'ink, '*tita*'? You t'ink I don' know nutting? One boy wen *da kine* one girl wit' his *da kine*. And, dat what make one baby!"

"Speak English!" Malia shouted.

"Fo' why?" Baby Jo cried. "What you take me fo'? I try talk li' you, folks t'ink I plenny *lōlō*!"

Yet teachers said in class her English was perfect. Her grades were excellent.

"Stop being ashamed to show you're *smart*." Malia shook her gently. "Don't let life slip through your fingers."

"Let go!" Baby Jo wrenched herself away. "Why you fuss wit' me so much? You not my muddah. You my '*tita*,' remembah?"

"I'm sending her to Sacred Heart Academy," Malia vowed. "Get her away from project kids."

"Put a lid on it!" Keo said. "She'll test you until the day you square with her."

"Sacred Heart?" Leilani sat down, shocked. "How you going get money fo' private school?"

"Watch me."

NOW MALIA SAT IN HER SHOP UNTIL MIDNIGHT, SEVEN NIGHTS a week. From across the street, an old woman with a cane watched her hunched like a racer, urging the Singer on as she called out resolutions.

"She will wear clothes that are pressed, and change with the seasons. And matching accessories. She will own leather shoes, not rubber slippers. She will have friends who live on paved streets, not rutted lanes. In real houses, not termite bungalows. She will have book bags, after-school activities. She will study languages. She will go to university."

Sometimes she sat back. What was the point of her daughter being educated if she starved to death? She bent to the Singer, calling out again.

"She will have a good business head. She will always have a bank account. She will not take men seriously. She will never compromise. Men will always step aside."

She wanted to save her daughter the debasement and debris of men, the scars that might be permanent. Her resolutions became like chants she shouted while she stitched, creating a blueprint for her daughter. A sequence and procedure. She knew that some stalled and aching twilight she would have to tell her who her father was. By then, Malia hoped, Baby Jonah would forgive her.

ʻAwapuhi Lau Pala Wale

Ginger Leaves Yellow Quickly; Things Pass Too Soon

One day, Jonah's watch, sent from Italy. Rusted, smelling strangely of manure. Keo sat in ʻAʻala Park, imagining combat, the watch flung into a ditch on his brother's severed hand. It had stopped at 3:15, the same time of day he was liberated from Woosung Camp. Thirteen years, and he was still returning and returning. Waiting for his mainspring—memory—to snap.

Now he held Jonah's watch, bereft. He stumbled into a church where small, fat candles in red jars pulsed like hearts. He knelt and lit a candle. The old woman watched as he left the church, so fit, impeccable, still so attractive. But something suddenly seen or remembered had struck him down with grief. She hung her head, wifed him out of habit.

. . . Come, dear one. Wipe your brow. Brush your hair. We'll walk along, eat roasted chestnuts by the Seine. Or put on soft pajamas, sit by our tiny window overlooking the rue, *and drink oolong from cracked china. Yes. Life slowly empties. But only in the way a teacup empties. Its concaveness still implies the tea. Tea-ness lingers. . . .*

She had become his unseen companion. Snail-shell knuckles humped round the handle of her cane. Shoes like beached amphibians. An old hard chair of a woman. Yet, something kindly in the eyes as she looked after him, following always at a distance. She never moved close. Never consciously moved close to anything.

He walked up Kalihi Lane, oddly at peace. It happened lately. For no reason, a mood would overtake him; he would feel safe, watched over. Now he studied the ebb and flow of family in his father's garage. Uncles drank beer and smacked their thighs, playing *hanafuda*. Aunties "talked story," cleaning just-caught squid. DeSoto's two boys practised judo while cousins, like running stitches, flew iridescent dragon kites. All tangled blood and sinew, falling across each other's lives like soft lightning.

Hours tapered down the lane. Folks gossiped in chop-suey Pidgin while, next door, Mrs. Silva's grandchild practised French. ". . . *il fait beau, il fait chaud, il fait froid* . . ." And somewhere from a dark, cool room, Gabby Pahinui singing "Hi'ilawe," then Aunty Genoa Keawe warbling "Ke Kali Nei Au."

Keo sat down and leaned his head back, finding comfort in this ancient groove, this old inherited taxonomy. He had begun to understand that nothing he accomplished would be as heroic as staying here, staying put. His parents were aging. He suddenly saw their narrow, unembellished world as rare. Life, to be cherished.

Some nights after playing at the club, he stood in their living room, looking hard at things, as if he had never seen them. He opened drawers that contained only bare necessities. A bottle of glue, a ball of string. Sepia snapshot of an ad for a DeSoto. In this dear house, even the simplest thing was shabby. Glue marbleized in the jar. The string crumbling, and the snapshot.

His parents' room was just as stark. Old *koa* wardrobe, double bed with threadbare sheets. A chest of drawers upon which lay a rosary, framed pictures of their children. On the wall, a crucifix. Windows hung with old crochet. There was nothing extra.

In this house his parents referred to "the bowl that holds the poi," "the pot for stew," "the chair for playing cards." There was one of everything, and only what they needed. It was only out in the world that Keo had learned objects had proper names. A T'ang vase, a Hiroshige print. Bavarian china. Here, he had grown up in the midst of, not poverty, but modesty bare as a knuckle. Nothing to see here, little to comment on, which left much space for feeling. A house many-peopled, deeply loved.

And in this house were his parents, almost childishly vague on what history and geography might be. They knew only that they inhabited an island in the ocean, that Japan and China were on one side, the U.S. on the other. An ocean they had never traveled, one they could not imagine the vastness of. They talked about Hawai'i becoming one of the United States, but did not know what that meant. They were not sure what a state was.

"How can be one state?" Leilani asked. "We not connected to da mainland."

Timoteo peeled a mango in a long, moist coil. "No mattah. Politics all mental."

She stared at a map, stunned by the isolated dots that were their islands.

"If we going be one state, U.S. going swallow us. Like *pūpū*! Like whatchoo call it—tidbits."

Keo smiled. He had once needed to escape this "ignorance," this place so narrow and provincial. Then life had grabbed hold of him and thrust on him more haunted beauty and evil than he would ever understand. Yet nothing but this lane was ever real to him. All else was spectacle.

Some nights he stepped out of the lane and hiked up to the heights, then deep into rain forests. The smell of swamp, sizzling ginger, the piss of barking deer. The sweetness of *kiawe* blossoms. He climbed past cane-moist, pasture-dry smells, past piny cypress, up into the fog zone where eucalpytus enveloped him.

Up here, great trees thrashed and howled as if containing all the tremors of the island, which had absorbed for eons all the tremors of the sea. The bark of each tree kept track of the robust logic of each wave of the ocean as it struck upon the sands. Keo fell asleep watching these giants bend in spasms, eclipsing great sierras of a plankton sky. *We are all touched,* he thought. *The sea has watermarked each island thing.* He felt life vibrate through his lungs, the sea vibrating through the lungs of land. He pressed his face against wet earth.

Days later, he would come down from the heights into the 1950s gleam of boomtown Honolulu. Bleached hulls of buildings blocked the skyline, bringing perpetual shade, northern gloom. Construction crews gouged out entire valleys. Beaches slowly disappeared.

Leilani wrung her hands and wept, watching crews demolish a store in Chinatown's Tin-Can Alley. It was her favorite shop for *char siu* duck, freshest ginger, and bok choy. Old women stood beside her wailing. Keo held his mother's hand, remembering the shop's rusty ceiling lights, fly-corpsed fans, exposed and oxidizing plumbing. Mr. Chock slaughtering pop-eyed carp while simultaneously reading the Chinese news. His apron calligraphed with guts and scales.

Keo remembered a ball of string on a spindle suspended from the ceiling over the counter, the mottled wrapping paper Mr. Chock used for purchases of fish and meat. He could still see the spindle jerk! jerk! jerking! with each pull of the string, still hear a rhythm in the constant motion—chop! pull! wrap!—of Mr. Chock's big hands.

He tried to comfort her. "The place was a firetrap. It's progress, Mama."

"I hate dis—whatchoo call it—prah-gress!"

That year he noticed how she who had been so beautiful, so awe-inspiring, was shrinking, growing frail. As if his mother had entered some frictionless medium and sped, without pausing, from youth to age. He hugged her more often, made her laugh, her laughter like fountains of colored glass that had lit his infant blindness. Each week he took her walking on King Street through Kalihi, Palama, cruising her old haunts—a favorite bakery, the crackseed store—barely one step ahead of the wreckers.

ONE DAY WHEN THEY REACHED HOME, DESOTO WAS SITTING with his father, both men looking stupefied.

"What is?" Leilani asked.

Timoteo shook his head. "His boy Teodoro."

She sank to her knees, terrified.

DeSoto finally spoke. "Dis t'ing called . . . polio. Can die from it?"

Keo put his arm round his shoulder, holding tight.

They gazed down at the boy, his eyes looking gnawed-at, the virus scrawling his skin a deadly yellow. His parents round the bright white bed, the bright white room, dabbing at him, brokenhearted attempts to push life back inside him. DeSoto humming, holding his wife and older boy close, the boy pressed against his armpit, smelling his briny father smell.

Sun shone on fizzy liquid in a tube snaking into Teodoro. He twitched, blinked rapidly in seizures, as if all of his will, his heart, were trying to defeat what stood between him and living. When he opened his eyes again, they were turned inward. He was already studying another life.

In the corridor, Malia sat with Baby Jonah.

"Da ditch," Baby Jo whispered. "We went swimming dere. Granny told us not to."

Near 'A'ala Park was Kapalama Canal, a thin ribbon of oily algae and metal that began somewhere in the rain forests of the Ko'olaus. It tapered down through Palama, collecting garbage from rain gutters, puddles, and ground wells until it was a swollen stream meeting the ocean out past the canneries near Honolulu Harbor. Kids from the projects fished and swam half-naked in the waters.

"You took him there?" Malia asked.

She nodded. "If Teodoro die . . . my fault! Granny warned ditch waters get plenny polio."

Malia had a fleeting moment of what life would be without this girl. The gaping hole. She held her tight and rocked her.

"Not your fault. Teodoro swam every ditch in Honolulu. Even that slimy Ala Wai Canal. Little ditch rat. He was warned a hundred times. Forty kids on Maui down with polio this year."

The girl sobbed. "He only ten. Cannot die. Cannot!"

In the bright white room, his limbs knotted and froze before their eyes, as if he were going through all the stages of the disease at an accelerated pace. Contracture. Thrombosis. Myocarditis. Respiratory failure. Then each of them held out their hands, feeling him pass through them.

They stood at his grave, a priest offering some version of a young boy's death they could live with. No one saw in the distance the old woman weeping softly, grieving for DeSoto. He had once rescued her, delivered her to Keo. Malia looked up, noticing the aged face, and something struck her. Days later, she would remember the fine antique kimono from her shop, which she had given Pono. The one embroidered with an old woman whose gaze was eerily familiar.

NOW CAME UNCEREMONIOUS GRIEF, AND NIGHTMARES. LEILANI climbed into each morning like a woman climbing from a coffin.

"Sixteen my babies die. Now my curse take Jonah. Teodoro. Next? Who next?"

She started sleeping with her eyes open, alert for what was coming.

"Seem my life only good fo' bring *make*." Death. "Mo' bettah I go *hiamoe loa*." Eternal sleep.

At night she wheezed. Her mouth became a laboring O. She sucked in air, sucking the house dry. She wheezed so hard, folks felt her inhalations pulling at their skin. Moisture disappeared. No one in Kalihi Lane could sweat or cry. Her wheezes grew louder. Overnight the lane turned parched, a morbid brown. Branches snapped, flowers died, sucked inward.

One night Leilani turned to Timoteo. "Air da bed each day. I be right here."

Grief walked up to her and pinched her heart. She went down like a petal.

‘OHANA

Family, Kin Group

ANOTHER BRIGHT WHITE ROOM. AT FIRST SHE THOUGHT SHE was already dead. Then she heard the *sssss!* of someone opening a beer. DeSoto, froggy-eyed from double mourning.

How long since he buried Teodoro? How long I been here?

Leilani's eyes were closed. Her body slept, her spirit wandered. It slipped out through her *lua ‘uhane*, spirit pit, the tear duct at the corner of her eye, gazing round the room.

Muddah God, look da crowd. So many here. Ooh, da smell. Machinery. Pineapple. Cooking grease. Folks coming straight from work. Fo' real I must be dying. Strange my body, nutting move. Maybe dis what folks call coma-kine.

She waved her arms, telling everyone go home, get on with their lives. She did this in her mind, her body paralyzed, her senses dripping at her side. People sat in little knots, whispering, nodding in and out. Doctors said the end was near. It had been arriving for three days.

Father Gerard stood in the doorway, florid skinned, just slightly cross-eyed. He smiled, handshook his way round the room, eyeing the beer cooler, paper plates of *manapua*, sushi, Coke bottles on the floor.

" 'Ey. Some party, dis!"

The old priest had always admired the Meahunas. Their physical beauty, their robust fearlessness. Oldest son DeSoto circumnavigating the world year after year. And that curvaceous Malia, the one who drew men's gazes. Look how she'd slimmed down so lazily no one even noticed. How smart a dresser, her own shop. That pale chubby daughter by her side, always seething a little. The one she passed off as *hānai*. One day, he must hear her confession.

There was the husband, Timoteo, grief-stricken but still handsome. Father Gerard studied him, thinking how that Shirashi widow always had her eye on him. Strange, how elegant women migrated toward the untutored and untamed.

Lastly, he gazed at Keo. The mystery. Some trouble in the war . . . his sweetheart disappeared. Still searching for her.

He signed the cross, performing extreme unction, then kissed his rosary to Leilani's lips.

Night fell, folks bent whispering last things to Leilani, then drifted up and down the halls. Slurp and drag of slippers. Someone in high heels clip-clopping like a horse. Again Leilani's spirit slipped out through her tear duct, looking round the room.

My beautiful Malia, nodding in sleep. How good you turn out. But listen me, one day what you do, not do, come round fo' haunt you. Time you tell Baby Jonah what and what. Give dat girl her birthright. Faddah waiting fo' his daughter. But proud like you. Nevah come fo' her until you say. I t'ink you both vain buggahs! We going talk plenny when I haunt you in da nights. . . .

O Muddah God. Here come my Keo. Favorite son, so talented, so smart. But quiet. Somet'ing in him make me shy. One day be lonely old man with puka-puka *socks. Even if famous jazz man, so what? Jazz cook yo' breakfast? Warm yo' feet? Jazz give you plenny kids?* 'Auwē! *I t'ink dis son da one most meant fo' love. Look how he hold Baby Jonah. Look how he hug his papa. Hug DeSoto's boy. Dat Sunny Sung, she mess Keo up real bad. I like see dat girl, shake her good befo' I die.*

Keo sat beside her bed for hours, whispering, falling silent, whispering again. Crowds thinned, people headed home. DeSoto woke his father, dozing in a corner.

"Papa. Time fo' go. Come back early in da morning." Timoteo bent, kissed and kissed Leilani's face. In her mind, she kissed him back.

Most precious Timoteo. Of all da men who stare at me, you drew my gaze. I knew dose big hands good fo' shield me from hot sunlight. Dose strong lū'au *feet good fo' clear da path. I knew dat big strong chest plenny wide enough to weep on. I knew you give me plenny kids. I only nevah know we birth and bury on da run. I nevah know life break us down child by child, year by year. Even tear down pride . . . war years when no work, not even mortuary sweeping, no one but daughter fo' look aftah us. Daughter wit' daughter of Krash Kapakahi. Yeah, my Timoteo, all dese years I know you knew!*

She smelled his hair against her face, wanting to feel it with her hands. And in her mind she did. In her mind they danced and dipped and were forever young, never running, or starving, never burying a child.

THEN IT WAS THE HOUR OF HIʻIAKA THE HEALER, YOUNGEST sister of Pele, fire and volcano goddess. Women of Leilani's family, keeping all-night vigil, summoned her. Kēhau Aho stepped forward, statuesque *kumu hula*, teacher of the dance and chanter of *mele*. Her voice, her face so lovely when she sang, folks felt rinsed clean of sin.

"Now we do *lāʻau lapaʻau*, herbal healing, but first we chant *kāhea*, the summons prayer." Her voice rang out:

"ʻ*O Hiʻiaka ke kāula nui, nāna i hana, nāna i palaʻau i nā maʻi apau.*" Hiʻiaka the great priest, she acts, she treats all ailments.

Chanting softly, they rubbed Leilani's hands with oil of *kukui*, rubbed it gently on her cheeks. Her eyes were closed. Her spirit watched and listened.

Kēhau Aho whispered, "This is good for *hoʻoponopono*, restoring balance in heart and mind."

Kauwealoha Ing carefully poured seawater into Leilani's mouth, and then each ear. Kauwealoha, handsome mother of five, rodeo champ, once addicted gambler. One night in Las Vegas she'd looked down at a deck of cards, seen the face of Mother God, and taken the first plane home to Honolulu.

"Seawater, original Mother juices running in our veins. Ninety-seven elements to clean the blood." She dabbed seawater on the lips. "Purifies of all bad words ever thought or spoken."

Pulling back the sheets, Lauwaʻe Desanto gently rubbed red dust of chili pepper on Leilani's chest.

"Shock the heart," she whispered. "Keep it beating on her voyage home."

Lauwaʻe Desanto, once Miss Hawaiʻi, runner-up Miss Universe. Eyes like green leaves, face Gauguin. Even in her forties, she was so beautiful, strangers followed her, entranced. She took up each of Leilani's small, cold feet and rubbed them with the chili pepper dust.

"Will swim in bloodstream," Lauwaʻe Desanto pronounced. "Keep feet warm while she follows footsteps of the ancients."

They were women joined by blood and legend, who found communion in the ancient ways. This gave them double mana, made their stride electric. When they walked the streets together, crowds stepped back. As if fearing some utterance, a fierce, implacable Hawai'ian truth that would snap the modern world in two.

Malia hung maile vines, turning the air fragrant and heady. Round the bed she assembled branches of eucalyptus, Leilani's favorite, from the highest heights of Tantalus. Finally, she wreathed her mother's head in ti leaves for safe journey to the next life.

Her clanswomen strummed 'ukulele, singing "'Ekolu Mea Nui"—"Three Greatest Things"—their voices blending in falsetto. Kēhau Aho, so great of height, stood lifting her voice so that even down the hall, patients turned, smiling in their sleep. Malia raised her arms in a graceful solemn hula of the ancients as they harmonized in communion to "Ke Akua Mana E"—"How Great Thou Art."

For hours they sang sacred songs, voices so deep and lingering that nurses stopped and listened. Throughout the building, elevators slowed, doors shuddering half-closed. Water fountains froze in mid-splash. Even the dying paused.

Kēhau Aho finally intoned: "*E mālama ia Kou makemake.*" Thy will be done.

Exhausted, they sat down and slept.

IN THE DEEPEST HOUR OF THE NIGHT, AN OLD WOMAN WITH A cane stood trembling in the doorway. She watched the women snoring in chorus, then moved past them and laid her cane beside Leilani. Gently, more gently than anything she had ever done, she dipped a tissue in water, dabbed Leilani's feverish and blistered lips. She bent and kissed the fallen cheek. She pulled up a chair.

Coming awake, Leilani felt gentle pressure, someone stroking her as if she were a child.

. . . oooh, plenny tired. Soon, time fo' hiamoe loa, *eternal sleep. Timoteo, precious, here beside me. Come to say goodbye.*

Her spirit hesitated, then peeked out from her tear duct.

Muddah God!

Sunny was holding her hand, talking softly. As if they had centuries. As if, in time, all would be explained.

". . . BELOVED LEILANI, YOUR BODY IS VERY TIRED. SOON YOU *will give in, and rest. My precious mama Butterfly taught me that our* 'uhane, *our soul, takes nine days to leave this earth. So you have time to listen. And I have much to say.*"

IN HER MIND, LEILANI SCREAMED. SUNNY SUNG, KEO'S BEAUtiful and spoiled love, had come back masquerading as a hag. Leilani's skin, her organs—every nerve end—recoiled.

"I KNOW YOU CURSE ME. YOU THINK I STOLE YOUR SON FROM *you, stole him from his islands. All I did was open doors, let him see what he could be. . . . I loved him more than life, but I was not enough. He was on the brink of things. He needed breath and I took up his oxygen. And so, I found my own breath. Saving my sister's life gave me importance. . . .*"

SUNNY TALKED THROUGH MINUTES INTO HOURS, WHILE BEHIND her the women slept. She talked of Paris, and sliding down the coast of Africa, learning she was carrying Keo's child. She talked of reaching Shanghai, finding her sister who helped midwife the child. She talked of trying to get Lili and the baby home to Honolulu. And how dismally she failed.

"KEO WAITED FOR ME TO COME BACK WITH OUR CHILD TO HO*tel Jo-Jo. I never returned. Afraid I would leave with him, leaving Lili to die. Because of my cowardice, I sacrificed both. My sister and little Anahola.*"

FALTERING AGAIN AND AGAIN, SHE TOLD HOW JAP SOLDIERS swept through Shanghai, herding women into trucks. How they took infants from their mothers' arms and threw them in the air, pointing their bayonets.

"I SAW MY BABY FLUNG INTO THE SKY. I SCREAMED, AND CLOSED MY *eyes so I would never know what happened. So I would always see her soaring upward like an angel . . .*"

AS SUNNY TALKED, A TEAR ROLLED DOWN LEILANI'S CHEEK. IT sat there, solid as a crystal. Quietly, Sunny spoke of her first "comfort station," in Shanghai. Men's bodies pummeling them, day after day, night after night. She told how she and Lili were kept in separate rooms. And how, one night, Lili was shot. Soldiers could not bear her clubfoot.

"THEY SHOT HER SEVEN TIMES. I HEARD HER DYING. I LEANED *against the wall and sang to her, until her wind stopped. That was my second death. Then one day they took me from that place, trucking me and many girls to military ships. We were sent with ammunition and supplies, deep into the Pacific. To a place called . . . Rabaul."*

SHE STUMBLED BADLY ON THE WORD.

Maybe it was Sunny's soft articulations, or maybe it was the discomfort of her hard-backed chair, for Malia slowly turned in sleep, shifting on her haunches. Hearing low murmuring, she woke, seeing the back of a head, an aged body, no one she recognized. But something familiar in the voice. Malia leaned forward, listening.

". . . HOW DID I ARRIVE HERE AFTER ALL THESE YEARS? ONE *day I turned, and I was facing home. Something beckoned. Beckons, still. Now I follow Keo, looking after him. Though he will never know. As you, Leilani, would not have known until one night I heard your wheezing. I felt your heart choke up with grief. How did I know? These things come to me. How did I know they brought you here? I only know I started walking. The way was clear."*

SUNNY TOUCHED LEILANI'S CHEEK, HELD THE TINY CRYSTAL IN her hand.

"SOMETIMES ONLY AMAZEMENT KEEPS US ALIVE. NOW, I WILL *tell you the rest. Knowing it, you might forgive me. . . ."*

OLA HOU

Resurrection

"WHO WILL EVER KNOW WHAT ALL THAT HORROR REALLY WAS? It was so long ago. And it was yesterday. Now there is only remembering. You see, after surviving, that's all there is. Remembering. Tidying up the details. Waiting to forget . . .

"When Allied soldiers brought us from the caves, they said the war was over. I didn't understand. If everything was over, why was I still alive? Rabaul had been mostly leveled by bombs. In hastily built clinics, medics deloused us, cut off our hair, and bathed us. We were quarantined. Officials came and looked at us through glass, and I remember thinking of a zoo—the tale told from the ape's point of view.

"After we were somewhat recovered, no longer in danger of infecting them with typhus, officers sat down with us. They spoke softly, trying to be kind. We didn't respond. You see, we couldn't. We thought they were telling us we were going to be shot for collaborating with the Japs. Some girls went blind. Doctors said there was nothing wrong with them. They simply stopped seeing. They had seen too much. A few white women, Dutch and Australians, broke down. I watched them cry. It came to me as wounded music. I wondered what was left in them that cared that much. . . .

"As we recuperated, we saw Jap prisoners in scorching sun scrubbing airfield runways with wire brushes. Some so thirsty they fainted. To get water they had to run, drink fast, run back. They were not allowed to walk. Many died of sunstroke, skin blistered like giant soap bubbles.

"Hundreds of Allied POWs had been taken underground to the tunnels, kept as hostages until the Japs saw all was lost. Now Japs were imprisoned in those same hostage cells, conditions filthy and bestial. They were made to lie down on the same diseased cots where POWs had perished. And they were stripped naked but for loincloths, paraded like that day and night. We watched them scrub latrines. We saw them kicked and beaten by Allied soldiers.

"Americans and Australians were now ensconced in the few officers' quarters left standing. The officers chewed gum and stared at us. Some of them looked bored. They had seen so much, what did a handful of sick whores matter? You see, they didn't yet understand we had been kept against our will, that some girls had been children, eleven and twelve when they were kidnapped, before they had even begun to menstruate. These men thought we had volunteered, that we were prostitutes. . . .

"A few officers even flirted with girls who had begun to gain weight and look human. Some girls, fearing rape again, went mad. Others of us hung our heads. This confused the Allies. They thought we were ashamed because Japan had lost the war. It was only when the white women spoke up, when they told what had been done to us, that officers began to look uncomfortable. They interrogated each of us alone.

"When it was my turn, my lips parted, yet I couldn't say the words. Visions weighted my tongue like stones: Rooms with hooks attached to walls, girls hanging by their necks like butchered game. Boatloads of girls blown up, so there would be no witness for the Allies.

"I remembered buckets in sunlight, from which water was scooped and poured over the blade of a fine heirloom sword. The sword raised in a sweeping arc, the bright hairy planet of a young girl's head. Trying to describe it, to articulate, I drooled. Someone gently wiped my mouth. Someone handed me a mirror, saying, 'Look what they did.' I was twenty-six, I looked seventy. I tried again, telling everything. Because nothing mattered now. . . .

"In time, the Allies understood what we had been. We were so used, and broken. One day, when some of us were strong enough, we were taken to a dining room set up especially for us. We sat at tables with tablecloths. There was fish and meat. Vegetables and bread. There was wine. Forks and knives. And napkins. They served us food like we were human. Some women laughed stupidly, already planning their suicides. . . ."

SUNNY SHOOK HER HEAD, STARING BLINDLY ACROSS LEILANI'S room, amazed that she could remember. That she was still here to remember.

". . . HOSPITAL SHIPS ARRIVED AT RABAUL, FULL OF RED CROSS medics tending Allied POWs. There were thousands of them, many taken aboard on stretchers. They were so lost, they cried out loud. Some men were suffering from wet beriberi, their limbs blown up like balloons. Some were blind, some hobbled on one leg. We had never seen these prisoners; they had never seen us, the P-girls. Two horrors kept apart. But they said sometimes they heard us screaming. And we had heard their torture. Ships departed. Others came, taking on more POWs.

"Red Cross nurses bathed us frequently. We were sprayed over and over with DDT. Then we were given proper clothes and proper haircuts, issued ID cards. We were questioned again and again. One day I sat in a room with a naval officer, his secretary recording what I said. I talked for hours. When I stopped, the man wiped his eyes. He took my hand as if he were my father. 'The war is over,' he said. 'You survived. Now you can forget, go home to your real life.' I laughed. Life seemed unbearable because suddenly the only thing real *was Rabaul.*

"I remembered little Kim, how we had held each other in the dark, living in our imaginings. Honolulu! Paris! Sometimes, from beyond our compound, we heard haunting, plaintive songs—a harmonica—that floated us a moment's peace. Why, even now, I sometimes hear an infinitely fragile tune skimming over the jungle, over barbed wire. And wind rattling through palms. I hear young Kamikaze pilots on their last nights, weeping, asking only to be held. They wrote us poems and died. You see, I am forever linked to that place. I am engraved.

"IN OUR COMPOUND AT NIGHT I WOULD HEAR TRAIN WHISTLES. The sound made me sob, reminding me of whistles of sugarcane trains rumbling into Honolulu during harvesting. I asked the American officer how it could be. Where would there be trains in the jungle? He said maybe it was passing ships. Maybe I imagined it. He told of a girl, imprisoned

for two years in the Philippines, how she had dreamed of her mother's baking. Nurses said she always smelled like flan. Another girl, chained inside a bamboo cage, dreamed of her bayoneted infant son. When Allies liberated her, she weighed eighty pounds. Her kneecaps and elbows had burst through her skin. Her eyes were gone. Yet even when they buried her, soldiers said she smelled of baby powder. . . ."

SUNNY SLOWED DOWN, RUBBING LEILANI'S HANDS, THE MOTION helping her to remember. Leilani's eyes were open, the whites immaculate as if they had been polished from the inside. What she felt now was harrowing grief bleeding into mother love. In her life, she had been made to run, sixteen babies' worth. At least they had left her feet for running. But all, all had been taken from this girl, who had not even been left the urge to live. Now she fell back into Sunny's telling.

". . . ONE DAY MPS HERDED US ON A SHIP TO SOMEPLACE CALLED *Okinawa. We lay across the decks like sticks, stopping at Guam, Saipan, Iwo Jima, picking up hundreds of other stick-girls. Women had been kidnapped and enslaved all over Asia and the Pacific, wherever Japan invaded. I began to see the magnitude. I wondered what would happen to us. What more could happen. In Okinawa, we were asked to look at groups of Jap officers behind barbed wire. To identify them. They said I fainted, yet I heard everything. Only vision left me. I was ashamed to name my executioners, ashamed to recognize a face. That's what shame does, that was the brilliance of it. . . .*

"Hospitals were huge in Okinawa. Surgeons were experienced at purging, carving out diseased and damaged things. My womb, for instance. Afterward, I felt lighter, full of air. My roommate was a Chinese girl from Honolulu, who had been at university in Peking when the Japs came. We talked about our wombs as if they were old handbags absentmindedly mislaid. There were other women there from Honolulu—a missionary, a doctor's wife—who had been enslaved in camps in China. I did not try to find them. What was there to say?

"They tested us again, like laboratory mice. X rays, heart, lungs, blood. We were put back in quarantine. Doctors were kind, but we were wary, still waiting for them to tell us we were going to be shot.

"This place, Okinawa, was where I overheard a doctor say most of us would not survive. Even the healthy ones. He was already burying us. 'Most of these women,' he said, 'can't return to their villages. Their families would stone them. Especially those kidnapped from Korea, a culture that demands virginity in women. The will has its limits,' he said. 'Many of them will find that what they have survived for won't be worth it. Hiding in new towns, new countries. Nothing left, no family or dignity. Only continuing disease, deterioration, physical and mental. And devastating memories. Many will find they've lived enough. They'll have no taste for more.'

"It began for me in Okinawa. Because, you see, daylight was repulsive. I wasn't used to all that light. In Rabaul, it was dim in the Quonsets. Dim in latrines. Even on bright days, jungle foliage surrounded us. That hell-year in the tunnels, we lived by candle, and kerosene. Now I shunned daylight. Yet, night brought phantoms. They rose laughing in my throat. And I began to understand that truly nothing mattered. All was over. I had died so many times. . . .

"My body didn't seem to understand. It continued fighting back. I would always limp with pain, but skin ulcers began to heal, scars faded. I gained a little weight. I decided if my body must live, I would reinvent myself. How could I return to Honolulu? I told the authorities in Okinawa that I was Korean, that I had lived in Shanghai, the old Chinese City. I spoke enough broken Korean and Chinese to convince them. I asked to be repatriated to Shanghai. Many women did the same. If they went home to Seoul or Panmunjom, they would be stoned as prostitutes. Some even chose repatriation to occupied Japan.

"While papers were processed, we were investigated, and hundreds of us were taken to the island of Tokashiki in the Okinawa chain. We were put in barracks next to camps with captured Jap soldiers. Though not called prisoners, we were guarded. Some women were interrogated repeatedly, suspected of having collaborated, turned spy, for the Japs.

"For almost a year we were detained on Tokashiki. They called it rehabilitation. Some women were trained as nurses' aides, typists. Many were still being treated for syphilis, TB, for chemical and surgical experiments performed on them by Jap doctors and researchers. Six girls committed suicide. Since we were the only women there, young Allied officers chose those of us who were the least ugly and least scarred. They gave us nylons and cosmetics. They offered compassion, willing to hear our stories. They offered

money in return for sex. Women who said no were forced. But how could a woman say no to her liberators?

"Since we were now housed and fed by the occupying forces, we were considered property of the U.S. Naval Operating Base on Okinawa. They were the victors, we were part of the spoils. Guards began to stroll our barracks at all hours. When women fought them, they were struck. Enlisted men began to come. They always asked first, they always paid. Some wanted sex, some just wanted talk. They were young boys, afraid to go home to the U.S. They had seen too much war and wouldn't fit in. I closed my eyes and held them. Japanese, American. I no longer cared."

SUNNY LOOKED UP, HER EYES LIKE DULL FIRES SEARCHING BEyond the room, beyond the night, for that young woman long past judgment, a girl she must not lose sight of.

"ONE DAY I WAS SHIPPED TO OCCUPIED JAPAN, THEN ISSUED PA*pers allowing me to go 'home to Shanghai.' There, war crimes were being tried before Allied courts. Most crucial were the trials of Jap officers who had commanded internment camps and POW camps just outside the city. 'Comfort women,' P-girls, what Japs officially called* jugun ianfu*—the thousands of women imprisoned as sex slaves—were never called to testify. Crimes against us were erased.*

"War trials were taking place in every country Japs had invaded. China, Indonesia, Malaysia, the Pacific Islands. But we, survivors of the hundreds of thousands of mutilated, murdered women, were never called upon to bear witness. We were the forgotten, the disposables of war. . . .

"Amazingly, Shanghai was its prewar self again. Foreigners strolled the Bund. There were nightclubs, cabarets. Gambling, opium. Back alleys were still sordid and seething. It would remain that way until 1949 when the Communists ended everything. I would then move to Hong Kong, live in a tiny room, sleeping all day, spending my nights teaching English, riding Star Ferry back and forth across Victoria Harbor. . . .

"Once I even followed Keo in Hong Kong. I sat near him on the ferry, and in a park in Kowloon where he talked to strangers. He was searching for the girl he knew as Sunny. The girl long buried . . .

"But I am ahead of myself. Now it was 1947, I had been 'liberated'

from Okinawa to Japan, processed my papers, and gone to Shanghai. Deep in my heart was the wish to find my sister and my child. The hope that, against all odds, they had survived. I was twenty-seven. The world was new. I would begin my life again. Except, how does one start over?

"One day I had tea on a terrace in the sun. A teahouse near the Bridge of Nine Windings sitting in a little lake. Around me there were young women and military men. The scene was tender. Everyone seemed a little shy, amazed that the war was over and they had survived. They spoke different languages, there was laughter. Couples heading off in open cars. I drank my tea, while sunlight slaughtered me.

"In that moment, the certainty of living, of life, was so acute, so stunning, I understood I no longer possessed the strength for it. All I had the strength for was remembering. Rabaul. The nights, the years. I had watched girls die and envied them. Even the beheaded. I guess we thought we would all die. Otherwise, there would have been more suicides. In the end, we didn't even have the strength for that. . . .

"In Shanghai I made no friends. I lived moment to moment, searching for phantoms. Existence had the strange, aloof acuity of dreams. I did not attach myself to things. I walked out of rooms leaving everything behind. I would walk through the years that way, attached to nothing. Until one day I turned, and I was facing home.

"And yet . . . after all, after all . . . there was a time of beauty that stays with me. A talisman I rub over and over.

"It was after the Allies, after the caves, when we began to recover on Rabaul. One day we took our first showers alone, without medics or nurses. Clean, spacious, disinfected showers. We undressed and entered slowly, like the blind. We touched white tiles, white faucets. Whole bars of soap. We became giddy, playful. We even sang, our voices pathetic and croaking. It was then, in those showers, that love, the capacity to love, was resurrected. You could see it in the eyes staring from our broken faces. Each woman there felt it for the other.

"We soaped, shampooed, rinsed each other tenderly like mothers. Some girls were still weak and had to sit down. We bathed them like children. We held them up to the showers, held their faces to the spray, their wristbones, little ribs and spines standing out like branches. For that while, we forgot the outside world. Just then—joined by our suffering, full of the fear of meeting 'normal' humans—we were lovers in the purest sense.

"We women fell upon each other, laughing, sobbing, embracing with

no need for words, no need even for gestures, yet not wanting to let go. We held on and on in those showers, water softening the corpses inside us. No one would ever know us quite as well, no one would enter that place again—that quiet room inside us where each of us housed the great thing we were feeling. In many ways, none of us would love again. . . .

"Afterwards, we looked at ourselves in mirrors. Legs like matchsticks, arms with no musculature. Heads huge on bony stalks of necks. From the back we looked like boys without behinds. From the front we were old women, our hair thin as spiderwebs, and gray. Our skulls shone through like bulbs.

"After the showers, we lay down on clean sheets. Liberation left us exhausted. And somewhere deep inside me was a wish I could not say out loud, even to myself: that the break in our lives could be postponed a while. Could we not live a little longer in our own, our only, world? So much of our lives, all of our youth, was buried in Rabaul. The world had changed, gone on ahead without us. All we had was each other. All we knew was here. How could we leave it so suddenly?"

SHE LEANED HER HEAD AGAINST THE BED, AND WENT AWAY FOR a while. A hand reached out, discolored and trembling. Leilani rested it on Sunny's head.

". . . I DREAM OF RABAUL. I DEPEND ON IT. CAN YOU UNDERSTAND? Barbed wire in moonlight. Watchtowers. Creaking gates opening their jaws to swallow us. Latrines made of planks, under which rise piles of steaming excrement. I smell it in my sleep. I hear feet running. I see fireflies caught in the bushy hair of natives staring through the fence. They throw us food, hold their babies up for us to see. . . .

"Even lying awake at night, sometimes I hear thrashing and know a python has caught a cassowary, or a child. I hear someone flapping sheets and know it's flying foxes coming home at dawn to roost. I smell mildew on my walls like condensation in the Quonsets. I remember how, in thirst, I licked those walls. . . .

"I dream of equatorial heat that made skin blister. I wake with searing arms and legs. Dreams can be so real. I dream of rains, torrential, endless jungle rains. I know they will end. They always did. I know the stars will come again. If only I lie still . . ."

Ka Huliau

Turning Point

He sat at his mother's grave, still in a wilderness of grief. There was nothing left to say, yet his lips moved rapidly, repeating and repeating. He had come here every day for weeks, until being here became so natural his mind wandered, he could have been playing cards, practising his horn. He sat plucking the grass, distracted, a man with no plot, no direction.

Among garish-colored wreaths on headstones, an old woman stood in the distance, dressed in gray. From the shadows of a tree she watched while Keo shielded his face from a sun stubbornly keeping abreast of him. An hour passed, or two. He heaved and groped in his personal darkness.

"Mama. I had such dreams. You never told me dreams grow old. Now I wonder . . . what next?" He shook his head. "I play, but there's a silence I can't fill. All the sound dies out inside me."

Approaching slowly with her cane, she stared at meek folds of his neck, hair now shot with silver, which would in time give him distinction. She had not been this close to him in almost twenty years. Dark skin still unwrinkled, lean, rather muscular physique. He was still a smart dresser, silk shirts, linen trousers. He still shunned rubber slippers, favoring leather shoes. There was still something electric, a tension in him.

He didn't notice her approaching, sitting near him on the grass.

He lay facedown on his mother's grave and dozed, not hearing her voice that spoke a long, soft time.

"KEO, DEAR, REMEMBER THE TEACUP. THOUGH IT EMPTIES, ITS *concaveness still implies the tea. Tea-ness lingers. As long as you remember her, she lives.*

"Days will come when you will without consciousness gather in all your wandering memories, and they will rebirth your mama. The day you and your papa did thus and such with her. The first time you and she went to church alone. The nights she watched you rebuild wooden hammers in your Steinway, trying hard to understand. The first time she heard you play trumpet. Her wild pride. These memories will all come home like prodigals.

"One day you'll remember walking toward that garage forever up the lane, a path of startling trees and drunk-making flowers. You'll remember the oil tablecloth and faces of loved neighbors sharing good-fun days of light and shade beneath that shuddering foliage. You'll always approach the memory from the entrance to the lane. Because you will always be coming home from a distance. . . .

"Time will be your prism, through which you distinguish features of relatives and friends, lips serenely moving in forgotten speech, in Pidgin. You'll remember nights in the garage, the wooden picnic table where you celebrated birthdays and namedays and confirmations. The table laid for modest meals. You'll smell your mother's cooking, your father's tobacco, fish smell of DeSoto's nets, Malia's French perfumes.

"You'll note the tweak of small green geckos brushing your hair, one falling to your sister's head, your sister leaping, neighbors bent with laughter. And lying across the table will be your father's arm, muscled, blue-veined, turned up in the bare-bulbed light of the garage. He'll fill a plate of food, keeping busy, so no one will see his eyes. You, his favorite son, are home. You'll hug your mother, brothers, sister, then almost lazily reach for the full plate from your father. No one will notice the look you two exchange, the way your eyes fill, your jaws clench with emotion. . . .

"And always in the center will be your mama, slow-moving and beautiful. In the place where a neighbor sits, there will be a succession of replacements. Mary Chang will turn into Rosie Perez who will turn into Mrs. Palama. Mr. Kimuro will become Mr. Silva, then Johnny Huli.

Tacky Cruz, the rooster, will turn into someone's mongoose, who will become the dog named God who always ran backwards. One of DeSoto's sons will turn into brother Jonah, and he will turn into his namesake, Baby Jonah, who will turn from a child into a young woman. The whole array of trembling transformations will be repeated, overlapping and disordered, for this is how we remember.

"But always there will be your mama, the center of your pattern. And just when colors and outlines and faces settle into a formula you can understand, a knob will be touched, a torrent of sounds will pour forth, voices Pidgining, singing. Ice rattling in DeSoto's beer cooler, someone strumming slack-key guitar. Sounds will ebb, then return as different sounds. Folks older now, remembering other folks, laughing, weeping. A dozen voices drowning yours, a dozen hearts out-thumping yours. A hundred doors swung wide, the sough and sigh of living.

"And out beyond your lane, Keo, there will be other lanes. And streets and avenues. And then above, behind, around it all, will be the sea, the Mother Sea, crashing and defying, destroying and rebirthing. Applauding all we know as life . . ."

STILL HE DOZED, ONLY HALF HEARING THE SOFT, SOLEMN VOICE. Later, much later, he would think her words had been his words, her thoughts his realizations, and it would bring a certain peace. She sat a while, smiling faintly. Her hand hovered over his sleeping head, just for a second, just close enough to remember. She limped away.

IN WAIKIKI, BANDS IMITATED ELVIS PRESLEY. CHUBBY CHECKER had arrived and people danced to something frantic called The Twist. At the Swing Club, jazz crowds ebbed and flowed; one night it was packed, the next night only four tables occupied. Some nights Keo and Endo drowned their frustrations in rum.

"You could alternate," Endo said. "One set jazz, one set rock and roll."

Keo shook his head. "I don't have the ear for that stuff. Or the stomach." He refilled their glasses. "Maybe that's what's wrong with us. Melancholy. Built strictly for jazz."

While they talked he studied Endo, the sad blue face, odd-shaped eyes like a man sobbing politely. In the last year he had started trembling, and complained of terrible headaches. Some days he seemed drunk when he wasn't. His coordination was failing. Keo wondered about his hearing. Some nights when Endo sat in with the band, no one knew what he was playing. It didn't sound like jazz. It didn't sound like anything. His skin was now a deeper blue, his fingernails almost black.

Keo hadn't spent time with him in weeks. The death of his nephew, then his mother. Time spent with his father and DeSoto.

"I'm sorry, man. This family stuff. Grief makes folks crazy."

"I understand." Even Endo's voice had changed, now hoarse and grating. "When I found out my family . . . Tokyo reduced to ash . . . I think I lost my mind completely."

They had touched on this before, Keo hoping talk might help him. "Do you remember surrendering? VJ Day?"

He shook his head no. "I remember jungle. . . ."

"Maybe we're not supposed to remember. I forget for months, then one night I sit up screaming, my fingers jerking wire round a neck. Another guy I smothered, sat on with a pillow—I feel him thrashing under my backside."

He shuddered, slugging back his rum.

"At least you have memories," Endo said.

"If I could just find out what happened to Sunny. Even if she's dead. Don't you remember her in Paris?"

"I'm sorry." He shook his head. "I remember so little now."

"A few years back, I learned she might have been kidnapped in Shanghai. Japanese soldiers."

Endo slowly nodded. "In every war, for every army—Allies, Japanese, a thousand years ago the Mongols—there are women used for that."

"Did you have kidnapped women in the jungle?"

"Oh . . . yes. We had thousands and thousands of men, extraordinary needs. There were women kept in barracks, huts, even hotels."

"Do you remember names? Nationalities?"

Endo looked through him. "They were given Japanese names. Nationalities? So many. I might have spent time with one or two. Relief, you see. I already knew we were losing the war. After Midway, we were finished. It was killing me."

He buried his face in his hands. "I followed my orders, sent thousands of our young men to their deaths. Sacrifices, all! The jackals running our war would not let us surrender. They lied to Hirohito, our emperor. He thought we were winning. They sacrificed millions of young boys all over Asia, the Pacific. They killed my parents, killed everyone!"

He swayed side to side, trying to wrench himself apart so that some human voice might cry out of its suffering.

A little drunk, Keo put his arm round Endo's shoulder.

" 'Ey, let's relax. Take time off. Go fishing in DeSoto's canoe . . ."

Endo reared back. "Not the sea! It horrifies me. I see bombed ships. Corpses boiling in blood."

Keo thought again. "How's about going hunting in the Ko'olaus. Good *pua'a*, wild pig, hunting season now. No rains, no mudslides. That's why you see so many trucks with pig heads mounted on the hoods."

Endo pulled himself together. "Uncle Yasunari and I used to go duck and pheasant hunting. Tramping out at dawn, smell of leather, oiled rifle stocks. I would like that, Keo, if you have the time."

One day before dawn with a cousin's pickup and two boarhounds, they set off for the jungles of the jagged Ko'olau Mountains separating Honolulu from the windward side of O'ahu. The Pali road was treacherous, two narrow lanes on hairpin curves balanced on the edge of cliffs two thousand feet high. Engineers had already begun the Pali Tunnel project, cutting through the heart of the Ko'olaus, which would make the cliff road obsolete. But even now, landslide boulders sometimes crushed the roofs of passing cars.

Twisting and turning up the mountain, Keo found the turnoff that took them half a mile into the jungle. He parked, and they began to hike deep into *pua'a* territory. After another mile they entered dense rain forest, beneath canopies of giant ironwoods and boxwoods. Keo pointed out trees vital to early Hawai'ians—*koa,* from which the hulls of great oceangoing canoes were fashioned. *Hau,* traditional wood used for outriggers. Breadfruit, whose sap served as binder with coconut fibers for the final caulking of canoes.

As the jungle deepened, Endo spun in circles, feeling something tap his back.

Keo grinned. "Playful *akua.* Spirits."

Two miles up the mountain, they saw in distant panorama the other side of the Ko'olaus. Flutings eroded by rain-fed waterfalls rippled the face of the Pali, the great jade cliff stretching twenty-two miles along windward O'ahu. Eons ago, pounding waves had carved the nearly vertical rampart as sea levels rose. When seas receded, volcanic rock on the valley floor weathered into soil. Over centuries, the valley spread out like a lush green carpet rolling on for miles, a vast amphitheatre for the jagged vertebrae of the Ko'olaus. Beyond it, the heaving sea.

Endo gasped. "Such violent beauty."

Somewhere, the squealing of a pig. They moved slowly now. Mist shrouded everything in gauze, streaking dark silhouettes of trees, softening rough edges of boulders in streams. In eerie half-light, owls ghosted from branches, drifting soundlessly. Light changed from indigo to violet, then shot the trees in fiery tapestries of sunrise.

The boarhounds had vanished, hunting in silence. Only when they cornered *pua'a* would barking begin.

"Then you run," Keo said. "And you keep running till you get there. If it's a sow, there's not much danger. But a boar can lay a dog open with one swipe of his tusks. The others will keep crowding in, insane. Look. See what tusks can do?"

Bases of trees and patches of forest floor were slashed and gouged where pigs had found choice beds of roots. Just beyond one of these, Keo broke into a run. Endo followed, hearing jungle sounds that confused him, made him think it was 1942.

He spun in circles. *My sword. Where is my sword? It must be near.*

The hounds had cornered a wild pig up a winding streambed. Lungs bursting, legs on the point of collapse, Endo reached the area minutes after Keo. The wind shifted, a giant leaf hung down, and in that moment Keo appeared headless. Endo screamed. The leaf swayed, and Endo saw the head connected to the body.

But in that instant, things came at him. *Sun glittering on a metal bucket from which I scooped water, pouring it over both sides of my sword blade. The sword arcing gracefully. Smell of gushing blood. Someone wiping clean my blade . . .* Remembering now, he staggered.

The snorting sow had backed into a culvert, holding the frenzied hounds at bay. Keo climbed a tree and shot her directly behind the ear. She shuddered, spraying excrement, and then collapsed. Endo felt chilled, felt mild excitement. He knelt, staring at the sow's thick neck. How cleanly, how easily, with one graceful swipe, the head could be cut from the body. His eyes darted to the hounds. Their necks were short and ugly, it would be hard to hold them still. *But with my sword, execution would be flawless*. . . . He would not look at Keo's neck.

Almost formally, he stood. "Well done. One bullet. As it should be."

Dogs scattered, hunting for another pig. The two men rested, Keo describing the vicious cloven hooves of *pua'a*, but Endo didn't hear him.

. . . I was such a master. They say I raised it to pure art. I could scan a crowd and in five seconds know whose neck was best. Whose fleshy composition would pose a sloppy job . . .

Later, he held the carcass while Keo cleaned and dressed it. The blood and gore did not excite him. The kill was over. Kneeling beside the sow, he drifted, remembering things. Things remembered him.

Afterwards, I was always numb for hours. I could put lit matches to my arms. Once, after taking a head, there were bombs; I was hit by shrapnel, yet did not notice. The time I took six native heads one after another, it was ballet. Later, I stood barefoot in that scorpion nest. They went berserk, stinging me, and I felt nothing. Nothing! So stimulated I was immune to their poison. They curled up and died from my adrenaline. Eleven years? Twelve? Why am I remembering?

They heard the howling dogs again. Leaving the female carcass hanging in a tree, they rushed through thorny *kiawe* that slashed their arms and faces. This time the hounds had cornered a huge young boar, nearly three hundred pounds, all flashing tusks and hooves. Only Keo's speed saved them from laceration. He fired shots into the air until the dogs fell back.

"Smell of blood makes them crazy. They're so high, they wouldn't know if he ripped into them."

The moment froze, the boar froze. For a second it twisted its head crazily, and Endo saw razor-sharp hairs part on its neck, saw the pink flesh beneath. *A good neck. It would be easy. One quick slice . . .*

The shot lifted the pig into the air. It landed grunting, wounded in the shoulder. Keo cursed, shot it again between the eyes. A messy shot, ruining the head for mounting. The men collapsed, exhausted, while hounds lapped at the blood. Keo saw their penises eerily erect. Why did living things do that in the face of death? Senses so keen and sharp, blood engorged the penis. His mind wandered, he thought how long it had been since *he* was engorged, since he felt bone-deep passion and desire.

He looked up self-consciously, as if the other man could read his mind. Then he remembered it was blue-faced Endo, whom, probably, nothing could shock. He suspected he had seen so much flesh in various contexts—tortured, dying, dead—his response to human bodies was boredom. He remembered Endo with beautiful Parisian girls, how they had loved his courtliness. Now he seemed to barely notice women.

Who did this to us? Keo wondered. *Who left us for dead?*

"Endo. Have you got a woman? Here in Honolulu?"

He looked down, shy. "Sometimes I go to prostitutes. Just release. I try, but I feel nothing. I only *feel* when I blow saxophone. Jazz, the way we play—the old, pure, searching way—it takes me back to innocence." He shook his head. "Whatever I once blew, I'm running out of it."

Watching the hounds lolling in blood, they talked until it seemed they had reached the bottom of things. A false bottom, certain things not touched upon. The fact that Endo was waiting to die. Though he had once been the enemy, Keo now saw his pain as ennobling, austere.

We're both empty shells. Loveless, childless. Except that he was wrenched from youth to serve his emperor. I was only searching for a girl.

"Endo . . . you ever think of suicide?"

He laughed softly. "That isn't necessary. All I have to do is wait." He pointed to his bluish face, his nearly black fingernails. "It's really rather dull, dying. One has to walk so slowly toward it."

"You've been to specialists. Can't they help you?"

"They want to put me under glass, a guinea pig. I have no sentiments to spare for science. My only fear is that insanity will take me first."

They stood and bent to the arduous task of cleaning and dressing the boar. Leaving the sow hanging in the tree for cousins, they dragged the gamy male down guava-laden slopes, skidding on their butts down slippery ravines. They made it to the truck by twilight, wrapping the carcass in rags and tarpaulin and ropes. Keo tapped each hound on the nose with his rifle, reminding them the carcass was *kapu.* He gave them pans of stream water, rubbing each one vigorously for being first-rate boarhounds.

In near darkness, heavy fog descended. It was like driving snow-blind. Twice Keo braked, blowing his horn at what looked like spectres spinning into their headlights. A flaming white bush flung itself across the hood, almost cracking the windshield.

"Iiiii! What is it?" Endo cried.

"Angry *akua.* We're driving the Pali Road with pork. It's *kapu!*"

Outside a shrieking. Even the dogs howled with terror. Keo stopped the truck, got out, and raised his hands, lifting his head to heaven, chanting in Hawai'ian.

"Noi e kala'ia! . . . Ho'okāmakamaka! . . . Kala mai! . . . Kala mai!"

He chanted it over and over until the spirits retreated, the road ahead grew visible.

"Kala mai," Endo said. "What does it mean?"

"To beg forgiveness."

NOW HEADLESS FIGURES IN RANDOM DRIFT HAUNTED ENDO'S dreams. Papuans in native garb, P-girls in filthy rags. His jackboots stippled. His sword stained red. He began to dread sleep, even twilight.

Sometimes he woke on his feet, poised in the *coup de grâce* behind a kneeling victim. He steadied himself, legs spread wide. He raised his sword. The graceful arc, the almost . . . ecstasy. But sometimes there was loss of face. A miss. Shoulder blade carved out like a quarter moon. Lung floating like a cloud. Now long-lost heads came bouncing back. A grinning mouth. A winking eye. He sat up in the dark, screaming. Even the full moon grinned.

Hotels evicted him. Each time a manager stood shouting in some distempered hallway under dingy light, Endo studied the man's neck. He started lingering in crowds, contemplating the space between a stranger's hairline and his shoulders.

. . . That neck would be easy. Pah! Pah! So little effort. That neck

too thin, real shakuhachi, *bamboo clarinet, neck. That neck* zenzen dame, *really terrible, much too fat. Would not be a clean cut, would get caught up in double chins . . .*

Some nights he crouched at his window, hearing Allied bombers approach Rabaul. He hid himself in a closet. When he stepped out, he stood in a military courtroom on trial for war crimes. Lost years, lost transitions. One night he woke scraping on his hands and knees. He had dreamed of the tunnels. A time he had never been able to recall.

. . . BODIES CARVED BY SHRAPNEL. NOWHERE TO PUT THEM, TO *bury them. Hollows scooped from clay walls. Niches of the living dead. Officers planning their suicides. Frenzied sex with crouching girls kept like animals. Conscripts sodomizing other conscripts . . .*

And all the while, beside me, tied to me, a talisman, a ragged girl. Softness, stench, disease. Who was that, tethered to me? Like two piles of dust enjoined. Maybe that is the way to come out of war. Someone to hold, to grasp, even though she's bone. Bones can be so clean, specific.

And deep inside me, always that morse of instruction. Lay my gleaming sword against her neck. But both so weak from leaking gas we simply lay there, unimpeachable. Yet, how hard she tried to die. To lift my sword in bird-bone hands. Who? Who was it? Name. She had a name. . . .

ALL THESE YEARS, HE HAD HOPED DEATH WOULD OUTRUN THE mad remembering. Now each day he woke from dreams like something skinned, muscles and tendons quivering, nerve ends alert and aglow. His skin deepened in jacaranda hues.

He walked the streets of Honolulu sideways, keeping his back against the walls. One day outside a barbershop, he went into convulsions. He thrashed about wildly, making funny sounds, then stiffened, losing consciousness. Strangers laid him on the grass, thinking he was epileptic. He woke exhausted, deeply confused.

After a while, he walked home slowly. A sense of being followed. He thought he heard a tapping cane. He thought he recognized a smell. He turned, but there was no one. Only the smell—extreme, abnormal, like wet rust. Like reservoirs of clay.

Ho'oikaika

To Gather Strength

She stood in morning pallor, then jerked the blinds, and in one blow the room was stunned with light. It always thrilled her, this ability to transform things. Materials. Environments. She plugged in the Singer, felt it come alive. Soon it would be chattering, connecting stitches like running fire.

Lately she and the machine seemed huddled in competitive seething. Her mind, its hum. Sometimes it stabbed her finger, drawing blood. A little juice in the fire, so the fabric seemed to sizzle. Now Malia reared back, grabbing its neck as if reining in a beast. The needle had taken off, stitching a word inside a seam. KAPAKAHI.

"I *know* his name. I won't forget that."

Osborn Kuahi "Krash" Kapakahi. She remembered how he had come home from war so full of plans. He was going to earn a degree. He was going to study law. He was going to be thus and such. He. He. He. His words had made her blood laugh. So male. So *he*-full. Well, she had accomplished something, too. Kept the best of him, the child. And not given back an inch.

So what if, for months and years, her bed had been weighed down with no one and nothing but his ribs, wrapped in soft white linen? And so what if sometimes loneliness impelled her to caress those ribs, rub them with *kukui* oil and oil of night jasmine, stroking them across her hips? And furthermore, so what if desire sometimes drove her fingers deep inside herself, holding the ribs against subsiding spasms of her body? Sobbing as she came. Ribs were bones, and bones stayed home. They could be counted on.

Now, some nights she felt yanked awake, felt Krash was dreaming of her, pulling her into his sleep. She sat up in the dark smelling his salty, oceanic skin, feeling his lips wet her thighs, fingers spreading on her like starfish. She held a mango, remembering the way he peeled them, viscous skin growing into one long, slippery coil, like a finger beckoning *come here*. The way he had slid his fingers into her mouth, feeding her two-finger poi. How ripe, succulent plums recalled the deep plum color of his sex. Even books slowed her down. The sigh of turning pages, the way he had let her watch him read. A thing so private.

When he went off to law school on the mainland, Malia had shut down like an eye. And when word came he had married a *haole*, she stood in the dark, in pieces. Only Keo knew her pain: one day he saw her downtown, all dressed up, in mismatched shoes. Years passed. Her daughter grew up, and she grew older, one half-living, the other half-watching. Now Krash was back, and Malia vowed he would not stroll into their lives at his leisure.

Then an old woman with a cane stepped from the ashes and stood beside Leilani's bed. What Malia had seen and heard that night haunted her. She convinced herself she had dreamed it, but the old woman's image stood coughing in the shadows. At night she watched Keo sleep, wanting to wake him and tell. Each time she knelt beside him, trying to begin, her tongue thickened, she could not speak.

She went to a store and studied maps. There, deep in the Pacific, north of Guadalcanal: RABAUL. Her back felt chilled. Tiny hairs stood up on her neck. One day the Singer took off on its own, inscribing inside a dart the name. SUNNY SUNG. Malia shuddered, remembering the delicate antique kimono she had presented to Pono as a gift. She remembered the old, eerily familiar face embroidered on the back. It was the face of SUNNY SUNG.

That night in Leilani's death room, Sunny had talked for hours. What Malia learned in that terrible night was what life could do to a woman, even a sheltered, privileged woman. She saw how badly a female needed guardians, protectors. She saw how desperately Baby Jonah needed her father.

She sat listening to her young-girl snores. She smiled. Her little *kanaka*, whose menstrual blood was already rinsing her into womanhood. Now she touched her daughter's foot, tracing the meticulous arch of one who could destroy her. She was still awkward, somewhat chubby, yet even in sleep her mouth was set, defiant. Malia squeezed her daughter's toe.

"What is . . . ?" Baby Jonah sat up, half alarmed.

"Listen, Baby Jo." Malia began to weep. "You are going to hate me. Maybe one day you will love me, too."

Frightened, the girl pulled the sheet up round her shoulders.

"I am . . . your mother. Yes. I birthed you. Now I claim you. Punish me a little, not too much. Life has taken care of that."

Across the hall Keo turned, moaning in his sleep. He frowned, dreaming of Baby Jonah.

He dreamed she sobbed out in the dark, "Tell me who my father is!"

He dreamed the dark responded, "Time . . . I need a little time."

KEO WATCHED HIS OLD FRIEND KRASH TRAVEL ROUND THE ISland addressing thousands of folks waiting to reclaim their lands. Lands that were stolen when the islands were seized and annexed in the 1890s. At such times Keo thought of Baby Jonah, wondering when Krash would claim the daughter that was his. They had never really discussed it, always talked round it until his marriage ended.

"When you going to face that girl?" Keo asked. "Like the man I know you are."

Krash's eyes were prideful. "You ever seen me beg?"

"Dammit. I'm the one who's begging. You and Malia, you folks are real *mākonā*. Cruel! Playing these ego games while your daughter grows up fatherless."

"What can I do? That *wahine* is too damned proud. She stills wants to marry *haole*."

"Nah. Nah," Keo cried. "She could have done that twenty times. A *haole* real-estate tycoon tried to court her, all real proper. She told him get lost, said she would marry him when he gave Hawai'ians back their land."

Krash smiled. "Still got her ways. But, don't tell me she's stayed alone."

"There's no one. I swear. She's watched Baby Jo grow up, and realized what she had with you was probably the best. It only happens once a life. Believe me."

Krash felt the sting of old resentments. "I came home from war, and was told that girl was Malia's *hānai* sister. Ho, man! How you think that made me feel? My features are written all over her. She even walks like me. Fact is, Malia didn't want to admit she had a *kanaka*'s kid."

"So you went off and married a *haole*."

"I did what I did."

Keo shook his head. "Funny thing, you're probably the only guy who could make my sister happy. You always kept her on her toes."

"Some women don't want happiness, Keo. They're after something else."

"Like what?"

"I'm not sure. You take a man with pride, he wants to build things, control things. You take a real proud woman, she wants to get under the skin of things. Find out what works, what doesn't, what she needs to keep the generations going."

"All I know is, together, you could give that girl a life. This pride thing . . . you folks make me sick."

Some nights Krash sat alone, wondering how much pride was enough. How much was too much. Fighting overseas, he had seen white soldiers bloated with arrogance and pride. And he had seen whites with no pride at all. They did menial jobs, kowtowed to higher-ups. In that way he had learned they weren't always superior. He was just as fearful and brave as they. Just as smart, often smarter.

In the late 1940s, while earning an undergraduate degree, he had applied to law schools on the mainland, one after the next, until he was accepted at the University of Chicago under a foreign student quota, even though Hawai'i was a territory of the U.S. and not "foreign." Studies were exhausting; some nights he thought he couldn't make it, he was up against superior minds. Then he thought, *Superior to me? Why?* It made him push harder, for himself, his race.

He was encouraged by professors who had been labor lawyers, aware of escalating labor disputes in Hawai'i, the coming of unions to sugar and pineapple plantations. These men taught him how to arm himself against sharp minds, when to advance, when to retreat. Amongst brilliant students, he learned to be quiet, listening and absorbing.

The sister of a classmate fell in love with him, attracted by his athletic body, his rough, handsome Polynesian face, and something deeper, more compelling—his sheer will to achieve. Liquid brown eyes, full, pouting lips, her languid movements drew him, reminding him of Malia Meahuna. Her name was Vivian. She was even wearing a gardenia when they met.

They married and lived in comfortable squalor while he finished law school. Looking back, Krash felt the whole marriage took place in the dark. He couldn't remember what they did, what they said. The sheer enormity of his ambitions overshadowed everything. By 1953, when he returned to Honolulu, they were already fighting, drinking, driving off in different directions. The marriage dipped and soared until it dawned on them it was over.

Admitted to the Hawai'i bar, Krash started his own practise, *Osborn Kuahi Kapakahi, Attorney-at-Law,* in a closet-size room in downtown Honolulu, augmenting his meager income by taking court-appointed cases other firms avoided. Criminal, divorce. Here he saw how his people had turned on themselves. He saw it in crowded courtrooms on Paternity Day, Juvenile Delinquent Day, the Day for Child-Abuse Cases. Native Hawai'ians beating themselves and their children down, on liquor, on welfare, on the run.

He took on suits to recover property, representing small landowners against plantations. In that way he learned the rules of law governing partition of real estate. Law was unique in Hawai'i: there were Hawai'ian, Pidgin, Chinese, Japanese, Portuguese, Filipino, and half a dozen other languages to contend with. It was also unique because, in less than seventy years, Hawai'i had gone from a monarchy to a republic to a U.S. Territory. Now it was on the brink of statehood.

Krash joined the Young Democrats Club along with a lot of returning war vets. Running for a seat in the Territorial House of Representatives, he was defeated. Even amongst the Young Democrats, he was considered "not electable." A Hawai'ian, with no political connections. The opposition called him the *Lū'au* Lawyer. Still, by 1956, he had begun to draw attention as a dramatic orator who commanded a courtroom.

He moved to a larger office and hired a secretary and law clerk, representing the elderly, war vets, plantation laborers arrested for supporting the ILWU. Not even the poorest were turned away. For the first time in Hawai'i's history, indentured workers had a voice.

"All these charity cases. You'll never get rich," Keo warned him.

"I'm not trying to get rich."

"Then how you going to set an example? A poor *kanaka* lawyer is just another poor *kanaka*, right?"

Krash studied him, his voice extremely calm and quiet.

"Keo. We both went out into the world. You saw more than me. All I saw was combat. For years I've listened to you talk about Louisiana, Alabama—Negroes hanging from trees. Hell, you were beaten with a baseball bat. You've talked about Gypsies in France, exterminated by the Nazis. Sometimes when we're drunk you cry, remembering coolies in Shanghai, kids eating garbage. . . ."

Keo's eyes shifted, not sure what was coming.

"You've been home a long time. Do you ever look around?" Krash leaned forward. "Man, the tragedy is *here*. Our people are being erased. It's done by stealing land, then wiping out culture, and Mother Tongue."

"I see it. I'm not blind—"

"But you never *say*, you never *do*. What did you learn in your travels? How do you apply that to Hawai'ians?"

"Hell, Krash, I'm not articulate like you."

" 'Ey! Trumpets talk, they cry. You know, I used to wonder why you weren't great. I mean, why you weren't *recognized* as great. Finally I figured it out. Keo, your music never represented your race."

He looked up, slowly. "Man, jazz is personal—not racial."

"Bullshit. Jazz is everything. It's slavery. It's massacres. It's black skin, red skin. It's crying for your mother. Your motherland." He shook his head, his voice grew soft. "I just never heard you crying for your people."

In the silence, Keo touched a cheek to see if it was there. He felt like something with its face cut off. After a while—because he loved him—Krash spoke out again.

"You were born with this freaky genius. Only I never saw you use it for anyone but you. Always searching. Jazzing. Sure, you've stretched the boundaries, broken new ground. When you're dead, folks will say, 'Hula Man! A genius on horn.' The real question is, how did you use that genius? Who did you help?"

In that second silence, they looked out at the sea, its movements so rhythmical, so intelligent, it seemed a huge impatient brain. When Krash finally turned to him, Keo was gone. He watched his dark form sucked into a wave, watched him carried almost to the reef. After a dozen waves had tossed him like a root, the ocean brought him back, gave him up so easily he strolled out of the water like a man strolling across a lawn. Skin wet bronze, he shook himself dry.

Then he sat down and squeezed his friend's arm.

IN THE HEADINESS OF THOSE YEARS, KRASH NEVER STOPPED thinking of his daughter, Baby Jonah. Mostly he kept his distance, knowing from Keo she went to Sacred Heart, knowing what her grades were, who her friends were. Occasionally he parked near the school just to see her coming and going. A sophomore now, plump and lovely, sloe-eyed like her mother. With school friends she spoke perfect English, but at the entrance to her lane, off came the shoes, and she was just "Baby Jo" slamming around with big *lū'au* feet, cussing and yelling in Pidgin.

He never went near Malia's shop. She never ventured within three blocks of his office. They knew their boundaries. But sometimes Krash drove slowly past Kalihi Lane. Late at night he walked up the lane, passed into the yard, and stood outside her window. *I want my daughter. I want you.*

And some nights in her sleep, Malia half woke, running her hands over her breasts, pretending they were his hands. Remembering her hands on *him*, his harsh and diffident erection, the physical gallantry with which he entered her. So slowly, so thoughtfully. How many years now? Could desire last that long? Maybe it had aged to something else. Maybe what she desired was to crawl into his bed and ask forgiveness.

KA ʻĀINA HĀNAU

Land of One's Birth

DAYS WERE SO HUMID, THEY SAW REFLECTIONS OF THEIR FACES in their forearms. Barefoot, they encamped in Krash's hallway—big, sweet-smelling Hawaiʻians, leaving sweat stains on his floor, ghostly sweat shadows of heads and shoulders on the walls. Whispering in Pidgin and Mother Tongue, they leaned damp cheeks against a door, just for the cold kiss of the doorknob. For days, sometimes weeks, they waited their turn.

In Krash's office, they stood tongue-tied, observing rows of thick, distempered law books, walls of yellow files. They stared at ceiling fans that echoed and echoed their unschooled tongues as they tried to explain how things were breaking down, how life was harsh, unsolvable.

Having no money, they brought him *koa* bowls, half a pig. Once, a whole barracuda. He sat cross-legged with them on *lau hala* mats, drinking guava from paper cups. Airing their grievances, their anger, their deep humiliation, Hawaiʻian voices dipped and soared. Arms floated rhythmically like dancers, then a fist slammed down emphatically. They used their heads, their legs, their feet, ribald and agile in their telling, so Krash was caught up in their drama.

They were elders "talking story" and he was a boy again, entranced. Sometimes he was moved to laughter, often tears. As he bent and wiped his eyes, they wrapped their massive arms round him, crooning. In their lavish, compassionate natures, they forgot who was seeking legal counsel, who was comforting whom.

"No, Krash boy, no mo' cry. *Pau* crying!" They hugged him like a child. "So sad you all alone, sad yo' wife left. You try come stay wit' us. I make you *'ono* pig and poi. Bumbye you feel real good!"

But hearing the same stories, day after day, he saw how native Hawai'ians were being ghettoized, slowly erased. Now, with the prospect of statehood before them, folks questioned the term "equality as Americans." In poll after poll, foreigners—island settlers—voted in favor of statehood. Most native Hawai'ians, now a minority in their own lands, voted against.

Week after week Krash stood before crowds, urging his people to stand firm and VOTE NO on statehood.

"They want to drain the ocean from our veins, turn our blood to stone, so we'll forget what was done to us!"

A woman shouted up at him. "I no agree wit' you! Statehood mo' bettah, give us one voice. Else, how we going get good jobs, how educate our kids? You like we stay on welfare fo' evah?"

He struggled for patience. "Have you forgotten our history? In 1893, white sugar barons overthrew our queen, stole all our lands . . . without the knowledge of the U.S. Congress! Five years later, the U.S. president illegally annexed all of Hawai'i. Statehood won't give us better jobs. Or educate our kids. It will only give them *total power* over us."

While locals stood shouting back and forth, a big, husky man in construction boots climbed onstage, grabbed the mike from Krash, and started yelling.

"You folks *lōlō*, or what? You like vote fo' statehood, den vote! Fo'get dis guy wit' fancy legal tongue. Nutting going bring back Queen Lili'uokalani. Time fo' turn da page! Fo' welcome statehood!"

An old Chinese man yelled up at him. "You one crazy fuckah, you. If lands stolen in da first place, how can be *legal* statehood? Dis statehood going benefit da rich, and bury da *kānaka*! And all us poor folks, too."

The construction worker danced across the stage, weaving and sermonizing. Krash gave him his five minutes, then tried to retrieve the mike. When the man pushed him away, Krash sighed, stepped back, and sliced the air with the edge of his hand, karate-chopping him in the neck. He folded like a paper doll. Bowing to the whistling, cheering crowd, Krash went on with his talk.

"My brother here is half right. We can't turn back the clock. But we can demand apologies, and reparations. The U.S. says statehood will improve our lives. If they want to improve our lives, give us back our lands! Give us a couple million dollars *cash*, for the years they've profited from those lands. Then we'll talk statehood."

While he helped the staggering man to his feet and off the stage, a priest stepped forward.

"Krash, I don't agree with you. A U.S. citizen has rights. People have to *listen*. Congress has to listen. If we get statehood, we can vote native Hawai'ians into positions of power. They'll give us representation in the state and federal legislature."

He looked down, shaking his head. "Father, I guarantee, even with statehood, forty-fifty years from now there won't be one Hawai'ian or part-Hawai'ian in Congress or the House of Representatives. Not one."

Keo stood amongst the crowd, only half convinced Krash was right. Whatever its drawbacks, statehood would give Hawai'ians dignity, a voting voice in U.S. politics. Some Hawai'ians felt that was important. They spat on Krash in the streets. A rock had been thrown through his window.

Now they shouted up at him. " 'Ey, bruddah. How's come all a sudden you fighting progress? Big education, now you t'ink you too good fo' be one state. Maybe you like Hawai'i be one monarchy again? Maybe you like be king!?"

He laughed, exhausted. Gaining their trust was like one-handed cat's cradle, a maneuver taking infinite patience. He stepped to the edge of the stage, half kneeling, leaning in toward the crowd.

"You folks remember me? I started out nothing, one lazy beachboy from Wai'anae. Then the U.S. Army sent me overseas. Said fight for *freedom*. I fought so good, I lost one lung. Then, I came home and looked around. . . ."

He spread his arms out dramatically. "You call this freedom? You want to stay fifty years in broken-down shacks? I got elders, family and friends—thirty-five years ago each one applied to the Department of Hawai'ian Homelands for a plot of land. Land that was supposedly set aside for native Hawai'ians, for one dollar per plot each year. Instead it's leased to foreign corporations, the U.S. military. All these years, those folks are *still* on the waiting list for land."

His voice reverberated across the grounds. "I guarantee you, even with statehood, *thirty years from now* when they are in their nineties, some will still be on that list, waiting for a plot of land. That's why they call it the *Hit List*."

People stood in knots, confused. They needed so badly to believe. To have something to believe in. By then they were already witnessing the slicing up of valleys for highways, resort development of dwindling shorelines that killed off old fishing villages. In the city, ghettoes grew.

Believing statehood would either save them or extinguish them, friends, even families, grew drastically divided. In Palolo, an angry wife bit off her husband's cheek. A man shaved his neighbor's hunting hound completely bald in Nanakuli. Near ʻAʻala Park, the owner of the Mango Luncheonette, vociferously in favor of statehood, watched his cousin open a new business just across the street. The Anti-Mango Luncheonette. Day after day, crowds taunted each other from opposite sidewalks. "VOTE NO! . . . VOTE YES! . . ."

TWO STREETS OVER FROM THE ANTI-MANGO LUNCHEONETTE, she watched an old *kahuna lapaʻau*, an herb healer, mash root of morning glory in sea salt. Then, softly chanting, the woman wrapped a ti leaf round Sunny's leg, spreading on the morning-glory poultice. Ti leaf kept the root from burning. Lastly, she covered the leaf with *kapa*, barkcloth.

The *kahuna* smelled of camphor, which always took Sunny back to Shanghai. Then, there was another smell, which took her to Rabaul. The sweet, damp odor of rot. In Rabaul maggots had eaten away infected flesh round her shrapnel wound. The wound had healed, but bone, too, had been infected. Each year when gourds called—when windy seasons, presaging winter storms, rattled dried gourds hanging in nets—her leg pain grew so intense, Sunny's body shook, even her hair trembled.

"I wait for death," she whispered. "What is the point of such suffering if it does not lead to death? But life does not oblige me."

"Life." The old *kahuna* sighed. "So short, is hardly time for laughter."

Sunny listened to crowds out in the streets. If one began to laugh, how would one stop?

The woman patted her shoulder. "Now I bring best medicine for bone." She came back with a bowl of *poi*. "Eat. You so skinny, almost mist."

"That is my Hawai'ian name. *Uanoe*. Gathering Mist."

She dipped her main *poi* finger in the bowl, swirled it round, and brought it to her lips. Soothing pounded-taro paste slid down her throat, her neck so thin the woman watched her gears shift as she swallowed. When she was full, the woman brought her *'awa* tea. Sunny drank in grandmother sips, feeling a mild narcosis as pain slipped across the room.

"Now, rest. See coco palm outside? When shadow of coco palm is longer than tree, I wake you."

Her eyes drooped. Outside, a young girl swung back and forth from a rope of bark fastened to a tree. She sat on a crosspiece at rope's end, holding firmly with hands and knees while her brother pushed her from behind. Together they sang, "*Pūhenehene no'a no'a*." Come, play the stone game!

She dozed, and it was small-kid time, and she was singing with her brother, Parker.

How fearless we were. Flying dragon kapa *kites, praying the wind would snatch us from the cliffs!*

He had gone down on a battleship east of Okinawa. The same week they had cut out her womb, an army officer showed her Parker's name on a manifest. She read his name, and blinked. Now diving deep, Sunny dreamed she found his body on the submerged deck. She wrapped him in ti leaves, packed hot sea salt round his body so he would sweat out death. She brought a full gourd to his lips.

"*Brother, here is juice of* limu, *seaweed. To strengthen you, rinse you back to life. So you can meet our sister, Lili. And little Anahola. I have brought them home. . . .*"

He pushed the gourd away. "*Go! I am at peace. Here among the* aku."

She woke up weeping.

"Crying very good," the old *kahuna* whispered. "How many years you never cry? Bumbye, Rain-Catcher Spider drink your tears! She weave cathedrals from your sorrow."

Turning her head, Sunny saw a graceful, ruby red spider mending the gossamer rigging of her web. She leaned very close. Smelling her tears, the spider paused and cautiously approached, eyes tiny golden broadcasts. Then, in a jeweler's hunch, she jumped from her web and ran across Sunny's cheek, nuzzling a teardrop. Glittering and growing a richer red as she sucked down the tear. A little drunk and dreamy, she ran back to her web, weaving human sadness into the arches and loggias of her universe. Sunny touched her cheek and watched.

How quietly she weaves. How patiently she bides her time.

KRASH AND KEO DROVE TWENTY MILES WEST OF HONOLULU TO an area of astonishing natural beauty. Miles of canefields, brooding emerald valleys. Up in the sharp, bold Wai'anae Mountain Range—paralleling the Ko'olaus to the east—were steep ridges, rain forests of double canopies. Here were sacred *heiau*, ancient temples, and caves, spirit dwellings of dead chiefs. Here was also a district where, within eroding houses, people's lives were endangered. This was what drove Krash back and back to Wai'anae, his birthplace on the island's arid leeward coast.

He spoke softly now, reminding Keo how, in the early twentieth century as land increased in value, native Hawai'ians had been forced out of Honolulu and Waikiki. Many had moved back to the plains and valleys of this rural coast. Strung with towns named Nanakuli, Lualualei, Ma'ili, Wai'anae, Makaha, Mākua, it was a haven where mountains and the sea shielded farmers and fishermen from outsiders. But this had not been an easy land. Much of it was barren, covered in *kiawe* and coral rock. There was little water.

Through the decades, love of *'āina*, land, had slowly changed the Wai'anae Coast from barren to fertile. Gardens grew, and fruit trees, fields of heart-shaped taro leaves blanketed the valleys. Day after day farmers waded knee-deep through rich, gravylike ooze of irrigated plots, weeding and nurturing, praying over tender young *lū'au*, taro tops.

Lives were once again based on the old tradition of bartering and sharing. It was still a hard and challenging land. It kept the people hard, wary of outsiders. *Haole* saw the Wai'anae Coast as primitive and dangerous, rebellious *kānaka* living in shacks of weathered wood and rusted tin. But this coast had one thing much coveted: broad white strands of beaches, the pure unblemished sea.

As they drove on, Krash told of spies who came sly-eyeing for resort developers and land speculators.

"They get caught by locals, their cars are overturned and set on fire. Trying to hitchhike back to the city, one guy was picked up by a sympathetic-looking couple. They left him on Farrington Highway stark naked!"

He pointed *mauka*, toward the mountains. "Still plenty hardship here. See those lush fields, Keo? Taro is thirsty, needs water for irrigation. Farmers need millions of gallons every day, or taro roots will rot. Already bad signs. One day farmers will be rationed. Taro, our staff of life, will be threatened."

That night they sat with Krash's family, as cousins told of waiting fifteen years for two acres of Homestead land. Then five more years before they were granted loans to build their house—under Hawai'ian Homelands contracts with substandard companies. Construction was so bad, within a year sewage backed up. Their house had such a dreadful smell, they slept outside in tents. They told how other Homestead folks were forced to use the same construction companies. Faulty wiring made their houses booby traps. A dog was electrocuted. A boy switched on a radio that blew up in his face.

"It happening all over dese damned Homestead lots," a cousin said. "Folks flush toilet, da house blow up!"

Krash's mother spoke up wearily. "I and Krash's papa ten years on Homestead waiting list. Finally get our lot in 1931, den get our house built . . ."

She dropped her head, and Krash continued for her.

"First night we moved in, my bedroom wall collapsed. Then the lights went. We moved round the house for months wearing headlamps like miners. Now, twenty-eight years later, Mama and Papa still get mouth sores from rusty water. They live in this house with year-round colds."

Each year during heavy rains his parents had to wear rubber boots, slogging through water leaking from ceilings and open junctures of walls. The water formed swirling reservoirs in every room.

"Like one indoor rivah," his father said. "Sometimes, ho man! you nevah seen such worms. Plenny good fo' fish bait."

Some Homesteaders had waited ten years for wells and electric hookup. Now, fearing for their lives, they slept in trucks beside collapsing houses. When they marched in protest, they were evicted by sheriffs and armed deputies. Landless, hopeless, Hawai'ians began to "squat" on beaches, under bridges. Living in crates, abandoned cars.

That night the two men sat silent.

"I know what you're thinking," Krash said. "If I'd married Malia, she would have ended up out here, wearing headlamps and rubber boots."

Keo shook his head. "No she wouldn't. And that's not what I was thinking."

"Well . . . ?"

"I was wondering what I can do to help you . . . to help our people."

NEXT MORNING, THEY HIKED UP INTO THE FIELDS TO A *LO'I* kalo, a taro patch.

"Come on, man." Krash rolled up his pants. "This is the sacred food brought by our first ancestors. You can't understand land rights, or water rights, or anything we're fighting for, until you're squatting in mud, planting and mulching and weeding taro."

Keo gave a shout, kicked off his shoes, pulled off his shirt and pants. Moving off alone, he slogged up to his knees in rich black mud. How many years since he waded through a *lo'i*, feeling wet earth coat his limbs? Not since he was a boy. Now, bending low, an elbow on one knee, other arm outstretched yanking weeds between plants, he remembered his mother "talking story," telling how ancestors had used only their strong hands and digging-sticks to build vast systems of irrigation ditches for their crops. Even now in certain valleys one could still see terrace after terrace of ancient *kalo*.

Hours passed, though Keo didn't know they were hours. He felt no ache from arduous bending and pulling, felt no thirst from the sun. After a while he felt nothing, he no longer existed as a singular thing. He and the land and the weeds he pulled and the heart-shaped glistening taro leaves and the mud and the air seemed one. He looked at his hand and no longer felt it, he could no longer name it. His hand flowed into leaf that flowed into earth that poured into the lava heart of his island pouring into sea.

He sat down slowly in luscious mud, his hands full of oozing earth. He had forgotten it. But, maybe it was waiting in him all the time. *'Āina.* Land. He had had to let the earth decide when to reclaim him, had to let it come for him, knowing when he was ready. He sat a long time, sun on his dark shoulders, mud drying on him like long gloves, the rest, the waist-down of him, deep in wet black earth. Mountains behind him, the ocean before him, forming a cradle. That was how Krash found him at day's end. A child, rocking in his cradle of taro fields.

IHU PANI

Closed Nose: Deep Dive into Knowledge

WITH STATEHOOD LOOMING FOR HAWAI'I, IT SEEMED EVEN NAture fought back. The sea grew more aggressive. Each night manmade beaches of Waikiki flowed back into the ocean so that, at dawn, waves lapped at terraces of smart hotels. While tourists slept in costly rooms, dump trucks brought in more sand, which the sea rapidly swallowed.

Sand rakers ran from their jobs, swearing they saw giant nightsquid come ashore, hoovering the sands, sucking down half a seawall. Under a full moon, three Filipino waiters watched the ten-story Reef Hotel sway like a dancer, as if from oceanic tremors. All warnings that Waikiki was on the heaving edge of collapse. VOTE NO supporters grew in small increments.

In spasms of uncertainty Keo stood before high school and college students. He even addressed marching bands, church choirs, urging them to get their elders to VOTE NO. This younger generation challenged him, Hawai'ians as well as other locals.

"Uncle, why you want to keep us from being first-class Americans? Our folks pay plenny federal taxes. They fought in World War Two, Korea."

A Chinese youth stood up. "We should *elect* our governor, not have him appointed by Washington, D.C. We should be allowed to vote for the president of the U.S. Otherwise, we're second rate!"

And then a Portuguese. "Uncle, we want dignity and prestige. When we go to college on the mainland, we want to be accepted as equals, not Territorians."

When Keo tried to argue, they shouted him down.

"You want us to go back to a monarchy? Class system and *kapu*?"

Sometimes when he addressed them, his bowels went soupy, he felt his heart beating in his throat. He had no idea what he was saying, he just wanted to save their lives.

"Don't you see, statehood can only be achieved illegally. Because we were made a Territory illegally. The U.S. government should officially return our lands. Then give us the right to *choose* to be a state."

His audiences were so young, even their parents didn't remember the monarchy, or forced annexation. The past was past. All they wanted was higher education, better jobs.

"Keep at it," Krash said. "Talk until they're so bored they start to listen."

He kept talking, on athletic fields, in parking lots, wherever youngsters gathered. His voice was honest, unabashed. What he had learned, what he had seen, what he thought progress was, and what it wasn't. Sometimes there were war vets in a crowd. A veteran, using his plastic hand as an ashtray, threw his butts in Keo's face.

"You telling me I can't be a voting U.S. citizen? What I lose my fucking hand for! I vote your way, what you going do for me? Give me back my hand?"

Keo brushed ashes from his hair. "No. But as an independent nation, maybe we can give you back your pride, so you can wipe your own behind."

One day a young Hawai'ian girl stood up. "Uncle, what's the difference how our families vote? We're such a small percentage, other groups will swamp us anyway. Most everyone but us wants statehood."

She was slender and lovely. She would have been his daughter's age. Something scrolled in his mind: images scribbled on his retina. He wouldn't look. It fed on looks: the past, always hovering. He snapped back to the here and now, leaning toward the girl.

"Child, I can only answer from the heart. The U.S. government doesn't give a damn about Hawai'ians. We embarrass them; they would be happy if we disappeared. To vote yes on statehood will encourage politicians and the rich to wipe us out. In my heart, I believe this."

In time, the sum of these small acts, formulating arguments, believing them, unified things inside him. He began to see himself in their eyes. He was older, maybe he was even wise. It was most obvious with youngsters hungry for advice. Though most did not agree with him on statehood, slowly, cautiously, they approached, asking other things.

Should they study classical *haole* music? Or authentic Hawai'ian music—ancient chants accompanied with gourds and drums? Should they concentrate on popular slack-key guitar, falsetto singing? Should they be rock and rollers? Should they even study music? Or go out and learn from life?

He made a pact with them. If they promised to sit down with their folks and discuss the pros and cons of statehood—if they promised to be informed and balanced in their views—he would teach them everything he knew about music. Most students agreed, and soon they were locked into rhythms of give and take.

He began feeling a strange sense of renewal, a resurgence of love for music, for musical instruments, the human relationship to them. He tried to convey to students how every quality a human possessed, every wicked or noble reflection, was mirrored in each note he played.

Sometimes while he talked, old folks drifted into the backs of auditoriums and churches. Their days were long. Now *pau* plate-lunch, it was time for midday snores. They sat on folding chairs, heads slowly drooping. An elder shouted in his dreams, shifted position and snored again. One old woman sat apart. Hands arthritic and scarred, elbows like cones of wrinkled bean curd. As Keo talked, she leaned forward on her cane, listening.

"WE'RE LOSING." KRASH STOOD TO THE SIDE OF A STAGE WHILE large crowds gathered. "Eighty percent of every crowd will vote YES." He shook his head, exhausted. "Maybe they're right. If we have to live in poverty, we may as well be a welfare *state*."

He pointed to a group of running, jumping kids, something haunted in their smiles. Teeth rotting to the gums from malnutrition. Legs calligraphed with open sores.

"Kool-Aid. Spam. That's all they know."

He'd lost weight. His handsome face was haggard. Newspapers had resurrected his campaign name, *Lū'au* Lawyer, accusing him of trying to keep his people illiterate and poor. Now he had organized a VOTE NO festival in the town of Wai'anae. Half a dozen bands volunteered. News spread up and down the Wai'anae Coast, and even those for statehood couldn't stay away.

School grounds were set up like a fair. Food and game booths, a stage for entertainment. Keo counted twenty different groups scheduled to appear. Blues and rock musicians. Slack-key guitars. *Kahiko* chanters and pre-hula *ha'a* dancers. Troupes costumed in Japanese, Korean, Filipino dress. Even groups for the Japanese circle dance, the *tanko bushi*. The air was electric. Whether folks wanted it or not, they felt their history changing.

By noon crowds numbered in the hundreds. Strolling the grounds, folks listened to old-timers harmonizing in sweet falsetto with 'ukuleles and guitars. They studied their neighbors, wondering how they would vote, no one really sure they wanted statehood as much as they wanted assurance that the new thing would be as good as the old.

Gazing at chaotic crowds, the thrust and jolt of bodies, Keo was jerked back to another landscape, of guards, watchtowers, starving, broken inmates. The gurgle of latrines. Crowds would always do that: in the blindman's buff of his senses, he would recall Woosung forever. He sat down, stroking his horn until he was back in the present, the thing he had to keep reaching for.

A broadcaster urged people closer to the stage. Full of food and drink, they settled down on mats and blankets, children beside them with cheeks stained shaved-ice blue and purple. A conch shell blew. An ancient chanter took her place onstage, beating her gourd drum as twenty dancers spread out before her.

She began to chant and slap the gourd as dancers bent their knees, dancing in unison. In low, controlled tones, she told of the fields and valleys surrounding them, once barren, now blessed with taro. She told how the sacred word *'āina*, land, came from the root word *'ai*, to feed, and how the sacred word *'ohana*, family, came from the root word *'oha*, sprouts of the heart-shaped taro plant, the staple and heartbeat of Hawai'ians, each family an offshoot of a larger stock. Thus, *'āina* nourished the *'ohana.*

She chanted praises to *akua*, gods living in stones that watched, in trees that listened. They were the guardians of the hard, dry soil of Wai'anae, helping it soften in rains, yield to the hands of *kānaka maoli*, indigenous Hawai'ians. In monotones she praised the hands and bent backs of *kānaka* that had labored for generations building taro terraces. She praised fish caught, *'opihi* gathered, that had strengthened those bodies that planted.

The dancers followed her words, moving in the nineteenth-century native style with bent knees, uplifted heels. Not the lazy, swaying motions of twentieth-century hula but the *hula 'ōlapa*, hula with chants, whose movements were emphatic and profound. Finally the chanter folded her hands, bringing the dancing to a close.

Then came *kachi-kachi* bands, *banduria* bands. Mounting the stage with his band, Hana Hou!, for a moment Keo paused, looking down at young and ancient faces, many on welfare, some living on beaches, in parks.

He leaned into the mike, breaking into Pidgin.

" 'Ey . . . *Howzit!*"

Whistles, applause, folks yelling "Hula Man."

"Real proud fo' be here wit' you folks today," he shouted. "First, going say one t'ing. Want you folks t'ink plenny hard fo' when you going vote on statehood, yeah? You vote yes, mebbe you voting fo' real junk-kine future. OK! *Pau* politics!"

Relaxing, he held up his horn. "Well, some of you folks know me as jazz kine. But what I going do now is, I going try make dis horn talk fo' you, Hawai'ian style!"

They cheered a little, quieting down as he began blowing trumpet in the softest way, songs reminiscent of the old days, of clacking stones, bamboo nose-flutes, sounds like wind through coco palms, through groves of talking jade-grass. Then he played "Papakolea," composed by blind Johnny Almeida, honoring an impoverished community in Honolulu. He played "E Hulihuli Ho'i Mai," Turn and Come Back. A song of longing and romance popularized by Hawai'i's songbird, Lena Machado.

He heard the crowd responding, singing the lyrics as he played.

He felt their emotion, that old Hawai'ian sadness, voices rising and rising as if drowning out fires of the death years. When he finished, there was silence in the crowd.

He inhaled, leaned into the mike again. "Here's somet'ing special. Hard to play. It's from one opera, *Turandot*, by dis guy named Puccini."

Opera? Tremendous boos from the crowd.

"Yeah, yeah. I know. But listen, dis part called 'Nessun dorma.' What da guy saying is . . . 'VINCIRÀ! I SHALL WIN!' Good theme for Hawai'ians, yeah?"

Then his trumpet began to soar, echoing across the grounds, the fields and plains, into the valleys and ridges of the Wai'anae Mountains. He soared until his sounds became so lost and seeking, people wept not knowing why. He finished slowly, like someone reaching understanding. Then he and the band eased out with pop songs, rock and roll.

AS BAND FOLLOWED BAND, MALIA'S EYES WERE DRAWN TO A certain booth. At intermission Krash was paged: they wanted him onstage telling folks how, and why, to vote. From inside the booth, he appeared, grinning broadly. Big shoulders stretching the fabric of his shirt, he strode forward, making his way toward the stage. Seeing them standing together he swerved, drawing himself up.

" 'Ey, great show, Keo. . . . Hello, Malia."

A nerve pulsed beneath her eye. She imagined the skin going dark like blue ravines. Something in her slowed and ached. She nodded silently, then looked away. He shook his head, defeated, walked into the crowd. Watching him, she thought she imagined that his back arched, his hands were thrown into the air. She thought she imagined that he folded in slow motion. The gunshot seemed to come as an afterthought.

She pushed Baby Jonah to the ground, covering her body with her own. Keo threw himself on both of them, then Malia struggled to her feet.

"Stay with her!" she cried.

With no sense of it, she pushed her way to Krash's side. Seeing blood flowing from his head, she knelt thinking how much they had wasted. How much of life they should have held against their faces. *We weren't careful. We didn't know how to live the fullness of each day that entered us.*

She looked up at the sky, begging for mercy for the father of her child. In that moment, she heard his watch ticking its lies, as if they still had time to court, and make amends. He lay facedown in the dirt. She saw blood spreading between his legs. *There must have been two shots. The head, the back.* She heard the whip of sirens. Squad cars circling the grounds.

And then it wasn't blood she smelled. In shock, his body had let go. Delicately, Malia moved his arm away from the puddle, then twisted his face into her lap. She slid a hand under his chest, trying to squeeze his heart and keep him alive. By now, the grounds were carpeted with human bodies, no one moving.

Police surrounded a thin Hawai'ian, wrestling him to the ground.

"Filthy Communist!" he screamed. "Trying to keep us from statehood. Keep us Territory trash."

A woman half stood and shouted, "Look that man! He shot Krash bad."

Malia ripped off part of her skirt, trying to wrap his head. She had the head turned now, resting in her lap. She wasn't sure what was in her lap. Bone, blood, a dead man. He moaned, it echoed in her ribs. In turning his head, somehow his body followed. Now he was lying faceup. Wet excrement stained her skirt beneath him.

Pulling his body close, she felt his waste run down her hand and over her wrist, run down her arm to the elbow. Blood from his head dripped into her palm. She wiped his dirty cheeks with spit.

He looked up, and his body trembled. "Malia . . . is it bad?"

"Please," she sobbed. "Don't die."

Crowds got slowly to their feet. Police dragged the man to a squad car while others patrolled, telling folks to stay back, stay back. Medics came running with a stretcher.

"Easy now. He may have a concussion. It's one big motherfucking rock."

"Big . . . what?" she whispered.

"There. Look at the size of it. Some crazy nut."

She shook her head. "I heard the gun. I saw the bullets knock him down."

Keo came up behind her. "Malia. A truck. A truck backfired."

She knew then she would never be rid of him. She could not stain herself with the waste and blood of a man, and not be haunted by him. She bent so close he felt heat from her forehead.

"Krash. It was a rock. Only a rock . . ."

He stared at her, struggling to comprehend.

Folks pressed forward and were pushed back. After a while he cautiously pulled himself to his feet. For a moment he just stood there, amazed to be alive. Refusing the stretcher, he leaned on his father and walked slowly to a first-aid trailer. Women led Malia behind a booth, where they sponge-bathed her and gave her clean clothes.

For almost an hour, crowds condensed in little groups, husbands holding wives, parents hugging children. A man announced Krash was all right, words echoing from the PA system.

. . . a rock. A truck backfiring-iring-iring . . . No one really hurt. The scary moment pau-pau-pau *. . . Now good-time music playing. Krash soon coming to address the crowd-crowd-crowd . . .*

She watched him step from the trailer in different clothes. Bandages covered the back of his head. A little shaky, he started for the stage, arms extended to the crowds. Then, seeing Malia, he stepped away from the police escorting him on either side.

He stood before her. "Thank you."

She held her daughter's hand. She looked down at the hand. To look up would be a final giving in. She still smelled what had been on her: his blood and other things. She smelled the curve of his back, his delicate heart-shaped earlobes. She felt his blood, hardening under her fingernails.

He sighed, turned back to the waiting crowd. Then she heard something call. Distant, unignorable. In that moment, Malia felt life come clean. She gripped her daughter's hand so hard, Baby Jonah winced.

"Go. Walk beside him."

The girl looked at her confused.

"Go!"

Baby Jonah turned to Keo. "Why? Why I should walk with Uncle Krash?"

Keo took her arm, and urged her forward. "Go. Walk with your *father*. Yes! He."

She turned and looked at Malia, her face going through configurations of shock. Her mouth hung, silent. Then, trancelike, she moved forward, falling into step with him. He stopped and gazed at her. She stood a little straighter.

He climbed the steps onto the stage and looked down into faces, knowing he had lost, his people had lost. Most of Hawai'i would vote YES on statehood. Still, he gripped the mike and talked. Of coming decades. Of the next generation who would resurrect and unify Hawai'ians.

"People think we are dying. But, no! We are only *resting*."

He never introduced her, but all the while he talked, Krash held Baby Jonah's hand. His hand was huge and warm. She felt it sweating, felt its pads and creases. She relaxed, letting the full weight of her hand, of her being, rest within her father's. He never let go. He stood in the day before a crowd, and held his daughter's hand.

Anahola

Time in a Glass

Her daughter's stares, like someone coughing in her face. Malia shuddered, imagining dark manias to come. The girl would try to kill her in her sleep. Or, worse, ignore her, totally ignore her.

Now she knows who I am, and who he is, and now I pay. I raised her, kept her warm and fed. She was held, adored. Maybe not enough by me, but I was always there, watchdogging from the shadows. Every night of every childhood sickness, praying, begging Mother God give me the pain, the fevers. I sacrificed, gave her eduction. Now she can go to him for glamour. She can hate me all my days.

There were long nights of weeping. Somehow she had wrapped herself up in this girl; she had become a mother. Now she was the voyeur, the one who stood aside to look but not partake, as father and daughter drove off together. Alone, they talked of books and life and how Baby Jo was going to be a surgeon. A judge. She wanted so badly to impress him.

Knowing the story of his ribs, his missing lung, when she heard her father's rattly breathing, she longed to nurse him, gather him in and stroke his brow. And when he brought her home and left her at the entrance to the lane, she stood taller because he was watching, his eyes walking her home. At such times Baby Jo showed pride, kept herself from running up and down shouting, Look, that is my papa! And she was quiet in the house, more loving, now that she knew she was loved and known by all who mattered.

In little ways she toned down her voice, so it wasn't as shrill. Her Pidgin grew softer, lilting, in the pattern of gracious island speech. She still called Keo "Uncle Papa." Timoteo was still, forever, Grandpa. Her uncle DeSoto still awed and impressed her with his quiet ways, his offhand knowledge of odd facts—that the octopus was closely related to the camel, that centipedes ran faster than cheetahs.

Only with her mother did malice show, each gesture cold and vacant. Her eyes pointed in the middle, darts dying to strike at Malia's heart. Since the day she took her father's hand, Baby Jo had not only retreated, she seemed to have erased herself completely from Malia's life.

One day, Malia entered her room and crossed the savage gulf between them.

"Go ahead, hate me. For waiting sixteen years to tell. Hate me for being proud. And making you a proud one. For giving you good and matching clothes, and for your private-school tuition. Hate me for scraping and saving, so you can go to university, not the streets or jail."

She moved closer.

"It doesn't matter that my youth is past. Or that you hate me. As long as you don't have to work the cannery, or bleed your arms into canefields. Because of me, there are things you will never have to do. Go! Go to your father. Maybe he can teach you extra ways to hate me."

Baby Jonah leapt at her. "You *lied*."

"I never lied. I never said. There is a difference."

The girl shut down, the room shut down. It was like standing inside a carcass.

At night she prowled the house, stood outside the door of this daughter who openly disdained her, who looked down her cheekbones at her. She walked the lane bereft, remembering the other reason she had led Baby Jonah to her father. So she would have a champion, a protector. So she would not be mutilated into an old woman with a cane.

One night she sat up calling, "Sunny!" Still wanting to believe the woman and the cane had been a dream.

Next day in her shop she couldn't work. Fabrics unstitched, scissors gasped open by themselves, attacking the air with snapping Xes. She thought PONO even before the Singer stitched the name. Seeing the letters, Malia laid her head against the machine's cool enameled surface, like leaning against hard black lava. She smelled the smog and sulphur of the Big Island, Island of Volcanoes, where Pono waited.

Taking the inter-island ship again, Malia watched Honolulu diminish in the distance, enormously relieved to shed this town that was her prison, her stagnation. Then she felt terror: what it would be like to watch Honolulu fade forever. To never again see silver-tasseled canefields, or smell the sweet-sticky odor of pines from the canneries, or see clouds thrash and tear over the Ko'olaus. To never again hear her daughter's purring snores, never smell the rust on the old screen door her father latched each night to keep them safe.

One rusty little latch. O Papa! It wasn't enough. The world broke in anyway.

Docking at the Big Island, Malia was struck once more by the landscape of black lava, where earth's crust still burped and parted, where its flesh overflowed, still giving birth. Then she felt Pono's touch, her hands reaching all the way down to the coast, fingers smelling of eucalyptus, soil, gardenia coffee-blossoms. It was even Pono weather—moody, tempestuous, rumbling skies. Then clouds were torn apart and, with piratic majesty, the sun stood blinding, plundering.

She looked up into the misty blue hills of the coffee belt, the old mountain towns called Holualoa, Kainali'u, Kealakekua. And Captain Cook, where Pono waited—a woman of uncompromise, who would not allow the world to walk right through her. Riding up and up into the hills of another era, Malia felt drugged, air so heavy with ginger blossoms that horses galloped sideways. She felt tension fold back like a fan, felt childlike and calmed.

Then came a slight burn to her nostrils, the Big Island smell of fog and volcanic ash, giving off a sulphurous, otherworldly odor. Somewhere on this island, mountains shuddered and spewed; somewhere the earth was unstitching, showing its boiling lava veins. Malia stood at the end of the rocky driveway off Nap'opo'o Road. Through a silent corridor of trees, once more she entered Pono's world, above the lawn, the brooding plantation house.

The small, wiry woman named Run Run, with a cheery little girl's face, stood in the cool gulf of a doorway. She stepped out on the *lānai*, deeply inhaling a cigarette, then puckered her mouth, exhaling perfect smoke rings.

"Who you?"

"Malia. I came before."

"So? Whatchoo want now?"

"The last time I was here, I gave Pono an antique silk kimono. . . ."

The woman's eyes danced, full of mischief. "What—Indian give? You like take back?"

"No, no," Malia cried. "I need to ask her to explain the face, there was a face—"

Run Run suddenly bent forward, shaking her finger.

"You da one! Dat kimono make Pono come real *pupule*. Every night she cursing, sobbing, rip out stitches of old face, sew in new face. Den change mind, rip out stitches ovah and ovah. Nevah seen her like dis. Pono not kine fo' sit in quiet corner, stitching. She of da sea and sky. Real WATCHOUT!-kine *wahine*."

Malia moved closer. "Run Run. I have to see her. Please. Tell her I have seen the living face . . . it's Sunny Sung."

The woman looked down the road toward the ocean, a tapestry of living indigos and jades.

"Walk da road. Stand da cliff. If she like see you, bumbye you know."

She walked down Napo'opo'o Road, then forked off into the forest toward a cliff overlooking the sea. She scanned the water, seeing no one. Then in the shattered mural of blues and greens she saw Pono surfacing, tearing herself from the lip of a wave. She paced the sands, chanting at the sky. She flung out her long black hair, unwrapped her wet sarong, bared her golden body to the sun.

She knelt, scrubbing her arms and breasts and hips with sea salt gathered in a lava bowl. Salt smoothed the skin, kept it firm and ever-thirsty for the ocean. Malia held her breath as Pono rushed back to the sea. She bowed her head, cupped her hands and drank, as ancestors had drunk to heal war wounds, as even now elders restored their health with daily drafts. She entered deep waters again, diving and soaring, graceful and hypnotic.

Malia lost track of time. Once she thought she saw her surface, finned and snouted. After an hour, or many hours, Pono reemerged, stood once more on the sand. Then turning in a slow, archaic way, she gazed up at Malia, a gaze like black stones laid upon her head. Malia fell back into a dream.

It was noon, when shadows were deep within each human, when *mana* was strongest. In Malia's dream, Pono walked up the cliff bent backward in a gravity-defying way and stood over her, giving off a prehistoric lime-fossil smell. Yet human warmth emanated from her sand-sugared calves, her thighs and sunstruck shoulders.

Malia sat up. That is, she watched herself sit up, the spiraling refractions of a dream. Pono held up the kimono Malia had given her with the face of the old woman.

"Look closely, the pained face is erased. You can see tiny holes in the silk where stitches were. The unstitching will be cured by time."

Malia looked close, not understanding. In the kimono, the woman's face was gone, as if digested. What was stitched there now was the back of her head, a slender neck, graceful as a geisha. She appeared to be gazing at the ocean. Such a simple landscape, it confused her.

"What about Sunny's nightmares?" she asked. "How will she go on?"

Pono answered slowly, for she had suffered for this woman, stitched and restitched, until the history and future of Sunny Sung rang true.

"Slow down! Time is not finished. It will have its say."

Malia slept again, and woke in the old plantation house, in a room of heavy liquid, nothing still. Sepia walls trembled as if the wood were feverish. She lay in a four-poster bed, feeling the glow of animate heat, feeling delivered into turbulence and throng. The room possessed a thousand tongues.

Pono held up the same kimono, and Malia resumed the conversation as if she had fallen back into the dream.

"What about the evil that left Sunny shattered?"

The woman stared from a window at the sea. "There will be a reckoning."

"I saw her," Malia whispered. "I was there. She told my dying mama everything. How can I help her? What should I do?"

Pono slowly sat down before her with a face that lacked awe for anything. She seemed to have grown in stature, in knowing. Malia felt she was looking into a face from a petroglyph, that she was breathing in the skin of the ancients.

"Listen now, Malia. You are going to help Sunny Sung in ways you cannot imagine. By letting the air become air. By not chaining each day, whipping each moment. By no longer running from emptiness to emptiness."

She sat up in the bed, as Pono leaned closer.

"I had four daughters. They are gone. I had a husband, he is gone. That is, life won't let me have him. I punished my daughters, wanting their father instead. I loved them with a love so strong I thought it was hate. I made terrible mistakes. Mistakes tell us who we are. . . .

"Now all I have are dreams. And, now and then, a man that life keeps taking back, because he is *ma'i pākē*. I have wounded him deeply by driving our daughters away. By chaining each day, whipping each moment. By bitterness and pride. I have destroyed the seeds we sowed together. Maybe one day the *daughters* of these daughters will forgive me. If I am ready to be human."

She touched Malia's hair, touched her cheek. She had never been this patient with another woman, except her friend and guardian, little Run Run.

"Look at your life, Malia. It is empty. Pride keeps passion locked in the closet of your midnights."

"But, what has this to do with Sunny Sung?"

"In your youth, you shunned her. She would have been a precious friend."

"But I have swallowed pride. I have even given my daughter her father."

"You have *half* given. You hold yourself back from the father. And so, you will tear what binds you."

Pono rose to her full height. "I tell you now. Take your pride and swallow. Ingest it! And excrete. Take the ribs you cherish. Polish them with oils of determination. Ask him to forgive you. If you push this man away, you will lose father and daughter for all time. And I myself will damn you."

Malia shook her head. "I can't. He humiliated me."

"Woman, you have lived! Did you think you could get through life with only scratches? That is not living. It's hiding."

"Then I'll hide. I don't trust love. You open up to someone, and they kill you."

"Listen now. Every decision we make—to love, or not love—is a death. Love doesn't kill or neuter. We do. We think too much. Talk too much. *Feel*, Malia, *feel.* We're women of blasphemy and recklessness. Life makes us pay. So, you have paid. Now, pick your life up, piece by piece. Remember what I taught you. Look for matching patterns, connect the seams. Brilliant designs will emerge."

Pono's voice softened. "Have you forgotten? The father of your child has suffered, too. Who knows what men suffer that they can't express? There is such feeling still alive between you. Rare. It is so rare. I tell you, take him up again. Let life begin."

Malia struggled, wanting to tell, not able. How she had tried to be honorable. To care. To tend and feed those who had birthed her. And whom she had birthed.

"I know everything," Pono said. "Your parents lived with dignity because of you. They never had to beg. One day your girl will know. Her father will tell her by and by. Can you believe that even now she weeps, thinking you have gone away? Your bed is made. Your shop is closed. She begins to understand you are the best thing that is ever going to happen to her.

"As for the father, he is tired, Malia, physically weary. He may not be as strong a lover as before. Nonetheless, he is a man of valor, fighting for our people. If you throw him away, you will walk the years a gutted woman. I tell you, be extravagant. Dare!"

Malia thought again of Sunny Sung. "How can I help her? How can I undo the years I was too prideful?"

"There is no need to do, or undo. The world changes us far more than we change the world. Just stand still. Things will unfold."

Malia lay thinking. When she spoke, her voice was sure.

"Pono. My daughter is now a young woman. She has outgrown her 'Baby' name. I never blessed her with a birth-name. Her *piko* still lies wrapped in linens."

Pono smiled, anticipating her words.

"I want to name her . . . *Anahola*. After Sunny and my brother's child. My daughter's blood flows in his veins. Keo is her father, too. He raised her. Perhaps she loves him most of all."

Pono took Malia's hand. "See? You are already growing kind. This naming will give your brother joy. And you will touch the heart of what is left of Sunny Sung."

She rose, looked out at the sea again. "*Anahola* . . . time in a glass. She will be a restless woman. Always searching. She will belong to each of you. And no one."

Malia seemed to need to ask again. "What about the ones who mutilated Sunny?"

"I told you. There will be a reckoning."

"And what about . . . Rabaul, where they imprisoned her. It still exists."

Pono's voice grew pitiless. "It represents too much evil to exist. One day Pele will reclaim it."

Now, gently, as if Malia were a child, Pono tucked a sheet round her shoulders.

"Rest. I have been generous today. Think deeply, Malia. Put down your whip. Let life begin."

A breeze like a shy, fragrant animal touched Malia's face, stroking her to sleep.

Drowsily she whispered, "Pono! When will my daughter forgive me?"

Pono smiled. "When will you forgive yourself?"

Maka Hakahaka

Sunken Eyes

He sat up with a tearing sound. He bent at the window, struggling to remember where he was. Trying to still his shaking legs, he moved to a mirror. Each day he looked more blue, more frontal. He sat on a chair, touching his saxophone, all that was left that was real to him. He steeped tea; holding the pot with both hands, trying to pour. Hands so jumpy he could hardly hold his horn, hardly control his breathing.

The only thing that calmed him now was walking through crowds. Studying necks. So few were desirable. Now and then one so perfect, so delectable, sweat stood up on his wrists. He felt a mild erection. Some days were pure disgust and hardship, crowds of imperfections. *Zenzen dame* necks, really terrible, yellow and brown slabs of fat. Or bamboo-clarinet necks, skinny stalks of bone. On such days he stumbled home, weak and famished.

Now, huge crowds in the streets, imbecile chanting! Parades, banners, speeches. The city in a fever over statehood. Keo said Washington could pass the bill any week now. In the subsoil of his being, Endo felt disgust. Here were people with houses, families to love, food to eat. Yet in their greed, they wanted more. What did they know of need? Of suffering? What did they know of incinerated cities? Origins becoming ash . . . *Mother! Father!*

He took walks in moonlight when Chinatown was quiet. He

looked up at stars and tried to remember being normal. But then the feeling of being stalked, the smell of rust, of wet clay. One night, losing his way, he paused at a shop for directions. Under glaring lights, a butcher slammed his meat-ax *pah! pah! pah!* Thirteen duck heads in a row. Bodies jerking and flapping. Endo stared at the pyramid of heads and screamed. The man wiped his hands and pushed him from his shop.

Maybe he imagined it. The only time he didn't feel stalked by the smell of wet clay was when he was with Keo. As if Keo were a shield, a thing that held the smell at bay. At the Swing Club, Endo's playing was reduced to mostly miming. He didn't solo anymore. Still, he came each night, and held his saxophone and studiously listened. Music was all he had left. His dread was the day his senses blurred, when jazz became for him just noise.

Increasingly, his vision wavered, the sun was crucifying. He wandered Chinatown in round sunglasses that, with his blue skin, brought to mind a large, fabled fly. Chemicals of lead were in ascendence, ravaging his nervous system. Food went down, and came back up harsh-colored. His limbs shot out independently. He had convulsions. Shopkeepers kept pencils ready so he wouldn't bite his tongue off. They scolded children who stared.

One day he stopped in a tea shop where it was dark and cool, tasseled lampshades, daily newspapers draped over bamboo rods. He drank tea through a straw, read papers by laying them flat on a table so his hands would not rattle them. Around the shop, through faint gyres of dust, people sipped from porcelain cups and read. Someone entered the shop behind him. In the sweltering day, he suddenly felt chilled, as if little hands had touched his spine. At a far table, an old woman with a cane and ugly orthopedic shoes sat and ordered jasmine tea.

For a time it was silent, the shop removed from noisy streets, occasional coughs stirring the dust. A child came to the doorway, hawking dried Java plums. The owner gently shooed her away. He smiled, his teeth big yellow tusks, and stared at Endo's skin, refilling his teapot. Across the room, a weathered hand shifted a cane.

Every thirty seconds, a neon sign outside the window tinted Endo pink. His intermittent glowing outraged a macaw in a rusty cage hanging from the ceiling. Maybe it reminded the bird of watercolored jungles of its origins, wings outspread in freedom. It started a commotion, scattering seeds, upsetting its water dish, its cage soaring back and forth like a pendulum.

Customers looked up, then went back to their papers. Water from the birdcage dripped to the floor beside Sunny's cane. She felt a drop against her ankle. She sipped her tea, her movements small and measured. But something in her gestures changed the air, the elements. The bird grew still. Across the room, Endo dropped his head and moaned, a blue man intermittently pulsing pink. He felt an odor rise up in the shop—rustlike smell of wet red clay.

People gathered, wondering how to calm him. His screams set off the bird again. His body shook and jerked. Someone offered a pencil for his tongue. He tried to explain it wasn't convulsions, it was the odor driving him crazy. Couldn't they smell it? Then it came closer. It put its hand on his shoulder. It leaned on its cane. Endo leapt up, reeling from the shop.

Beside him, remembrance, like a running ghoul.

. . . Miles of chambers carved from clay. Chambers for starvation. For suffocation. Chambers full of malarial mosquitoes, whining and relentless. Like kamikazes flying to their deaths. Millions of young boys sacrificed . . .

He ran out into traffic. "THE EMPEROR HAS ORDERED THIS!"

AS HIS FRIEND SLOWLY DECLINED, KEO SPENT MORE TIME WITH him, watching him drink through a straw, eat from his plate like a dog, no longer trusting his hands with forks and knives. Week by week, his skin grew bluer. His eyes receded into deep, dark throats. Keo began to think of his skull as something scholars dipped their pens in.

"We've got to find you a specialist."

Endo shook his head. "I told you. I will not end up a microbe, a thing under glass to pinch and probe."

"But, look. You're getting worse."

"I'm not getting worse. I'm dying."

He studied Keo, even his neck, a good neck. He felt great affection for him. "Don't be sad. I've lived enough. You've been a good friend. You have humored me."

Then he really looked at Keo, eye to eye. "You're a first-class trumpeter. The real McCoy. I wish you the recognition you deserve."

Keo looked off, embarrassed. "I don't think about that now. Those dreams are past. So much going on here, we need so much. One day Krash told me I had lost touch, my music lacked the *cry* of our people. Supporting them seems more important now than recognition."

Endo sighed. "There are always voices crying out."

"Maybe. I only know I had muscles, and nerves, that were dead for years. Now they ache, they tingle. I feel alive. Teaching kids, I feel connected. When Mama died, I saw life speeding up, our elders starting to fade away. We were the new generation of elders. But I was still living in the past, the present zipping right by me. I've lost the need for certain things. Even the need to travel."

"And . . . what of the girl you were trying to find?"

"A wise friend told me life would find her. Now, when I think of her, I feel the *memory* but not the pain." He watched the ocean for a while. "Sometime, she's so vivid, I think I hear her heartbeat."

"I once knew such love. Well, passion. A little Mongolian named Udbal." Endo smiled. "She taught me concupiscence. I was a virgin till I met her."

Keo frowned. "You were no virgin. After all those girls in Paris?"

"Child's play. I was a boy, really, until the war. Udbal took my cherry, as they say. She introduced me to a . . . particular addiction."

He closed his eyes, remembering his first brief tour in occupied Manchuria.

. . . winter so cold his teeth cracked. Wolves fighting over corpses. The little Mongol beauty Udbal. Captured at fourteen, when his soldiers massacred her village. Each time before he raped her, he had made her sing. It was said music was born in Mongolia. Sometimes, while inside her, he heard screams. Prisoners of war being used for live experiments—their bodies sliced open, injected with bacillus of cholera, bubonic plague.

One day he found sores on her of syphilis. He looked down at his penis, imagined it covered with pustules. He wept, loving her a little. Then took her outside, making her kneel in the snow. The arc of his sword. Her young head soaring. After, there was nothing but wolfprints. They came like silver flashes.

Udbal, his first ecstasy. In two months he took down five more syphilitic girls. He began to study necks, even those of fellow officers, their heads bent meditatively at chess. A captain grew uneasy. Endo's eyes had too keen an edge. He was transferred to Rabaul, deep in the Pacific. . . .

Now he opened his eyes. "I suppose, remembering our first love is a way to keep innocence safe from decay. It is not allowed to rot before we do."

Keo had trouble imagining Endo driven by passion or addiction. A man so damaged, his exhalations smelled like burning metal.

"What happened to the girl, Udbal?"

Endo looked away, lips moving in small whispers. "*Gomen nasai. Gomen nasai.*"

"What are you saying?"

"A simple phrase. It means the same as your *kala mai.* Forgive."

Keo patted Endo's arm, and sighed. "That war will never leave us. But seems to me you've suffered enough. Soon as this statehood thing is over, we'll get you to a specialist. Maybe all you need are vitamins."

Endo threw his head back, laughing hysterically. "Vitamins! Ah, my friend—you are original."

Then his expression changed. He leaned closer.

"You should begin to think of my remains. Cremate them. Then, if you will, bury my ashes in the Koʻolaus, where the soil is calm. Keo, I *beg* you! Don't throw them in the ocean. I have such a horror of that place, such ghastly memories. Even my ashes would know. It would be like boiling forever in a red, wet hell."

Hānau Hou

Rebirth

ONE BALMY MARCH DAY, MALIA HEARD SIRENS OUT ON MERchant Street. She saw women with their hands reaching toward the sky. The radio announcer seemed to be laughing and crying. Both houses of Congress had voted in favor: the Hawai'i Statehood Bill was passed.

Moments later, church bells sounded across the city, a tolling that would last twenty-four hours. Traffic stopped as folks jumped from their cars, cheering and embracing. Men ran through the streets, tearing their shirts off. She stared at the Singer, imagining crowded tenements and Homestead shacks where Hawai'ians sat silent.

She patted the machine, wishing it could tell her what was coming. She sighed, looking round her shop. Sometimes she grew weary, nothing in life but work. Yet work relieved her of freedom she would not know how to use. It kept her from admitting there was nothing else to yield to.

She thought of Sunny Sung, wondering where she was, wishing she could go to her. She thought of Leilani who had said if statehood came, the U.S. would swallow their islands. *Mama. Who never learned to read or write. Who poured pride into me, and arrogance, so no one could break my back. Mama. What now? What now? . . .*

She closed her shop and started for home. Streets were rivers of people, cars and buses abandoned. It took four hours to reach Kalihi, only a mile west of downtown Honolulu. The lane was one big celebration, folks hugging and dancing. The Silvas and the Changs. The Manlapits. Rosie Perez and her brood. Mr. Kimuro who had sold his bed. Fourteen years after World War II, he still slept on his knees, praying for his boy's return from battle. Only the Palamas, against statehood, drew their shades and stayed inside.

"Come, come celebrate," neighbors called. "Plenny fo' eat and drink."

Even a small band was set up in the lane. Malia kicked off her shoes and drank a beer with her father. Split in his views on statehood, he looked euphoric in a lost way.

"If only yo' mama be here. Wondah what she say. So many years running from *haole*, now dey got us by da t'roat."

Malia patted his back. "Papa, statehood will bring good things, too. I just don't like the way white folks treat it like a *victory*."

She kept looking down the road for Baby Jo. It could be hours. She slipped into the house and showered. She washed her hair, scrubbed her nails, everything so gritty. Then she slid into a long lime-colored sheath, padding around barefoot.

Hours passed. She brushed her hair, turned up the radio, bands broadcasting from Waikiki. She danced alone. Late afternoon now, her father and neighbors in the garage harmonizing over Keo's old piano. In the lane, rich smells of barbecue, *chow fun*, pungence of *bagoong*.

Out beyond King Street, beyond Kalihi, the sky turned flamboyant reds and purples. Soon dusk, real celebrations, fireworks and cannons. Malia thought of Baby Jonah somewhere in those mobs. She began to perspire. Her daughter moving at a motherless gait, a stranger following. She perspired so profusely, a breeze dried her sweat to salt tattoos. She looked round for a weapon.

. . . Needles. Scissors. What a woman needs . . .

She had not taught her daughter these vital things. Baby Jo was out there unprepared. She thought of all that could happen to her. She was soaked, as if she'd sprung a leak. She drank another beer, trying to calm down. She looked in the mirror. Glowing skin, thick, dark hair held back on one side with plumeria. Her not quite slender body poured into the long green sheath.

I have never looked so good. While my daughter is somewhere being mutilated . . .

She ran to the window, calling to her father. "Papa! She's not safe. Not safe!"

He waved, mishearing her in the growing din. She moved out to the steps, searching the crowded lane, then went back inside to her nightmares.

. . . His hand stroking his penis. Stalking her. The way snakes hunt by smell. Her virgin smell. She pictured her daughter's bright white panties tied round her neck. . . . *With which she has been strangled.*

Malia screamed. Folks in the lane screamed back, thinking it was singing.

Maybe it was the crowds, the chaos—something had reared up in her. Fear, conjuring the history of Sunny Sung.

"Where is her father? Please. Let him reach her in time."

She thought of him then, without letting herself think his name. Right now he would be out there in the thick of it, being a sensation. Utterly useless. Malia grabbed up a large, lethal pair of scissors. She would rescue her daughter herself. She would slash her way through crowds, roam the earth to find her, to avenge her. She would be a walking blade.

She called out again through the window. "Papa. I'm going out! To find her."

That's how she would recall the moment. She would recall her father in the garage, suddenly staring down the lane. Her father rising, moving forward. She would remember turning, going to the screen door, would remember them walking up the crowded lane. Baby Jonah and her father. They walked slowly as if treading glass, saw her standing at the door. She heard blood lapping in her veins. She stepped outside, and felt her father move beside her. She heard his heart, or was it hers?

Folks went on singing, celebrating, but much attention was paid. Faces turned toward Malia, waiting to see if she would yield. Baby Jo looked terrified, eyes like cocoa saucers. She seemed to be pulling Krash, but then he saw Malia in the light of the doorway. Her lush black hair and glowing skin, the lushness of her naked arms. Halfway up the lane, he and his daughter stopped, and waited.

"No be proud," Timoteo whispered in Malia's hair. "Go, meet dem halfway."

It seemed the whole lane waited.

Timoteo pinched her arm. "In da name of yo' mama. Go!"

She hesitated, then moved like a woman trollied, flowing across the green lawn in her lime green dress, seeing nothing but her daughter's eyes. The man beside her daughter slightly rumpled, but alert, like someone hungry but extremely proud. She moved down the lane, clutching the scissors in her fist.

Folks stood back on either side, staring. She walked up to the father. He was watching what was in her hand. She gazed at her daughter, touched her face and shoulder, everything intact. She flung the scissors to the grass, then turned to Krash. She would not remember if they spoke. They must have. She would remember only Baby Jonah walking between them, holding their hands like children as they passed down the lane.

Miles of moving humans. They floated through them, and over them, as if the three of them were winged. Ships in the harbor shot off cannons, making the ground beneath them shudder. Malia would remember looking down, laughing at her bare feet, and pausing somewhere, drinking something cold.

Years hence, in between rushing out to see the world, then rushing home, then rushing off again—a woman forever going *makai* and *makai* and *makai*—Baby Jo would tell the story. She would begin by saying how there were, in each life, certain moments that are pure. Moments sculpted so precisely they are fitted to one's hand, so one carries them always. She would say that such moments were like a first glimpse of something extraordinary when a veil is thrust aside.

The moment she first realized her sister was her mother. The first time she looked into her father's face, understanding who he was. The pads and creases of her father's hand. The actualness of him, never quite describable. She would carry these moments like rare jewels.

With them she would carry that statehood night, when she walked between her parents, holding their hands. Her father's labored breathing, her mother's needle-scarred fingers. She would recall it as holding tight to her two children, so they would not evaporate.

As they pushed on toward Waikiki, police, recognizing Krash, gave them a lift in a squad car. Siren wailing, folks throwing flowers thinking they were famous. Although the Statehood Bill was passed in Congress, people of Hawai'i still had to vote in favor, or against.

One of the cops now turned and asked, "'Ey, Krash. Hawai'ians going lose on statehood. Most folks voting YES. What we do now?"

His voice was deep and clear. "We keep marching. Keep shouting. *Ha'ina mai ka puana!*" Let the story be told.

Just after McCully Bridge, they entered Kalakaua Avenue in Waikiki, the street sealed off to traffic. By midnight more than a hundred thousand people would be gathered, turning the avenue into a spinning ballroom where couples danced straight into morning.

Taking their hands again, walking between them, Baby Jo looked up at the face of her golden, full-lipped mother, hair going wiry and electric in humid air, and her big, bronzed, rough-skinned father, perspiring profusely so his skin seemed a suit of mirrors. Dusk made them both a little darker. In torchlight and Chinese lanterns lining Waikiki, in moonlight and spotlights from a dozen bandstands, through streamers and confetti, their teeth and eyes jumped out, the two of them so tall and regal, people stared.

They found Keo on a bandstand in front of the Royal. He was up there leading Hana Hou!, snapping fingers while a sax and clarinet went crazy. Baby Jonah closed her eyes, breathed in deeply, took her mother's hand, and carefully placed it in her father's. Then she climbed up on the stage. They were alternating island songs with rock and roll, World War II, anything the crowd yelled out. Just then they struck up "Moonlight Serenade."

She slid into her uncle's arms, then pointed down at the crowd, her parents there, together. They weren't talking, they were looking in opposite directions. But they were holding each other, dancing. Keo looked at them amazed, then turned his back to the crowds, to Baby Jo, his hands busy at his eyes. After a while he turned back to his niece, watching her parents together.

"Remember this," he said. "Remember."

All night, Chinese dragons would leap and slide down Kalakaua Avenue. Ten thousand firecrackers would be ignited. Every half hour, navy destroyers would split the night with rocket fire and thundering cannons, so buildings seemed to sway. An army artillery division would fire cannons in fifty-round salutes. On Sand Island, across Honolulu Harbor, a mammoth Victory Torch was lit, a bonfire sending flames one hundred feet high, visible from miles at sea. Each hour, army helicopters would add firewood sent from countries round the world.

BABY JONAH WOULD REMEMBER ALL THESE THINGS. SHE WOULD remember her parents dancing, her uncle watching them. Years later, in a lover's arms, she would tell how her mother and father never married. Her mother refused, knowing if they married, they would be competing to outshine. And maybe she refused because she could never forgive him for the *haole* wife.

Yet they would be more than man and wife. They would be each other's passion and devotion. They would be each other's conscience and raw heart. And so it would transpire that several nights a week, Baby Jo's father would tiptoe up the lane and slip into her mother's room. She would hear him rushing down the hall, closing the door, as she lay smiling in the dark.

Through the years, she would continue the saga of her parents, telling how one night her mother came to her with her *piko*, her umbilical cord, looking like a dried-up pig's tail, explaining how, though Baby Jo had been given several names, until her mother swam her *piko* to the reef, she was not condoned or blessed by *'aumākua*, ancestor gods.

One day Malia would swim out to their resting place, chanting aloud, asking if Anahola would be a fitting name for Baby Jo. Her father desired this, honoring the sixteen years she never knew him, years of life set aside, waiting to be lived. And Malia desired this, in honor of the child of Keo and Sunny Sung. Baby Jo would tell of watching her mother swim, holding the *piko* between her teeth, her father paddling a canoe, watching over her. And how in that moment—her cord between her mother's teeth—Baby Jo felt a painful tugging on her navel, pangs of rebirth.

She would tell how her mother called out to *'aumākua*, releasing her birth-cord to waves which took it down, its blood and cells flowing into theirs. She would remember her parents waiting for a sign, the sun beating on her father's back, making his bullet scar grow tender. Then the sound of *'aumākua* chanting from beyond the reef, their sacred *mana* flowing back to Baby Jo.

And she would tell how her father half adopted her, because she was half his. And how her name officially became Anahola Meahuna Kapakahi, which roughly translated as Time in a Glass–Hidden in Secret–All Askew. Which might explain why her life would be spent restless and wandering, seeming to some folks nonsensical and all askew.

And through the years Anahola would continue telling how she heard her father, just before dawn, slipping out of the house. And how, if she was quick, she could dart across the hall and watch him through a window, her big, handsome father running down the lane, trying to outrun the dawn. He was in politics, she said, and cared about his reputation.

She would remember how sometimes he woke up late, light already pouring over the Ko'olaus, and how he dashed down the lane, struggling with his trousers while workers passed with lunch pails. She would remember a particular dawn, when she was still at university, how she tiptoed to Malia's room, put her arm round her mother, and together they leaned laughing at the window, as her father ran down the lane with half-buttoned pants.

She would tell how, for years, her father campaigned for office, defeated as the *Lū'au* Lawyer, until a new generation of Hawai'ians rose up, helping elect him to county office, and then to the state supreme court—young attorneys he had inspired and apprenticed. He would bring radical reforms to state government and land allocation. But he would be best remembered as the orator who ignited courtrooms, defending his people.

In time, Anahola would tell how her parents celebrated their tenth, and then their twentieth un-anniversary. And then their silver, with a *lū'au* in Kalihi Lane. Both still so in love, so wary, her mother smelled his clothes for the scent of other women, and he searched her body for the imprints of strange hands.

And somewhere in Hong Kong, Sydney, or New Delhi, still going *makai* and *makai* and *makai*, Anahola would continue their story as they approached their forty-fifth, and then their fiftieth un-anniversary. There would be many storms, breakups, and heartaches between them, because they were both of the same strong *kapa* cloth, both proud *kānaka*.

In time, she would turn her lovers into listeners. She would captivate with words the way her uncle had with trumpet. Men would lie beside her like children, beguiled. They would recall her as a "talking story" woman. But sometimes her tales would grow dark, her eyes would narrow. By then she was already leaving them. And when she left, their beds would resonate with stories.

Her lovers would sleep, dreaming of her islands. Of blue cliffs called Pali of the Koʻolaus, and giant ti leaves dripping dew on sleeping boar. They would dream, too, of taro fields thirsting to extinction, of pure streams bubbling to sludge. Of children sleeping in exploding houses, people growing old in packing crates. People who, in time, would rise up prideful and outraged, in towns named Waiʻanae, Nanakuli, Lualualei, Makaha, Mākua, Papakolea.

And when her lovers woke, they would touch the hollow in her pillow and still feel her heat. And they would know her stories were not fables.

Ho'opa'i

Revenge

She dreamed of women bobbing facedown in the sea, stirred in the wake of exploded boats. She dreamed of hanging corpses shimmering like earrings. Then, too, she dreamed of pink-cheeked Allies, offering food and penicillin and, later, hints and vacillations. They were the victors, they owned the spoils. She shrieked herself awake and sat all night beating dreams to death with her cane.

She rose, looked out at the dawn. It seemed to promise a new beginning, as it often did, before daylight turned up the noise of humans. She gazed round her simple room, her putty-colored jade hare walls. From outside, the hotel looked decrepit, sunlight snagging on its cracked façade. Yet she had grown comfortable here.

The day already felt electric. Something had awakened her, called her from her bed as if she were being led to a showplace, unsure what was going to be shown. She lingered at her window. Someone in another room was reading; she heard a brown sleeve turn a page. She had come to imagine her neighbor as an ancient woman with no tongue. Their silences spent time together. Sometimes the woman vanished into slumber. Sunny heard her book groping for her hand, heard it hit the floor. She imagined one eye on sleep, the other on unread pages at her feet.

From small shops below, the virulent smell of coffee brewing, sweet *mochi* buns side by side with pig's cheeks. Some days she forgot how long she had been back in Honolulu. Time was no longer part of her existence. Outside, light grew across the city, roofs palpitated, palm trees trembled into flames. Then everything was glare, the sun's alchemy. She drew her shades.

She had thought it would be another church day, sitting in shadows in hard pews, listening to Keo coach kids on horn and piano. Maybe he would play some Ellington, a little Chopin. Sometimes leftover tar—incense from masses—made her head ache; she would leave the church before his playing ended. But always, if the jacaranda man was there, she waited. Patient, attentive.

Even if she was dying, even if she had no feet. She would follow him forever. To restaurants, tea shops. To the ripe moment. One night she stood so close, she smelled his breath, a crackling deep inside him. She was not going to let life burn him to a crisp. Not let his ashes blow round a corner. It was not enough.

Now and then, when she grew weary of crowds at the Swing Club, she walked the streets of Honolulu. Inside little shops, the human tableau. Butchers meticulously carving fowl, bakers kneading rice paste. In the background, mothers crooning, nursing their infants. She touched the sad, shriveled skin of her breasts hanging like taffy.

Some nights she stood across the street from the shop called Malia Designs. Inside, a woman driving a sewing machine like a race horse, fabric flying like pennants. Sunny could almost feel the red-hot needle's hum as Malia urged the Singer on, sometimes even shouting at it. Watching her brought Sunny a moment's laughter, peace. She touched the label on her dress, and, in her shop, Malia looked up as if someone had touched her neck.

One night Malia breathed in sharply, feeling chilled. A presence in the shop behind her.

"Forgive me . . . for intruding. . . ."

She cried out, knowing who it was.

"Please. Don't turn around."

Malia waited for she knew not what. Finally she spoke. "I named my daughter Anahola. In memory of your child."

"I know. . . ."

"She loves Keo like a father. He'll never be alone."

"I came to thank you, Malia."

She kept her head down, terrified. "Sunny, let me be your friend. Let me help you!"

Sunny answered with profound tenderness. "Only . . . remember."

The shop was still again. Sunny continued walking the streets, ending up in Chinatown. She haunted a dozen little shops crowded with jars of the endangered and the rare. Head of an albino king cobra. Freckled penis of a rhino. Bound feet like little hooves. A pygmy fetus. Under swaying paper lanterns, vials of deadly poison oils. *'Oliana,* oleander. *Nānā honua,* angel's-trumpet flower. Snake venom. Anti–snake venom. And in quiet yards between the shops, temples, gongs, the look and smell of saffron.

And shopkeepers telling her how two hundred years ago captains of opium and tea ships, ignorant of the value of jade, used it as ballast when sailing back from the Orient. And how at night coolies carried off the jade, burying it for decades, so their children's children might not starve. Wizened men and women who told such tales were aunties and uncles of shopkeepers she had lived among in Shanghai. Hearing their voices made her think of her sister, Lili, and Sunny grew very still. They comforted her, patting her arm with cracked, seamed hands, refined with the labor of centuries.

Some nights she and Lili stood outside their father's house, watching through the windows.

"He was so dynamic," Sunny whispered. "Now, see how he sits bone-idle."

They watched as their mother, Butterfly, cut his hair, lathered his jaw and shaved him. Some nights he and she played cards like equals, tenderly slapping each other's hands. And sometimes while he slept, his daughters stepped into his dreams, twice-forgiving him.

Always Sunny went back to Chinatown, sitting in herb shops and seed shops with jars of dried fruits in fourteen different colors—*li hing mui, si mui, hum lum, mango seed, sweetsour salty crackseed.* Shop owners smiled, having grown used to her, and went on reading their papers. Some invited her to tea, and talked in scholarly ways of herb cures and root cures, poisons and balms. Most often she sat at the Anti-Mango Luncheonette, across from a certain small hotel where she watched the coming and going of a blue man.

Now she sat in her jade hare room, chilled by air that felt electric. It was midmorning when she heard the bells, the cheering. Her neighbor in the next room stood and gasped. Sunny parted her blinds, and shuddered.

HE DREAMED HE WAS HOME IN TOKYO, HAVING JUST COMPLETED officer training. Wearing his thousand-stitch belt made by his mother and sisters, he was dancing British-style with a beautiful Japanese girl who spoke three horizontal languages.

He bragged about his training. ". . . judo, bayonet-fencing, swordsmanship, horsemanship."

She laughed in his face. "You are going to war, not on holiday!"

In his dream, the ballroom was suddenly overrun by tanks covered with nets that made him think of glamour-girl snoods. Allies pointed machine guns from the turrets. Endo reached up with his sword, taking the head of one of them. His dance partner screamed. He turned, studying her neck, feeling his sword-arm quiver. The sound of war planes, bombs whining down, turning the city into an inferno.

He woke up screaming. "Mother! Father!" His blue cheeks stained with snot.

Fully awake, he still heard planes, then sirens, tolling bells. He shook so hard, his bed bounced. He burrowed under sheets, counting explosions. He hid for hours. The bells grew louder, sirens grew louder, outside, people running like rivers.

They will turn us to ash. The city will burn for fifteen miles. I must save my parents.

He rose, reaching for his sword. There was nothing, not even his uniform. Now people screaming in the halls. Out in the streets it was late afternoon, so many fires in the hills, so many explosions, the city was fogged and dusklike. He heard cannons from warships out at sea, he saw buildings sway. Outside, he started running against the tide of thousands. Trying to reach his parents before the Allies.

He headed west in their direction, but nothing looked familiar, no one hurt or wounded, just madness in their faces. So in shock they were grinning, even dancing. With each explosion he threw himself against buildings. Still, the church bells tolled. Far in the distance, he saw planes approaching, trucks of soldiers.

Tokyo is lost. Already invaded.

Endo looked between buildings to the sea: destroyers, aircraft carriers, massive cannons pointed at his city. Now and then a BOOOMM! that tore up streets, threw crowds against each other. Yet they kept flowing forward, smoke everywhere, the rat-a-tat of guns. A car blew up. A city expiring.

He pressed on, trying to outrun the fires that would roll right through them. He called out for his mother and father, his sisters, knowing he could never reach them. People momentarily fell back, aghast at Endo's face, his screams. Fluorescent colors overhead, lights coming on like fractured jewels. A sun hideously dying.

At dusk, in the distance, over a place called Sand Island, he saw planes dropping log-shaped bombs. Then, all of Sand Island exploded, flames shooting skyward. From somewhere, infantry divisions fired off countless rounds. He threw himself to the pavement, feeling nothing as crowds ran over him. He shimmied to his feet against a wall.

Time stood still. He stood still, mobs rivering against him. Then he was on a bridge, looking at the full horror of Sand Island, an inferno leaping a hundred feet into the sky. It looked contained, they would probably stoke it with gasoline until it was a fury, then unleash it on the city accompanied by bombs. Where were his men, his forces? He saw destroyers and carriers massing, moving closer to land, saw fire from their cannons split the dusk. He continued running west.

Mother. Father. I will die with you. The emperor has ordered this!

Up a street going *mauka*, toward the mountains, he saw behind a fence an open field, a hillside slouching to a stream. Thirst, he felt such thirst. He would drink, then press on. Behind him, Allies in the streets, advancing. Folks would soon be dying by the thousands. If he could just get home.

He staggered to the fence, ripped his shoulder crawling through barbed wire. He crossed the field, looking down a rocky embankment. His body snapped back, struck by a stench that had haunted him. The city was threaded with streams from upland mountains that collected algae, dirt, and sewage as they deepened into flowing currents on their journey to Honolulu Harbor. In the stench, he smelled red clay.

He slid down the rocky embankment, knelt at the dirty stream, cupped his hands and drank. Then he looked up. The mouth of a tunnel gaped at him. A rusted, clay-packed metal pipe ten feet high, through which mountain water gushed in flood seasons, emptying into the harbor and the sea. He stood, and moved closer, peering into the opening.

. . . *We are going underground. The tunnels of Rabaul, last sanctuary.*

He advanced two steps. A place of rust and decay: walls looked bloody, the water was scum.

Inside, the stream narrowed, the uplands weren't flooding now. There was just a quiet trickling within. Dim light showed silt along the walls, gathered in lumps of filth and weeds. He heard voices, echoes, walls behind walls. Large rats skittered on ledges beside him, staring into his eyes. He thought if he stuck out his tongue they would take it from his head.

He heard footsteps behind him. Someone breathing. He plunged deeper into the tunnel. There were soldiers he had to save, officers he had to warn. The Allies were here, and soon they would mine their way through the tunnels. He tripped on a large, shredded dog. He saw bones in the shape of a human doll. He retched, and slogged forward. Rounding a corner, he saw what looked like a passage branching off.

Down there our fortress begins. Three hundred miles of hidden tunnels!

"They are coming!" he shouted. "Command your posts! Ready your ammunition!" His voice echoing and echoing.

Again, he heard footsteps. And breathing. He turned; light hit him in the face.

"Who is it? The enemy?"

She moved the flashlight back and forth. Her hands were muddy where she had slid down the hillside after him. She wiped them on her dress. Outside bombs burst, ship's cannons exploded. The walls of the tunnel shuddered, so that rust peppered their faces. Overhead thousands of humans running. Now he smelled fires of the city. The bells went on and on.

"Who is it?" he cried again.

She stepped closer, shining the flashlight up at her face. "Look at me. Do you remember?"

Leaning close, he studied her, then studied the walls, clay walls. He studied her again. The past stood up, inhaling.

"Moriko!" For that was what he had called her.

"My name is Sun-ja. Moriko was your whore."

"Where is she?"

"Dead. And so am I."

She shone the light in his face again. "I have followed you a long time. Do you wonder why?"

He was insane, yet something in him understood. "I have outlived curiosity."

Another explosion, screaming crowds. A hot wind rushed through the tunnel, so their skin felt singed. Heat of the burning above them.

Suddenly he grabbed her hand. "Rabaul is finished! They will capture us like this. We must retreat. Look, where the passage branches off to deeper tunnels, then hidden chambers. Allies will never find us."

Was he pretending, or had he gone mad? She slapped his hand away. Her flashlight flew around, illuminating eyes of watching rodents. Outside, sounds like columns of soldiers in sturdy boots. Planes, bombs. The dying. Her mouth was so dry, she could not swallow. Her tongue like bark, lips cracked, her juices evaporated. She felt drops. Condensation on the walls. She was a whore in a Quonset hut.

. . . Very carefully she rises, gliding like algae through humid air. She bends, licks condensation from the wall, then moans, listening for the sea. For that is what she longs for—waves cataracting, corroding her to crystals. . . .

Leaning, she put her tongue against the filthy wall. The walls trembled and bulged, as if her tongue were against a man. Endo's face was in his hands. Was he sobbing? Or moved to be with her? Cannons in the harbor, tearing the city apart.

"We will be buried. Gas will suffocate us like before. My sword. Where is my sword?"

Another shocking heat wave. Then she, too, heard voices in the walls. Jap soldiers crying, P-girls moaning, locked deep in airless chambers of red clay. Every scar, every stitch in her body screamed. Every organ cut out, every cell diseased and dead, every part of her already buried.

He went down on his knees. "Moriko, take my hand. Quickly! We must go deep where they will never find us."

He looked down, shocked by his erection. He remembered bucking and hollering inside her.

Already starving, diseased, but still enough left of her to desire. Still warm and wet, a sucking fruit closing on me, clasping me. Me flooding, not in coming, but anticipation. Thinking how afterwards . . . ahh! after, there was still her neck. . . .

She swung her light at him. On his knees, he was holding his erection, his face grotesque.

I am so tired, she thought. *Maybe I've come far enough.*

She felt her big shoes sinking. Slowly she sat down in filth and mud, thirsty and exhausted. She laid her cheek against a wall and thought of cool, wet clay. She heard crowds singing far away. She thought of wasted, haggard girls entering a shower for the first time in years. She thought of them touching clean, gleaming white tiles, fingering them like the blind.

She thought of them touching soap like precious hunks of ivory. Soaping and rinsing and soaping again, singing ever so softly. Holding each other like mothers, like children, praying to cascading water baptizing their faces, their broken bodies, as if it could rinse them young and clean. Rinse everything away. Some would survive, some would find they had lived enough. She wept. Only a little, there was so little left.

The man before her begged, all blue and babbling.

"Moriko, come! If they find us, they will kill us. Bring my sword."

He was gone. She had no further purpose here. And yet. Some things could not be permitted without redress. She thought again of Quonset huts in the Pacific. Typhoid barracks in Jakarta, Manila. Frozen tents and boxcars in Manchuria, Nanking. Kidnapped P-girls forced to march into blizzards, into swamps, into battle, defending their executioners. And when they were raped to death, diseased and finished, their bodies were split open, their warm organs used to thaw cold feet, or feed the army's livestock. Thousands of young girls. Hundreds of thousands.

Sunny hung her head remembering how her mother, Butterfly, had told her long ago of the ancient *koa wāhine*, women warriors of Hawai'i. She told how these young women had followed their men into battle, carrying calabashes of food and gourds of water to replenish them, their wails and chants urging warriors on. She told how, when a husband or father was killed in battle, the women took up their clubs and battle-axes and javelins. With fierce war cries, *koa wāhine* rushed forward to destroy the enemy.

"That how a girl became a woman," Butterfly had said. "When she learned *ho'opa'i*. Revenge."

Now her mother's words were like an army marching behind her. Sunny put down the flashlight, opened the pouch at her waist. The vial, the hypodermic needle. The Chinese herb man had instructed her so patiently, so meticulously, she could do it in the dark. When the needle was ready, she aimed the flashlight and moved closer. He saw the needle, his eyes yawned wide.

She plunged it deep into his neck, saw blue flesh suck down deadly juices of *nānā honua*: angel's-trumpet flower. She saw him freeze, deafened in the trumpet's blare. It would take time. Death would come in slow, staccato riffs, piercing cell by cell, paralyzing limb by limb. He would watch his body die in segments like a worm.

He lay still. He saw her sit. She was waiting for something. The trickling stream beneath him nibbled at his skin. While streets outside exploded, while humans ran in waves, high in the Ko'olaus it began to drizzle. Drops gathered in rivulets, which gathered in slow streams. In time, the stream beneath him would rise, imperceptible and sly. In time his heels and buttocks and shoulders would begin to sink.

She sat attentive, hour after hour. By dawn, city fires smoldered, exhausted crowds retired, thundering cannons had died. In the silence, an older thunder shook the earth. He saw her look up toward the sound. He saw her smile. Thunder would bring rains, incessant rains. And they began. It rained a full day, then a night. Ditches flooded, streams began to swell.

He was dying upward. His legs were stone: angel's trumpet blowing deadly juices. He could barely move his arms.

Sunny climbed to a slight rise up against the tunnel wall. What she was waiting for began to dawn on him. Horrified, he screamed, he thought he screamed, but something else came out instead. Currents rose, deep enough to float him. They swayed his body side to side. He screamed again, tried to grasp the walls with dying arms.

Rapids suddenly rushed in, spinning his body, floating his face up close to hers, a blue and gruesome, grinning mask. His cries almost mortal in their anguish. Then rapids shot his body forward, so the living brain of Endo Matsuharu saw the ocean waiting in the distance. Red, and boiling, and patient.

ANOTHER DAY PASSED. RAINS SLOWLY SUBSIDED. AN OLD WOMan stepped from a tunnel, muddy and steaming. She squatted, eating a few blades of grass, so fresh and crisp, she smacked her lips. She held her face up to the rain. Holding on to banyan roots breaking the earth like organ pipes, she climbed slowly up the embankment. Now and then she paused, resting her head against a tree. She breathed in deeply. The bark smelled clean, and earth smelled clean.

ʻĪNANA

Life, Anew

IN JUNE 1959 STATEHOOD WAS VOTED IN, AND IN JULY A NAtive Hawaiʻian became the first elected lieutenant governor. On that day folks stepped out prideful, but in years to come they would retreat back into silence, the argot of the poor, the invisible. In August Hawaiʻi was officially made the fiftieth state of the Union, and for a short, euphoric time local politicians kept their promises.

Electric saws felled rotted trees lining the streets of Kalihi. With morbid haste the lane seemed to suddenly breathe and expand. Workmen came with vats of boiling pitch and trucks of gravel, and folks tiptoed down narrow planks beside bitter, carbon-smelling tar. Keo was shocked by the sudden sky, missing the canopied ceiling of palms and giant ferns that kept them hidden from the world.

Now the lane stood out black and straight as a boar's hair. Suddenly families owned cars, great shining scarabs whose flashes of chrome snatched children's shapes as they passed. Overnight the slack-key rhythms of strolling couples disappeared. Now folks sat out in their cars between faded bungalows, encamped there through the evenings, drinking, "talking story."

And with the alchemy of time, a faster pace of living, neighbors no longer leaned at fences recording the ebb and flow of the Meahuna family. They had no time to gossip about Timoteo and Kiko Shirashi, the elegant mortician's widow, and how he dragged home at all hours. They hardly noticed when he collided with that politician, Krash Kapakahi, grappling with his trousers in the lane at dawn.

Each night in front of flickering TVs, foreign faces leapt into their living rooms, blasting them with such strange communiqués. Folks sat stunned, losing track of funerals, marriages, baby *lūʻau.* And because each generation seemed more independent and outspoken, folks would not think it strange when Baby Jo shed her kid-name for Anahola. Or when, after university, she would choose not medical or law school but a freighter, taking off into the world. Living for two, she would say, living out her mama's dreams.

Neighbors were so preoccupied, they would hardly notice when she came home every other year, crashing up the lane, because next week there would be another son or daughter coming home, dragging luggage, a degree, a wife or husband from the mainland. Elders would lose track of which child was at university and which was backpacking in Honshu, Fujian, the Azores, tracking down ancestral roots.

The Territorial years were gone, and folks paid less attention to the comings and goings of Keo, still charioting the sea with his trumpet, still playing his midnight piano. Some nights he sat with Anahola, laughing, talking his head off. Other nights, neighbors thought they saw him talking to an empty chair. No one was shocked. The world was now so *huikau*, confusing, a lot of folks sat up all night arguing with their shadows, shaking their poi fingers at the moon.

One night, as Keo sat musing over the dissonance and pacing of a piano composition, someone swaggered up the lane.

"Hula Man. Howzit! Long time no see." Oogh stood there in a cowboy hat, little boots, and Levi's.

"Oh, my God." Keo stood up, laughing. "Don't tell me you're a *paniolo* now!"

Oogh strolled into the garage and climbed up on a chair, hugging Keo. "Nah, nah. This outfit just fo' show. Selling tickets at rodeo over Wahiawa way. *Mon ami*, I hear you doing real good things. Teaching serious kine music to students."

Keo dipped into a cooler, pulled out two beers.

"Well, it kind of happened with the statehood thing. Krash got me started. You know, teaching kids excites me. Keeps me on my toes."

The little man removed his hat and gazed up at his friend. "Meanwhile, you still one dynamite horn man."

"I still blow. But jazz is fading, Oogh. Most of my gigs are backup on piano. Look, I want to hear about you."

He sipped his beer, banged the pointed toes of his boots together. "I got one real dream job, Keo. Traveling wit' rodeo boys. Dey like my style, put me in one kiosk, selling tickets to da crowds."

Keo shook his head impatiently. "When are you going to get a job to match the superior brain God gave you?"

"'Ey! One t'ing you fo'get," Oogh said. "I always wanted folks looking up at me, remembah? Like one judge. Inducing anxiety wit' his gavel!"

He stood up, pantomiming, explaining the dramaturgy of intimidating.

"Dis job, see, I sit on one high stool inside kiosk, look like I seven feet tall! Folks drive up, got to look *up* at me. I tell 'em, 'OK, ROOM FO' YOU FOLKS.' Or 'SORRY! ALL FULL UP.' Dey start to beg! Sometime I give da stink eye, check out how many folks stuffed in backseat, even in da trunk. Den I tell 'em, ''EY! YOU PAY TWENNY DOLLAH EXTRA, TOO MANY FOLKS IN DAT ONE CAR.' Sometimes I tease 'em, 'NO PAY, I T'ROW YOU IN DA BULL PEN.' Ooh, funny, der expressions! Keo, you gotta come see me work. All height, and authority. Da best!"

Keo laughed, shaking his head. "I promise. Now, tell me, how's your papa?"

Oogh slipped from Pidgin to English, his voice grew soft and thoughtful.

"Papa. What a guy! He's teaching me net-making, poi-pounding. How to listen when gourds call. When certain winds blow through empty gourds, means it's deep-sea-fishing time. And, too, he's teaching me our secret wandering stars, Following-the-Chief Star, Red Star, Dripping-Water Star, and what their journeys mean."

"And what are *you* doing in return?"

Oogh looked up and smiled. "One day he saw me writing a letter to *ma mère* in Shanghai. Papa began to cry. He told me their story. She came here a picture bride, already sold to another man. But when the ship docked, all she saw in the crowd was Papa's big brown shoulders, his golden cheeks and taro-tough teeth. They didn't speak each other's language. But when he put his hand out, she placed hers there, and when he left the crowd, she followed. . . .

"They loved each other very much. But, in time, she ran away, shanghaied me back to China. Why? Because she was greedy, wanting more than to be a country wife. And he was too proud to learn to read or write. That is what I teach my papa. Reading. Writing. Even a soupçon of French. Maybe I will make him a taro-farmer scholar! He is making me his *kua'āina* son—real country-jack."

Keo shook his head. "You're amazing. Even standing still, you find adventures."

"This one is the most exciting," Oogh said. "Family. Mystery. Unriddling. I love this *kanaka* more than life. He is even teaching me to love *ma mère*, that old profiteering goat!"

Keo threw back his head and roared. Across the way, Noah Palama, the twelve-fingered neighbor, looked out of his bedroom window. Keo seemed to be talking to a hat.

Oogh sat up importantly. "Also, I am learning to play gourd drum, and bamboo nose-flute."

" 'Ey. You may end up more *kanaka* than me."

"I think never, *mon ami*. You are more Hawai'ian than you know. In the end, we are what we were intended to be."

Oogh smiled again, thinking of his mother.

"Now I help Papa write letters to *ma mère*. He is still *kanaka* proud, but in a better way. I know they cannot go back in time, but maybe they are building something new. I think there is a bit of Wai'anae budding in Shanghai, and in the taro fields of Wai'anae, there is the laughter of a too-young girl whose papa sold her for a pot of tea. . . .

"She is still cunning. But I see tearstains in letters from Shanghai. I see Papa cry when I read them to him. I put the letter down, blow puffs of air like kisses, drying his tears. When cheeks are wet, air kisses feel cool. He shivers and we giggle. He says *ma mère* used to blow air kisses, too. Who knows? Maybe I am a bridge reconnecting them. Papa's emotions, Mama's drive."

Keo leaned forward. "Oogh, I believe you're growing sentimental."

"Ah, yes. Maybe we are all dwarfs, the sentimentals of the world. I am learning how good it is to *feel*, to not be always cynical and clever. I have even outrun my nightmares. Of waking up caged, someone's souvenir. Papa also teaches me how good it is to be alone. There is so much of life we *live*, but never examine. For that we need solitude. To quietly fill it with ourselves.

"But there is more! It is not all whatchoo call it—bed of roses. *Ma mère* is still a profiteering goat, oh yes! Her letters are tear-stained, but they are also demanding. Send this, send that. Cartons of cigarettes. Jack Daniels. In return she sends us garbage. Empty chocolate boxes from before the war, filled with crumbling, blood-stained crochet. What are we to do with that? Probably dug up from her bombed-out brothels. A filthy placemat from the old Cathay. Dead singing-crickets. My God! While she still sweeps around in silks and jades.

"So? Papa and I conspired. We collected giant centipedes, four, five inches long. We sent them AIR MAIL. Two dozen ugly, poisonous devils. You have to love her, to admire her. Now living in Communist Shanghai, but still mercantile as a pharaoh. What did she do? Was she insulted? No!

"She dried the centipedes, painted and lacquered them. Fashioned them as beautiful *objets* to be worn. Brooches, bracelets, charms. She sold them for enormous sums. Now she is sending us huge orders, for more and more boxes of . . . yes, centipedes! Ah, what you can do? Even Papa says, and with great pride, she is still one *akamai*, very smart, *wahine*!"

Oogh looked down, somewhat shy. "Hula Man, without you I might never have reclaimed my birthsands. You were trying to come home and, helping you, I found my way. I'm only sorry that it took a war."

Keo sighed, thinking of the losses. "A Gypsy friend believed the human race was squalid, start to finish. He said it was *war* that made us human. It made people kinder, more thoughtful."

"And you, *mon ami?* Were you kind?"

"A little. For a while."

Oogh shook his arm. "My God, don't talk as if it's over! We're still youngsters, hardly fifty. Why, it takes fifty years just to step back and get a running start."

Keo slowly shook his head. "I don't think—"

" 'Ey! Don't *think* yourself to death. Relax, let life age you to perfection. There will be epiphanies, moments that will make you gasp with beauty. And there will be the slow drip of the quotidian. Let it come. Throw your arms wide. Now and then there will even be a woman who will look your way. Blow your trumpet for her."

"Sometimes I think blowing is just a way of screaming for help."

"Hula Man. When you want to scream, be still. Be still. Deep within you is a place where everything's all right. As for your music . . . it articulates life. Makes it bearable."

He tapped Keo's arm. "And you must pay attention to Anahola. Like your sweetheart, Sun-ja, she will always be searching, driven to extremes. Perhaps it was those fatherless years. She will hurt herself time and again, living by the intuition of the instant, flying blindly into the frozen heart of things."

"She has parents now. She'll go to them."

"Never! She's too proud. And it may be she loves *you* most of all. One day, you will save her life. Is that not something to live for?"

Keo looked down. "It's strange. Each time I'm with her, I'm struck by . . . similarities. She's so much like Sunny, it's like Sunny's come back to me."

Oogh nodded thoughtfully. "There are so many voices we never hear. So many meanings we never get. Perhaps we are *all* lost, and found, and lost again. Perhaps only amazement keeps us alive."

He checked his watch and jumped up, hugging Keo.

"Come see me at the rodeo. And, Hula Man, be *ikaika*, strong. Remember, after everything, there is still *'ohana*, family. And all this!"

He flung his hand out at the night, then dashed down the lane, singing out, "*Hi'ipoi ka 'āina aloha!*" Cherish the beloved land.

Twelve-fingered Noah Palama sat up in his bed again, peering out the window. He saw what looked like a miniature cowboy running by, a little singing buckaroo. Or maybe he was dreaming.

HA'INA MAI KA PUANA

Let the Story Be Told

SOME DAYS THE OCEAN COMES TO GET HIM, WAVES SO WHIPPED and frenzied, he can hardly hear his horn. On such days he still "feels" notes through vibrations of his fingers, as if he were a deaf man. Today the sea is calm. He feels a gentle rocking as waves inhale, exhale. Moist air lifts his skin, so he looks luminous. He has a sense of well-being, a sense that, though things are missing in his life, what he has might be enough.

He lifts his trumpet, presses it to damp, scarred lips, and quietly approaches the "Nessun dorma" aria from *Turandot.* He plays it slowly, with consideration, as if mining the aphorisms and crystallized griefs of his life. In quiet exaltation, he blows like a man seeing the world through a mind gone sane. Almost dignified, restrained. But there's still something wild and haunted in his playing. Something that, long ago, was almost touched by genius.

From the beach, in the shade of ancient palms, an old woman watches and remembers. Once, in Paris, they listened to Puccini's opera while a Gypsy told the story of *Turandot*, how in legendary times in Peking, a prince won the hand of a haughty princess by naming the three enigmas, Hope, Blood, Love. Keo had vowed one day he would play the aria to perfection.

The old woman suspects he no longer seeks that perfection. Now he comes to the aria out of habit, like a man sitting down with a comforting friend. At the end, he lingers, then lowers his horn. She sees his shoulders slumped in meditation, allowing the aria to reverberate within him. Then he brings the trumpet to his lips again, trying to capture the sweet, intricate patterns of an old Hawai'ian song.

She wipes her forehead. It has been hot and dry for weeks. Fields are scorched distempered brown, and in the *pali* of the Ko'olaus, even waterfalls are still. The heat has kept her sleepless. Everywhere a brittle sound—clattering palms, stones cracking in sun, the crepitation of large insects like humans opening leather wings.

Now, listening to Keo play, she feels mist gather that will turn to gentle rains. Rains that will mature to torrents, quieting everything. All will be forced to lie still and listen. For soon they will enter island autumn, a *kōkō* slung between two seasons. Then the *'iwa* bird will fly. Clouds will walk the coast like royalty. The sea will deepen, land will soften. Winter will bring hurricanes.

She feels she could sleep forever. She rouses herself and heads to her jade hare room, passing a pond where brilliant-patterned carp, like loaves of brocade, rise to the surface. Long nights are waiting, and dreams. Some will be unbearable. But there will be other dreams to salvage her.

Healing hands of the mothers of her mother, ancient *mele* chanters and tale weavers chorusing in Mother Tongue. They will gently bathe her, soothing her bones. They will rinse her hollows. Swaying on the ocean floor, they will turn, passing her nightmares from hand to hand like heirlooms. Her pain will be made bearable; they will bear it with her.

Listening closely in those dreams, she will hear her mother's mother and that woman's mother, chant out how Sunny Sung became a woman, how she exacted *ho'opa'i*, revenge. And broken girls, that army of women in her blood, will rise beside the elders. In nights of sleeplessness, they will keep watch, turning the darkness womanful.

One day, when winter rains are *pau*, she will wake and see the greening all around her. The green veil of rootless plankton, like marine pastures on the face of the sea. Green jewels permeating fields and uplands, feeding them oxygen. The bronzed, verdant haze on rock and sand. The indelible green of her islands. She had seen it in her youth, yet not seen it. Now it will leap up in her second sight. And in that reborn greening, she will take up her cane again, following him at a distance.

She will see him with Anahola, once called Baby Jo. How quietly he will sit, telling her the history of Sunny Sung. Telling of his infant daughter, never held. She will see Anahola weeping in her hands. Her story will be Anahola's burden, and redemption: after this, she will always look behind her. She will draw closer to her uncle, watching over him. Time will be their prism.

On the Big Island, Island of Volcanoes, Pono will slowly unstitch a worn kimono, erasing the old woman. There will be nothing left but surrender. Life letting go with forgetful hands.

. . . ONE NIGHT SHE HEARS THEM CALLING, *E HO'I MAI! E HO'I Mai! Come back. Come back. Women massing like weather. Women whose scars are radiant with light. They come for her—Lili, with her clubfoot shriveled and intent, and little Kim, her wrists and ribs like branches. They stand beside her sleeping form and take her hand. She rises like mist. They pass through walls like groves of talking jade-grass, and for a moment jade hares turn and stare.*

They lead her to the uplands, following footsteps of the ancients, so she will see, and always remember, how her island is stored like a morsel in a great wet cheek. Rising higher and higher, they pass ironwood and cypress, then the fog zone where eucalyptus envelops her. Trees yawn and sway, containing all the tremors of the island which have absorbed for eons all the tremors of the sea.

Looking down, she sees how the island is enfolded, how each thing is watermarked. She kneels, presses her face against the soil and drinks, because it is the sea and only intermittently the land. Something expires, something is born. Now Sun-ja Uanoe Sung dissolves in mist that settles in the lowlands, that rolls down to the beaches. Mist that jewels green veils of rootless plankton, like marine pastures on the face of the sea . . .

And into that sea she pours. Down, down to the arms of mele *chanters and tale weavers. To that army of young women swaying on the ocean floor. Women who died voiceless, and will never stop telling. Women whose memory ripples the skin of soldiers' dreams. Women whispering at our nerve ends. A hand on each other's shoulder as they walk away from time.*

Hawai'ian-English Glossary

'AHI (ah-hee) . . . Yellow-fin tuna fish
AKU (ah-koo) . . . Skipjack, Bonito fish
AKUA (ah-koo-ah) . . . Spirit, ghost
AKAMAI (ah-ka-my) . . . Smart, clever
'ĀINA (eye-nah) . . . Land, earth
ANAHOLA (ah-nah-ho-lah) . . . Hourglass
'AUMĀKUA (ow-mah-koo-ah) . . . Family gods, deified ancestors
'AUWĒ! (ow-way) . . . Alas!
'AWA (ahh-vah) . . . Tea, mildly narcotic
BENTO (ben-toe) . . . Japanese word. Box lunch
CHAR SIU (char-soo) . . . Chinese word. Bits of roasted duck
DA KINE (da kind) . . . Pidgin for "You know what I mean"
E HO'I MAI! (ey-ho-ee-my) . . . Come back, come back!
E KIPA MAI! (ey-kee-pah-my) . . . Come, enjoy hospitality!
FLIP (flip) . . . Pidgin for Filipino
GO FO' BROKE (go-fo-broke) . . . Pidgin for "push to the limit"
HANAFUDA (hah-na-foo-dah) . . . Japanese card game
HĀNAI (hah-ny) . . . Adopted
HANOHANO (hah-no-hah-no) . . . Dignified
HAOLE (how-lee) . . . Caucasian, white. Literally, one without breath
HAOLEFIED (how-lee-fied) . . . To act white, to have airs
HAPA-HAOLE (hah-pah-how-lee) . . . Half-white. Also, "touristy"
HIGH MAKA MAKA (hi-mah-kah-mah-kah) . . . Pidgin for pretentious
HILAHILA (he-lah-he-lah) . . . Bashful, shy, shamed
HŌHĒ (ho-hey) . . . Coward
HO'O PONOPONO (ho-oh-po-no-po-no) . . . Restore balance of heart, mind

HOWZIT! (howz-it) . . . Pidgin for "hello." Common local greeting
HŪPŌ (hoo-po) . . . Ignorant, stupid, a fool
HUHŪ (hoo-hoo) . . . Angry
HUIKAU (hoo-ee-kow) . . . Confused, mixed-up
HUKILAU (hoo-kee-lau) . . . Net-fishing party
ʻIWA (ee-vah) . . . Frigate, or man-o-war bird
KAHIKI (kah-hee-kee) . . . Tahiti
KAHIKO (kah-hee-ko) . . . Ancient, long ago
KAHUNA (ka-hoo-nah) . . . Sorcerer, seer
KALAHALA (kah-lah-hal-lah) . . . To ask forgiveness. Also *KALA MAI*
KALO (kah-lo) . . . Taro. A yamlike corm with large, green heart-shaped leaves. The staff of life for Hawaiʻians
KĀLUA (kah-loo-ah) . . . Baked in earth oven
KANAKA (kah-nah-kah) . . . Hawaiʻian person, human being (Plural: KĀNAKA)
KANAKA MAOLI (kah-nah-kah mah-oh-lee) . . . True native Hawaiʻian. Both terms of great pride to Hawaiʻians
KĀNE (kah-nee) . . . Male, husband
KAPA (kah-pah) . . . Tapa cloth made of pounded mulberry bark
KAPAKAHI (kah-pah-ky) . . . Partial to one side. Also bent, askew
KAPU (kay-poo) . . . Taboo
KEIKI (kay-kee) . . . Child, offspring
KIKEPA (kee-kay-pah) . . . Sarong
KOA (ko-ah) . . . Bold, fearless. Also large, native tree
KŌKŌ (ko-ko) . . . Hammock
KOʻOLAU (ko-oh-lau) . . . Sawtooth mountain range separating windward side of Oahu island from leeward side
KUAʻĀINA (koo-ah-eye-nah) . . . Country, rural
KŪKAE (koo-ky) . . . Excrement
KUKUI (koo-koo-ee) . . . Candlenut, from that tree. Also lamp, torch
KULIKULI! (koo-lee-koo-lee) . . . Be quiet!
KUPUNA (koo-poo-nah) . . . Grandparent, ancestor
LĀNAI (lah-nigh) . . . Porch, veranda, balcony
LAUHALA (lau-hah-la) . . . Leaf of the hala (pandanus) tree
LAULAU (lau-lau) . . . Steamed ti leaf–covered fish or pork
LILIKOʻI (lee-lee-ko-ey) . . . Passion fruit
LIMU (lee-mu) . . . Seaweed
LOʻI (low-ee) . . . Taro patch
LŌLŌ (lo-lo) . . . Stupid, feebleminded
LŪʻAU (loo-ow) . . . Heart-shaped taro leaves. Also feast
LUA ʻUHANE (loo-ah-oo-hah-ney) . . . Tear duct where spirit hides
MAʻI PĀKĒ (my-pah-kay) . . . Leprosy. Literally, Chinese sickness
MAKAHIKI (mah-kah-hee-kee) . . . Ancient Hawaiʻian autumn festival
MAKAI (mah-ky) . . . Seaward, in direction of the sea
MAKE (mah-key) . . . Death
MANAKA (mah-nah-kah) . . . Boring, dull, monotonous
MANA PĀLUA (mah-nah-pah-loo-ah) . . . Possessed of double mana

MANAPUA (mah-nah-poo-ah) . . . Pork-filled bun, popular island food
MANŌ (mah-no) . . . Shark
MEAHUNA (mee-ah-hoo-nah) . . . Secret
MELE (may-lay) . . . Song, chant
MOE MOE (mo-ee-mo-ee) . . . Sleep
MOLOĀ (mo-lo-ah) . . . Lazy, indolent
NĀNĀ HONUA (nah-nah-ho-noo-ah) . . . Big, white flowers of the angel's trumpet tree. Poisonous to eat
NU'UANU PALI (noo-oo-ah-noo-pah-lee) . . . Literally, the "cool-off cliffs"
'OHANA (oh-hah-nah) . . . Family, kin group
OIA NŌ (oh-ee-ah-no) . . . So it goes
'OKOLE (oh-ko-lee) . . . Buttocks
'ŌKOLEHAO (oh-ko-lee-how) . . . Homemade rice wine, or pineapple wine
'ONO (oh-no) . . . Delicious, savory, good
'ŌPAKAPAKA (oh-pah-ka-pah-ka) . . . Blue snapper
'OPIHI (oh-pee-hee) . . . Limpets, mollusks, a delicacy
PĀKĒ (pah-kay) . . . Chinese
PALI (pah-lee) . . . Cliff
PANIOLO (pah-nee-oh-lo) . . . Hawai'ian cowboy
PAU (pow) . . . Finished, ended, all done
PEHEA 'OE? (pe-hey-ah-oy) . . . How are you?
PELE (pey-ley) . . . Goddess of fire and volcano
PIKO (pee-ko) . . . Umbilical cord
PILAU (pee-lau) . . . Foul, rottenness, to stink
PILIKIA (pee-lee-kee-ah) . . . Trouble, distress
PŌHAKU (po-hah-koo) . . . Rock, stone
POI (poy) . . . Paste made of pounded, cooked taro corms
PONO (po-no) . . . Goodness, balance, morality
PUA'A (poo-ah-ah) . . . Pig
PUA SADINIA (poo-ah-sa-dee-nee-ah) . . . Gardenia flower
PUKA (poo-kah) . . . Hole
PŪPŪ (poo-poo) . . . Snacks, tidbits
PUPULE (poo-poo-lee) . . . Crazy, insane
SAIMIN (sy-min) . . . Japanese noodle soup
SHOYU (shoy-oo) . . . Japanese word for soy sauce
TITA (tee-tah) . . . Pidgin for sister
TŪTŪ (too-too) . . . Grandmother (informal)
UANOE (oo-ah-no-ee) . . . Misty rain, fog
'UHANE (oo-hah-nee) . . . Spirit, soul, ghost
'UKULELE (ook-oo-lay-lay) . . . Literally, leaping flea. Hawai'ian guitar
'ULI 'ULI (oo-lee-oo-lee) . . . Seeded rattle gourds for dancing hula
WAHINE (vah-hee-nee) . . . Woman, lady, wife
WAHINE U'I (vah-hee-nee-oo-ee) . . . Beautiful woman
WIKI WIKI! (wick-ee-wick-ee) . . . Hurry up!

Acknowledgments

Eternal gratitude and affection to my distinguished agent, Henry Dunow, who championed the book in its early drafts, and to Peter Borland, my brilliant and intrepid editor, whose sensitivity and perseverence carried me through the final revisions. For patience and caring, thanks also to Emily Grayson and Jennifer Carlson.

For generous support and assistance, I am indebted to the Lila Wallace–Reader's Digest Travel Fund, and the staff of the Schlesinger Library, Radcliffe. I salute my sisters of the Bunting Institute, Radcliffe, especially Dr. Janet Talvacchia.

Mahalo ʻa nui to the following for their love, support and encouragement:

On the U.S. mainland: Patricia Powell, Isabel Allende, Alix Kates Shulman, Dr. Joseph Chang, of Honolulu and the University of Wisconsin-Milwaukee, Lois Rosenthal of *Story* magazine, Lis Harris, Anne Greene of Wesleyan University, Tina Howe, Gretchen Simpson, Polly Kreitz, Sara Reinbold, Patsy and Harry Harsh, and especially my daughter and son-in-law, Anita and Robert Yantorno.

And to the Boston Hawaiʻian Club, *Wahi Ku Moku*, especially Al Kuahi Wong, Pat and Joe Neilson, Lei-Sanne Doo, and Vernon Freitas for reading my manuscript, and for his love of literature and jazz.

In Hawaiʻi: Special *alohas* to my Houghtailing family, especially cousins Evelyn Liu, Raenette Kauwealoha Ing, Rosemond Kahau Aho, and Aunty Carrie Chang, for their memories of World War II. And to Sister Malia Domenica for strength.

Holomua to my fellow artists and educators of Hawaiʻi Nei, who have fed, housed and inspired me, and who are reviving and advancing our people, *nā kanaka maoli:* Puanani Burgess, Dr. Manu Aluli Meyer and family, Polly Roth, Su-su Hokulani, "Brash" Nainoa Cobbs, Napoleon Keawe, Balthazar Makua, Luana and Craig Busby-Neff, Auliʻi Mitchell, Leo Akana Anderson, Laka Morton, Elizabeth Lindsey, Steve Soone, Lani Kealoha, Karin Williams, and many more. And to Kupuna Mikala Kekahu and "Butch" Kekahu for their *onipaʻa.*

Also thanks to the staffs of the Hawaiʻian State Archives, and of the Hawaiʻian Historical Society Library.

In Shanghai: For help in researching the mills, internment camps, and the "comfort stations," thanks to Robert Chu, Tommy Lou

Tong, Letitia Lum and family, and LuLu Savage. And to Sam Sam Soong, Cheng Yueqiang, and Mr. Zhou for their memories of Shanghai jazz bands in the 1930s.

In Australia: Thanks to the staff of the Australian War Memorial, the Victoria Museum, Melbourne. And again to Peter Kafcouladis, of Brisbane, indefatigable researcher and friend.

In Papua New Guinea: Thanks to the staff of the Papua New Guinea War Museum, Port Moresby. And in Rabaul, New Britain: Deepest affection and gratitude to the Toimanapu and Sanka-Sanka families, their elders and friends, for their hospitality, memories of World War II, their correspondences, and their guidance through the tunnels of Rabaul.

I am also indebted to Dr. Alice Chai, former Professor of Women's Studies, University of Hawai'i, for her lectures and materials on "Comfort Women, the Chongshindae Movement." And to the "Asian Pacific Women in Solidarity for Human Rights, Justice and Peace," and the "Korean Council for Women Drafted for Military Sexual Slavery by Japan" for their materials, suggestions and guidance during my stay in Seoul, Korea.

Many books were helpful to my research, most especially *Native Lands and Foreign Desires, Pehea Lā E Pono Ai?* by Lilikala Kame'eleihiwa, *Sisters and Strangers, Women in the Shanghai Cotton Mills, 1919–1949* by Emily Honig, *Japan At War, An Oral History* by Haruko Taya Cook and Theodore Cook.

For inspiration while writing this book, for their Slack-Key Guitar brilliance, and for taking our music out into the world, *mahalo* to: Ray Kane, Keola Beamer, Cyril Pahinui, Ledward Ka'apana, George Kahumoku, Dennis Pavao, the golden-voiced Loyal Garner, and Robi Kahakalau. *Hana Hou!* to Gabe Baltazar, alto saxaphonist *non pareil.* Also thanks to Mick Mason for dusk-to-dawn trumpet lessons.

Last and most important, my deepest gratitude and love to those women who were imprisoned in World War II, and who have survived to bear witness. I thank them for their time, and their courage in resurrecting painful memories. Though most choose to remain anonymous, this book could not have been written without their words.

E Pūpūkahi

Song of the Exile

KIANA DAVENPORT

A Reader's Guide

A Conversation with Kiana Davenport

Q: A number of narrative traditions coalesce in *Song of the Exile*. You seem to interweave strands of Greek mythology, Christian mythology, regional folklore, and, most prominently, the enduring myths of Hawaii. What sort of challenge did you encounter in spinning many stories into one?

KD: The challenge for me is always restraint. Hawaiians come from an oral tradition, so for generations, nothing was written down. Now my generation is writing and being published, and the stories are just pouring forth, based on our oceanic history, our families, our spiritual beliefs.

It's a constant struggle to stay focused, and not incorporate some of these fabulous stories into each book I'm working on. This was an issue with my last novel, *Shark Dialogues*, which is a bigger book than *Song of the Exile*. *Exile*, by the way, is based on an actual story. Had I made it up, I would have simplified it. Fewer locations, for a start.

Q: Please comment on the interplay of experience and imagination vis-à-vis the genesis of *Song of the Exile*.

KD: My Hawaiian mother died when I was around ten, and one of her older sisters raised me. My Aunty's husband, Ayau Kam, was pureblood Chinese, so I was raised in a Hawaiian-Chinese family. Uncle Ayau, who died recently at the age of ninety-five, had played drums in a jazz band in Honolulu in the 1920s.

As an old man, he used to walk me up and down the lane, talking about that era when jazz was big in Honolulu. Occasionally Uncle mentioned this Hawaiian musician who had taught himself guitar and trumpet. A real jazz virtuoso.

Evidently, the man was so talented, he played with black musicians at the army bases. When they mustered out, they gave him a ticket to New Orleans. Eventually he joined them, and they all ended up playing in Paris in the 1930s. The story goes that this man returned to Honolulu after World War II, and spent the rest of his life traveling around Hong Kong, Shanghai, and Singapore, searching for the sweetheart he'd left behind. He had been told that she was "taken" by the Japanese in Shanghai, where she had gone to find her sister.

Through the years, I half-forgot this story. Then in 1992, I read an article in the *New York Times* about former prisoners of the Japanese called "comfort women." After fifty years they were demanding reparations from the Japanese government. That was the first time I heard that phrase, "comfort women." Reading that article, I felt something tap me on the shoulder. I cut it out and saved it, not sure why.

Then, in 1993, just as I finished *Shark Dialogues*, I read that several former "comfort women" were speaking at Harvard University. They wanted to educate people to what had been done to them by the Japanese. Of course I attended the lecture, which was very emotional. People in the audience cried. I learned that "comfort women" was a term despised by these women for it suggested prostitution. Since eighty percent of all women kidnapped and raped were Koreans, they preserved the Korean word *chongshindae*, which means "conscripted worker."

Of the hundreds of thousands kidnapped, an estimated 90 percent of the women had been killed while imprisoned. These aging survivors were part of the small number who had survived.

That night was an epiphany. Sitting there, I remember the story of the Hawaiian jazz man who had lost his sweetheart to the Japanese. During that lecture, I was already starting my novel.

Q: **Given the gravity of the reality in which you situate a significant part of your novel, i.e., the tragedy of the *chongshindae*'s life, were you caught in a conflict between fidelity to facts and the novelist's predilection to play, however seriously, with them?**

KD: Well, I'm a novelist, I prefer to invent. But in deference to these heroic women—their imprisonment and torture, which had been kept secret for fifty years—I did not want to deviate from what actually happened. I felt a moral obligation to honor them, to portray their lives pretty much as they had described them to me.

I knew I would have more "authorial freedom" in the second half of the novel, more room to imagine and conjure, because I don't know how the actual story ended. Evidently the real-life musician played in dives up and down the Asian coast, searching for his sweetheart. No one knows how he died.

Q: **Would you elaborate on that a little?**

KD: For instance, I wanted to bring Sunny back. I didn't want her to die in the camps. Since many of the survivors I interviewed still feel great rage, I wanted some kind of closure for her. So I brought the Japanese lieutenant back, too. Novelists are always asking themselves, "Is this logical, or probable?" At first, I was afraid his reappearance would not be believable. In my research, however, I discovered several former Japanese officers who had settled in Honolulu after World War II. Readers, certainly critics, could complain that Lt. Matsuharu's reappearance after the war is too coincidental, but life, like fiction, is full of uncanny coincidences.

Q: That view seems reflected in the structure of the novel. You present us with a narrative that owes its shape more to the fortuitous workings of memory than the simple chronology of a linear telling.

KD: I realized early on that this was not a story I could tell chronologically. The minute these women began talking about their imprisonment in camps, they were back there. They described the smells, the taste of rotting food. They trembled, they broke down. That juxtaposing of past and present is something we do everyday of our lives. You recall something in your past, and instantly you're back in that precise moment. I tried to convey that in the novel.

Also, I think a story has much more impact when told in the present and in the first-person voice. The camp scenes would not have had such impact if told from the perspective of fifty years later, in the voice of a third person.

Q: How did your past play itself out in *Song of the Exile*? In particular, how did time away from your home in Hawaii enable you to create it on the page?

KD: Well, the book is about exiles, longing for home. Living apart from my islands, and my "native tongue," is often painful. Sometimes I don't feel quite real. I miss talking "pidgin," the island-Creole language I grew up with. When you give up your native tongue, part of you dies a little. You grieve. But, I think that kind of pain is important for artists. What Shakespeare called "The growth of the soul under stress."

I try to incorporate that longing into my novels. I think of James Joyce, Milan Kundera, Vladimir Nabokov, and how love for their homelands added enormously to the expression of what they lost.

It deepened the humanness of their work. Also, distance has given me enormous perspective. The challenge for me now, is not to write so elegiacally about Hawaii. In recent short stories I've attempted something darker.

Q: The reach and limits of wordless expression appears as a motif of *Song of the Exile*. Did you wittingly present characters who turn to something other than words to communicate?

KD: I did not consciously approach the novel that way. But I realize now—at this very moment—it must have been in my subconscious. Most of the characters in *Song of the Exile* are not particularly verbal. Keo is uneducated. He speaks through his horn. Sunny is essentially mute after her experiences as a "comfort woman." Her life is one of silence. Malia expresses her rage through her sewing machine. Lt. Matsuharu is traumatized, half-insane. Somehow, though, it all works. As in life, folks often communicate without words.

Q: I'm reminded of a scene early in the novel in which Malia encourages Keo to take up the trumpet, to acknowledge the need to scream. To what extent has writing enabled you to scream—if that verb is the apt one?

KD: Yes, yes. I think for me, writing is a way of screaming. I have a lot of rage inside. Probably, if I weren't writing, I'd be a very dangerous woman. I felt this especially while researching and writing this novel, because of the unspeakable things that happened to these women. There were days I could not walk out on the street, afraid I would attack someone. I think most women harbor a certain amount of rage, with good reason when you look at history. Thank God we find ways to channel it.

Q: Among the more emotive, colorful passage of the novel, are some rather tragic scenes rendered in a sparse, quiet prose.

KD: I knew when discussing the women in the camp that the writing had to be as simple and as pure as possible. It was very difficult. The first drafts were an absolute assault on the reader! I wanted to tell everything, hit the reader over the head with every atrocity committed on these women. Thank God for good editors.

The first draft of *Song of the Exile* was something like fifteen hundred pages. It was overblown and gory. By the twenty-fourth draft,

I was very conscious of how every word counted. Still I never got it down to that diamond point perfection. What writer ever does? I am learning book by book that what you don't say has the most impact, what you let the reader imagine.

Q: At what point did your undertaking seem most daunting?

KD: The book became complicated in ways I never imagined. First of all, it seemed too ambitious—the whole World War II background, the years covered, the distances traveled. I didn't want to write a novel of that scope. And the more research I did, the more emotionally involved I became with these women and what happened to them. There were times when I thought I could not write the book. I hadn't been imprisoned as they had, I didn't have the right. But they encouraged me, even begged me, to write it. Most are now in their late seventies and eighties, and are so psychologically scarred they will never write their own stories.

Q: How have they responded to the novel?

KD: I have been humbled by their approval, and their gratitude. Some of them have bad eyesight now, so my book has been read to them. Their letters mean more to me than anything. They write to thank me for the novel; whereas I should be on my knees thanking them, for their strength, their courage. One woman wrote that—I'm not sure I can get this out—that by telling their stories, I had given her back a measure of her dignity, that I had given her back her life. A book is so small. It fits in your hand. You don't think of it as giving someone back their life.

Q: In what ways have these women remained in your life?

KD: People ask me how can I write a book like this and just walk away? What does one do after writing such a book? I'm reminded of William Styron and his novel, *Sophie's Choice*. I remember thinking "How could he write such a book, then walk away from the Holocaust." The answer is, you don't. I think all the years Styron was writing that book, and the inability to let go of the horrors, contributed to the massive depression he experienced and chronicled in *Darkness Visible*.

I had a lot of dark nights, periods of depression while writing this novel. I do believe there is such a thing as too much knowledge, too much research into horror. You should stop at the point where it begins to damage you. I still have dark nights, a part of me will always be haunted by these women sacrificed in World War II.

I'm also asked what more I will do for these women. I don't know. I go on lecture tours. I talk about the few other books written on the subject of "comfort women." I make donations to their cause. Organizations, such as the Asian Pacific Women in Solidarity for Human Rights, Justice, and Peace, are fighting for legislation that will give these women some kind of financial reparation.

Whatever we do will not be enough. How do you compensate a woman who was kidnapped at the age of ten, or twelve, raped day and night through all the years of the war? What is the reparation for someone so physically and psychologically damaged that, fifty years later, she still cannot function without five medications?

I'd like to remind readers that it was not only Asian and Pacific women who were used as "sex slaves" by the Japanese. There were also white women—Dutch, English, Americans—who were students, nurses, wives of missionaries. Imprisoned and raped when Japanese armies invaded Indonesia and China. I have met some of these women. Most wish to remain anonymous.

Q: What role, if any, can fiction play in the face of such trial?

KD: Often I'm asked what the novel is essentially about. It's about many things, but ultimately it's about survival. That heroic drive in each of us, the human will to go on. And, I believe that art, music, literature help play a role in our survival.

May I share with you one of my favorite passages of writing? It's from John Gardner's *The Art of Fiction*. He writes, "To write with taste in the highest sense is to write with the assumption that one out of a hundred people who read one's work may be dying or have some loved one dying. To write so that no one commits suicide, no one despairs. To write as Shakespeare wrote, so that people understand, sympathize, see the universality of pain, and feel strengthened if not directly encouraged to move on."

Isn't that beautiful? That's the level of writing I want to achieve, one book at a time.

Reading Group Topics and Questions for Discussion

1. Keo's jazz mentor emphasizes the importance of knowing a tradition before experimenting with it. To what traditions is *Song of the Exile* indebted? How does Kiana Davenport borrow and blend various narrative traditions—Greek mythology, Hawaiian folklore, chronicles of war—to create her own?

2. Discuss how the structure of the novel mirrors the workings of memory. What does the novel show us about the past's place in the present?

3. A number of landscapes are traversed throughout the course of the novel's action; some seem to exert a greater influence on character than others. What do we learn about the extent to which place shapes character? And how can character shape place? Also, how does the novel challenge or uphold traditional notions of home?

4. Much of *Song of the Exile* chronicles characters' attempts to bring their interior lives into some sort of harmony with the exterior world, the world of others. What sort of obstacles most often appear between the two? Which prove the most formidable, and why? What resources do Keo, Sunny, or Malia find or find lacking when confronted with trial?

5. What was your understanding of the term "comfort women" before reading this novel? From where did you derive your knowledge? What notions were undermined or supported? To what extent can a work of fiction color one's consciousness or effect social change, however modestly?

6. Kiana Davenport has spoken of the importance of resisting the temptation to depict the Japanese lieutenants as utter villains, noting the inherent humanity each of us possesses—however damaged it may be. Does she succeed in avoiding caricatures of evil? What light does *Song of the Exile* shed on the nature of cruelty and violence, particularly during wartime?

7. The novel is replete with exiles. What are the various songs of each one, and what is the significance of singing or at least making the attempt? What are the perils of silence?

8. Threats to freedom appear throughout the novel, some more conspicuous than others. Provide examples of the way notions of freedom differ from character to character. What restraints are imposed

internally, and externally? How? Which prove most difficult to break?

9. Follow the shifting role of music in Keo's life, and explain the ways in which it opens up or limits his character. How does his means of expression compare to Malia's or Sunny's? What might Davenport be proffering about the role of creative self-expression in one's life? Or the extent to which one person can comprehend another?

10. How pointed are the politics in *Song of the Exile*? Do you see this as a novel with an agenda? If yes, what? Does a novelist have a responsibility to engage the politics of the time he or she chronicles? Why?

11. Hawaii itself emerges as a character in the novel. What sort of transformation does it undergo? How does its evolution compare to that of the central characters? What forces are at work on each? Which are unique to place?

12. Kiana Davenport has said that the writers she admires most get at the truly difficult themes through the subject of family. What is the role of family in *Song of the Exile*? How do abstractions such as freedom, happiness, and meaning find expression in the author's handling of family?

13. What is the dominant tone of the novel?

14. Samuel Johnson famously remarked that "the only end of writing is to enable the reader better to enjoy life or better to endure it." How does *Song of the Exile* measure up to his criteria?

15. At the novel's close, Oogh reminds Keo of the many voices we never hear, the "many meanings we never get." He then adds, "Perhaps we are all lost, and found, and lost again. Perhaps only amazement keeps us alive." Look at *Song of the Exile* through the lens of Oogh's wisdom.

ABOUT THE AUTHOR

Of Native Hawaiian and Anglo-American descent, KIANA DAVENPORT was raised and educated in Hawaii. She is the author of four previous novels, including the internationally acclaimed *Shark Dialogues,* a multi-generational saga set in Hawaii from the nineteenth century to the present. Her short stories have been included in the Pushcart Prize collection in 1998, and the O. Henry Awards Anthologies in 1997, 1998, and 2000. Recipient of a fiction grant from the National Endowment for the Arts, she was also a 1992–93 Bunting Fellow at Harvard-Radcliffe, and the 1997–98 Visiting Writer at Wesleyan University.

Davenport has traveled extensively throughout the Pacific and Asia researching her novels and short stories. *Song of the Exile,* based mostly on fact, took five years of research. Her travels were a very personal journey as well as fodder for her writing: "As I traveled throughout the Pacific and the Pacific Rim, interviewing World War II survivors, I began to understand what my father had experienced fighting at Midway and Guadacanal. I also saw how war damages humans irreparably. During interviews, men and women broke down and sobbed even after fifty years."

More Praise for Kiana Davenport

"An overwhelming experience. . . . Davenport's prose is sharp and shining as a sword, yet her sense of poetry and love of nature permeate each line. . . . Haunting."

—Isabel Allende

"An incredible novel . . . profound, lyrical, insightful."

—*Booklist* (starred review)

"Davenport writes with exquisite intimacy . . . [she] weaves into her lush narrative indelible portraits of Honolulu's narrow back streets."

—*Elle*

"Passionate . . . *Song of the Exile* transports the reader into an often-magical world by the power of its story. Its language is at times a song, and sometimes a cry in the dark. . . . Davenport's imagination and vision will haunt you for a long time."

—*Chicago Tribune*

"Lyrical . . . The success of *Song of the Exile* lies in Davenport's commitment to telling a story that has been shamefully silenced."

—*San Francisco Chronicle*

"Captivating . . . [A] rich tapestry of myth and history, of the political and domestic spheres, of brutal desire and rare moments of exquisite joy, the final song played is, if not entirely triumphant, then at last and completely transcendent."

—Elizabeth Haas, bn.com

"*Song of the Exile* is written to be a popular novel, which is to say it has a story that sweeps across three continents and is fired by a flaming romance. What separates it from its genre, however, is its intensity of feeling, its body of sensuous detail present on every one of its pages, and its dedication to a level of writing very few bestsellers possess."

—Norman Mailer

"Nuanced and haunting, *Song of the Exile* reveals the emotional truths hidden beneath the World War II euphemism 'comfort women.' A half century later, this important and powerful novel gives these women a way out of the perpetual exile of the forgotten."

—Gloria Steinem